The Sign of the Cross

A NOVEL

DAVID HORTON

ChariotVictor
PUBLISHING
A Division of Cook Communications

Victor Books is an imprint of ChariotVictor Publishing,
a division of Cook Communications, Colorado Springs, Colorado 80918
Cook Communications, Paris, Ontario
Kingsway Communications, Eastbourne, England

Designers: Andrea Boven; Bill Gray
Editors: Susan Reck; Barbara Williams
Cover Illustration: Kazuhiko Sano
Maps: Daniel van Loon

1 2 3 4 5 6 7 8 9 10 Printing/Year 01 00 99 98 97

To Ryan and Melissa

"All people should strive to learn before they die:
What they are running from, and to, and why."

— James Thurber

Acknowledgments

Tracking down the interesting details that make for credible historical fiction is seldom easy. My task would have been even more difficult had it not been for the kind assistance of people such as David Pavey, Craig Glass, Paul Luedtke, the staff of the Swiss National Military Archives, and the staff of the Palatine, Illinois Public Library.

I am also indebted to Greg Clouse and Jim Elwell, who provided me this opportunity; to Sue Reck, whose editorial skill I have come to count on; to Barb Williams, Andrea Boven, Bill Gray, and the ChariotVictor Publishing staff, for caring for the details; and to Don Pape, whose prayers and encouragement helped me keep going.

A very special note of thanks to my wife, Jennifer, who encouraged and supported my efforts, listened to my ideas, and gave me the time to do what I love.

To all of you, un grand merci.

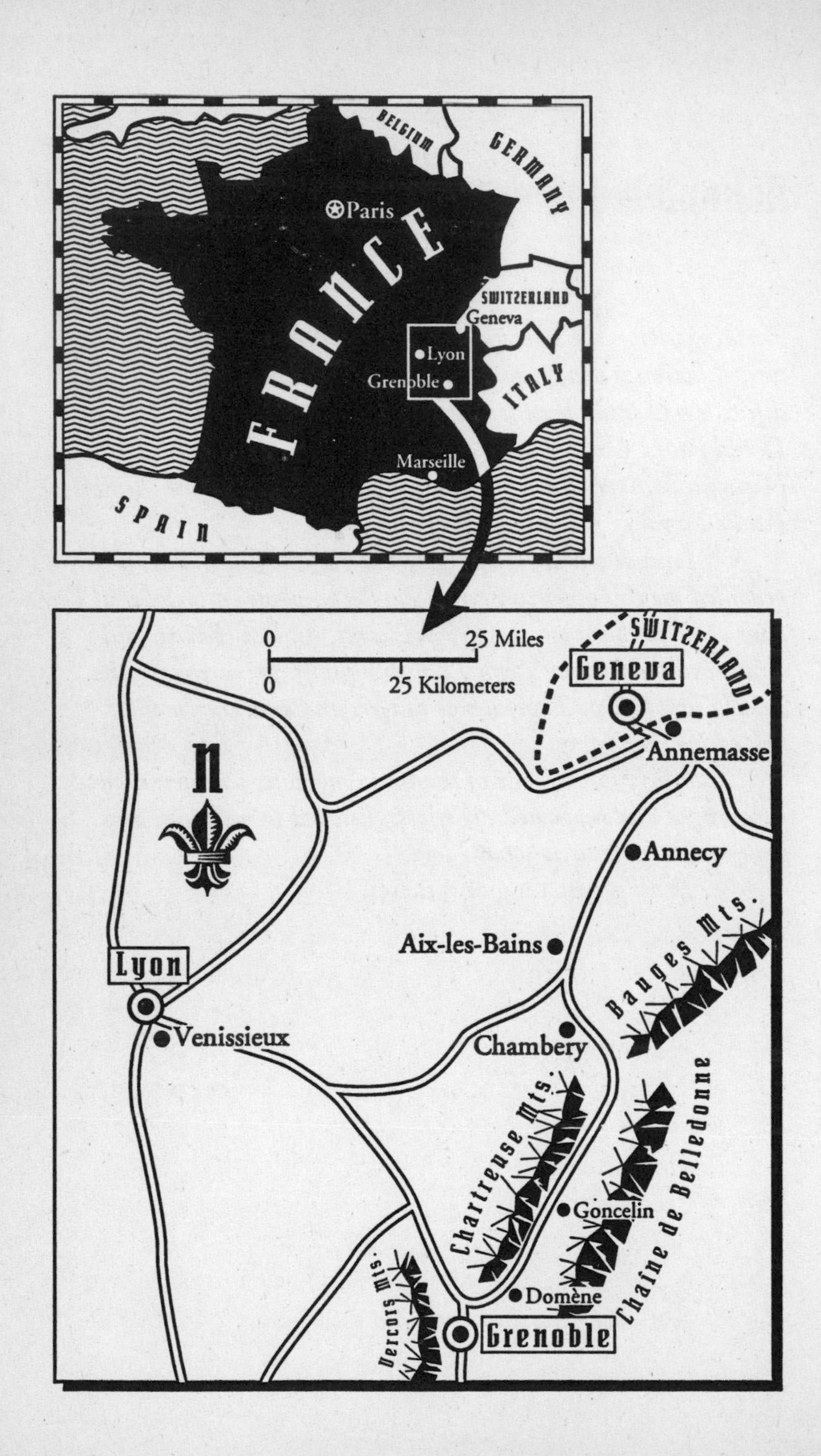

BELGIUM
GERMANY
Paris
FRANCE
SWITZERLAND
Geneva
Lyon
Grenoble
ITALY
Marseille
SPAIN
0
25 Miles
0
25 Kilometers
SWITZERLAND
Geneva
Annemasse
N
Annecy
Bauges Mts.
Aix-les-Bains
Lyon
Venissieux
Chambery
Chartreuse Mts.
Chaîne de Belledonne
Goncelin
Vercors Mts.
Domène
Grenoble

Prologue

Lyons, France, May 1943

Awakened to the sound of jackboots on the hard stone floor outside his cramped cell, Marcel Boussant jerked halfway to a sitting position and peered around. Harsh slivers of incandescent light forced their way through the cracks in the cell door, piercing the musty blackness. Squinting, he could just make out the others—all three of them—like large lumps of coal, still as death. They too were wide awake, these "enemies of the state," though they gave every appearance of sleeping. It was the same every morning. And no one ever made a sound until the jackboots went away.

"Delacroix."

The hair stood up on the back of Marcel's neck as the name was called out.

"*Pas de bagage.*"

He put his hand to his mouth as the taste of bile rose in his throat. He'd only been in the Montluc Prison a week, but he understood all too clearly what "no baggage" meant. He didn't know Delacroix, probably wouldn't even recognize his face. But he felt sick all the same as he tried not to listen to the sound of a nearby cell door creaking open and someone stumbling into the corridor. That would be Delacroix.

"Blanchet."

Marcel cringed. Blanchet he knew. They had been brought to this ancient military prison on the same truck. They had never really had a chance to talk, though they managed a vague sign of recognition during the few minutes of exercise the prisoners were allowed each morning.

"*Pas de bagage.*"

Marcel glanced up as the first faint glow of dawn seeped in through the cell's tiny broken window. Suddenly, even the promise of morning light offered precious little solace. Blanchet had seemed so gentle, almost harmless. Surely they would let him go once they had interrogated him! What crime—real or imagined—could he possibly be guilty of?

Dear God, is this how it will end for me as well? I thought I was doing what You wanted. . .

Then a key was rattling in the lock outside, and the battered door swung rudely open. Half blinded by the electric torch the guard held aloft, Marcel crouched low to the straw-strewn floor, finding it suddenly difficult to breathe. Just twenty years old, he had scarcely stopped to consider what might become of him should he be arrested. But in just seven days in the hands of Oberstürmfuhrer Klaus Barbie, he had seen one grim example after another of the lengths Lyons' Gestapo chief would go to crush the Resistance. Marcel knew he was about to pay for his "crimes" as hundreds had in the past few months.

"Hernandez."

The sound of a cell mate's name didn't register immediately, so certain was Marcel that his own fate was sealed. He remained on the floor, motionless. And so did everyone else.

"*Allez,* Hernandez! On your feet!"

Only as Hernandez, a Spanish communist come to the aid of his French brothers, rose slowly to face the open door did Marcel realize that somehow he had been spared. Then he felt someone beside him, tugging him too to his feet. They were all standing now, reaching, touching Hernandez, saying nothing, saying everything. Hernandez forced a wan smile, then reached for his tattered bag of personal belongings.

"No baggage, Hernandez. You'll have no need where you're going." The SS guard seemed almost cheerful as he pushed Hernandez toward the corridor. The young Spaniard never looked back. Too stunned even to feel anger, Marcel still couldn't believe his own name hadn't been called as silence fell over the cellblock.

Minutes later, over the rhythmic clomp of jackbooted feet in the courtyard, a tenor voice, strong and clear, lifted the opening strains of "La Marseillaise" into the cool dawn air.

Allons enfants de la Patrie
Le jour de gloire est arrivé.

Joined by first one trembling voice, and then another, the defiant tenor was soon drowned out as the prisoners in the cellblocks took up the anthem, singing as one man.

Contre nous de la tyrannie
*L'étendard sanglant est levé.**

Marcel, unable to hold back the tears, sang for all he was worth, hoping desperately like all the others to somehow muffle the inescapable chorus of rifle shots.

---

*Arise, children of the fatherland, the day of glory has arrived.
Tyranny has raised its bloody standard against us.

Chapter 1

Lyons, France

The two young children lying on straw mattresses in the sweltering attic slept fitfully, overcome by their fatigue. Théo Lévy, however, would allow himself no such luxury. Sitting on his own mattress, leaning his back as comfortably as he could against an old pine bureau, he alternately pinched his arms and bit his lower lip in an increasingly difficult struggle to remain alert. There would be time enough to sleep, he kept reminding himself, when they were all safe. But as long as the children were his responsibility—and as long as they were within reach of the authorities—he couldn't afford to let down his guard. If anything happened to them . . . He pushed the thought from his mind.

Théo yawned in spite of himself. It seemed as if they had been in the attic forever. Maybe when Tante Elise and Oncle Louis returned he could take a nap—a very short one—while Tante Elise watched the children. The couple had been so kind, even insisting that they be called "aunt" and "uncle."

Surely she wouldn't mind watching the children while he closed his eyes for just a few moments. If only it weren't so stifling hot in the attic. But the more he fought sleep, the more he felt his eyelids sag lower and still lower, and soon he too was overcome.

"Théo!"

His eyes snapped open at the loudly whispered sound of his name. There, peering anxiously into his face from no more than a foot away, kneeled little Léa. Her dark hair was damp and matted, her face gleaming with a thin film of perspiration. Inwardly, Théo cringed at the changes in her. She had seen more than a six-year-old ought to, and it showed most in her eyes. Each day it seemed that she resembled less and less the spirited, carefree girl he knew and loved. He forced a thin smile to keep from betraying his thoughts.

"Théo," Léa rasped again, rubbing her throat, "I need a drink of water."

Théo nodded without saying a word, then turned and reached up behind him to where a carafe of water sat atop the pine bureau. Their hosts' ten-year-old son, Matthieu, had climbed the narrow stairs to the tiny attic room just before noon to deliver bread, chocolate, and ice-cold water.

Handing the now-tepid water carefully to Léa, Théo watched as she tilted the carafe to her mouth. Watching the sparing way she drank made him wonder if she understood instinctively that it might be all the water they would have for a while. Oncle Louis was at work, of course, and Matthieu at school after his midday break. It seemed hours since Elise had gone out, and there was no telling when she might return. Of course, maybe Léa just found it unpleasant to gulp lukewarm water. Whatever the reason, she lowered the container after only a couple of meager swallows.

But just as she reached out her too-thin arms to return the

carafe to Théo, it slipped from her grasp and crashed noisily to the attic floor beside the mattress. Both she and Théo gaped helplessly as shards of glass scattered in every direction and what remained of the water disappeared into the cracks of the thirsty floorboards. Léa quickly covered her mouth to stifle a sob.

"Wha—what's the matter?" Eight-year-old Victor, as sweaty and disheveled as his sister, had bolted upright on his bed and was looking wildly about for the source of the noise. "What happened? Where's Tante Elise?"

"Shhh." Théo put his finger to his lips and then motioned that he thought it best to lie down again. Léa had begun to cry silently, so putting an arm about her thin shoulders, he helped her back to her mattress. She was tired, he knew, in spite of the nap. He tried to soothe both children as best he could without making a sound. It wasn't easy. As far as he knew, no one was home in the house below, but secretly, he too feared that someone had heard the glass breaking. And after having seen what happened to people in their situation, discovery was unthinkable.

Once he was sure Léa wouldn't continue crying, Théo began to collect the broken glass as best he could in the rather dim light of the attic. Someone should be home before long. Then perhaps they could return to the comfortable rooms below where the heat was more bearable, the water plentiful. He glanced at Léa and Victor, both pretending to sleep, but still very much awake. Maybe soon they could all sleep soundly.

It seemed to Théo that he hadn't enjoyed a good night's sleep in months, though he knew that it must only be a few weeks. And most of the time, when he did sleep, he dreamed scenes he wished he could forget.

The dreams had started right after the police came for his

parents. They had been given just enough time to pack a few belongings. Then after a tearful farewell, the elder Lévys had been hauled off in the back of a truck like common criminals. Criminals—the very thought made him burn inside! And for no other reason than that they were Jews. No matter how he tried, he just couldn't get it out of his mind. His father's family had lived in Lyons for three generations. Three generations! They were as French as anyone he knew—as French as the officers who arrested them, that much was sure. It wasn't fair. Especially when the government had assured them that they were only concerned with foreign Jews.

He certainly didn't want to forget what had happened—couldn't forget if he tried. But the dreams . . . Sometimes the only way to keep them at bay was to stay awake, something he found harder with each interminable day that passed.

The sound of someone pounding on the door to the house below gave Théo a start. A quick glance at the wide-eyed children confirmed that they too had heard the noise.

"Shh. Don't make a sound." He mouthed the words silently. It might be nothing, just a neighbor. But Oncle Louis had warned them not to give themselves away, even to the neighbors. "You don't always know who you can trust," he had cautioned Théo more than once. Not that Théo was likely to forget. He was pretty sure that his parents had been denounced by a long-time neighbor—a neighbor they had always thought of as a friend.

The pounding startled him once again, only it was even louder this time, as if someone were using a maul, or a timber, to break it down.

"Open up, do you hear?" The voice from the street below was muffled, but plainly understandable.

What should I do? The look of fright in the children's eyes no doubt mirrored Théo's own fear. He really had no idea when their hosts would return. He didn't even really know them—or if they would return. No! he reproached himself. Of course they'll come back. They haven't put themselves in danger only to abandon us.

The problem was that neither Elise nor Louis was here now, and someone else was. Was it the police? Or worse, the Milice? Did they know that Jews were hiding here? Is that why they were here? Would they put Léa and Victor in the camp at Vénissieux like so many others, in spite of their young age?

The pounding was becoming insistent along with the shouting, and it now sounded as if someone were around the back trying to break down that door as well. It wouldn't be long before they succeeded, whoever they were. Théo prayed they wouldn't think to look in the attic. There would be no escape if they did.

Ignoring his prior warnings not to move, Léa and Victor crushed against him now, trembling, seeking his strength. Théo put his arms about them both and held them tight. For the moment, there didn't seem to be anything else a twelve-year-old brother could do.

Hands clasped behind his back, Captain Jean-Claude Malfaire paced unhurriedly back and forth in front of a gray stucco house just a half block north of the Place de l'Europe, on Lyons' near west side. Before him, five men in blue trousers and sweat-stained khaki shirts attempted to break down the stubborn front door. He could hardly suppress a smile. Even the temporary annoyance of this delay couldn't dampen his enthusiasm for his work on this sun-drenched spring day.

It had been a mere four weeks since he had taken the oath to devote all his strength to the triumph of the revolutionary ideal of the Milice Française, to accept its discipline, to sacrifice his life, if necessary. Such a pledge was no small thing, to be sure. But for Jean-Claude it was a privilege, an honor, a sacred duty. And he was where he knew he could serve his country best—an officer in the Milice's intelligence service. More than ever, he was convinced that his old friend, Joseph Darnand, knew what he was doing when he recruited him to serve in his new paramilitary police force.

Leaving the Lyons' police had been a difficult thing to do after nearly twenty years. And Marie hadn't been as supportive of the change as Malfaire had hoped. Even now she voiced reservations, which he found disappointing. But then, she had expressed doubts about his continuing with the police too, after his brush with death at the Swiss border just after Christmas. Marie was convinced that he took far too many risks.

What he couldn't tell her, of course, was that he had had little choice but to leave the police after the December incident in which he had been shot and left for dead by a band of terrorists. The plain fact was that he had been well outside his jurisdiction at the time of the incident. His superiors, though somewhat sympathetic, felt that they could no longer trust his judgment. So, to avoid official embarrassment, they quietly allowed him to drop out of the force. Fortunately, Darnand's offer of a Milice commission had come just before his savings were completely depleted.

Marie would see things as he did, eventually. In over fifteen years of marriage, she always had, more or less. And she would again when she caught the vision for how much better France would be when the undesirable elements were eliminated.

Yes, the Milice was the place to be when France took her rightful place as a world leader once more. And it would be Joseph Darnand's Milice who would play the key role in restoring the former glory of the fatherland. With force and determination, Malfaire, and others like him, would demonstrate to the German authorities that occupation was unnecessary. Right-thinking Frenchmen could govern themselves in a manner compatible with the aims of the Reich.

"*Capitaine!* We've broken the lock." Malfaire's thoughts were interrupted by a uniformed youth whose deep-blue beret and black necktie were both slightly askew.

"Very well, then, Sergeant Poulain. Search the house—top to bottom. And make sure someone guards the entrance to the alley. I don't want anyone slipping through our fingers this time."

The trouble with the police was that there had been too few morally and physically fit young men like Poulain willing to accept strict discipline. Not so, here. Military-style discipline seemed to suit these fellows—they appeared to want it, in fact. And it pleased him that in spite of the fact that his duties dictated civilian attire, the men accorded him every military courtesy. He sometimes wondered how he had put up with the nearly unmanageable police bureaucracy for so long.

Malfaire strode up the steps to the entrance of the aging residence. He had traced three fugitive Jews to this address, thanks to a patriotic informant, and he wanted to be present when the outlaws were dragged out of hiding. He would make an example of them for the entire neighborhood to see. The sooner France was rid of the Jewish menace, the sooner social and economic recovery would take hold.

The family who owned this house would also pay a heavy price for their complicity in this affair. These soft-headed, liberal Jew-lovers had to be dealt with harshly to discourage others from taking up their misguided cause. When he apprehended them—as he most certainly would—he would make them sorry they ever looked at a Jew, let alone helped any. He might even hand them over to the SS. Yes, that's what he would do. His reputation with Lieutenant Barbie was badly in need of polish, due to a bungled manhunt last fall while he was still with the Lyons police. Of course, that wasn't really his fault. He'd been sold out by one of his own men. But perhaps this would make up some lost ground with the Gestapo chief.

Once inside the splintered front door, Malfaire found the home more Spartan than he had expected. It seemed pleasant enough and spotlessly clean. But the furnishings and decor were simple—even austere. It made him all the more proud of his own home, a short drive away, which Marie had decorated with charm and style—not an easy thing to do on a policeman's salary.

"There's no one here, *Capitaine*." The powerfully built Poulain had entered the salon and was once again standing at attention. His thick lips twitched nervously.

"What?" Malfaire's voice rose in spite of his effort to remain calm. "That can't be! The old woman across the street assured our office that three Jews arrived two days ago. She claims they're still here."

"*Oui, mon capitaine*, but—" began Poulain.

"I want them found!" roared Malfaire, his composure slipping. "Turn this place upside down and inside out if necessary, but find them." He glared at the young subordinate who remained frozen, as if trying to decide what to do next. "Now!"

As Poulain scrambled from his presence he added angrily, "And send someone across the street for the old woman. She'll pay if we've been misinformed."

Deciding that there was nothing for it but to have a look around himself, Malfaire ascended the stairs to the second floor. Under his watchful eye, armoires were unceremoniously emptied, beds ripped apart. The home's owners would have quite an unpleasant surprise when they returned.

Walking slowly from room to room, he made a mental note of each detail of the home's interior: dark hardwood floors, blue cornflower wallpaper in this room, rose paper in the next one, plastered swirls on the ceiling—

"Sergeant!" he bellowed, his eyes suddenly fixed on the ceiling. "Come quickly!"

Poulain nearly tripped over a child's wooden toy as he entered the room.

"See there?" Malfaire pointed to a shiny spot in the cream-colored plaster.

"What is it?" The sergeant looked puzzled.

"It's water, Sergeant." Malfaire tried to sound as matter-of-fact as possible.

"Yes, sir." The young man obviously didn't understand its significance.

"When was the last time it rained, Sergeant?"

Poulain paused before answering. "I think it's been nearly a week, *Capitaine.*"

"So where do you suppose this water came from?" Malfaire made no attempt to hide his irritation. "Perhaps you think Madame takes her bath in the attic?"

Poulain colored. "I'll get a ladder, sir."

"Never mind that. Let's find the attic door first." Malfaire shook his head. The lad's allegiance was beyond question. Perhaps in time his investigative powers would improve. One could only hope.

They found the entrance to the attic in the next room behind an enormous old pine armoire. Though the men had already spilled its contents on the floor, they hadn't bothered to move it away from the wall. When, under Malfaire's direction, their efforts sent it crashing to the floor in the middle of the room, a narrow wooden door was revealed.

Malfaire unholstered his semiautomatic pistol and carefully

edged the door open a crack. "Come down the stairs one at a time with your hands on your head!" he shouted into the darkened stairwell.

His command was greeted with total silence.

"You in the attic, do you hear? Come down or we'll come up!"

No answer. Only a faint scraping noise, like the sound of one empty flowerpot rasping against another in a neighbor's garden. Someone was up there!

"Wait here," Malfaire said, and strode quickly into the room where he had first seen the water spot. Raising his pistol, he fired three shots in rapid succession through the ceiling. Great chunks of plaster smashed to the floor beside him, disintegrating on impact and leaving gaping sections of lath exposed to his view. Still no response from above.

Turning on his heel, he returned to the attic door. Without a word to his men, he flung the door wide, nearly ripping it from its hinges. Taking the cramped stairs two at a time he ascended into the dark. Other than the sound of his own breathing, all was silent.

"Bring me a torch!" he called down to Poulain.

Standing on the top step, Jean-Claude Malfaire turned full circle, aiming his pistol with the beam of light as it reached into the farthest recesses of the well-kept room. He swore softly, and then again out loud. Except for three mattresses and a few odd pieces of furniture, the attic was empty.

Chapter 2

Geneva, Switzerland

Isabelle Karmazin shifted nervously in her chair, trying not to disturb the sleeping Alexandre as he lay cradled against her breast. The steady rhythm of his breathing reassured her that in this, at least, she was succeeding. She had begun to wonder if he would ever stop crying in the unfamiliar surroundings of this office of the International Committee of the Red Cross. But she had been waiting nearly an hour outside Mr. Blanchard's office, and for the past twenty minutes her little boy had been snoring lightly.

She glanced at the well-dressed woman seated next to her who gazed longingly at the slumbering child, her obvious admiration tinged with an edge of sadness. Isabelle had seen that look a hundred times before, and each time she was reminded of what an incredible gift she had been given. Alexandre was the sun, his smile banishing the clouds from her otherwise gray existence.

"Would you like me to hold him for a while?" the woman

asked in a low whisper without taking her eyes off Alexandre. "You must be getting tired."

Justine de Rocher and her husband Robert had so far been unable to have children of their own. At thirty they had not yet given up hope, of course, but it was clear to Isabelle that the lack of a child of her own weighed heavily on Justine. Being a mother seemed so right, so natural, something Isabelle could hardly have imagined prior to giving birth nearly six months ago. And Justine would make a great mother. Isabelle was sure of it. It hardly seemed fair that her friend should be denied such happiness.

"Just be careful not to wake him," she replied softly as the two women joined in the elaborate dance required to pass a sleeping infant from the arms of one to those of the other. They both held their breath as Alexandre stirred and stretched, and then exhaled together when his breathing resumed its cadence.

Isabelle rubbed her arms to restore the circulation to normal and then smoothed the wrinkles from the front of her dress as much as she could. She wanted to look her best for her appointment, but after sitting so long, and with a baby to tend—surely, Mr. Blanchard would understand.

The small waiting area outside the office of the Refugee Resettlement Bureau chief was crowded with worn-looking people of all ages. Some spoke to one another in hushed tones, but most just sat in silence, stealing nervous glances at Blanchard's office door with its translucent frosted-glass window. Directly in front of the door was a nondescript gray metal desk of the type seen in institutional offices everywhere. Behind the desk sat an equally nondescript gray woman who answered the occasional ringing of the phone, and who called out the names of those whose turn had come to see Mr. Blanchard.

"How much longer will it be?" Isabelle asked Justine, more from nervous energy than in anticipation of a reply. Though it had only been an hour, she felt as though she had waited five long months for this appointment. Today was the day she hoped to find out if her application for emigration to the United States was to be granted.

"It shouldn't be long, now." Justine nodded in the direction of a middle-aged couple across the room. "They're the only ones still ahead of us."

Us, Justine had said. As if her future, too, were somehow linked to the outcome of this appointment. Isabelle smiled to herself. That was just like Justine. Always putting herself in someone else's shoes. What a mess she would be in if the de Rochers hadn't found her wandering—babe in arms—at the edge of the woods near the border five months ago. Five months? Yes, when Justine and Robert took her in, Alexandre was not quite three weeks old. *And now look at him. How he's grown!*

"You seem awfully deep in thought, Isabelle." Justine's voice broke the melancholy spell. "What are you thinking about?"

"I—I was just thinking about the night you found me." Isabelle leaned toward her friend so as not to be overheard by others in the packed room. "It still amazes me that I didn't die of exposure, as wet and cold as I was. It's even more amazing that Alexandre didn't at least get sick!"

"You did seem remarkably healthy, all right," Justine smiled, "but you were so frightened that you almost ran from us. Do you remember?"

Isabelle nodded without offering a reply. That entire night had replayed itself over and over in her mind almost every day since: the pursuit by the police, crawling across a snow-covered field with Alexandre strapped to her back, wading waist-deep across an icy stream, and then passing through the barbed wire and onto Swiss soil. It had, at times, seemed like a nightmare.

The worst part was that she hadn't expected to come alone with her baby. Marcel Boussant had promised to accompany her into this mountain-ringed land of freedom. Marcel, whose strong arms had held her tight, whose tender lips had kissed away her tears, whose simple faith had buoyed them both. But Marcel hadn't come across the frontier like they'd planned. Something went wrong. Something must have gone wrong! There could be no other explanation. She only hoped he hadn't been arrested—or worse.

"Isabelle, are you all right?"

Isabelle dabbed self-consciously at her moist eyes. "I'm fine," she said quickly, avoiding Justine's gaze. "Really, I'm fine."

Everyone in the room suddenly seemed to be staring at her and she felt her face grow warm. What was taking Mr. Blanchard so long? And why did she feel like crying every time she thought about Marcel Boussant? Sooner or later she would have to stop thinking about him. She certainly couldn't go on like this forever. Soon she would be in America making a new life for herself. She would just have to put the past behind her.

"Monsieur and Madame Bloch," intoned the gray woman behind the desk. Immediately, the middle-aged couple rose and were ushered into Mr. Blanchard's office.

Justine reached over and patted Isabelle's hand. "We're next," she said, forcing a wan smile.

Isabelle gave her friend's hand a squeeze and breathed a prayer that this meeting with Mr. Blanchard would go well. It just had to.

Michael Dreyfus rose quietly from his seat, steadied himself against the gentle swaying of the train, and exited the compartment without disturbing the other travelers. What little noise he might have made was masked by the incessant clacking of the train's wheels on iron rails. Grasping the polished wooden handrail that ran the full length of the passenger car just beneath the window frames, he took a few stiff steps toward the rear and stopped. The narrow aisle was deserted except for a lone man in a gray business suit having a smoke at the far end near the door to the WC. The man nodded slightly in Michael's direction, and Michael returned the gesture before turning his gaze toward the magnificent countryside gliding by the windows.

The farms nestled into the steep hillsides didn't look any different from here than they had from the window inside the crowded compartment, but at least here he could stretch his legs. He'd been sitting so long he had begun to go numb.

The trip from Marseilles had taken much longer than he had anticipated, longer than anyone had anticipated. They should have reached the border hours ago, and probably would have had it not been for the delays caused by a damaged section of track just outside Grenoble. The work of local *maquisards*, one of the other passengers had informed him, just to make life miserable for the Italian occupation troops. But the Italians Michael had seen didn't seem all that perturbed by it—not perturbed enough to speed the repairs, anyway. The passengers had been forced to stay aboard the Geneva-bound train for three hours as it sat on a siding, waiting for the damaged rail to be replaced. Michael was certain that he wasn't the only one wondering if they would ever reach their destination.

Catching a movement out of the corner of his eye, Michael turned to see the door to his compartment open just wide enough to allow another passenger to slide into the aisle. A playful smile flitted across Gerard Richert's face as he joined his colleague at the window, lurching for the handrail as the train swayed around a curve.

"Doesn't look much like New York, does it, Michael?" The forty-five-year-old Richert grinned.

"You can say that again," Michael replied. The fact of the matter was that it didn't look like anything he could remember seeing. Films and photographs were poor imitations now that he was seeing this alpine wonderland in person. Gerard, he knew, had seen this all before—many times. In fact, judging by the stories he told, there wasn't much left on earth that he hadn't seen. But this was Michael's first overseas assignment in his new position as Gerard Richert's assistant. And, except for a couple of trips to Canada, it was his first time outside the United States since his family had moved there from Switzerland nearly twenty years ago.

"How much farther to the border?" he asked Gerard. "It seems like we've been on this train forever."

"That's what you said about the plane ride to Algiers," the older man teased. "Now you know why I laugh whenever the girls in the office go on about how romantic it must be to travel as I do. It's a lot more monotonous than they think." He paused, as if he were thinking about something else, then added, "It won't be long, now."

Almost as if on cue, the train began to slow. Within a few minutes, several other passengers had ventured out of their compartments into the long aisle, yawning and stretching. Michael admired the apparent ability of so many to sleep while the train ground its way through an occupied land. But for them, this wasn't unusual. Most of the passengers seemed to be either Swiss or French. In fact, Gerard too was Swiss, though he was married to an American and had worked in the States for more than twenty years with the Red Cross.

"Let's go back inside," Gerard suggested, motioning toward

their compartment as the train came to a complete stop. "The border police will board here for a passport control while we're still on the French side. That way, if your papers aren't in order, they can simply kick you off the train and be done with it. If they wait until the train stops on the Swiss side, then they have to transport you back across the frontier."

Michael said nothing, but he wondered whether Gerard were telling the truth or simply playing on his already frayed nerves. Richert seldom missed an opportunity to needle him about his lack of travel experience. Still, he'd be glad when they were safely over the border. After forty-eight hours of travel, he was ready to stretch out in a hotel somewhere and sleep for another forty-eight. But knowing his boss, there would probably be a flurry of meetings scheduled the moment they arrived.

The other four passengers in their compartment hadn't moved in their absence, allowing Michael and Gerard to reclaim the window seats facing each other. From this side of the train, the two-lane road leading into Switzerland was plainly visible, and by craning his neck Michael could just make out the welcome sight of a Swiss flag. A dozen or more automobiles were lined up along the roadway, awaiting their turn to cross the frontier. Looking back the way they had come, he could see the Italian border post, bristling with machine-gun toting *carabinieri*. The train, it seemed, was in no man's land.

He was going home, in a way, though he couldn't remember living anywhere but New York. His parents had decided to leave Berne when his grandparents died, and they had never returned together as a family. His father's machine tool business had prospered in New York, and the elder Dreyfus had occasionally traveled back to the old country. But it was as if Michael would be seeing it for the first time.

Again, the wait seemed interminable. All the other passengers looked increasingly uncomfortable, except Gerard, who had opened a copy of Rostand's *Cyrano de Bergerac* and had begun reading. Michael passed the time trying to identify the makes and models of the waiting automobiles.

He was silently bemoaning the fact that the cars were all facing away from him—making identification more of a challenge—when a commotion in the middle of the road ahead caught his attention. A cluster of people was inching its way past the line of waiting cars away from the Swiss frontier. Michael leaned forward to tap Gerard on the knee.

"What do you think it is?" he asked Gerard, pointing toward the approaching jumble of what now appeared to be eight or ten people.

"It doesn't look normal, whatever it is." Gerard's demeanor was suddenly serious for the first time all day. "Are some of those people in uniform?"

"I can't tell." Michael squinted in a vain effort to see through the window glass more clearly.

"*Passeports, s'il vous plait!*" a nasal voice sang out in the next compartment.

His attention diverted for the moment, Michael fumbled with his passport, checking for what must have been the twelfth time that his papers were in order. Satisfied that everything was as it had been the last time he looked, he refocused on the group in the road.

"They're border police," Gerard muttered, as though talking to himself.

Outside, the little group was drawing nearer. And Gerard was right. Two of them wore the gray uniform and *képi* of the border police. The others—Michael counted six of them—were civilians. And with each faltering step they took, he realized that three of the six were children, clinging pathetically to the adults who walked beside them.

"*Passeports, s'il vous plait.*" The Swiss officer stood stiffly in the doorway to the compartment, motioning with his upturned hand for everyone's travel documents. Michael glanced up at him fleetingly, then at Gerard, who was handing over his passport without taking his eyes from the scene unfolding no more than a few dozen yards from where they sat.

"What are they doing?" Michael blurted out loud, unable to contain himself any longer. "Where are they taking them?"

"Michael." Gerard sounded apprehensive.

"Your passport, please." The officer reached out a hand, but Michael's mind was on the children.

"Where are they taking them? Why won't they let them across the border?"

"Monsieur, I must have your passport!" The officer's eyes flashed from beneath the brim of his *képi*.

"Michael," Gerard fairly growled at him, "give the man your papers."

Michael felt the muscle in his jaw twitch as he handed over his passport. Didn't it bother this man that these children—this family, by all appearances—were being forced back into a hostile country?

"Monsieur," the officer gave a little sigh of exasperation. "Many people wish to come to Switzerland, but we cannot accept them all." He glanced quickly over the documents in his hands, returning each to its owner. "If we allowed everyone to climb into our little lifeboat, there would be no more room for us Swiss."

"But the children," Michael began, ignoring the stern look from Gerard Richert. "I thought we Swiss prided ourselves on giving refuge to the oppressed."

"And would you have us take in all the stray cats and dogs too, monsieur?" The officer returned Michael's passport last, a hint of condescension playing across his lips. "These people are probably just stateless Jews, not political refugees as you might imagine, *Monsieur Dreyfus.*"

Michael slumped back into his seat, comprehending all too well the officer's ulterior message.

As he turned to go, the officer added, almost too politely, "I trust you will enjoy your return to our peaceful little country." And with that he touched two fingers to the bill of his *képi*, turned on his heel, and disappeared down the aisle.

No one in the compartment said a word. Each passenger went back to napping, or reading, or whatever had occupied him before the train stopped. The fact was, except for Michael and Gerard, there hadn't been much conversation the entire journey. But now, Michael sensed that his anonymous traveling companions welcomed the silence as a means of distancing themselves from him. Perhaps Gerard too was embarrassed. He was as silent as the rest.

Reluctantly, he permitted his gaze to return to the window just as the train jerked noisily at its couplings and crept into motion. The refugees were no longer in sight. Only the two policemen were visible now, walking briskly back to their post along the car-lined road. For a moment, Michael thought he saw one of the officers looking back over his shoulder toward occupied France.

Chapter 3

"And which one of you ladies is Madame Karmazin?" Monsieur Blanchard smiled pleasantly from under a handlebar mustache and stood to his feet as Isabelle and Justine entered the room. As he stepped out from behind his desk, his worn gray suit appeared to Isabelle to be a perfect match for his surroundings.

The inside of Monsieur Blanchard's spacious office seemed to Isabelle only slightly less dull than the waiting area just outside his door. Three identical gray metal filing cabinets sat in a neat row along the left wall. Opposite the cabinets was a door, apparently an exit since none of the people Isabelle had seen entering this office had reappeared in the waiting room. A large map of the world hung at eye level behind the Resettlement Bureau chief's desk, but otherwise the yellowing walls were entirely unadorned. The top of the desk was equally bare, but for a telephone and a single unopened manila dossier. The desk chair, and the pair of wingback chairs facing the desk, all upholstered in burgundy leather, looked wildly out of place.

"I'm Isabelle Karmazin." She hoped he wouldn't notice how nervous she was. She also hoped Alexandre would remain asleep in her arms for a while yet. She turned slightly to indicate Justine. "And this is my friend and sponsor, Madame de Rocher."

"*Mesdames, bonjour,*" he said as he inclined his head in a polite bow and gestured to the wingback chairs. "Please, won't you both sit down."

As the two women seated themselves, Blanchard returned to his own leather chair and leaned his elbows on the top of the desk. Steepling his fingers under his chin, he peered intently at the slumbering Alexandre.

"This must be your son," he said after several moments of silence.

Isabelle nodded. She had filled out almost as many forms for Alexandre as for herself since arriving in Switzerland. And the Red Cross was nearly as meticulous as the Swiss government. They now knew almost as much about her son as she did.

"He certainly seems to have found a moment of peace," Blanchard said, his tone thoughtful. "It's a shame the rest of the world is not so fortunate these days."

Isabelle waited, not knowing what to say in reply. The burgundy leather creaked softly as she tried to find a more comfortable position without disturbing the sleeping child.

Blanchard looked down at his desk then, and opened the manila dossier. He leafed through a couple of pages before looking up again.

"Am I to understand that your residence here in Switzerland is legal and regular in all respects?"

"Yes." Isabelle shot a quick glance at Justine. "With the

help of Madame de Rocher and her husband, I have complied with all the government regulations for refugees."

"Since you have legal refugee status here in neutral Switzerland, what made you decide to appeal to the government of the United States?"

"I met some Americans when I first came here, and they offered me a place to live and even a job. But more than that, I want to live in peace, where I won't have to worry about being arrested or deported. I understand that even though America is at war, her citizens do not live in fear of such things."

"Surely you don't fear arrest here in Switzerland?"

"Germany is just across the border, monsieur. Do you think I will be safe here if Switzerland is attacked?"

Blanchard dismissed the idea. "I don't think Germany has any intention of invading our country, madame. And I'm sure that you are perfectly safe here."

"All the soldiers I see make me wonder if your countrymen are as certain as you are, Monsieur Blanchard. And I want to be as far from danger as possible."

Blanchard was silent for a long moment as he made some notes in the dossier. When at last he spoke again, his question caught Isabelle by surprise.

"You are not married. Is that correct, Madame Karmazin?"

Isabelle felt her face grow warm. "I was married," she said, feeling a little defensive. "My husband was killed by the Gestapo in Paris—without a trial, I might add. It's all there in the dossier." It had taken hours to fill out the application, answering question after question until she had felt completely exposed. It seemed that there was nothing about her life that she had not been required to divulge. But now she was beginning to wonder just how much of it this man had actually read. Or could it be that he was looking for discrepancies in her story?

"Madame, please forgive me if I seem indiscreet," Blanchard began again, looking up momentarily from the sheaf of papers he fingered nervously, "but I must ask if the boy is your late husband's child."

"Really, monsieur!" Justine was suddenly on the edge of her seat. Color infused her fair-skinned cheeks and her steel-blue eyes flashed fiercely. "Of course the child is her husband's. Do you mean to suggest otherwise?"

"Of course not, madame," he soothed, raising his hands as if in self-defense. "But you see, we are required to establish the parentage of all minor children, as far as it is possible, especially in cases where parentage plays a role in one's refugee status. Truly, I meant no offense, and I apologize if any was taken."

"It's all right, Justine," Isabelle said quietly. She didn't like the questions any more than Justine, but she was beginning to sense where they were leading.

Justine relaxed ever so slightly and slid her slight frame back into her chair. Her knuckles, however, remained white where she gripped the chair's arms.

Blanchard's gaze returned to the dossier. "Your husband was a Jew, Madame Karmazin?"

"Yes." Now she was certain where his questions were leading.

"And your parents?"

"Yes, and my grandparents, and their parents—"

"Please, madame. I understand how difficult this must be." His face bore a pained expression. "However, I am required to verify in person certain information that is contained in your dossier. I have only a few remaining questions."

"I understand, monsieur," sighed Isabelle, even though she would have preferred to simply end what seemed more like an interrogation than an interview. But it wouldn't do to alienate such an important man and ruin her chance for a new life in

America. She managed a weak smile. "Please continue."

Blanchard returned her smile before studying the papers in front of him once more. "So," he continued, "you do not deny that both you and your son Alexandre are Jews."

"I have no wish to deny my heritage." Isabelle looked down at Alexandre and then back at Blanchard. "Both my son and I are Jews."

"And is it on the basis of your race that you have made application for refugee status in the United States of America?"

"It was because of my race that I was hunted by the police in Paris." She fought to remain calm as she spoke. "I was arrested, put in a detention camp, and slated for deportation to God only knows where—because of my race. I had to live in hiding for months, never able to walk outdoors in the light of day, and I was hounded by police all the way to the Swiss border—all because of my race." She paused for a moment, trembling, before continuing. "So, yes, in answer to your question, I am seeking refuge in America because of my race."

Blanchard lowered his eyes. "I understand, madame, and I am sorry. Truly I am."

Sorry for what? she wanted to retort. Sorry that my life was made miserable these last few years, or sorry that I am a Jew? But she bit her tongue. It wouldn't do any good to vent her anger on this poor man. After all, he was only doing his job, even if he was rather exasperating. He couldn't be expected to really care what happened to her—not with the dozens of people whose cases he saw every day. She drew a deep breath to try to restore a bit of calm, outwardly, at least.

"One final question, Madame Karmazin." Blanchard looked directly into her eyes for the first time. "Is there anything regarding your application that you wish to change at this time?"

Change? She had gone over all the forms two and often

three times, and had given all the information requested, everything she could think of. She had been as truthful as she knew how. What could she possibly wish to change?

"No, monsieur, there is nothing I wish to change."

Blanchard looked down and cleared his throat before speaking again. "In that case, Madame Karmazin, I have been instructed to inform you that your application for emigration as a refugee to the United States of America has been denied. I'm very sorry."

Isabelle stared uncomprehending, first at Blanchard, who did not return her gaze, and then at Justine. She couldn't believe what she had just heard. Was it possible, or had she simply misunderstood? She tried to speak, but no words came. It was Justine who broke the silence.

"Denied?" she asked hoarsely. "What do you mean 'denied'?"

Blanchard cleared his throat again. "We have been informed that the United States is not accepting any Jewish refugees at this time. Based on that, and on what your friend has just told me regarding her situation, there is nothing I can do."

"But she was told—"

"I'm sorry if she was given some false hope," he cut Justine off in mid-sentence, "but if someone—anyone—told her she could easily emigrate to America, they were mistaken."

He rose to his feet then, and slowly handed a copy of Isabelle's application across the desk to her. With Alexandre still asleep in her arms she dared not reach for it, but even from where she sat she could see the words "Request Denied" stamped across the page in large red letters. It was official, yet it didn't seem possible.

Numb with disbelief, Isabelle was barely aware of anything else that Monsieur Blanchard had to say. Five months of hoping and dreaming had come to an abrupt end.

Dinner should have tasted better. At least that is what Michael Dreyfus was thinking after two days of near-constant motion. He had so looked forward to dining at a table that was not only well appointed, but also stationary. And he had imagined with great anticipation the delights of a French-Swiss meal—especially after the way Gerard Richert had gone on and on about the cuisine of his native city.

But here he sat, across from Gerard, in the dining room of the Hotel des Cignes in downtown Geneva, tracing the lacy edges of romaine lettuce leaves with his cocktail fork. The salmon filet—which came from nearby Lac Léman, as the maitre d' informed him—had not yet arrived, and already he was no longer hungry.

"Something wrong with your salad, Michael?" asked Gerard between bites. His appetite seemed perfectly healthy.

"No," Michael replied quickly. "Just not as hungry as I thought I was, I guess." He picked at a forkful of *salade niçoise*, eventually bringing the fork to his lips.

"Well, I suggest that you eat hearty tonight," said Gerard. "We won't be eating this well every day on our Red Cross budget. It's expensive, you know."

"I'm sorry, Gerard. It's just that, well, ever since we arrived I haven't been feeling too well."

"Really? You seemed fine earlier." Gerard looked at him for several moments. Only the clinking of glasses and the clank of silver disturbed the tranquillity of the smallish dining room. "Is that situation at the border still bothering you? Is that it?"

"I don't know—"

"Because if it is, you are going to have to get used to things like that. The more you see of this war, the more you'll discover that all is not right with the world. But, Michael, that doesn't mean that you have to take every incident personally. You'll worry yourself sick if you try."

"It just seems so cruel and—well, unjust, to turn away people who are in danger." He couldn't get the image of the refugee family out of his mind.

"Look, I was just as upset by that as you were, but you've got to stop dwelling on it. If you don't, it will keep you from doing what we came here for." He smiled at Michael. "You've got a big heart, and that's good. You just need to build a sort of fence around it—protect it a little—so you won't get hurt. That's what I've had to do. If I hadn't, I'd never have made it in this line of work all these years."

The waiter came just then with their salmon. They sat in silence while he busied himself removing the salad plates and refilling their glasses. When he had finished, he left them alone again.

"Try the salmon," Gerard suggested as he savored his first bite. "You won't believe how good it tastes."

Michael forced himself to chew and swallow a couple of bites before speaking again.

"Is there nothing we can do for people like that?"

Gerard dabbed at the corner of his mouth with the linen napkin. "You mean the refugees at the border?"

"Yes, and others like them. There must be others."

"I'm sure there are many others. But in wartime we're severely restricted, as you well know. We can't operate freely inside German or Italian-occupied territories. The Germans only allow us access to prisoners of war. And that's because there are German and Italian prisoners in Britain and the U.S., and they count on us to look after their people as well. Beyond that, our hands are pretty well tied."

"What about the refugees already outside the Nazis' sphere of influence?"

"Refugees are a very sticky issue—and a very political one—even in neutral countries like ours, as you will soon find out. We can't do any more than the government and the military allow. And right now that makes it hard to do anything but try to feed and clothe the ones who are here."

Gerard returned to attacking his salmon, while Michael, lost in thought, sat silently by. There had to be something he could do. It just seemed unacceptable to sit idly by while men, women, and children were sacrificed to a devilish Nazi agenda. And it was unthinkable that anyone should deny refuge to innocent people when, in doing so, they were delivering them into the very hands of their tormentors. How could such a thing be happening, especially here, in this land long renowned for its promise of refuge—the land of his birth? And what could he do about it?

After dinner, as he looked out the window of his third-floor room, Michael wondered if indeed there was anything he could do. Growing up in America as he had, he was frustrated by that country's stingy policy on Jewish immigration. But returning to his native land to find that it too seemed to be turning a deaf ear to the cries of the forgotten, left him with a sense of heaviness he had never known.

As a Jew, he felt a special affinity—even a responsibility—for those whose fate was linked solely to their race, his race. It was more than a general need to stand against anti-Semitism. Now that he had witnessed the evil firsthand, it had suddenly begun to feel personal. One day it might be him or someone he loved.

It wasn't as though the Swiss had turned away all Jewish refugees, of course. He had read reports regarding the thousands of Jews among the many refugees here already. But for him, one Jew in need of refuge was one Jew too many. Perhaps if Gerard were a Jew he would be able to see the gravity of the situation far more clearly. But Gerard was a pragmatist. That, above all, was what had enabled him to accomplish so much for so many years for the Red Cross. Still, to see his boss respond to people with more outward compassion would have cheered Michael enormously.

Glancing down the empty but well-lit street toward the dark shimmering waters of Lac Léman, he thought about his afternoon stroll with Gerard along the tree-lined Promenade du Lac. The lake had been a deep blue mirror to an even bluer sky, and the marigolds in the adjacent Jardin Anglais fairly exploded in starbursts of bright oranges and yellows. Scores of other people had milled about the lakefront too, carefree, even jovial, seemingly heedless of anything but the glory of spring. And it had been glorious, Michael had to admit. But long after he drew the curtain closed and turned out the lamp beside his bed, he lay awake, unable to get the image of the refugees out of his mind.

Chapter 4

Sitting for days in his damp, dingy hole of a ground floor cell in Montluc Prison had convinced Marcel Boussant of one thing: that it is not prisoners who insist that there are never enough hours in a day. Each sunrise began a seemingly endless day, followed by an even longer night, and the cycle repeated itself with agonizing slowness. With nowhere to go, nothing to do but think, and little to look forward to but judgment, every day contained far too many hours to suit Marcel.

When he first arrived at Fort Montluc, now a Gestapo prison, Marcel had assumed that he would pass the time in conversation with his cell mates. They would make the most of a desperate situation, he figured, sharing information, offering encouragement, perhaps even plotting an escape. The hours would pass quickly as he prepared himself mentally and physically for whatever lay ahead—whether a chance to "go over the wall," or some less appealing fate.

But watching a fellow prisoner receive a blow to the jaw with a rifle butt, merely for talking, had been all the encouragement Marcel needed to keep his mouth shut whenever there was any danger of being overheard. And it had made clear to him why so many of his fellow prisoners seemed unusually taciturn.

It wasn't long before he had changed his ideas about exercise, as well. The primitive cell, a mere five feet wide by nine feet long, with a rotting wooden bunk under the smallish opaque window, would have been crowded with one occupant. With four—that is, until this morning's executions—it was hard to move at all without jostling a fellow captive. And with little more than twenty minutes of walking allowed in the prison courtyard each morning, it was going to be difficult to maintain his strength and agility.

Escape, of course, was out of the question once he had actually seen what he was dealing with. Guards, armed and alert, patrolled the cellblock corridors, the courtyard, the roof. Those prisoners who attempted evasion were subject to summary execution, a decidedly effective deterrent in Marcel's judgment. Especially effective because of how often it was actually carried out.

So mostly Marcel and his remaining two companions sat on lice-infested straw mats on the floor, or stood to lean gingerly against age-blackened, mold-covered stone and concrete walls, each lost in his own thoughts. Mid-morning they ate in silence their one meal of thin soup, a small hunk of stale bread, and an occasional bit of sausage. The rest of the day was spent waiting—for nighttime, as much as anything. At night, they stuffed bits of old clothing under the door in a futile attempt to keep out the rats and roaches. Then, wrapped in their blankets—more for protection from vermin than from cold—they lay atop the disintegrating straw, thinking, praying, hoping for another sunrise.

Today the sun had risen the last time for Hernandez. There would be no more endless waiting for this quiet comrade from Spain. Marcel didn't even know his first name—just that he had survived Franco's fascism in his own country, only to die trying to combat it on foreign soil. And now, as afternoon was turning toward evening, Marcel gazed at his two remaining cell mates and wondered what it must be like to die—and which of the three of them would be the next to find out.

Increasingly pale and weak as the days wore on, Mouyon—as the guards referred to him—appeared to be in his early thirties. He seldom spoke, even when he had the opportunity. His frequent absences from the cellblock corresponded to new and ever more severe bruises, burns, and lacerations, ample evidence that he was a regular—and evidently uncooperative—"guest" of *Obersturmführer* Klaus Barbie's interrogation room.

Marcel had only seen Barbie once, and even then it had been from afar. One morning a couple of months previously, as he was leaving the Perrache train station, he had passed a couple of baggage handlers who had stopped work momentarily. They were watching the Gestapo chief as he strolled carelessly through Lyons' Place Carnot with his Alsatian dog.

"Gorilla ears," they had snickered to Marcel, "that's what everyone calls him." Somehow, from a distance, Barbie had seemed more arrogant than dangerous, even though his reputation as a brute, a Nazi's Nazi, was growing rapidly. But try as he might, Marcel was unable to get Mouyon to confirm or deny any of the rumors about their captor. Perhaps Mouyon's deteriorating condition was all the confirmation he needed.

The cell's third occupant was a man Marcel remembered seeing once or twice before on the train from Grenoble to Lyons, though they had never actually met. Didier was not much older than Marcel, and slightly owlish in appearance.

Little round spectacles stubbornly resisted the slight man's repeated efforts to push them into place, slipping back time and again to the midway point on his straight, thin nose.

Unlike Mouyon, Didier talked whenever he could get away with it—and whenever anyone would listen. He would whisper at night especially, when the presence of guards nearby was less frequent. He was from Grenoble, he said, though he never mentioned having seen Marcel on the Grenoble-Lyons train. Perhaps he didn't know that Marcel was from the same area. In any case, he never asked, and Marcel thought it best not to volunteer any such information.

Didier seemed rather proud of having been arrested, recounting more than once how he had helped to sabotage a munitions factory that served the Luftwaffe. The details of his capture, though, remained pretty sketchy. Marcel supposed that the circumstances were probably less glorious than Didier thought he deserved. Like the man he'd recently heard of whose embarrassing arrest had occurred in a bath house.

Marcel let him talk, but kept his responses to a minimum. Didier seemed an unlikely terrorist, so much so that it was hard to take his war stories seriously. Marcel often wondered what the real reason was for his cell mates' imprisonment, but he tried not to let on that he had doubts.

Didier remained in the cell day in and day out, except for the twenty minutes or so allowed for exercise out in the courtyard. And, like Marcel and Mouyon, he took his turn emptying the chamber pot whose contents had to be discarded each morning. But unlike Mouyon, at least in the week since Marcel's arrival, Didier had not once been taken to the Ecole de Santé Militaire, where the interrogations were carried out.

Of course, neither had Marcel—at least not yet—and it made him wonder whether or not his case had already been decided. If not, then interrogation was certain and he would be called out soon enough. If a decision had been made, then it was probably only a matter of time before he ended up like Hernandez, listening to "La Marseillaise" in front of a firing squad. The thought of it made him shudder.

Not that he was any more afraid to die than the next man. It was just that contemplating death, now that it was a very real possibility, was suddenly far more daunting than ever before. There had been ample time to reflect on the hereafter these past few days, and he hadn't really tried to avoid such thoughts. Denial was difficult when most mornings began with an execution.

Knowing that any pain he felt would only be momentary didn't really help. Nor did the fact that if he did end up being shot, it wouldn't be the first time. Even now, when he flexed his shoulder a certain way, there was a twinge of soreness at the point where a policeman's bullet had penetrated it. That cold December night was etched indelibly, painfully, into his mind. And it wasn't just the memory of a terrifying hail of gunfire and the chaos that followed.

It had been five months ago, almost to the day. In the woods near the Swiss border, not far from Annemasse, Marcel had caught his last fleeting glimpse of Isabelle Karmazin. Moments earlier, he had held her and assured her that everything would be okay. But it hadn't turned out as he promised. Yes, she was free, and he was grateful for that. But she was far from him. And now, every time his shoulder throbbed, he thought of Isabelle and felt another kind of ache—an ache he couldn't put into words. And no matter how hard he tried to put it behind him, it refused to subside. Even here in this dreary anteroom to death it continued to gnaw at him.

"Boussant!"

Marcel had been so absorbed in his thoughts that he hadn't fully heard the approaching footsteps. The clatter of keys against the cell's rusting iron lock mingled with what sounded like a flurry of German oaths. Several seconds followed in which the guard continued to fumble with the aging mechanism before the door finally swung open. Marcel, his pulse quickened, was already on his feet.

"Boussant, come with me," the guard said flatly, remaining in the corridor.

Marcel looked from the German soldier to the faces of his cell mates. Neither of them said a word, but Mouyon looked back at him with flashing, defiant eyes. Didier avoided his gaze altogether.

"*Schnell*, Boussant!" The guard had been joined by another, taller one. "Let's not keep the Lieutenant waiting."

Marcel felt suddenly dizzy with the double realization that though his life would be spared yet a few hours, he was about to be interrogated. And the Lieutenant could be none other than Barbie himself. He stumbled on rubbery legs out into the corridor. The taller of the two guards pulled Marcel's arms roughly behind his back, and ratcheted a pair of handcuffs down over his wrists. Then, with one guard walking five yards in front of him, the other prodding him from behind every few steps, Marcel filed past the long row of cells to the stairwell. It took all his concentration to keep from stumbling on the three broad steps as he descended into the courtyard. All he could think of besides staying on his feet, was the way Mouyon looked each time he returned from the Ecole de Santé.

A gray-green German military truck sat in the Montluc courtyard, its diesel engine idling. The truck's tarpaulin cover was rolled up on its frame to reveal a half dozen somber prisoners already seated on rough wooden benches in the back. Two soldiers stood just inside the lowered tailgate, their automatic weapons slung over their shoulders. Two more sat in the front of the truck, seemingly oblivious to their human cargo.

Half-lifted, half-shoved into the back of the truck, Marcel struggled vainly to keep his feet as one of the guards clamped a heavy hand on his shoulder and propelled him toward the nearest bench. The guard and his buddy laughed loudly as Marcel crashed headlong into a grizzled old man, nearly toppling them both over the side.

It took several seconds before Marcel regained his balance and managed to sit somewhat tentatively on the broad wooden plank. It took a bit longer to regain his composure. He avoided looking at the guards, but tried to mutter an apology to the old man.

"Hey! No talking!" Both guards glared at him threateningly, as if expecting him to continue.

Marcel felt his temperature begin to rise. He looked away again. It wouldn't do any good to let them get to him.

"Don't worry about me," said the old man aloud. Holding himself erect, he looked straight at the nearest guard. "I've survived tougher men than these."

The guard merely returned the old man's steely stare, and snorted disdainfully as the truck rolled out through the arched prison gate.

Anxious to think about anything but his present situation, Marcel gazed out at the city as they rumbled along the streets. Lyons was an old city, he knew, dating back to before the birth of Christ. Once a handful of buildings huddled against the hill where the garish, dominating basilica of Notre Dame de la Fourviére now perched, the city had gradually spilled across two rivers and out onto the open plain. The heart of Lyons remained the Presqu'île, a narrow spit of land running north and south between the Rhône and Saône Rivers. Its quays lined with plane trees, Presqu'île was where visitors found the best hotels, and where residents and guests alike enjoyed the most elegant restaurants, spacious shady parks, and fine old seventeenth and eighteenth century mansions. It was no wonder the Germans had found it so attractive.

Even the presence of the Gestapo, however, did not diminish Lyons' claim as capital of the Resistance. Old Lyons, its slummy hillside neighborhoods laced with *traboules*—nameless alleys and narrow passageways that cut right through the courtyards and hallways—had become a natural hideout for numerous *maquis* figures, and a source of irritation to the Nazis.

Within minutes the truck pulled off Avenue Berthelot into the central courtyard of the Ecole de Santé Militaire, once a French army medical school. A solid structure of dirty gray-brown stone, the Ecole de Santé stood just east of the Rhône River, a few hundred yards from the Perrache train depot through which Marcel had arrived and departed numerous times over the previous months, and where he had narrowly averted arrest once, months earlier. He wondered if this would be his last visit to Lyons—or anywhere else, for that matter.

Once inside the enclosed courtyard and cut off from the outside world, the prisoners were taken into the building. As they passed a stairwell, Marcel could hear loud voices coming from the next flight up, but he couldn't understand what was being said. Prodded through another door, he and his fellow prisoners descended a short flight of stairs into a spacious basement room where three large cells awaited. The blank stares of a dozen men and women greeted them from behind the cell bars.

"Pigs!" The grizzled old man fairly spat the word the moment the guards disappeared back up the stairs. "The dirty *boches* won't get anything out of me, I guarantee you."

"Don't be too sure, old man," replied a haggard man sitting on the floor nearby. Leaning his back against the wall, he didn't appear to be looking at anyone in particular as he added,

"Herr Barbie and his friends will make you wish you had something to tell, even if you don't know a thing."

The old man tried to look unconvinced without really succeeding, but said nothing more.

Marcel sat on the floor with the others and looked around. Two of his new cell mates had just arrived on the truck that brought him here. Of the other four, two were women. And although none of the four looked as battered as Mouyon often did when he returned from his sessions here, there was something dejected—almost hopeless—in the expressions they wore. How long they each had been here was anybody's guess. But if vacant stares and unkempt appearance were any indication . . .

"How long before they come for us?" Marcel rasped half-aloud to the thin man on his left. The reality of what might happen next was beginning to set in. Would the terror begin right away or not until morning?

Without turning to face him, the thin man mumbled, "Try not to think about the time. It'll only make things worse. Just be thankful for every minute they leave you in peace."

No one spoke again for some time, so Marcel waited and prayed silently that he would be able to remain true to his comrades no matter what happened. Gilles and Babette weighed especially heavy on his mind. But by now they should have gotten the latest Jewish family to safety and returned to their respective hideouts. And hopefully, his own arrest had served as a warning to the entire network to stay out of sight—and certainly out of Lyons—for a while.

Gilles Théron had grown up with Marcel, their families both members of the tiny Protestant community in Grenoble. There were differences, certainly, for while the Boussants farmed a small plot of land near the village of Domène, the Thérons ran a lucrative import-export business in Grenoble.

Still, the two boys had always valued their friendship over social or economic status. Now comrades-in-arms as well, Marcel was determined to protect Gilles at all costs. He knew in his heart that Gilles would do the same for him.

Babette was a more recent acquaintance. An expert in passing refugees undetected over the Swiss border, it was the middle-aged Babette who had made Isabelle's escape possible, and who, along with her husband Hervé, had rescued a wounded Marcel and nurtured him back to health. They treated Marcel like a son, having lost all three of their own in the German blitzkrieg. Their way of grieving such a devastating loss had been to resist the invaders however possible, in honor of their sons. Hervé, a brick mason in peacetime, commanded a growing unit of youthful, armed *maquisards*, while Babette directed rescue efforts for a number of groups assisting Jewish refugees. Marcel considered himself in their debt, and maintaining silence about their activities would be the least he could do.

He would need a story of some sort for his interrogators. That much he knew. Simply trying to hold out against their brutal measures—as Mouyon had apparently chosen to do—seemed useless. But what could he say that the Nazi inquisitors would believe? Or that they didn't already know? Obviously, Barbie and his henchmen had enough information to have him arrested, but how much did they really know? And what if they didn't believe his story? From where he sat, his situation looked bleaker by the minute.

Unfortunately, he had been carrying his actual identification papers at the moment of his arrest, so there was no point in trying to establish a false identity. He only hoped that his identity wouldn't lead to problems for his family as it had once before. Maman had been forced to flee to her parents' home in Ardeche along with his brother, Luc, who was almost ten, and his seventeen-year-old sister, Françoise. There, they hoped to remain out of harm's way until the rumored Allied invasion swept the Germans out of France. And though it had been over a month since he had last seen them, he said a prayer for them every day. He hoped it would be enough.

A single exposed light bulb, hanging by a thin pair of wires from the ceiling outside the cell, glared relentlessly like an all-seeing eye as long minutes turned to hours. And while some of the prisoners fell eventually into an uneasy slumber, most, like Marcel, kept a silent vigil, their eyes on the door at the top of the stairs.

Chapter 5

It was noon the next day before they came for him. Hearing his name called as if from a great distance, Marcel struggled to his feet as first one and then a second SS guard descended the eight steps into the basement of the Ecole de Santé. Weary from lack of sleep, he made no effort to resist as the two Germans cuffed his hands behind his back and led him back the way they had come.

After mounting yet another flight of stairs, they trod the length of a corridor which divided two rows of offices. Glancing through the windows as his guards hurried him along, Marcel could see dozens of people seated at desks—both men and women. Some were uniformed, while others were dressed in civilian clothes. But they all seemed completely unaware of Marcel's passing, absorbed rather in their forms, their telephones, their typewriters. It struck him that except for the uniforms, these offices had the look of any ordinary place of business. And he wondered just how much these functionaries actually knew about what went on here.

The guards paused momentarily to knock before entering the door at the end of the hall, and Marcel took a deep breath. He had no way of knowing what awaited him on the other side of the door, but all his instincts told him to prepare for the worst.

God, I don't know if I can do this, he breathed silently. And then the door opened and he was ushered inside.

Looking up at him from behind a large but plain wooden desk was the man he immediately recognized as Lyons' Gestapo chief, Klaus Barbie. To Marcel's surprise, the *Obersturmführer* was dressed in civilian attire, his fashionable deep-blue tie neatly knotted over a gleaming white shirt. His office, though sparsely decorated (a picture of the Führer was all that graced the wall behind him), was as neat and clean as he was. The top of the desk too was very neatly organized, with an ordinary black telephone, a matching pair of small easel frames, and a dossier lying open on top of a dark gray blotter. Off to one side was what appeared to be a riding crop.

"Please have a seat, Monsieur Boussant," a smiling Barbie offered politely in excellent French. Caught momentarily off guard by the unexpected gesture, Marcel hesitated. Within seconds, however, he was thrust unceremoniously into a straight-backed chair by the two uniformed SS men who then remained standing behind him.

"Relax, gentlemen," Barbie scolded the men in a mild voice as he rose from his chair. "We don't want to give our young friend here the wrong impression, now do we? This doesn't have to be unfriendly at all." Still smiling, he sauntered around the side of his desk, seating himself on its front edge directly in front of Marcel.

He wasn't as tall as Marcel had remembered, but then he had only seen him at a distance. And his hair was dark, almost black. But what struck Marcel most were his piercing blue eyes—not just the color, but the fact that they seemed to be in constant motion. And though he found the man's gaze a bit unnerving in spite of the easy smile, Marcel wondered if all the rumors of brutality could be true. This polite German officer simply didn't look capable of the savagery of which others accused him.

"So, Monsieur Boussant," the Gestapo chief began again, "I hope you haven't been too uncomfortable at Fort Montluc these past few days, but I've simply been too busy to have this little talk any sooner. You understand, don't you?"

Marcel looked down at the worn rug on the floor without acknowledging the question. There were stains here and there on the rug, and he wondered briefly if any were bloodstains.

"Do you have children, Monsieur Boussant?" Barbie chuckled softly when Marcel didn't respond, then twisted around and reached for one of the picture frames on the desk behind him. "No, of course you don't," he replied to his own question. "You're much too young."

Extending the framed photograph to within a foot of Marcel's face, Barbie revealed the black and white image of a small child. "This is my daughter," he said. "Little Ute Maria. Isn't she beautiful?"

Marcel looked first at the photo and then at Barbie. He was puzzled. Why was this man showing him a picture of his daughter? And why was he being so cordial? There was something very strange about all this.

Barbie gazed lovingly at the image of his daughter's face. "I'm a very good father, you know," he said rather absently. "Everyone says so." He replaced the photo next to the telephone, then swiveled back to face Marcel. Several seconds passed before he spoke again.

"I imagine you must be hungry. Would you care for something to eat?" He looked quickly at one of the guards. "Kurt, bring some bread and cheese for our friend." He sounded as though it were the most natural thing in the world for him to say under the circumstances. "Oh, and some wine too," he added as the guard left the room.

"No, thank you," Marcel rasped, his voice sounding strange to his own ears. He wasn't about to lunch with Klaus Barbie. He looked down again at the rug beneath him.

"What's that you say?" Barbie asked. The smile had disappeared from his face.

Marcel cleared his throat and looked up at the German officer. "No, thank you, Lieutenant." He tried to sound firm, resolved, unafraid. But inside he braced himself.

Barbie studied him for a long moment. "Nonsense, Monsieur Boussant," he said at length, as the smile once again softened his features. "Everyone has to eat. When Kurt returns with the food, you can have whatever you like."

Marcel had to admit that the idea sounded tempting. He hadn't eaten a decent meal in over a week, and he had been given nothing more than a few sips of stale, tepid water in the past twenty-four hours. Food—any food—sounded good just now. Still, it wouldn't do to eat with the enemy. He reminded himself that it was indeed what Klaus Barbie represented—the enemy—no matter how cordial, no matter how humane he might appear.

"Perhaps we can be helpful to one another, you and I," Barbie was saying, seated once more behind his desk. He began toying with his riding crop as he leaned back in his chair. "Yes," he continued without looking directly at Marcel, "I think we'll get along very well."

There was something in the way he said it that made Marcel bristle. He had no intention of being helpful, and he didn't see how there could ever be any cooperation between them. Klaus Barbie stood for everything Marcel despised. So, what made him think—how could he be so arrogant as to think that Marcel would cooperate? And yet, there he sat, smiling his beady-eyed smile, waiting for what? For Marcel to tell him everything he wanted to know? Well, the little Nazi was in for a big surprise, Marcel told himself. He hated being underestimated, especially in such an obvious way.

"Ah, there you are, Kurt." Barbie rose from his chair as the guard entered the room with a tray of food and a bottle of red wine. Kurt placed the tray and the bottle on Barbie's desk as the lieutenant indicated, and then retreated to join his colleague who stood silently behind Marcel's chair. The tray held Marcel momentarily spellbound, for on it lay not only the requested Camembert cheese and *baguette* of bread, but there were several large slices of sausage and what had to be the first ripe cherries of the season. He could feel the saliva begin to flow inside his parched mouth.

Barbie, meanwhile, busied himself uncorking the bottle. When he had finished, he poured the ruby liquid into two glasses which he produced from a desk drawer.

"Remove his cuffs," he ordered the guards. "He can't very well eat with his hands behind his back, now can he?"

Rubbing his wrists to restore the circulation, Marcel couldn't take his eyes off the food. If only his cell mates could see this—they would never in a hundred years believe him. In fact, he could hardly believe it himself. He had lain awake all night in anticipation of a day of terror, and here he was in front of more food than he had seen in weeks!

"Please, Monsieur Boussant, help yourself." Barbie raised his glass. "To good men everywhere," he said almost solemnly. "May they work together for peace and prosperity." Both guards murmured something in German that sounded vaguely affirming as Barbie put the glass to his lips and drank deeply.

"Now, then," he said as he set his glass down and leaned forward on his elbows. "As long as you're here, why don't you answer a few simple questions? That way you can walk out of here freely and do whatever you like. As you can see," he gestured with open hands toward the untouched food, "I am not such an unreasonable man. Just a tiny bit of cooperation and you are free to go. How does that sound?"

Marcel cleared his throat again. "I'm sure I don't know anything you'd find very useful, Lieutenant." He hoped the tremor in his voice wasn't noticeable to anyone but himself.

"Come now, Monsieur Boussant. I'm confident that you know a great deal more than you let on." The smile was fading. "Perhaps you could begin by telling me about your little rendezvous at the Café de la Marine. Who were you meeting there?"

So this was how it was going to begin. Marcel's mind began to whirl as he tried to decide what to say. He knew if he refused to say anything at all he would end up like Mouyon, beaten senseless every few days until he caved in, or until Barbie tired of the game and had him killed. On the other hand, if he cooperated too willingly Barbie might become suspicious and kill him anyway. What he needed was time—time to figure out what to do.

Instead of answering right away, he reached tentatively for the hunk of bread nearest him on the tray.

"Yes, yes, go on. Eat!" Barbie suddenly seemed a little impatient.

Marcel chewed slowly, savoring each morsel. The bread was fresh, obviously baked this morning, unlike what he received in his cell each day. There was no telling how old that bread was, or where it had been before it came to the prison. But this was different, better, and at the moment, it tasted as good as any *baguette* he could remember.

"The Café de la Marine." Barbie would not be put off for long. "Who did you go there to meet?"

Marcel swallowed the last bit of bread in his mouth. "I didn't meet anyone," he protested. "I had just sat down to eat lunch when—"

"Really, Monsieur Boussant. What sort of fool do you take me for?" Barbie's smile was completely gone now, replaced by a look of indignation. "I not only know who you are and where you live, I know a great deal about you. I know that you take the train from Grenoble to Lyons more frequently than is customary for a farmer. I also know that you have been seen before at the Café de la Marine, which is nothing more than a cesspool of criminals and terrorists. I know you were there to meet someone. Given that and the fact that you were arrested in possession of falsified ration coupons, you have some explaining to do."

Marcel wasn't sure whether to be frightened or relieved. The fact was, Barbie knew more than Marcel had expected. How did he know about the travel to Lyons? Had the Gestapo been watching him, and if so, for how long? As for the Café de la Marine, he had been there before, but only once. So how did Barbie know about that? Unless he had been followed by the Germans over the past month or so, the only explanation was that he had been betrayed by someone in the Resistance—someone who knew him. But who?

What gave him some small sense of relief, however, was the fact that Barbie had mentioned nothing of his activities on behalf of Lyons' Jews. Fortunately, his contact had failed to show at the café as planned, or he too would certainly have been arrested.

It had seemed simple enough. But then it always did. All he had to do was deliver the forged ration coupons to a contact person who would then distribute them to Jews in hiding, as well as to the families who hid them. It was the only way most of them could hope for even a meager supply of food. And even then it could hardly be considered adequate. With coupons in hand, they would be able to purchase Spartan quantities of bread, cheese, meat, butter, and other staples—except when the stores ran short, of course. Without the coupons they would be forced into the black market—if they had money. And unless they were willing to steal, slow starvation was the only other option.

Marcel had been delivering the false coupons without incident for weeks. Even the fact that his contact was not always the same person had not proved too great an obstacle. His friend Gilles meticulously prepared the coupons which Babette had promised to needy families. Marcel's part was to carry the valuable papers to their destination. A meeting place was arranged—usually someplace public like a park or a café—a prearranged code was exchanged, and the coupons were handed over discreetly. When it was all over, Marcel would get back on the train and head back to Grenoble. It was dangerous—as he had since discovered—but it was simple.

Of course, sitting around for weeks on end in a frigid, makeshift *maquis* camp in the Chartreuse hills had also been simple. But Marcel had had his fill of that. Waiting for the weather to improve, waiting for more airdrops of arms from the British and Americans, waiting for orders from de Gaulle's London headquarters, always waiting. And when they weren't waiting, they were moving camp from place to place to avoid being discovered by the Nazis or the Milice. It was enough to drive a man crazy.

Far less simple, and far more dangerous, were the times he and Gilles had transported Jews in the trunk of Gilles' car, delivering them to Babette Chassin for the final dash over the Swiss border. Or the time they had broken into a sub-prefecture office, along with several of Hervé's men, looking for ration coupons. They had only narrowly escaped, and forging the coupons had seemed much more sensible after that, even if it was less exciting.

When the Gestapo raided the Café de la Marine, Marcel had been taken completely off guard. Everything had gone so smoothly up to that point that he had perhaps become a little careless. Normally, when a contact failed to show at the appointed hour, he would wait an additional ten minutes or so and then leave the area. This time, however, he had decided to stay for lunch and watch the nearby Rhône River roll by on its way to the Mediterranean.

"I'll ask you again," said Barbie as he rounded the corner of the desk. "Who were you to meet at the café, and where did you get all the false coupons?"

The coupons themselves were sufficient evidence to insure that Marcel would remain in prison for years at the very best. There was nothing to gain by denying that he had been caught with them.

"The coupons were for my friends," he began slowly.

"Yes, go on!"

"I have a couple of friends who are hiding to avoid the S.T.O. They can't get any food without the coupons."

Barbie said nothing. Marcel hoped desperately that he would buy his story. Enough of it was true that he didn't really have to invent much. Hervé Chassin's *maquisards*, with whom he served, were largely made up of young men fleeing the *Service du Travail Obligatoire*. The S.T.O., as it was commonly referred to, was a program in which young, able-bodied Frenchmen were drafted and shipped off to work in German factories. These "volunteer" workers were supposed to help alleviate the acute labor shortage resulting from the huge number of German men in uniform. But few participated, and fewer still were truly volunteers.

"Your friends are idiots!" Barbie made no attempt to conceal his disgust. "If they had any sense at all they would go to work in Germany. At least there they could lead honorable lives. And they would be fed without resorting to crime."

Marcel said nothing. He wished they could talk about something besides food. The bit of bread he had eaten had tasted wonderful, but it had failed to satisfy his hunger. He eyed the tray filled with food. Perhaps he could eat just a little more, before Barbie changed his mind. He reached out his hand for a slice of sausage. But just as his fingers closed around it, Barbie's riding crop came to rest across the back of his wrist, pinning his hand to the tray. Barbie leaned his face close to Marcel's, his breath hot and stale.

"Suppose you begin telling me the truth," he hissed, "and the sooner the better. I assure you I can be very persuasive." He lifted his riding crop and Marcel withdrew his empty hand immediately.

"Now," Barbie continued, his voice rising, "where do you get the coupons? Who is your contact? How do you know where to meet him? Who is your leader?"

Marcel tried hard not to let the rapid succession of questions confuse him. He had to keep his story straight at all costs. A slip-up could cost him dearly.

"I—I get a note in my mailbox telling me where to meet someone," he said slowly, trying to think ahead as he talked.

"Who delivers the note?"

"I don't know."

"And who does the note tell you to meet?"

"No one. It just tells me when and where to go."

"How do you know who to give the coupons to?"

"I—" Marcel hesitated for an instant, sensing a trap. "I told you I give them to my friends."

Barbie's riding crop caught Marcel just above his left ear, knocking him off balance and sending him crashing to the floor. Dazed and shaken, he tried to regain his feet. Kurt and the other guard grabbed him roughly from behind and slammed him back into the chair.

"Cuff his hands behind him," growled Barbie. His face seemed suddenly twisted and discolored. "I treated you like a gentleman, offered you food, and how do you repay me? With lies, contemptible lies!" He shrugged off his jacket and began rolling up the sleeves of his white shirt. "You will talk to me, Boussant. I guarantee you that. And this time you had better tell me the truth."

Marcel felt cold drops of sweat breaking out on his face and neck as the guards clasped the handcuffs around his wrists. This was the real Barbie, no pretense, no mask of politeness. From here on out it would be more than just a struggle of wits; it would be a test of resolve—and perhaps physical endurance.

"Let's begin again." Barbie seemed to have gotten control of himself once more. "Who do you give the coupons to?"

"I told you, I give them to my friends."

Barbie slapped Marcel across the mouth with the back of his hand. This wasn't going to be easy.

"Who gives you your instructions?"

"I don't know. I just get messages in my mailbox."

Again the knuckles across his lips. This time he tasted blood.

"Who's the leader of your terrorist group?"

"I'm not a terrorist. I just have some friends who don't want to go to Germany."

This time Barbie's closed fist connected with Marcel's cheekbone, sending both him and the chair over backward. Immediately, the guards righted the chair with him in it. He shook his head to try to clear his thoughts. He wasn't sure how much more of this he could take. Eventually he would have to give Barbie some answers that satisfied him, but he didn't want to arouse suspicion by caving in too easily.

Two hours later, as he was being lifted off the floor yet again, Marcel wondered if there were any places on his body which Klaus Barbie and his guards had not yet slapped, slugged, kicked, or flayed with the riding crop. There were moments when he thought he would lose consciousness, only to have one of them throw water in his face. He was wearing down, unsure as to how long he could hold on, and not knowing if or when Barbie would give up. The Nazi was certainly showing no signs of relenting. If anything, his rage only seemed to mount with the passage of time.

"Ready to talk yet, Boussant?" Barbie sneered down at him, "I can keep this up for a long time, you know. And when I get tired, Kurt and Erich will be only too happy to give me a break. Right, men?"

The two guards laughed and slapped playfully, menacingly, at the back of Marcel's head.

Barbie was right. He could keep this up indefinitely. And Marcel could feel his own strength—even his resolve—dwindling rapidly, dramatically, with each successive blow. How much more could he take? He really didn't have a good answer for that. All he knew was that he didn't want to keep getting hit.

"I've had enough," Marcel mumbled through parched, swollen lips. "I'll tell you what you want to know."

Chapter 6

Something wasn't quite right. Jean-Claude Malfaire had come home early to enjoy some well-deserved time with his family. Shirt sleeves rolled up, tie loosened, he slouched in his favorite chair on the terrace behind his house. He sipped a tall *pastis* and watched absently as Marie fussed over her red geraniums a few feet away. It was a perfect afternoon, he told himself. Or it would have been, except for the nagging puzzle of yesterday's botched arrest that he had so far been unable to solve.

It should have been routine. These things usually were. A call came in from some civic-minded soul, he took a few men to the given address, arrested the Jews or suspected terrorists, put some fear into the neighborhood, and that was that. At least that was how it usually went. Oh, occasionally things didn't go quite as smoothly as he hoped. But most of the time a little planning and a healthy dose of intimidation was all it took to ensure success.

Yesterday had been different, and for some reason he couldn't get it out of his mind. Three Jews. That's what the old woman who called had said. Three children, he had since discovered. Children. It should have been as easy as falling down.

Once he and his men managed to get inside the house, it seemed clear that someone had been hiding there. And even with Poulain's gun to her head, the woman who had denounced the children swore by everything holy that she had not seen them leave the house. Apparently, they had vaporized into the warm spring air. And that was what was troubling him. How could he and five trained *miliciens* have been outwitted by three children—and Jews at that?

"Dédé will be ready to come home from the *maternelle* soon," Marie said softly. "I'll get washed up and walk down to get him."

"I'll go, *chérie*," said Malfaire, putting his drink down. "I don't get the chance very often."

"Are you sure? I don't mind, really."

"I'm sure, Marie. Besides, it'll be fun to surprise him." He rose from his chair and walked to where she knelt on the terrazzo tiles, tending her beloved potted plants. "The garden looks lovely," he said as he leaned over and kissed her lightly on the forehead. "Almost as lovely as the gardener."

Her pleasure shone in her eyes. "Go on, flatterer, and get your son." Then with a wink she added, "You can tell me more lies later."

He smiled. "In fifteen years I've never needed to resort to lies, *chérie*. Why would I start now?"

"Sixteen," she chided playfully. "Maybe your eyesight is as faulty as your memory."

He chuckled and cast one last look at her as he started off toward the *maternelle*. She was something, his Marie. There was no mistaking that.

Dédé, as they had nicknamed their soon-to-be-six-year-old son, André, would start primary school in the fall. For now, however, he attended a nearby *maternelle*, a sort of kindergarten. He was a bright boy. Even his teacher said so. And his father had high hopes for him. Dédé wanted to be a policeman, but Jean-Claude was sure he was destined for even greater things—a general, perhaps, or a prefect.

One thing was certain, however. Whatever the boy chose to do, he could count on his father to stand behind him, even to pull some strings if necessary. Young André would be the one—the only one—to carry on the family name. And it was important that he have every advantage.

There had very nearly not been any heir at all. After ten years of frustration, Jean-Claude and Marie had given up hope. Then, seemingly out of nowhere, their prayers were answered. Well, truthfully, Marie's prayers were answered. Jean-Claude didn't pray much. "God's going to do whatever He wants to do, no matter what I say," he always told Marie. Apparently, God had meant for him to have a son all along. That was all there was to it.

"Papa! What are you doing here?" André bounded down the front steps of the *maternelle* to meet his father, his little schoolbag draped over his shoulder the way older schoolchildren did it.

"*Bonjour*, Dédé," Malfaire said, planting kisses on the boy's ruddy cheeks. "I took the afternoon off just so I could come walk with you." He took the boy by the hand and they started off toward home.

"So, what did you learn today?" he asked André, after they had walked a few yards.

"Well, today the *maîtresse* told us about the Ten Commandments."

"That's very good, Dédé. Everyone ought to know about

the Ten Commandments."

"Do you know about them, Papa?"

"Of course, Dédé. Since I was a boy like you. Only I learned them from the priest."

"You mean Father Benoit?"

Malfaire ground his teeth almost as an involuntary reflex. Old Father Benoit was the priest at St. Just where Jean-Claude had attended since boyhood. But Benoit had become rather outspoken since the German invasion—outspoken against the occupiers and against their anti-Semitic policies. It irritated Jean-Claude that this old cleric whom he had long admired should stick his nose into affairs that clearly did not concern him. The government should decide issues of racial policy, he reasoned, not the church. The worst of it was that the aging priest had actually had the temerity to admonish him to his face about his own involvement in carrying out government policies. He considered it an outrage of the worst kind, though nothing would be served, of course, by burdening his son with all that.

"Yes, son. Father Benoit taught me the Ten Commandments."

"Hey, Papa. The *maîtresse* said that Moses was the one who gave us the Ten Commandments."

"Your teacher is right, Dédé. Moses was a great man."

"But my friend Jules said that Moses was a Jew."

Malfaire cleared his throat. "Well, er, perhaps—that is, I suppose he was, but that was a long time ago. Anyway, he was certainly not like the Jews we have here in Lyons."

"Oh." He looked thoughtful. "Are all the Jews in Lyons bad people?"

"Jews aren't like us, Dédé. They're dishonest, they're greedy, and they don't even believe in God—not the real God, anyway."

André looked puzzled. "Even the children?" he asked.

"It's not really their fault, son. It's the way they're taught, even when they're little. It's quite shameful, really."

"Is it true that Marshall Pétain is sending all the Jews far away from here?"

"Who told you that?"

"My friend Jules."

"Well, you don't need to worry about things like that." He patted his son reassuringly on the shoulder. "No Jews are ever going to bother you. I can promise you that."

They walked along in silence for a minute or two before André spoke again.

"Papa, is the war almost over yet?"

"Pretty soon, Dédé," he sighed. "Pretty soon."

"Are the Germans winning, or are we?"

"We're not fighting the Germans anymore, son."

"But Jules said—"

"Sounds to me like Jules does all the talking at the *maternelle.* You shouldn't listen to everything he says."

André grinned sheepishly up at his father. "That's what the *maîtresse* says too."

When the two arrived home, Marie Malfaire was still in the garden, organizing several new plants in their terra-cotta pots.

"Why don't the two of you go play *boules* in the park while I finish up here?" she suggested. "I'll come join you after a while."

"Can we, Papa?" André looked elated.

"Why not?" Malfaire smiled indulgently at his son. "You run along inside and get the *boules*, and I'll meet you out front."

As André dashed inside to fetch the steel balls with which the popular game was played, Malfaire turned back toward his wife who was sliding several empty clay pots over the terrazzo tiles and up against the garden wall. The scraping sound caught him up short. There was something peculiar, almost weird about the sound. Where had he heard it?

And then it came back to him in a rush. The attic. Just before he entered the attic yesterday he had heard the same sound. And the only thing in an attic that could possibly make such a sound was one roofing tile scraping against another. Why hadn't he thought of that before? The roof tiles. Of course! The children hadn't vanished at all. They had simply found some loose tiles and climbed out onto the roof!

"Jean-Claude, are you all right? Jean-Claude?"

He stared blankly at Marie for a few seconds. "I, I—uh, I have to go, *chérie*," he stammered out at last. "Some—something has come up." He turned to go.

"Jean-Claude! What about the *boules* game?" she called after him. "What about André?"

Jean-Claude Malfaire didn't answer. If he hurried he might just find the three Jewish children before they got too far away.

Théo Lévy crouched low behind a pile of empty packing crates as a nearby door opened inward to reveal a brief but tantalizing view of a restaurant kitchen. He barely noticed the boy who stepped out into the alley and prepared to light a cigarette. Instead, his eyes were fixed on the chef inside, busily preparing for the dinner crowd which would begin filing in through the front door in a couple of hours. Then, as quickly as it had opened, the door swung closed, banishing him from the feast of sights and smells.

Moments later, the acrid smell of tobacco smoke reached his nostrils, just as his stomach growled audibly. He immediately hugged his sides tightly, as if doing so would keep him from being overheard. With nothing to eat since yesterday's lunch, his stomach had been complaining all day. But the unknown youth, carefully exhaling a long thin plume of smoke into the air, didn't seem to take any notice of him at all.

Victor and Léa were probably wondering why he hadn't returned yet, and by now they would be worried. He hadn't intended to be gone this long. It had just taken far longer than he expected. Hopefully the children weren't crying. It wouldn't do for them to be discovered in his absence.

He had found the perfect hiding place for the three of them last night under the west end of the Pont de la Feuillée, a bridge spanning the Saône River away from the heart of Lyons. Fortunately, he had made the discovery before twilight. Finding his way back in after dark had not been easy, but it would have been nearly impossible had he not known the way already. So he was confident that as long as Léa and Victor kept quiet they would be safe.

At length the unknown boy took one last long pull on his cigarette, flipped the butt onto the paving stones, and turned toward the restaurant door. Slowly, so as not to attract any attention, Théo rose from his hiding place and crept forward. As the boy stepped inside, Théo rushed forward on cat's feet and reached out a hand to keep the door from swinging completely shut. He pressed himself against the doorpost and listened.

"Oh, it's about time you came back in!" The deep voice probably belonged to the chef. "I pay you to work. *Non*?"

Théo couldn't make out the boy's mumbled reply.

"*Allez*," the chef continued his scolding, "I told you I wanted the dining room ready early this evening. A *wehrmacht* officer will be along any moment to check on preparations for the dinner party. And I'm warning you, everything had better be spotless."

This time the boy's response was plainly audible. "I don't see why we should go to any special effort for the stinking *boches!*"

"You'll do as I say, or you'll be out on the street," the chef retorted. "Besides, if you're nice to them, they'll probably leave a big tip. Anyway, if we don't serve them, they'll just spend their money somewhere else. Is that what you want?"

Théo waited for the reply but heard none.

"I'll show you what I want once more," the chef continued, his tone somewhat softened, "but then I've got to finish preparing the *coq au vin.*"

The chef's voice trailed off until Théo was no longer able to hear him at all. So carefully, gingerly, he eased the door open a few inches and peered around it into the kitchen. Just as he expected, there was no one. He squeezed his wiry body through the narrow opening and crept silently inside.

Standing in the kitchen, surrounded by the sights and smells of more food than he had seen in weeks, Théo suddenly felt a surge of rage welling up inside of him. At this very moment some German officers were waiting to fill their bellies with French food and wine, while across town, Léa and Victor were huddled under a bridge, hoping for a scrap of bread—anything to relieve their hunger. How could this be? It wasn't right. It just wasn't right. Léa and Victor were too young to suffer this way, especially when others—Germans, no less—had plenty. Whatever small reservation he still harbored about stealing food dissipated in the heat of his anger.

Théo padded softly to the squat black stove where steam escaped in little puffs from beneath the lid on a huge pot. That would be the *coq au vin,* he decided. He couldn't very well carry that away, so he began looking around. He would have to hurry before the chef or his helper came back. The trouble was, he hadn't really planned what he would do if he actually did manage to get inside. Now that he was virtually surrounded by food, he couldn't decide what he should take.

This wasn't his first attempt of the day. But the long line in front of the *boulangerie* this morning had kept him from getting inside at all, let alone stealing any bread. And then the grocer had caught him trying to conceal two cans of sardines under his shirt, and had taken him by the ear out into the street where he insulted him in front of all the passersby. This was his last chance for a meal today, the last chance to get something, anything, for the children.

Suddenly frantic with that realization, Théo began grabbing things from the counters. He bit off a big chunk of sausage and shoved the rest into the pocket of his trousers. A couple of bites of paté followed and then a mouthful of cheese. Still chewing, he stuffed a handful of olives in his pocket without eating any.

Just as he reached for a long, thin *baguette*, he heard the chef's voice again. It sounded much too close. Quickly, he broke the *baguette* in half and pushed both halves down inside his shirt. Then, as he headed for the back door, he stopped in front of the stove. Grasping a pot holder with his left hand, he removed the lid from the simmering pot. With his right hand he picked up the salt shaker and rained its contents down on the wine-soaked chickens inside. He set the shaker back atop the stove as the door to the dining room opened.

"What do you think you're doing?" The chef's eyes were bulging, his face crimson.

For the briefest instant, Théo thought that the chef would explode, but not wanting to find out, he dashed for the back door. As the chef screamed obscenities at him, he fumbled with the latch for what seemed like the longest time before finally bursting free into the alley.

Ignoring the threatening voices behind him, Théo ran down the alley and into the street beyond, dodging pedestrians as he went. Car tires shrieked and their horns blared in alarm as he crossed first one street and then another. All he could think of was to get as far away from the restaurant as possible as quickly as possible. So he ran—blindly, wildly—until he could run no more. His breath was coming in great ragged gasps, making it hard to focus on anything else, when he realized that he didn't know where he was. He wanted to sit down and get his bearings, but his pockets were so full he could hardly bend at all. Finally, he found an alley where he could lean against a wall unseen, at least until he regained his breath and his bearings.

Minutes later, his breathing was more even, his pulse less intense, Théo felt almost calm. He chewed off some of the baguette, smiling to himself as he thought of a bunch of Germans sitting down to the saltiest *coq au vin* they would ever eat. It had almost got him caught, his last-minute prank, but right now it seemed worth it. He wished he could be there to see the look on the chef's face. Perhaps he wouldn't be serving any more Germans after tonight!

In another half hour he was scrambling along the catwalk under the Pont de la Feuillée on his way to where Léa and Victor were hiding. Tonight they would eat well. He only regretted that finding food had kept him away from the children for so long.

"Victor! Léa!" he called, as he jumped down off the catwalk. "I'm back."

There was no answer.

"It's me—Théo," he tried again, peering into the gloomy concrete cave that served as their temporary home.

But Léa and Victor were not there. Instead, rising from the place where the children should have been, was the biggest man Théo had ever seen. Théo didn't move—barely even breathed. But he felt as if he were going to be ill.

"So, there you are, *petit*," the giant rumbled gruffly. "We've been waiting a long time for you."

Chapter 7

"Wh—where are they?" Théo felt as though his lips were numb. "Where are the children?"

"Now, don't you worry about them, *petit,*" said the giant, reaching out a big paw to pat Théo on the head. He smelled of garlic. "They're someplace where no one can find them."

"What have you done to them?" Théo was angry. He resented being called *petit*, though from the giant's point of view it probably made sense. Nor did he appreciate being patted on the head like a mere child. But he was scared too. Scared that he might not see Léa and Victor again. "Tell me what you've done to them!" he demanded, drawing himself up to his full height.

"Well," the big man said slowly, "to begin with we took them to a safe place. We gave them a bath and some clean clothes. Then we fed them some lunch." He laughed, a big, hearty laugh. "That boy, he sure can eat. I've never seen anything like it."

"Then you're not with the police?" Théo was confused.

The giant laughed again and seemed to look right past Théo. "Do you hear that, Hugue? He wonders if we're with the police."

Théo, his thoughts swirling, wheeled around to find a second man, of normal proportions, standing just a few feet behind him. Arms folded across his chest, he too was smiling.

"Now that is a good one, Pepin," he chuckled. "There's never been a uniform cut large enough to fit the likes of you. That I am absolutely sure of."

"Who are you?" Théo was more confused than ever. If they weren't with the police, then why were they looking for him? Why would they take the children? The police would not have bathed or clothed the children, though he guessed they might have fed them something.

"Let's just say that we're your friends, Théo," said Hugue.

"H—how do you know my name?"

"Your sister Léa told us. She said she would only go with us if we came back to get you. And Victor agreed." Hugue sounded matter-of-fact. "So here we are."

"I'm not going anywhere with you," protested Théo. "How do I know you really have them?"

"I thought you might say that." Hugue held up a dress that looked remarkably like the one Léa had worn daily since their parents' arrest.

Théo grabbed the dress from Hugue's outstretched hand. As he turned it over and over in his hands there was no doubt in his mind that it was indeed Léa's dress. How would he ever look himself in the mirror again if something terrible had happened to her or to Victor. His parents, if they all survived long enough to be reunited, would never forgive him. How could they? So what choice did he have but to go with these strange men? At least that way he might find out for himself what had happened to the children. No matter what, he had to try to see them again.

"Okay," he said at last. "I'll go. But you'd better not have hurt them."

Pepin the giant chuckled again. "You'll see, *petit.* You'll see."

They waited until twilight fell before leaving the hideout. It was a good thing, Théo decided, for in broad daylight Pepin would surely have attracted attention from passersby. His huge body was dressed in rough peasant clothes and he clomped along the sidewalks on wooden-soled *sabots,* the likes of which Théo had almost never seen in the city. The big man certainly looked out of place, though he didn't seem particularly ill at ease.

A short distance on foot brought them to where Hugue's car was parked along a narrow side street. They put Théo in the back seat by himself, and within minutes Hugue was guiding the car slowly up a steep winding street and pulling to a stop along the curb. Théo looked up at the large house that loomed high above him, perched on the hillside overlooking the street. It looked even bigger than his grandfather Lévy's house. In the dark, it looked big enough, and foreboding enough, to be a prison. *Are Victor and Léa being held captive here?* he wondered. He looked up at the windows, trying to imagine where their cell might be.

Pepin held the car door open for him and led him up the sharply inclined walkway to the front entrance. Théo tried to hang back, but the big man urged him on. When they reached the door, Pepin rapped twice with his massive fist. Moments later, the door was opened by a girl who appeared to be nearly Théo's age.

"*Bon soir*, petite," Pepin said pleasantly. "You have another visitor."

"*Ah, bon soir*, Monsieur Pepin," replied the girl, smiling up at the giant. Then to Théo she said, "Please, won't you come in? We've been waiting for you."

Théo stepped gingerly over the threshold and into the front hall. He had to admit that so far it didn't look like a prison. Still, he was reluctant to venture too far from the door.

"Maman!" the girl called out excitedly over her shoulder, "he's here! Monsieur Pepin found him!"

Almost as soon as the words were out of her mouth, a woman appeared with Léa and Victor in tow. And as his eyes met theirs, each in turn, Théo felt an almost indescribable relief. They were grinning from ear to ear, and they looked happy for the first time in a long time. They ran to him without a word, and he knelt and embraced them both. Tears stung his eyes as he held them, and a feeling washed over him like a man on death row who has been granted a reprieve. He hadn't lost them after all. They were together again—all three of them. And no matter what, he wouldn't let them out of his sight again.

"Did that giant man find you?" Léa asked at last, looking over his shoulder toward the front door.

"Yes, he did," replied Théo, still holding both children in a tight embrace.

"He's very nice," she whispered, "but he smells too much like garlic."

Théo couldn't hold back a grin.

"We thought you weren't coming back, Théo," said Victor. "You were gone so long, and we were afraid. And so hungry." The eight-year-old looked around him as though suddenly uncomfortable. "Well, especially Léa," he corrected himself.

"I know," whispered Théo, "and I'm sorry."

"That's why we went with those men. They said we could have all the food we wanted. And they promised they would find you and bring you here too. They said it wasn't safe to stay under the bridge."

"It's all right, Victor," Théo soothed. "I'm here now."

"Are you hungry?" asked Léa, her eyes shining. "They'll give you lots of food if you are. They're real nice, Théo. And they have lots of children."

Théo looked up at the woman and her daughter. They had been joined by several more children, who smiled silently as they watched the reunion.

"There's plenty of food," said the woman, "and you may stay as long as you like. You'll be safe here."

Théo nodded his head, unable to get the right words to come out. He wanted to believe her—that they would be safe, that is—but a part of him wanted to grab the children and run back out into the night. Once again they were at the mercy of people they didn't know—Gentiles who, though they seemed to want to help, might not be so generous once they found out that the police would be looking for them. It had happened before, and there was no reason to believe that this time would be all that different.

"Ooh, Théo!" Léa interrupted his thoughts. "What is all that stuff coming out of your pockets?" A look of disgust clouded her face.

Théo looked down to see that his trousers were oozing a strange-looking mixture of cheese, olives, and sausage. His heart sank, and he could feel an uncomfortable wave of heat flooding his neck and cheeks. "I, that is, um, I found some food, and I was bringing it to you," he managed to stammer, hoping everyone else was not staring, but pretty sure that they were. "I guess you're probably not hungry anymore."

Léa covered her mouth with her hand and almost succeeded in stifling a giggle. Victor too looked amused. "We're not that hungry," they said, practically in unison, and then both burst into a fit of laughter.

Soon everyone in the room had joined in, unable to resist the children's infectious merriment, in spite of the awkwardness of the moment. Before long, even Théo began to laugh, partly at himself, partly out of the sheer joy of seeing Victor and Léa happy and relaxed—though he knew it wasn't likely to last.

⚜ ⚜ ⚜

Montluc Prison never looked so good. Even the sight of his bedraggled cell mates was a welcome relief to Marcel after the punishment he had absorbed at the Ecole de Santé. But judging by the way that Mouyon and Didier stared at him through the late evening gloom, relief was not what they were feeling.

The door to the cell clanked noisily shut and the sound of the guards' jackboots diminished slowly down the corridor before anyone spoke. As usual it was Didier.

"What happened?" he whispered incredulously.

"What does it look like?" Every muscle, every square inch of flesh on Marcel's face begged him not to speak.

"Barbie?" Mouyon, who seldom spoke, rose from the sagging wooden bunk, concern evident in his hoarse voice.

Marcel nodded slowly.

Mouyon, his own face bearing the signs of several beatings, motioned him to the bunk. "It's yours tonight," he said solemnly. "You've earned it."

Marcel sat down gingerly on the edge of the rotting boards. His thighs, his ribs, his shoulders, all protested each new movement. When at last he had seated himself, and rested motionless for a moment, the pain subsided a little.

Didier crept close, examining Marcel's face in the dim light that seeped in through the cell door.

"Aiee!" he breathed aloud, cringing at the sight. "They really did some work on you."

Marcel resisted the urge to reply. He was in no mood for a stupid conversation, or any other kind, frankly. But he would accomplish nothing by lashing out at Didier—nothing, that is, but inflicting more pain on himself. It simply wasn't worth it.

"So what did they want to know?" Didier wasn't going to give up, it appeared.

"Everything."

"Shut up, Didier!" hissed Mouyon. "Just shut up!"

Didier wheeled around to face Mouyon, who stood between him and the cell door. "What if he told them something important?" he croaked. "What if he burned one of us?"

"You're crazy!" Mouyon advanced menacingly toward the agitated Didier. "Why would he do that? He doesn't know anything about me."

Marcel felt a sudden chill in the silence that followed, and questions bombarded his mind. What was Didier getting at? And why did he seem so nervous about what Marcel might have said? Had he guessed at what had happened in Barbie's office? Or did Marcel simply look guilty?

But guilty of *what?* he wondered as he watched the two men squaring off like fighting cocks in the center of the cell. He hadn't breathed a word about Didier to Barbie. He had only seen Didier on a couple of occasions. They had never even . . .

"I want to know what he said about me." Didier's rasping whisper was filled with anxiety.

"I—" Marcel began.

"By the looks of him, I'd guess he didn't say much," interrupted Mouyon.

Marcel looked at the straw scattered across the cell floor. He wondered if Mouyon would so readily defend him if he knew what he had actually said to his interrogator. Judging by the numerous beatings the other man had already suffered at Barbie's hands, he doubted it.

"I didn't say anything about you—either of you," Marcel said through teeth clenched against the pain.

"There, now leave him alone." Mouyon relaxed visibly.

"Look," began Didier, looking directly at Mouyon, "I don't know you, and you don't know me. So we can't really hurt each other with the *boches*, right?" He turned and pointed an accusing finger at Marcel. "But he's seen me before. More than once. He won't say so, but I know he has."

"So?"

"So when people start getting slapped around the way he has, they talk, that's all. And I don't want to find out that he's been talking about me."

"Are you saying that I've talked just because I've been beaten?" Mouyon took another step closer to Didier.

Didier didn't answer immediately.

"And if you're so worried that people will burn you, why do you talk so much? If it weren't for the guards, you'd never shut your ugly *gueule* up with all those wild stories." Mouyon's twisted face was just inches from Didier's. He hadn't said this much in the week that Marcel had known him.

"You know what I think?" Mouyon obviously wasn't going to let up until he had had his say. "I think you're scared the *boches* will make you talk. And so you assume that everyone else is just as weak as you are." He spat disgustedly on the ground at Didier's feet. "Well, you're wrong. Some of us are men—real men. And we don't burn our friends or talk to the *boches*."

Didier was silent, evidently stunned by the quiet man's

uncharacteristic outburst. Perhaps what Mouyon said was true. Perhaps Didier was reacting out of some deep fear. They were all afraid, Marcel reasoned, even Mouyon. Each just had his own way of showing it. But maybe they weren't all afraid of the same things.

For his part, Marcel was afraid to meet Mouyon's gaze. Somehow he just knew that this impassioned *maquisard* would be able to see right through him. And he was just as certain that Mouyon would never condone, nor even understand, what he had done. He wasn't entirely sure that he understood it himself. But it was done now, and he would have to live with the consequences, for better or worse. He could only hope and pray that if the worst should happen, somehow God, at least, would forgive him.

Chapter 8

Isabelle brushed at a wisp of hair that a light breeze had swept across her cheek as she strolled aimlessly up the hill near the University of Geneva. If she continued in the same northeasterly direction a few more blocks, she would soon crest the hill where the cathedral stood. From there she could descend directly to the lakefront via the Vieille Ville, Geneva's Old Town. Or she could turn left and wander down the hill, past the synagogue, to where the Rhône River began its long, winding journey to the Mediterranean. Either way, nearly the entire city, and a good deal of Lac Léman, would be within sight in a few minutes—if she could find an unobstructed view between buildings. Justine always said that the best view was from the top of the cathedral, but Isabelle had never been there. She imagined it would be a little bit like seeing Paris from the Eiffel Tower, which she had ascended once with Adam. She had experienced vertigo and had vowed to stay closer to the ground after that.

Still, she enjoyed what she had seen of Geneva, with its tree-lined lakefront harbor, where sailboats bobbed placidly at anchor and the *jet d'eau* blasted its stream of water hundreds of feet in the air, providing a picture-postcard foreground to distant mountain ranges. She squinted against the mid-morning sun as it played hide and seek with lazy puffs of cloud that skidded harmlessly across a deep blue sky. The spring air was fresh and warm on her face, and for just a moment she closed her eyes and imagined she was a little girl again, holding on to her mother's hand, skipping along the sooty streets of Warsaw.

It hadn't been a perfect childhood, of course, but Isabelle looked back on it with far more fondness than regret. She was the only child of a university professor and his wife, and though Isabelle had been too young to fully appreciate it at the time, she had since recognized how her father's position had spared her family the ravages of poverty suffered by so many in Poland in those years. So while other children were working or begging to help support their families, she was taking piano lessons and making her parents proud with her marks at school.

But a dark cloud had descended on the Rayski family when Isabelle's mother contracted tuberculosis. Doctors came and went and her mother seemed to spend more time in hospitals and sanitariums than in their Warsaw apartment. Then, shortly after Isabelle's twelfth birthday, her mother slipped away and life was never the same.

A mere six months later, her father accepted a teaching post at the prestigious Sorbonne University in Paris, and over the protests of family members and friends, he took his daughter to the City of Lights. Scared and excited all at the same time—and too young to know the difference—Isabelle accompanied him willingly, unable to bear the thought of another separation. And though it took time to heal from the loss of her mother, and time to adjust to new ways and new words, Paris eventually felt like home to her. She never saw Poland again.

From a nearby steeple came the melodic peal of a church bell, tolling eleven o'clock and the end of her reverie. Overhead the clouds were growing thicker, darker, and the breeze was no longer gentle. She should be getting back, she knew. Justine would be anxious, as Alexandre had the habit of making his hunger known to anyone within reach of his healthy voice. But for once it was good—really good—to be alone. And after yesterday's disastrous news Isabelle needed some time to think, to sort things out.

Thinking about her father made her wonder what he would do in her place. She bit her lip at the thought. In some ways, he *had* been in her place. He had lost a spouse, just as she had, though the circumstances were quite different. And he had done his level best to raise a child alone, just as she was trying to do. Like her, he had found a kind of refuge in a city, a country, far from his home.

But her father seemed to have shut out the past, almost as though it had never happened. He seldom spoke of the old country, and Isabelle knew that the letters that arrived from family and friends in Poland went largely unanswered. Perhaps he avoided the synagogue, too, to avoid running into fellow Polish expatriates who might somehow remind him of his former life. It was as if he couldn't face the pain of it.

And as for the future, when the Parisian authorities stripped him of his teaching post—the one thing he truly lived for—he had chosen to end his life. No note, no explanation, just a body floating in the Seine River.

Isabelle shuddered. Was that what lay in store for her too? Now that her dream of life in America was officially over, could she go on? But, go on to what? To wait helplessly in a tiny country ringed by an enemy bent on destroying her kind? Or would that great comforting void of death beckon her the way it must have called to her poor father? Was that the only way out?

Raindrops had just begun to fall lightly as Isabelle entered the cobblestone courtyard which surrounded the cathedral of St. Pierre. A quick glance at the sky over the church's twin towers was all she needed to know that the weather was probably going to get a lot worse. She jogged quickly up the steps between the great Romanesque columns that formed the cathedral's portico just as the clouds unleashed their flood.

Standing in the lee of the sudden storm, Isabelle ran her fingers self-consciously through her damp hair. She regretted not having tied it back this morning as was her usual habit. But unless the rain stopped soon, she would have more than wet hair to deal with. She sighed and took a couple of steps farther away from the droplets that splashed against the granite steps and onto her shoes.

She turned at the sound of giddy laughter punctuated by soggy footsteps to watch as a young couple, hand in hand, dashed through the downpour and up the cathedral steps. Soaked to the skin, the youthful lovers seemed oblivious to Isabelle as they embraced just beyond the reach of the shower, giggling at the caprice of nature and their own comical appearance.

When several moments had passed and the rain showed no signs of letting up, the pair fell silent, her cheek lying softly against his chest, his chin resting on the top of her head, both staring dreamily out into the rain-spattered courtyard. Only when at length they turned curiously toward her, however, was Isabelle conscious of the fact that she had been staring.

Feeling her face suddenly grow warm, she retreated toward the cathedral door. She hated it when strangers stared at her, and now here she was doing the same thing. Perhaps she could make amends by offering the couple some measure of privacy, though she guessed that if privacy were their goal they would not have been out in the courtyard in the first place. Whatever the case, she needed to get away from them.

It had never occurred to her to enter St. Pierre's, just as it had not really mattered to her which direction she took when she left the de Rocher's house this morning. It just happened. But as the massive carved door closed behind her, as her eyes struggled to adjust to the dim light of the austere gray interior, she could feel her embarrassment begin to subside. Perhaps when she stepped back outside the couple would be gone.

It wasn't simply the fact that she had been caught staring that bothered Isabelle. Rather, it was the bittersweet memory of a certain embrace, strong arms about her, the tender brush of lips on hers, promises whispered in her ear. Sweet because his love had rekindled hope for the future in spite of all she had lost. Bitter because she would never know his touch again.

Marcel, she mouthed his name soundlessly as a tear slid down her cheek. *Oh, how I miss you!* And she felt sad and angry all at once as she had many times over the past months. Where was he? Why hadn't he come? Yet she knew that there had been little chance that the Swiss would have let him stay even if he had managed to make it over the border with her. Perhaps he had been prevented from coming. She clung to that thought, knowing it gave him a reason for not appearing. Still, the pain she felt often crowded out reason. She needed him now, and he wasn't here.

Justine and Robert de Rocher were kind, as kind as anyone she had ever known, and she had grown very fond of them. But their kindness alone was not going to resolve her present difficulties. And it would never replace the love she had once felt for Alexandre's father, certainly not what she still felt toward Marcel Boussant. How could she resign herself to remaining here where she didn't feel free from fear, when her heart was elsewhere? She just didn't know.

"Is there something wrong, mademoiselle?"

"No!" she blurted as she spun around to face a rather ordinary looking young man in a dark suit. "I—I mean," she stammered, swiping at the moistness on her cheek, "I only came in to get out of the rain. I'll just go back outside."

"No, please, mademoiselle, make yourself comfortable for as long as you like. It's still quite stormy outside. I only thought perhaps you were . . ." His voice trailed off and he looked quite uncomfortable.

She shouldn't have come inside. She just knew it. If he found out she was a Jew he would probably ask her to leave. And perhaps he would be right. This was no place for her.

"I'm fine, really," she said hurriedly, sniffling just a little. "But thank you, anyway, monsieur—er, father." She recalled how her friend Ginette had referred to her priest back in Paris. But by the time she remembered that St. Pierre's was a Protestant church, it was too late.

"You needn't call me 'father,' mademoiselle. I'm only a seminary student. Anyway, here we refer to our ministers as 'pastor.' "

"Of course," she mumbled, feeling awkward. "How stupid of me."

"Not at all. It's perfectly understandable."

Isabelle was puzzled.

The young seminary student smiled. "Lots of people visit St. Pierre's, mademoiselle. We don't expect them to know all about the church and its customs just because they walk in the front door."

"Then you don't mind if I'm only here waiting for the rain to stop?"

"On the contrary, you're welcome anytime, for any reason—or no reason at all."

"I—" Isabelle hesitated. "I'm not Protestant."

He smiled again. "Whoever comes to Me I will in no wise cast out."

"I don't understand."

"It's from the Bible," he said, "and we take it seriously here at St. Pierre's. If you need shelter, someone to talk to, or if you just want to pray. Or," he added with a little chuckle, "if you just need to come in out of the rain."

Isabelle couldn't help but smile, and she relaxed a little. "I had no idea that Protestants had such large churches," she said, gazing around at the immense sanctuary, with its towering vaults and massive stone pillars.

"Oh, yes. Here in Switzerland, you'll find some even larger than this one. But this one is famous because it's where Jean Calvin used to preach."

Isabelle nodded. She had heard Marcel's family speak of Calvin. Something about French Protestants having fled to Switzerland to avoid persecution. Perhaps she wasn't the only refugee to stand on these very floor tiles. Suddenly, strangely, she didn't feel so out of place.

"Well, anyway," the seminarian said, looking at his watch, "I have to go now, but stay as long as you like." He hesitated before adding, "I do hope you're all right."

Isabelle forced a little smile to reassure him, then followed him with her eyes until he disappeared through a side door.

She returned to the door she had entered and pushed it open just enough to see that the rain was still coming down, though not as hard as before. She'd have to leave as soon as it stopped. She had to get back to Justine's.

Then, as if drawn back in by some unseen force, Isabelle let the door close behind her and walked slowly down the center aisle of the cathedral, the sound of her cautious footsteps reverberating off the sturdy stone walls. Slipping silently into one of the age-darkened pews, she looked around to see if anyone else was there. Except for her, the big church was empty, much to her relief.

The stained-glass windows high above her gave off a somber light, no doubt reflecting the darkened skies outside but matching Isabelle's mood. She sat in gloomy silence for several minutes, trying to decide whether or not to give voice to her fear and disappointment. Maybe she'd find more understanding in the synagogue she had seen a few streets down toward the river. But somehow, she didn't think she would feel any more comfortable there. Maybe it didn't matter.

For years, ever since her mother died, she had refused to believe that the God she had often heard about—this powerful yet benevolent supreme being—could actually exist. If He was so good, then why did He allow her mother to die? And why all the pain? Why didn't He just heal her—especially if He was so all-powerful? If He did exist, what kind of God could He be, anyway?

Her father certainly hadn't encouraged any such belief. Superstition, he called it. Unscientific. A crutch for the weak and uneducated. Even her husband, Adam, was disdainful, especially of orthodox Jews. He simply could not understand blind adherence to some rigid set of arcane rituals. And Isabelle's own skepticism had been reinforced with each new tragedy in her life: her father's death, Adam's execution, her own flight from the authorities, her arrest and brief stay in the detention camp.

But somehow, living on the Boussant farm for those months in the fall had made her think that she might have rushed to judgment. Marcel's family was different from any she had known. They too had known heartache and loss, and yet their faith in a loving God remained firm. In fact, it had been that faith that had driven them to give her shelter, in spite of the danger. They spoke of their God—and *to* Him—as if He were some kind of all-wise friend. And it seemed so natural for them. How she had wished it were that easy for her.

Then, when Alexandre was born, it was as if she just knew instinctively that this pink, squalling, little treasure was a gift. Something inside her could not fathom his existence in any other terms. Yes, she understood clearly all the biology involved. But there was a sense, a bond, a knitting of souls that surpassed mere biology. She had loved Alexandre instantly, unconditionally, completely. And science would never be able to explain that to her.

Alexandre was a gift. And surely such a gift had to come from the hand of a giver far beyond her understanding. Nothing less made any sense. And it never ceased to amaze her that her tiny, helpless child had helped her understand what no amount of persuasion could.

Still, it was hard to act on it, even if what she suspected were true. No one could expect her years of skepticism to simply melt away at the sight of a newborn child, could they? And she had questions, dozens of them. There were so many competing views of God. Which was true, and which was merely wishful thinking? It was all so very confusing.

"God," she said at last, in little more than a whisper, "are You there? I need to talk to You."

She waited for what seemed like a very long time, but heard nothing in response. Several more minutes passed in silence as the glow from a thousand multi-hued panes grew brighter by degrees until the entire church was bathed in warm light. The storm had passed.

In the beginning, Isabelle had been in awe of Robert and Justine de Rocher's spacious mansard-style home, with its white stucco exterior and black wrought-iron balconies. Its two large stories, topped by long-vacant servants' quarters, provided more than ample room for the childless couple, yet all the rooms had that "lived-in" look that made it easy to get comfortable there. She had imagined she would be sleeping in the servants' rooms, but Justine had insisted that carrying a baby up and down one flight of stairs would be work enough, let alone two flights.

Downstairs was a large paneled salon, Robert's study, the dining room, kitchen, and water closet. At the top of the broad staircase were four bedrooms, each larger than any Isabelle had ever occupied, and two full baths. For the first time, she had slept in a room separate from her infant son, and hard as it seemed at first, she had gotten used to it.

The de Rochers had gone to great effort to insure her comfort, and in spite of all her other fears and concerns, Isabelle felt welcomed and wanted here.

"There you are! I was beginning to worry about you."

Justine looked relieved as Isabelle entered the front door, and it wasn't hard to tell why. Alexandre's plaintive wail could be plainly heard from the nursery upstairs. He was apparently unhappy, and as she looked at the clock on the wall, Isabelle didn't have to guess why. It was nearly half past noon.

"I'm sorry," Isabelle said over her shoulder as she hurried up the stairs to Alexandre's side. "I lost track of the time, and then the rain came and I had to take shelter until it was over." She picked her son up out of his crib and held him close, wiping huge tears from his cheeks. "There, there, my darling boy," she soothed, "Maman is here. No need to cry."

Seating herself in a nearby armchair, she balanced the still-sobbing baby on her knees, fumbling with the buttons on the front of her green and white printed cotton dress. "Has he been fussing long?" she asked Justine, who had followed close behind her.

"Not long," replied Justine. She smiled down at Alexandre who was nursing ravenously between sniffles. "He's been very content all morning—until just a few minutes ago, that is. What I was beginning to worry about was you, Isabelle."

Isabelle looked up from her suddenly contented son. "I didn't mean to worry you," she said. "I just got lost in thought. Then when the rain came I took shelter in the cathedral. I hadn't planned to stay so long, but—" She wasn't sure how to explain herself.

"The cathedral?" asked a surprised Justine. "You mean St. Pierre's? Are you sure it's wise to be wandering alone that far from the house?"

"What do you mean?"

"I just think that it might be better not to go alone, next time. I'd be happy to go with you, you know. It's not as though I've never offered."

Isabelle said nothing. Justine and Robert had never pushed her, but she had always found a reason not to attend church with them. But this was different. What was so wrong about going alone?

"Maybe I'm being too careful," Justine continued, "but I couldn't bear the thought of you and Alexandre going to one of those dreadful refugee camps. And if the police stop you too far from the house without an escort—"

"I know," sighed Isabelle, finally grasping the cause for Justine's concern. "I guess I just wasn't thinking." It seemed so unfair. All she had wanted was to take a walk, but refugees—with few notable exceptions—were not allowed to wander unaccompanied in Geneva—or anywhere else in Switzerland, for that matter. It was only because the de Rochers had offered to be her sponsors that Isabelle wasn't already confined to a camp of some sort.

"Someday," she said, more to herself than to Justine, "someday I want to live where I can come and go as I please, where they won't always be threatening to put me behind a fence. It's not right."

"It's the war, Isabelle. It will be different once this is all over," Justine assured her. "You'll see."

Alexandre, his little belly apparently full, was falling asleep, so Isabelle stood carefully and carried him back to his crib.

Justine waited for her out in the hall. "Why don't you check the letter box while I put lunch on the table?"

Outside the front door, Isabelle grasped the handful of letters the mailman had left in the box. Walking back inside, she glanced at the first two or three to see if there was something for her, more out of habit than anything else. What she found was certainly meant for her—though not at all what she expected. A plain white piece of paper, folded in half, opened to reveal a handwritten message. Isabelle stared at it in disbelief as icy fingers clutched at her throat. It was happening all over again.

"Isabelle?"

Unable to speak, Isabelle simply lowered the paper and stared at her friend.

"Isabelle, what is it?"

Woodenly, Isabelle handed the page to Justine.

Her face suddenly ashen, Justine's voice trembled as she read, "Send the filthy Jew back to the Germans. They know how to deal with tramps like her. Switzerland is for the Swiss."

Isabelle turned without a word and numbly climbed the stairs. She wasn't hungry anymore.

Chapter 9

"Where to, monsieur?" The taxi driver peered at his passenger by way of the rearview mirror.

"Well, I'm not exactly sure," replied Michael Dreyfus, seating himself wearily in the rear of the black Peugeot. A day of meetings at the International Red Cross headquarters had worn him out. "I thought perhaps you could help me find someone."

"I'm a taxi driver, monsieur, not the police."

"I already tried the police. They weren't much help."

"So who are you looking for?" asked the graying driver.

"A French refugee."

The driver twisted his head and shoulders around to face Michael. "You must be new here, monsieur. Geneva is filled with refugees, poor devils. But unless you have an address, I'm afraid I can't help you."

"Where would they take him if he just came across the border yesterday?"

"That depends, monsieur. How old is your friend?"

"About like me, twenty-four." Michael wondered how detailed his invention would have to get before he found what he wanted. The police officer he had spoken with at lunchtime had seen right through it, and had warned him not to interfere with the government's programs and policies. The worst the taxi driver could do was refuse to take him anywhere.

"Is your friend a Jew?"

Michael hesitated. "Yes," he said finally, sighing. "Yes, he is."

The driver turned back to face the steering wheel. "You probably won't find him," he said matter-of-factly.

"Why not?"

"Well, the way I hear it, most Jews over sixteen are turned back at the border, that's why. Look," continued the driver, turning partially around again, "I'd like to help you, but I really have to go. Times are tough. If I don't drive you somewhere, I don't make any money. You understand."

Most Jews over sixteen are turned back! Michael hesitated for a moment with his hand poised on the door handle. "Do you know where they take the ones who do manage to get in?"

"Well," the driver scowled and scratched his stubbly chin, "there is a camp over in the area we call Le Bout du Monde. I haven't been there for years, but I know where it is. It used to be a home for girls." His scowl became a grin. "My friends and I used to go over there all the time when we were boys, just to peek in through the windows."

"Will you take me there?" Michael asked.

"Why not?" The driver slipped the Peugeot into gear and gunned the engine. "It won't be cheap, you know," he added over his shoulder as he pulled away from the curb. "It's not exactly next door."

Relieved, Michael sat back in his seat and watched out the

side windows as the driver wound his way skillfully through the late afternoon traffic. The streets showed faint evidence of the morning's downpour and the sky, now a brilliant blue, held only a handful of cotton ball clouds. Maybe the day wouldn't be a complete loss, after all.

A sharp left just past the train station brought the deep blue of the lake into view. Michael had already seen it several times since his arrival, yet it stirred him with awe at each new sighting. As they descended the Rue du Mont Blanc toward the waterfront, he could see the *jet d'eau*, its powerful white plume of water forcing its way skyward, only to return to the lake's surface in a misty cascade.

"You see that?" the driver was pointing at the water jet. "More than 400 feet high it shoots this water from the lake. You will find nothing like this in all the world. That is why our government guards the secret of how it works like a national treasure. No one can copy this. They must come here to see for themselves. *Magnifique, non?*"

Michael had to agree. Though it seemed that nearly every postcard in the city featured this marvel of Swiss ingenuity, nothing compared with seeing it in person. He couldn't help but wonder how it worked.

Beyond the *jet d'eau*, an endless row of five-story buildings rimmed the lake, housing shops, businesses, and hotels, separated from the water only by a tree-lined boulevard. Rising gently behind the lakefront properties were row upon row of commercial buildings, apartments, churches, and schools, each seeming to peek above the next for that coveted view of the lake. And, as though surveying the city from just across the French border, the scarred cliffs of Mont Salève provided a ruggedly dramatic backdrop to the whole scene. After living in New York, it seemed almost surreal to Michael Dreyfus. He couldn't imagine ever tiring of the sight.

"Elle est belle, cette ville. N'est-ce pas?"

His driver was obviously—and understandably—proud, and Michael had to agree: the city was indeed beautiful.

Crossing the bridge over the mouth of the Rhône River, the driver guided the Peugeot along the quai of the Left Bank and then turned south along a series of narrower streets. More like a tour guide than a taxi driver, he prattled endlessly, pointing out the many historic buildings and monuments as they passed.

St. Pierre's Cathedral, with its two stone towers and metal steeple, dominated Old Town from its perch atop the hill. But there were also museums, the Hotel de Ville, the university, and too many others to remember, only blocks away. Michael knew he would need to return on foot if he were ever to see it properly.

Soon the narrow streets and mansard tile roofs gave way to the sprawl of suburban Geneva, the driver's chatter subsided, and Michael's thoughts returned to the reason for this little side trip. He had been purposely evasive when Gerard had asked about his plans for the evening. Perhaps it would have been wise to have someone more experienced along, but he was convinced that Gerard wouldn't understand why he needed to do this. Gerard wasn't a Jew, after all, so how could he understand? It was better just to leave him out of it.

Gerard had his hands full as it was, trying to sort out the difficulties the International Committee of the Red Cross was experiencing getting parcels to American prisoners of war. The problem lay not so much in getting the parcels from Switzerland to the POW camps in Germany and Italy. To be sure, there were hazards inherent in such deliveries, not the least of which was the Allied bombardment. But the Red Cross convoys were clearly marked for proper identification, both from the ground and from the air, and the Axis powers had their own reasons not to hinder the deliveries. Not only were they concerned about potential reprisals against the thousands of their own soldiers held in Allied prison camps, but every Red Cross delivery meant less that they would have to supply from their own resources.

But getting the vital parcels from the United States to neutral Switzerland without enormous losses due to pilferage seemed to be the more difficult problem. That was why Gerard Richert was here: to take part in a task force charged with minimizing the losses.

Michael was committed to doing everything possible to assist Gerard in this critical task. But ever since the border crossing, he couldn't put the refugees out of his mind. And the realization that many of them were Jews only served to intensify his desire to help them.

That in itself seemed more than a little surprising to him. His parents had seen to it that he and his sister, Beatrice, were "raised Jewish," as his mom always said, but their circle of friends and acquaintances was by no means limited to the Jewish community. Nor was their life defined by strict religious observance. They attended synagogue on many major holidays, though not necessarily all of them. And of course, Michael's bar mitzvah at age thirteen had been a day to remember.

But when Bea decided to marry a Gentile, the Dreyfuses, proud of their open-mindedness, agreed to the match, provided the children would be "raised Jewish." Michael himself had dated several Gentile girls while at Columbia University. And though his parents had never raised an outright objection, his mother more than once had offered to introduce him to "a nice Jewish girl."

Something happened, however, when stories of the Nazi atrocities against Jews began circulating in New York. For perhaps the first time in his life, Michael began to identify with his heritage. His people were being threatened—slaughtered, if the reports were true—solely because, like him, they were Jews. He didn't suddenly have a religious awakening. He simply decided that anything driving thousands to their deaths had to be important.

And now, here he was—against his parents' advice—in the eye of the Nazi storm. He hadn't come here to rescue Jews, of course. His job was to assist Gerard Richert—whatever that required. But while he would do his job to the best of his ability, he would not—indeed, could not—ignore what he saw happening to fellow Jews. He only hoped he would be here long enough to do something about it.

"*Eh, voilà!*" The driver's exclamation broke the silence. "There it is up ahead."

Michael leaned forward in his seat and craned his neck to see what the driver was pointing at. "I don't see anything," he said.

"There. Just to the right of the road."

"The villa?"

"That's it." The driver began to slow the Peugeot as they wound down the narrow lane toward a large gray villa. "You were expecting something more grand?"

"I don't know what I expected," replied Michael, "but this isn't it."

As they drew closer to the old villa, he could see that the house and yard had been completely encircled by a high barbed-wire fence. Soldiers, clad in gray-green uniforms and armed with machine guns, patrolled the perimeter of the fenced yard. In the yard were several dozen people in civilian dress. A few paced aimlessly back and forth, like animals in a pen. Others leaned against the front of the villa, staring out into nothing. Still others, children mostly, clustered in little groups, chatting or playing games.

The driver stopped the car about fifty yards from the entrance. "This is as far as I go, monsieur," he said. "I don't like the looks of this place."

"Are you sure this is it?" asked Michael. Somehow, he had expected something much more humane looking than what he was seeing.

"Positive. Like I said before, it used to be a home for girls, and there wasn't any barbed wire or soldiers, but it's the same place all right."

Michael considered for a moment. "Wait here for me," he said as he slipped the man several franc notes and slid out of the car.

"Fifteen minutes, no more," the driver replied through his open window. "And be careful. Some of these refugees are dangerous!"

Michael only half-heard the warning as he strode toward the "camp" gate. One way or another he had to find out what went on inside this place. And the best way was to go inside and see for himself. The trouble was, he had no idea whether the guards would let him pass or not. An ominous sign on the fence warned that anyone coming too close could be fired upon. But surely they wouldn't shoot a Swiss citizen. An idea struck him then and he reached for his wallet with about ten yards to go before reaching the gate.

"*Arretez-vous, monsieur!*" barked one of the two soldiers standing behind the wrought iron entrance. "Don't come any closer!" The other soldier was fingering the trigger mechanism on his machine gun, though to Michael's great relief the muzzle was still pointed toward the ground.

Michael stopped in his tracks, pulled a card from his wallet and held it aloft. "I'm with the Red Cross," he called out. "I'd like to come inside and have a look around."

The guards exchanged puzzled glances. "We were not told

to expect you, monsieur," said the first one. "You'll have to come back another time."

Not so easily dissuaded, Michael took a step forward—only one. But as he did so, the barrel of the second guard's gun rose almost instantly to point directly at his chest. Michael felt a sudden chill and stepped back. Maybe this wasn't such a good idea after all.

"Please," he said, trying to disguise the fear he suddenly felt, "I'm unarmed." He held his arms wide. "It's very important that I see inside the camp."

"Get back in your car, monsieur. No visitors are allowed without the *capitaine's* permission."

By this time, a number of the refugees inside had gathered near the barbed wire to see what was going on. "He's from the Red Cross!" Michael heard one woman exclaim. "At last, someone's come to save us from this awful place."

"Please," wailed a little girl, "I need to find Maman and Papa. But no one will tell me where they've taken them." She started to cry.

"We've nothing but straw to sleep on," rasped a grizzled old man, pushing his way to the front of the group and shaking his fist. "And we aren't even allowed to contact our families."

"Get back! All of you!" shouted one of the guards. "Get away from the fence or we'll shoot!" As if to add credence to his threat, he pressed the muzzle of his machine gun against the old man's chest.

The crowd began to disperse as Michael watched, stunned into silence by what he was hearing and seeing.

"What's going on here?" A uniformed officer bolted from the front door of the villa, followed closely by a portly man in a dark civilian suit. "Why are these people all gathered around like this?"

"*Capitaine*, this man at the gate claims to be from the Red Cross, and some of the refugees gathered when he refused to leave. We were just dispersing them, *mon capitaine*." The guard's face was ashen as he stood at attention before his superior.

Michael watched apprehensively as the captain strode toward the gate without so much as acknowledging the guard's response. And as he came—the man in the dark suit in his wake—Michael heard the squeal of tires. Turning to look behind him, he watched in dismay as the taxi sped back up the narrow lane toward Geneva. It would be a long walk back—assuming he got out of this unscathed.

"What do you want?" The captain, dispensing with any semblance of courtesy, was obviously in no mood to be trifled with. He glared at Michael from under his cap. "Well? I haven't got all day. They say you refuse to leave. What about it?"

"I never said I refused to leave," Michael began in a choked voice. He cleared his throat and tried again. "I didn't refuse," he said more emphatically. "I simply said I was with the Red Cross and that it was important that I see the camp, that's all."

"Red Cross?" the captain sneered. "Red Cross? And you think you can come to my camp any time you please?"

"We're concerned about the welfare of the refugees, *capitaine*." Michael knew as soon as he said it that he should have quit while he was ahead.

"The welfare of the refugees?" the captain fairly exploded. "What about the welfare of the Swiss? What about us? We can't take in every stray in Europe, can we?" He paused to take a breath, then motioned toward the man in the dark suit. "Do you see this man? Herr Rosen is just like you, worried about these cursed refugees. Only in his case he's only concerned with the Jews. What a waste!"

The man in the suit looked embarrassed by the whole scene. And as for Michael, he wanted to scream, to erupt in indignation. But he couldn't think of a single thing to say.

"Now, Herr Rosen, go on back to Geneva, have a couple of drinks and tell your people that if they continue to whine and complain, I will forbid all access to the camp." He signaled the guards to open the gate. "And as for you, Monsieur Red Cross, find something else to do with your time. As a military commander, I am in no way obligated to answer to you or your superiors. For anything. At anytime." And with that said, he turned on his heel and strode back to the villa.

Michael watched him go, and for the first time in his life he wanted to kill someone. Never had he met someone who touched him off like this petty tyrant did.

"Monsieur?" The German accent was evident even in the pronunciation of a single word. "If you like, I can give you a lift back to the city in my car."

"Of . . . of course," Michael stammered, suddenly feeling embarrassed by his own thoughts. "That's very kind of you, monsieur." At least he wouldn't have to walk back.

The two were silent for a long time before Rosen spoke. "What you said about the Red Cross, is it true?"

"Well, yes," said Michael, a little sheepishly, "but I was bluffing. I wasn't there on official business. I was just trying to find out what happens to the refugees who actually make it across the border."

"Mmm, I see."

More silence.

"And you?" Michael was curious to know how Rosen had managed to get into the camp, in spite of the fact that the captain obviously didn't like him.

Rosen smiled. "Heinrich Rosen, monsieur, and I'm just a simple businessman," he said. "But I represent a committee of concerned Jews. We're trying to help these poor people all we can."

"I'm Michael. Michael Dreyfus." He reached for the hand that was immediately offered and clasped it firmly. "Is there any way I can be of help?"

"Where are you from, Michael?"

"I was born here in Lausanne, but I've lived in the United States since I was a little kid."

"And you know what happens to those Jews who don't make it into Switzerland?"

Michael nodded solemnly.

"Then perhaps you will not be surprised when I tell you that my committee is trying to reduce the pressure on the Swiss borders."

"I don't follow you."

"The Swiss government is afraid of being overwhelmed with refugees, especially Jews. But what if we were able to open another route of escape from these devilish Nazis? If we can do that, we will accomplish two things. One, we will give the refugees themselves an option to crossing into Switzerland. And two, if the Swiss see that another option exists, they may be inclined to accept more refugees, knowing that their stay will only be temporary."

"But how is that possible with Germany controlling all the surrounding countries?"

"I am a German, as I am sure you can tell. But I will make no bargains with the Nazis. They cannot be trusted. But the Italians—now that's another matter." He paused. "There are plans, Michael, big plans. And if you are interested, we can use all the help we can get."

Somewhere deep inside, Michael Dreyfus felt a spark of hope ignite into a tiny flame.

Chapter 10

"So, Capitaine Malfaire, just how long have you been harboring a terrorist?"

Leaning back in his chair, *Obersturmführer* Klaus Barbie uttered the accusation coolly, almost casually. Only his small eyes, darting back and forth beneath heavy brows, belied his intensity.

"I . . . I'm afraid I don't understand, Lieutenant."

Jean-Claude Malfaire was confused. His lunch with Marie and André had been interrupted by a knock at the front door, and two plainclothes Gestapo had politely, but firmly, suggested that he accompany them to the infamous Ecole de Santé. They had offered no explanation other than to say that Barbie wanted to see him immediately. After reassuring an obviously shaken Marie that everything would be all right, he climbed into the rear seat of the Germans' car and they sped off.

When they arrived at the Gestapo chief's headquarters, the two men led him up the stairs and down the long hallway to an office where Klaus Barbie sat waiting behind his desk. Malfaire was left standing in the middle of the room. From the time he left his house, no one had spoken a single word—until now. And he had absolutely no idea what Barbie was talking about.

"Come, *Capitaine,* I'm a busy man. Let's not play games." Barbie leaned forward, placing his forearms on the desk. In his right hand he gripped a leather riding crop. "I want to know about this terrorist."

Malfaire felt the muscle in his jaw begin to twitch. "I have no idea what you are talking about, Lieutenant, and I resent any suggestion that I would have anything to do with a terrorist."

Barbie laughed. "Do you hear that?" he said to the two plainclothesmen who remained standing beside the office door. "Our friend resents my suggestions." Then, boring his chilling gaze into Malfaire's eyes, he lowered his voice. "I assure you, *monsieur le capitaine*, that I am suggesting nothing. One of my prisoners claims that a certain man in your employ is an important operative in a terrorist network."

Malfaire's mind scrambled desperately, trying to think which of his men could possibly be playing him for a fool. Poulain and the others seemed more than dedicated to the twin tasks of rounding up Jews and ferreting out subversive elements. The idea that any of them could be a closet resistant was practically unthinkable.

"Well?" Barbie was impatiently tapping the butt of the riding crop on the top of his desk.

"I assure you, Lieutenant," Malfaire began slowly, "that none of my men are in any way associated with this cursed terrorist movement. Each man has pledged his honor—even his life—to our cause. And if any one of them were somehow slack in his duties, the others would report it to me. I'm certain of it." He hated the idea of having to justify anything to this little German, least of all the loyalty of his men.

"What then am I to make of this prisoner's accusation?" Barbie leaned back in his chair once more.

"He's lying. That's all there is to it."

"Perhaps you should see my work, *Capitaine*." Barbie smiled a broad, rather sinister smile. "Very rarely do my prisoners manage to lie convincingly. You see, I give them a great deal of incentive to tell the truth."

Malfaire felt a surge of anger welling up in him. He was being set up! "It's simply not true," he said flatly. He was not about to cower, even before this notorious torturer.

"Please, have a seat, *Capitaine*," said Barbie, indicating a chair with a wave of his hand. "Haven't we met before?"

Surprised by the sudden shift, Malfaire sat down. "Yes, I believe it was last fall," he replied cautiously.

"As I recall, you were a police inspector at the time."

"That's right."

"I understand you were pretty good at your job."

Malfaire held himself erect in his chair, but otherwise tried not to acknowledge the compliment. He was not about to be any more civil than necessary after being falsely accused of complicity with the cowards of the so-called Resistance!

"I also understand that, unlike many of your colleagues, you had a driver."

Malfaire could feel the blood drain from his face. It had been months since he left the police, and up to this very moment, he hadn't even considered that the ghost of his driver might come back to haunt him.

"Your driver's name was Dominique Raspaud, wasn't it, Capitaine Malfaire?"

Dominique Raspaud had been his driver for five years. In fact, Malfaire couldn't imagine a better driver or mechanic.

And he had trusted the man implicitly. Every investigation he conducted, every time he made an arrest, Dominique was there. He heard everything, saw everything, knew everything.

But Malfaire's surprise had been complete when, on a cold December night just a few hundred yards from the Swiss border, his arrest of a fleeing Jew and her French accomplice was foiled—by Dominique's treachery. And not only had his trusted driver thwarted him, he had also betrayed him into the hands of a small band of terrorists. There was no telling how long Dominique had been passing information to the Resistance, but looking back, his double game had certainly explained why so many cases had gone sour in the last year or so—especially cases that involved Jews.

"Did this Raspaud work for you or not?" Barbie insisted.

"Yes." There was hardly any point in denying it. Even a cursory investigation would reveal that it was true.

"And is it true that you gave him information which he passed on to his terrorist network?"

"Absolutely not! I had no idea he was a traitor until just before I left the police." It sounded lame even as the words escaped his lips. How could he have missed it, after all? He was with the man day after day, for five years. The idea still galled him.

"Your former police colleagues consider you quite a brilliant investigator, Capitaine Malfaire." Barbie's smile twisted into a sneer. "So how do you explain such utter stupidity? Unless, of course, you happen to be playing the same game as your driver."

Malfaire bolted to his feet. "What are you saying—that I too am a traitor? I am a Frenchman!"

Barbie waved him off. "And so is Raspaud."

"I have pledged my allegiance to Marshall Pétain!"

"Better you should be loyal to the Führer," growled Barbie,

motioning Malfaire back to his seat.

Malfaire tried to ignore the remark. The Germans, of course, served a useful purpose, but sooner or later, France needed to govern herself without any outside interference. And any suggestion that a true Frenchman could be loyal to anyone other than another right-thinking Frenchman was insulting.

"So where is your friend Raspaud, now?" the Gestapo chief continued.

"Dominique Raspaud is dead," said Malfaire flatly, "and don't think for a moment that he was ever my friend."

"Dead?" Barbie was visibly upset. "The man's family claims that he is on a police assignment somewhere. The police are still paying his salary, and I have a prisoner who says that Raspaud is his contact. What do you mean, he's dead?"

Malfaire was incredulous. "I know he's dead because I shot him!"

"When?"

"Five months ago when I discovered that he had betrayed me."

Barbie sat for several moments without saying a word, slapping the riding crop into his open palm. His eyes, normally darting about, were bulging and still, as if he were staring down some unseen adversary. Crimson flooded his face and neck. "Get Boussant," he rasped at last to one of the plainclothesmen. "And I want him here within the hour."

"Boussant?" Malfaire blurted. "Marcel Boussant?"

"Yes. Why?" Barbie was impatient.

"Marcel Boussant was with the men who tried to kill me!"

"Well, then, *Capitaine,* you'll be happy to know that I intend to return the favor."

Jean-Claude Malfaire almost smiled in spite of his anger at Barbie. Marcel Boussant was within his grasp at last, and already the taste of revenge was sweet.

⚜ ⚜ ⚜

"Hey, Boussant!" One of his two SS escorts prodded Marcel in the kidneys with the muzzle of his automatic rifle as the three made their way across Montluc Prison's courtyard to a waiting truck. "Your fiancée came to see the commandant today."

Marcel kept walking. Whatever the guards could do or say to make a prisoner's life miserable, they usually tried. Sometimes they would report that a spouse or a parent had died suddenly. Or that a family member had been arrested. Or anything else likely to cause anguish to a man cut off from the outside world. But the more they did it, the less it bothered the prisoners, except the newcomers, of course.

"She's very beautiful, I hear," offered the second guard. "I wonder what she sees in you, Boussant." Both guards laughed.

"Too bad you won't live to enjoy your wedding," said the first, clucking his tongue.

"Or the wedding night," snickered the second. Both men burst into laughter once again.

Marcel had more important things on his mind than some fictitious fiancée. The reprieve he had hoped for had been short-lived, and that could only mean one thing—that Klaus Barbie had discovered his story to be a lie. He knew he ran that risk from the moment he uttered the words, but he found it hard to believe that he had been found out so quickly.

Barbie wasn't going to be satisfied with anything less than a betrayal of Marcel's Resistance connection. And finally, nearly numb from the pain of the beatings, it had come to him. Why not give up someone who couldn't be hurt by it? Why not give up a dead man? And that is how he decided to make Dominique Raspaud his scapegoat.

Marcel had hoped that the length of time needed to unravel his story would be greater than Barbie's patience, and that the Gestapo chief would simply give up and let military justice run its course. A few years in prison—sooner if the Allies succeeded—for illegal possession of ration coupons, and Marcel imagined he would be back on the family farm again. Prison wasn't ideal, certainly, but it was an option he could live with. And it seemed like the only option at the time.

It was strange, really. Had he been asked to divulge information concerning Isabelle's whereabouts a few months previously, he would have said anything, true or not, to keep her from the Nazis. But somehow, when it came right down to it, he felt guilty about lying to save his own skin. You shall not lie. Wasn't that what the commandment said? And yet, what was he supposed to do, tell Barbie the truth and face a firing squad? Of course, chances were good that the same fate awaited him no matter what, now. As far as he knew, the only person outside the network who knew of Dominique Raspaud's dangerous game had been Inspector Malfaire. And Malfaire was long since dead. He just prayed he hadn't put anyone else in jeopardy in his effort to save himself.

The handcuffs cut into flesh still raw from the last time he had been obliged to wear them. His ribs ached, as did his still-swollen face, from the blows rained on him by a furious Klaus Barbie. Had he given in too easily, he wondered, or should he have said what he had to say from the very beginning and avoided the whole painful ordeal? He had asked himself the same question a dozen times already, and each time had arrived at the same conclusion: it wasn't until he was half-unconscious that it had occurred to him what he should say. Maybe he just needed to stop torturing himself any further. *God forgive me,* he whispered again for what seemed like the hundredth time.

Surprisingly, Marcel and his two guards were the truck's

only occupants, except for the mandatory driver and front seat guard. Apparently they didn't want to take any chances with him, a thought which brought him no comfort at all. He sat on the bench that ran along the right side while the Germans sat opposite him, eyeing his every move, guns held at the ready. The truck lurched forward as soon as they were all seated, passing through the arched entry to the prison and out onto the street. A dark, sinking feeling enveloped Marcel at the thought that a second—and probably final—meeting with Klaus Barbie was only minutes away.

Chapter 11

Jean-Claude Malfaire strode north along Lyons' Rue de Marseilles at a furious pace, here and there jostling a slow or inattentive pedestrian unfortunate enough to get in his path. The pounding in his temples nearly kept time with the rhythm of his shoes on the sidewalk, and droplets of sweat had begun to dampen his collar. Ignoring the puzzled, fearful stares of people he passed along the way, he was only slightly aware of the sounds of traffic in the busy street. Not until the resonant bells of St. Andre's broke into his consciousness, sounding the half hour, did he realize just how far he had come, or exactly where he was.

Suddenly aware of his surroundings, he slowed to a stop, loosened his tie and collar, and turned to look back along the street toward the Ecole de Santé. It was all he could do to keep from cursing aloud at the arrogance of Klaus Barbie and his entire coterie of *boches.* But the Nazis had informants everywhere, and he was all too familiar with what happened to people who voiced contrary opinions in public. Better to just swallow his pride for the moment and await the right opportunity to get even. And get even he would. Lieutenant Barbie had not heard the last of Jean-Claude Malfaire.

It was bad enough that he should be escorted from his own home—without warning, no less—for an audience with the Gestapo chief. But, after all the years he had faithfully served his country, to be accused of being a traitor was too much. How could anyone in his right mind possibly suspect him of collaborating with the ragtag assortment of Communists, ne'er-do-wells, and opportunists that pretended to fight for France's "liberation"? What were they thinking?

Even stranger, the fact that he had already disposed of the man who *was* the traitor hadn't seemed to please Barbie at all. In fact, Barbie had turned sullen, as if his little game had been spoiled. Then he had simply dismissed Malfaire, as though he didn't matter at all.

"That's all," he had said. "You can go now." Not a word of gratitude for the information provided. No apology for the patently false accusation. Not even an offer to have someone drive him back to his house. Just "that's all, you can go now," as though he were some ordinary stoolpigeon. Well, Herr Barbie was going to pay for his arrogance. One way or another, he would pay.

The cruelest blow of all, perhaps, was that someone else would have the privilege, the pleasure, of killing Marcel Boussant, Barbie or one of his grinning goons, probably. Boussant had lied to them, of course. But it wasn't as if they should have expected otherwise. Malfaire, on the other hand, had a personal score to settle—a matter of honor. Why couldn't they have seen that and let him deal with the boy?

Malfaire took a deep breath, swiped at the perspiration on his face and neck, and then let a long slow sigh escape. Turning back toward the north he began walking again, his pace more measured this time. Just a few short blocks and he would reach the Cours Gambetta where he could catch a bus for home.

Up ahead a German military truck turned the corner and lumbered into the southbound flow of the Rue de Marseilles, and the normal automobile traffic parted automatically to clear a path for it.

Then, as the truck rumbled to within a hundred yards of him, Malfaire heard the sudden squeal of tires and watched in disbelief as a black sedan roared out of a side street to his right. Narrowly avoiding what appeared to be a certain collision with another southbound car, the sedan catapulted headlong into the driver's side of the truck, pushing its nose up onto the sidewalk where both vehicles screeched to a shuddering halt against a swaying light pole. A stocky man, brandishing a pistol, bounded out of the sedan and onto the truck's running board. He began yelling something as he aimed the pistol through the open window.

Instinctively, Jean-Claude Malfaire bolted toward the scene. Then, as if struck by lightning, he stopped in his tracks and waited. *This is Barbie's problem,* he mused with a strange sense of satisfaction. *Let him clean up his own mess.* Then he heard the sharp report of a gunshot, followed quickly by another.

Marcel had been watching the traffic out the rear of the truck when the crash came. The panicked shout of the guard in the front was his only warning, and it was quickly drowned out by the wrenching impact. The truck lurched sideways so violently that all three rear passengers were thrown from their seats in a tangle of arms and legs. Gunshots pierced the early afternoon air as Marcel found himself pinned on his back, his handcuffed arms beneath him, the struggling body of one of the guards threatening to cut off his wind.

Unable to see anything, each passing second increased his alarm. Something blunt pressed hard on his ribcage, but there was no way to tell if the soldier atop him was still in control of a weapon, or if one of the benches had been splintered by the impact and was somehow pushed against him. He wondered if the German guards were injured, if they felt the same panic he himself was feeling. Marshaling all his strength, he twisted to one side to try to see, only to find the face of one of the soldiers just inches from his own, eyes rolled back grotesquely. He gasped for breath and tried unsuccessfully to twist his body in the other direction. A wave of white-hot panic threatened to submerge him.

The grinding squeal of metal against metal had stopped, and in its place there was shouting, a tumult of voices—some German, mostly French. Somewhere, muffled in the distance, someone was repeating his name, now shouting his name, and then hands were on his arms and shoulders, separating him from the body that was pinning him down. Air rushed into his aching lungs as a voice urged him to hurry, but he couldn't seem to get his bearings, let alone move with any speed.

Dazed and coughing from the sudden intake of air, he felt himself being dragged by the armpits from the back of the truck. His legs felt wooden and when his feet thudded sharply to the ground he was unable to stand. He looked wildly around, trying to focus on someone, anyone, but everything and everyone was moving too fast, spinning in a circle around and around him. The shouting continued, more gunshots, the squeal of tires. Half-dragged, half-shoved into what vaguely seemed like the back of a car, he could feel something wet beginning to trickle down his forehead, and then a thick warm darkness covered him like a blanket.

⚜ ⚜ ⚜

Malfaire stood next to the disabled German truck and seethed as two Citroën sedans sped down a side street and out of sight. A third car, an aging Peugeot abandoned by its driver, sat nearly perpendicular to the truck, its front tires flat, a geyser of steam gurgling up from beneath its torn, crumpled hood. For the moment at least, the fugitives appeared to have succeeded in prying a man from the grip of the Nazis. And unarmed, Malfaire had been unable to do anything to stop them.

Like all policemen, there were certain faces etched into Malfaire's brain as surely as if they had been put there with hammer and chisel. And one of them belonged to Marcel Boussant. Boussant, who undoubtedly fancied himself a great humanitarian for all his help to the Jews, was little more than a hooligan—a lowlife. Sure, the boy was responsible for nearly ruining his career—and had almost succeeded in getting him killed—but he was a lowlife Jew-lover, nothing more.

But seeing Boussant's face again, though just for an instant as he was dragged from the truck into one of the waiting Citroëns, made Jean-Claude Malfaire's pulse race, his temperature rise. He had been that close to fulfilling his months-old dream of vengeance, and he had stood stupidly aside until it was too late. He couldn't even take much pleasure in the fact that Barbie was being denied his revenge as well.

Furious, he wheeled and kicked the door of the truck, nearly losing his balance, sending a spasm of pain shooting up the length of his leg. As he hopped a couple of steps backward on the other leg, the truck door groaned open and the limp, bleeding body of the German driver sagged against it, slumping heavily onto the running board, and then twisting grotesquely onto the pavement. From where he stood, Malfaire couldn't be sure, but it looked as if the young soldier were dead and his heart sank. This could mean nothing but trouble, especially when Barbie found out.

The humiliating truth was, he had been so filled with rage at the Gestapo that he hadn't even tried to intervene until after the first shots were fired. And by then it was over. He cursed himself for letting Barbie get to him so thoroughly. Now, there were sure to be questions—questions for which he could envision no good answer.

Behind him, a handful of civilian cars crawled past in single file on the far side of the street, their occupants agape at the sight of the sprawling soldier as much as at the wreckage. A small crowd of pedestrians had gathered on the sidewalk, and a few edged cautiously toward the truck, straining to catch a glimpse of a dead German.

"Get back, all of you!" Malfaire hoped his voice conveyed an authority he did not feel at the moment. It was simply his years of police training taking over. He wanted out of there as quickly as possible, but he had a feeling that unless he stayed, the crowd might turn ugly. He took a step toward the gathering civilians to reinforce his command.

"Milice," he said, his voice more steady now, "and I said back away!"

An uneasy murmur swept through the crowd, and those in front backed up a few steps. Malfaire circled around behind the truck to survey the damage there. What he found surprised him only slightly. Two uniformed soldiers lay awkwardly across the floorboards in the back, one moving slightly, the other still as death, his eyes staring unseeing at the sky overhead.

"Somebody phone for an ambulance," he called out.

No one moved.

"The filthy *boches* deserved it, that's what I say," someone in the crowd said, a bit too loud.

Malfaire looked in the direction of the voice, though from where he stood it was impossible to tell who it belonged to. But as he turned his gaze back to the soldiers, other voices joined the first.

"So much the better if they're all dead."

"The Milice is no better than the *boches.* Let's treat him to the same fate!"

Malfaire looked quickly around at the fringes of the crowd. He stood with his back to the truck, and they were beginning to close in on him. No one said a word now as they pushed in from three sides, cutting off any route of escape. They were a pathetic lot, he decided, emboldened only by the fact that he was alone. Well, in his experience such people were easily dealt with. But as he reached instinctively under his jacket, his hand found nothing resembling a semiautomatic pistol and instantly he remembered why. This was no time to be without a gun.

For the first time in his life, Jean-Claude Malfaire was really scared—scared of what would happen if the Gestapo knew he was at the scene, but even more scared of the murmuring crowd facing him. Bulling his way past the weakest of his antagonists, he ran as fast and as far as he could.

The insistent rumbling sound coming from somewhere beneath him pushed at the fuzzy edges of Marcel's brain. He could feel his prone body swaying, and the smell of leather assaulted his nose. Slowly, as if still half in a dream, he tried to open first one eye and then the other. His efforts were rewarded with a close-up view of some sort of upholstery, caked with blood, directly in front of his face. Startled and still disoriented, he tried to sit up, but his hands seemed to be pinned behind his back.

"I'd stay down if I were in your place. It wouldn't do to be seen now."

He obeyed the familiar voice, and at the same time tried to will his mind into a state of consciousness. The events of the afternoon were all jumbled together, and he needed to sort them out. Maybe the voice would help. He tried to replay its sound in his mind, to attach it to its proper owner, but the fog in his brain was making clear thinking almost impossible.

"Where am I?" he managed to mumble through lips that seemed uncooperative.

"Welcome to the land of the living, Marcel," said the voice. "For a while there, I thought the Germans had done you in."

It was Gilles' voice he was listening to. Yes, that was it. But what was Gilles Théron doing here? And where was *here*, anyway? The last thing he remembered clearly was riding in the truck from Montluc Prison to the Ecole de Santé. That would explain his hands. He was apparently still handcuffed. Everything else was all very confused.

"Where am I?" he asked again, louder.

"We're still in Lyons," replied Gilles, "but you're not easy to rescue, you know. I've been trying for nearly half an hour to find a safe way out, but the *boches* have all the roads covered."

So that was it. The truck accident had been planned. He had been rescued, or so it seemed. And not a moment too soon, either.

"What are you going to do?" Marcel's head was clearing. He twisted his body around to where he could see the back of Gilles' blond head.

"I'm supposed to go to the Rue Lanterne if all else fails. Hervé says there's a pastor there who may be willing to hide you."

"His name is de Pury," Marcel offered. "I've worked with him before."

Gilles turned and shot a quick glance into the back seat. "Are you all right? I mean, are you comfortable? You don't look so good."

"I'll be okay as soon as I can get rid of these." He strained against the handcuffs.

"We'll get them off of you as quickly as possible. That, I promise. And then we'll get a doctor to examine you. You look awful."

"Thanks!" He almost smiled.

"Seriously, what did they do to you?" Gilles was looking back over his shoulder again.

"Oh, they slapped me around a little," Marcel felt his face grow suddenly warm, "but it's not the end of the world. I'll be fine. What I want to know is how you found me."

"Well, we knew you'd been arrested, of course, and since it was the Gestapo, we assumed you'd end up in Montluc. That was the easy part."

"Easy for you, maybe."

"You know what I mean. Anyway, the hard part was finding out when you would be taken to Barbie's headquarters for questioning. We figured the only way to get you out was to try something while you were being transported. But as you know, they don't exactly announce their intentions to the public."

"So how did you find out?"

"I'm getting to that. Dominique Raspaud's widow got in touch with Hervé last night and said the Gestapo had been around asking questions."

Marcel's blood turned icy in his veins. "Dominique Raspaud's widow? I—I didn't know he was married. I mean, I didn't think. . . . Is she all right?"

"She's safe. Hervé moved her out of the city last night."

"What did the Gestapo want from her?" Marcel was pretty sure he knew even before he asked.

"They wanted to know where Dominique was. It seems that Madame Raspaud, with the help of a sympathetic friend in the police department, had not reported her husband's death and had continued to collect his pay. Since he reported only to Inspector Malfaire, no one else ever caught on."

"And of course Malfaire is dead too."

"Not exactly."

"What do you mean by that?" The scene replayed itself immediately in Marcel's mind, just as it had dozens of times over the past several months. After walking into Hervé's trap, Malfaire had sat quietly on the floor of the abandoned farmhouse near the Swiss border. Then without warning, he had pulled a pistol from inside his boot and the place had fairly erupted in gunfire, smoke, and flame. When it was all over, Dominique lay dead inside the burning house, while Malfaire made it outside before collapsing in the snow. And though Marcel had been wounded himself, he had never doubted that the inspector was dead.

"Apparently he survived, somehow," said Gilles. "The Gestapo threatened Madame Raspaud with exposing her secret by letting Malfaire in on it. When she told them he too was dead, they laughed at her. He's not only alive, he's a captain in the Milice!"

Marcel could hardly believe what he was hearing. It was just too crazy. The story he told Barbie had been simple, even if it weren't entirely true. So how could it have gotten so complicated? And how could Malfaire possibly be alive?

"Anyway," Gilles continued, "the Gestapo led Madame Raspaud to believe that someone had confessed to a secret association with her husband, which is why they were investigating him. That's why she called Hervé."

Marcel closed his eyes. "And Hervé knew?" he asked quietly.

"There aren't many people who were aware of Dominique's role. And you were the only one in custody."

Marcel fell silent, not wanting to further expose his shame—even to his dearest friend. He hadn't even considered that Dominique might have a family, hadn't thought beyond his own need to survive. And now he had put an innocent woman in jeopardy. Yes, she was safe for the moment, but for how long? Would she have to live in hiding? And what if the Gestapo had arrested her first and then asked their questions? He hated to even think what might have become of her in the hands of the sadistic Klaus Barbie. His reputation with female prisoners was enough to make anyone sick.

"Look, Marcel," Gilles' determined voice broke into Marcel's thoughts. "What's done is done. Besides, Madame Raspaud is safe, and we got you out in time. That's all that matters, isn't it?"

Marcel didn't respond right away. At the moment he wasn't at all sure that Gilles was right. What did matter, after all? He knew that he would have to live with the decision he had made, that he couldn't go back. But he couldn't get over the fact that he had nearly ruined someone's life in order to alleviate his own pain. Could he undo it? He knew he could not. But somehow, some way, he would have to make up for it. It simply could not be forgotten.

"You still haven't told me how you knew I'd be moved to the Ecole de Santé this afternoon," he said, suddenly fearful that the hole he was digging for himself was about to get deeper.

Gilles chuckled. "We sent a girl into the commandant's office at Montluc to inquire about you."

Marcel grunted. "My fiancée?"

"She had to tell them something."

So that was what the guards had been talking about. And he hadn't suspected for even a moment that there was anything to it.

"The funny thing is," continued Gilles, "while she was pleading with the commandant to tell her whether or not you'd been condemned to death, a driver arrived from Barbie's office demanding that you be transferred within the hour. It couldn't have worked better, though we did have to scramble to get into position in time."

"Who was she?" Marcel asked. "Is she safe?"

"A local girl. And you needn't worry about her. Hervé says she's very experienced."

Gilles had steered the car into a shadowy alley and was pulling to a stop when he spoke again. "There's a man Hervé knows here who can remove your handcuffs," he said. "Once that's done we'll rest until dusk. Then we'll go find Pastor de Pury."

"Will Hervé meet us there?" asked Marcel.

"No. He doesn't want to risk being seen in Lyons too much."

"Is he angry with me?" Marcel was almost afraid to ask, but he needed to know.

"You know Hervé," said Gilles, a little too somberly. "It's hard to tell what he's thinking."

Chapter 12

"Are you sure about this?" Justine asked for at least the fourth time. "It's not too late to change your mind, you know."

Isabelle nodded. "I'm sure," she said. "One way or another, I have to stop thinking only of myself and my problems."

"Isabelle!" Justine frowned just a little, but her tone conveyed more than a hint of reproach.

"No, I'm quite serious," Isabelle insisted. "It seems that all I've thought about for the past five months is getting out of Switzerland and going to America. But I'm beginning to realize just how unlikely that is—and how ungrateful I must seem to you, after all you and Robert have done for me here." She held up a hand in polite protest as Justine opened her mouth as if to interrupt.

"It looks as though I'll be staying here for quite a while," Isabelle continued, "whether I like it or not." She smiled wanly at Justine. "I really am grateful for all you've done for me. I hope you know that. Alexandre and I probably wouldn't be alive if it weren't for you. But there are others who are much less fortunate than I am, and I think it's only right that I should do something for them."

"But you already do so much," said Justine, sounding a little defensive. "Your hard work around our house certainly hasn't gone unnoticed. And with Alexandre to care for—well, I don't think you've been idle. And certainly not selfish!"

"I know what you're trying to say and I appreciate it," said Isabelle, "but you work hard too, Justine, and you still find time to give to others. I'm just asking to have the same opportunity. I don't want to be a charity case anymore. I want to contribute too."

"Oh, Isabelle! I hope you don't think I see you as a charity case. I took you in because you needed help, it's true. But how could I have done otherwise and still call myself a Christian? Besides, you've repaid me a hundred times over, anyway."

"Repaid you? How?"

"By your friendship. By your honesty. By letting me help you with little Alexandre." Her cheeks colored ever so slightly. Isabelle knew how her friend had grown attached to the baby.

"How could I not be your friend, Justine? You've accepted me just the way I am. And you're the reason I'm still alive."

Justine cast a quick glance heavenward. "He's the reason you're still alive, Isabelle. He just allowed me to play a small part."

Isabelle nodded. "A part, yes, but not so small, after all."

She was more convinced than she had ever been that Justine was right—Someone had orchestrated her rescue. If only she could know what He wanted from her in return. Somehow, the answers to such questions always seemed to elude her, though they apparently came easily enough to others. Perhaps if she focused on other people and their problems, the solution to her own situation would become more clear. Sometimes life was like that, she reasoned. And maybe that was how people discovered their destiny, learned what they were supposed to do. In any case, it couldn't hurt to get her mind off the fact that she was stuck here in Geneva.

"And you're not still too upset by that awful note?" Justine probed, referring to the paper they had found earlier in the post box.

"There are racists everywhere," Isabelle said, trying to sound matter-of-fact. "I don't know why it should surprise anyone to find a few on Swiss soil too."

But it *had* surprised her, she admitted to herself. It had surprised her a great deal. Someone's hatred had been directed specifically at her. It hadn't been aimed at the Jewish population in general. It wasn't some racist diatribe in an anti-Semitic newspaper. It was some unknown, flesh-and-blood person—maybe even a neighbor—lashing out spitefully, hatefully at *her*. *She* was the target—*personally*. And that had frightened her.

But as soon as the initial shock had worn off, she had resolved not to allow her fear to paralyze her. Next to leaving the country, that would suit her antagonist very well, she imagined. And that had made her all the more determined to attend Justine's Refugee Aid Society meeting tonight. Maybe there she could find a way to help meet the needs of some fellow refugee. She prayed that at the same time activity would keep her own fear and disappointment at bay.

Gerard Richert stared incredulously at Michael Dreyfus and set his empty wineglass on the low table that separated the green upholstered chairs in which the two men sat. Gerard's cramped hotel room seemed suddenly humid.

"Are you crazy?"

Michael winced reflexively. He had suspected all along that this conversation wasn't going to sit well with his boss. He just hadn't expected it to go this badly. For a second he wondered if it had been such a good idea to tell him at all. But sooner or later Gerard would find out, he knew, and it was better that he should hear it firsthand.

"What were you thinking?" Gerard continued, his voice rising steadily, splotches of color beginning to dot his pallid cheeks. "No, what *are* you thinking? Did you leave all your common sense behind when we left New York?"

"Now, Gerard—"

"It's not enough that you stick your nose into some refugee camp where it doesn't belong. Now you're planning to promote some ridiculous scheme to get Jews out of Europe?" Gerard laughed derisively. "I can't believe you're actually serious about all this."

Michael felt his own cheeks grow slightly warm, and he wanted to return fire. Didn't Gerard see how unreasonable he was being? Instead, he drew a deep breath before saying a word.

"It's not such a ridiculous scheme, Gerard," he said, trying to keep his feelings under control as well as his voice. "Mr. Rosen and his committee have enough money to purchase several ships, and they have a promise of cooperation from the Italian government."

"Cooperation with the fascists? They'll never agree to anything that doesn't involve lining their pockets."

"I don't know all the details, but Mr. Rosen says that it's in the Italians' best interest to cooperate. His plan could mean the evacuation of as many as 30,000 refugees. And that would mean 30,000 fewer people to police, 30,000 fewer mouths to feed. I would think that would look pretty attractive when

Italian resources are being stretched so thin by the war."

"So, let me see if I understand all this," said a slightly exasperated Gerard, leaning forward in his chair. "These Jews, or this committee, as you call it, is going to buy some ships, dock them in an Italian port, load them with refugees, and set sail for an American-held port in North Africa. Is that what you're telling me?"

"Well, yes, that's the basic idea."

Gerard shook his head slowly from side to side. "Unbelievable," he said.

"Why unbelievable?" Michael wondered if there were something he was missing in all this. It certainly hadn't seemed unbelievable when Heinrich Rosen had explained it to him.

"Because it's impossible, that's why." Gerard poured himself another glass of wine. "I can't believe you're letting yourself be taken in by these people. What are they after, anyway? Have they asked you to wring some money out of your father?"

"It's not like that at all!" Michael felt a wall of anger rising inside him. Gerard could be so pigheaded sometimes. "They haven't asked me for a dime. They're just trying to get as much support for their plan as possible, and I offered to help. What's so blasted impossible about it, anyway? The Italian government has already agreed to let the ships dock. All they have to do is get the U.S. government to give permission for the landings in North Africa."

Gerard looked taken aback momentarily, but quickly recovered his composure. "This Rosen fellow told you this?" he asked.

"Yes."

"And did he also tell you about the attempts to ferry Jews to Palestine?"

Michael wasn't sure where this was leading. "No, he didn't. Why?"

"Well, maybe he didn't tell you because those attempts have been a nightmare. Everything that could go wrong has. They've been forced to use decrepit old tubs instead of proper ships because of the demands of war. And when they do find something more or less seaworthy, it leaves port poorly equipped and overcrowded—if it is able to leave port at all."

"What do you mean 'if'? "

"I mean that the Axis powers are always threatening, and the British themselves don't want any more immigrants in Palestine. So the port authorities are inclined to think twice before letting ships leave.

"And even if a ship does manage to slip out of port, there's no guarantee it will reach its destination. The British are maintaining a blockade off the Palestinian coast, and when they catch an unauthorized passenger ship, they impound it and detain the passengers in camps on Cyprus. Very few people have actually been able to get to Palestine, Michael. And I suspect that your Mr. Rosen's group is equally unprepared—and equally doomed."

"Well, Mr. Rosen's group isn't trying to take anyone to Palestine," argued Michael. "Besides, they've already taken care of the kind of problems you're talking about. All they need is U.S. permission and Mr. Rosen says that's a mere formality."

Gerard snorted derisively. "Nothing is a mere formality with the U.S. government, Michael. You should know that by now." He took another small sip of his wine. "In any case, I don't want you to let this nonsense interfere with your work. Just stay out of trouble—and believe me, this crazy scheme is nothing but trouble."

"No trouble, Gerard," Michael sighed, holding his hands up in front of him, palms outward. "I promise there won't be any trouble."

In the hallway outside Gerard's room, Michael screwed his

face up into an exaggerated frown. "This crazy scheme is nothing but trouble," he mimicked in a sarcastic whisper. He shook his head disappointedly as he descended the stairs to the lobby. Gerard didn't understand the urgency of the situation. That much was obvious. Perhaps he would see it differently if he had seen the faces of those poor refugees at Le Bout du Monde. Or maybe, if he were a Jew. Well, he would just have to worry about Gerard some other time. Right now he was late for a meeting with his new friend, Heinrich Rosen.

Isabelle scanned the modestly appointed room as discreetly as possible from her seat in the fourth of five rows of wooden chairs neatly arranged before a small lectern. A handful of people were hidden from her immediate view, but those she was able to see seemed completely engrossed in the animated speech of the portly, middle-aged man behind the lectern.

Herr Rosen, as he had been introduced to this gathering of the Refugee Aid Society, was an invited guest representing the Jewish Committee for Refugee Relief. He was apparently informing the forty or fifty people in attendance of his committee's activities, although Isabelle could not be entirely certain since he had asked to address the group in Schwitzerdutch. Obviously, he was far more at ease in the Swiss German dialect than in the laborious French with which he had begun. Unlike Isabelle, most of his audience, though French-speaking, understood Schwitzerdutch well enough to follow what he was saying. Isabelle only caught a word here and there, but since Justine had promised to fill her in as soon as Rosen was finished, both her eyes and her mind had soon begun to wander.

Justine had introduced her to several Society members in

the few minutes between their arrival and the start of the meeting. A few of the women she had already met over the course of the past months when they had visited Justine. Nearly everyone she talked to inquired about Alexandre, which pleased her immensely. Robert was watching the baby this evening, a job he had volunteered to tackle, surprising everyone who heard about it.

The evening's first speaker had been an officer of the Aid Society making an appeal for help with the shortage of children's clothing in the camps and "homes," hostel-like establishments for refugees scattered throughout the country. Isabelle was excited to have an opportunity to use the skills she had honed as a seamstress in the prestigious Parisian dress shop of Madame de la Court. The idea, however, that she would be catering to the most basic needs of indigent children rather than the whims of finicky society ladies, made her smile. If Madame de la Court could see her now!

The prospect of once again being useful helped to dull the disappointment that seemed to define her existence lately. If she were going to be stuck here—and it was now clear that she was—then working to improve the existence of a few children would in turn make her own life seem better.

She was already beginning to plan what she could do to make the most of the limited resources of the Aid Society when she noticed the handsome young man on the far end of the fourth row of seats looking in her direction. Suddenly self-conscious, she averted her eyes, though she felt sure that his gaze had not shifted. She didn't recall ever having seen him before, but then the same was true for more than half the people in the room.

Heinrich Rosen was just then stepping away from the lectern to the accompaniment of the audience's polite applause. He was smiling, evidently pleased to have made his point with such an important group. Isabelle, of course, had almost no idea what point he had been trying to make, but leaned toward Justine in anticipation of an explanation.

"It's very exciting," Justine whispered as the applause faded. "Monsieur Rosen and his committee have devised a plan to evacuate 30,000 Jews from Italy."

"But where will they go?" Isabelle asked. "Will the Swiss let them come here?"

"Unfortunately, no," Justine replied with obvious chagrin. "I seriously doubt that many more Jews will be allowed in at all, let alone 30,000."

"Then where?"

"That's what's exciting. They plan to resettle the refugees in the American-held territories of North Africa."

"Can they do that? I mean, is it even possible?"

"I don't know for sure, Isabelle, but it just may work."

Isabelle fell silent as the meeting began to break up. It would be wonderful to be one of the chosen 30,000, she mused. If only she were in Italy instead of Switzerland. And that is when she happened to notice that the handsome, chestnut-haired stranger was still watching her.

The sound of applause broke the spell, and Michael glanced forward to where Heinrich Rosen was shaking hands with several members of the Refugee Aid Society. Apparently, his little speech had been a success. Michael had remained attentive for as long as he could, but the longer Mr. Rosen spoke, the more difficult it had become. Even though he was Swiss, Michael did not understand Schwitzerdutch, having attended school in the United States. His parents could understand it and even spoke some occasionally—especially when they wanted to keep something from Michael and his sister, Beatrice, but neither he nor Bea had ever learned more than a few words.

Eventually, his mind had wandered to other things—that is until his eyes chanced to focus on the girl seated at the opposite end of his row of chairs. So captivated was he by her natural beauty that he had felt unable to stop watching her. Once, just for an instant, she had looked his way, and he saw the hint of a smile on her full lips—or had he only imagined it?

Now the young beauty and the woman with her were wending their way through the small crowd toward Mr. Rosen, probably to congratulate him, as seemed to be the case with everyone in attendance. And rightfully so, as Rosen's plans did have the audacious air of genius about them. Michael didn't have to wonder what the plump little businessman had said to these people. The very reason they had come was to drum up support for the evacuation of Jews from Italy.

Quickly, but without trying to appear too hurried, Michael made his way to Rosen's side, touching him lightly on the elbow. Rosen turned, beaming his pleasure.

"So, my friend," he said discreetly in his heavily accented French, "how did I do?"

"Great, Mr. Rosen," Michael replied softly, smiling. "You were just great."

"You understood, then?" Rosen looked surprised, bemused.

Michael felt his cheeks burn. "Well, uh, not every word, but all you have to do is listen to the response. I think they were very impressed."

Rosen turned to greet yet another member of the assembled group while Michael scanned the crowd trying to catch sight of the girl again. Somehow, in the brief time it took for him to move from his seat to the front of the meeting room, she and her companion had disappeared. They had to be here somewhere. The room simply wasn't that large.

"And this is my colleague, Michael Dreyfus, from the Red Cross," he heard Rosen say.

"Ah, the Red Cross! What a marvelous organization."

"How do you do, monsieur?" asked Michael absently, as he shook the hand of an elderly gentleman whose name he hadn't quite caught. Mercifully, the old man hadn't tried to start a conversation with him. The last thing he wanted was to get tied up in some meaningless discussion while the most beautiful girl he had ever seen walked out of the room. But try as he might, the girl was nowhere in sight, and two dozen or more people were queued up to greet their guests. For the moment at least, he was stuck.

It was just possible, of course, that from where he had been sitting, his eyes had deceived him somewhat. Perhaps it was the lighting that had imbued an average girl with Olympian qualities. And he was forced to admit that just maybe his desire to meet her—whoever she was—was as much as anything due to the fact that his social life had been practically nonexistent for months on end. There were plenty of reasons to doubt his feelings, but not one of them seemed particularly compelling at the moment.

And then, as if to reward his instincts, she appeared in the line, just behind her companion who was introducing herself to Mr. Rosen. He suddenly felt as nervous as a schoolboy, and he hoped his mouth wasn't gaping open in awe.

"I'm Justine de Rocher, Mr. Rosen," the friend said as she clasped Rosen's hand, "and this is my good friend, Isabelle Karmazin."

"*Enchanté,* madame, mademoiselle," purred Rosen, bowing ever-so-slightly first to Madame de Rocher and then to Isabelle

Karmazin. "I hope the evening wasn't a complete bore."

"Quite the contrary, monsieur," Madame de Rocher assured him. "It was most informative." She dug into her handbag and pulled a card from deep inside. "Perhaps my husband and his associates could be of service. I'm certain he would be interested in your work."

"Thank you, madame," he said, bowing slightly once more and accepting the card. "Now, please allow me to introduce my colleague, Monsieur Dreyfus, from the Red Cross."

Michael took the hands that were offered, each in turn, but found himself utterly speechless. Isabelle Karmazin was even more than he had imagined from a distance. Slender and shapely, she melted him with her smile. Her straight brown hair was pulled away from her intense gray-green eyes and held neatly by a small black bow at the nape of her neck. Her creamy complexion was nearly flawless.

"It's nice to meet you," she said shyly, pulling back gently the hand he realized he had held a moment too long. And then she was gone, along with her friend, out the door and into the starry Geneva night.

Michael didn't remember another thing that happened all evening.

Chapter 13

Filled to overflowing with Sunday worshipers, St. Pierre's cathedral took on a completely different ambiance than when Isabelle had come all alone. The morning sun, diffused by a kaleidoscope of stained glass, added an air of joy and celebration to a place she had previously found somber. And though a feeling of reverence still permeated the austere gray stones, the muted voices of several hundred parishioners conveyed a kind of anticipation that Isabelle found as fascinating as it was unfamiliar.

Her previous visit to St. Pierre's, entirely unplanned on her part, had nonetheless prompted her decision to return. And yet she did not wish to return alone. There was so much she did not understand, and simply returning on her own would do little to correct that. So, she had asked to accompany Justine and Robert at the time of their regular worship on this last Sunday in May. They seemed genuinely pleased that she had asked, and were now seated next to her.

"Shhh," she whispered to Alexandre, who was squealing his apparent delight at making an all-too-rare public appearance. Two fashionable ladies in the pew in front of them turned at the sound and smiled adoringly. Isabelle smiled back, but secretly worried that what the ladies found charming now might become an annoying distraction if it continued for long, especially once the service began. Thankfully, Justine produced a small rubber toy which Alexandre grasped from her hand and immediately began gnawing contentedly. She hoped the quiet would last longer than it usually did.

From the moment the first melodious notes of the organ prelude sounded, it was as if Isabelle had entered a foreign country. It wasn't that she didn't understand the language, though not everything was perfectly clear. Nor was she made to feel particularly ill at ease by those around her. Rather, it was the customs that were the most confusing. All that standing up, and sitting down, and praying, and singing on cue. For much of the first half hour she felt as though she were mostly rushing to stay in step with everyone else. And trying to keep Alexandre calm didn't make things any easier. When at last the pastor climbed the steps to the imposing pulpit, she was relieved to hear Justine whisper that she could relax and remain seated for a while.

"This morning," the dark-robed pastor intoned, "we read from the Gospel of Luke the familiar story of the Good Samaritan." He paused briefly, and then began to read.

"A lawyer stood up and said to Jesus, to test Him, 'Master, what must I do to inherit eternal life?' Jesus said to him, 'What is written in the law? What do you read there?' He replied, 'You shall love the Lord your God with all your heart, with all your soul, with all your strength, and with all your mind; and your neighbor as yourself.' 'You have answered well,' Jesus told him. 'Do that, and you will live.' But wanting to justify himself, he said to Jesus,

'And who is my neighbor?'"

The pastor paused at this point as if to allow the lawyer's question to sink into the consciousness of his listeners. After a moment, he resumed his reading.

"Jesus spoke once again and said, 'A man went down from Jerusalem to Jericho. He fell among some ruffians who robbed him, beat him, and went away, leaving him half dead. A priest who chanced down the same road, having seen the man, passed by. A Levite, who also happened on the scene, having seen him, passed by. But a traveling Samaritan who came there was moved with compassion when he saw him. He came near and bandaged his wounds, pouring oil and wine on them. Then he set him on his own mount, led him to an inn, and took care of him. The next day he took two coins, gave them to the innkeeper and said, "Take care of him, and whatever you spend in addition to this, I will repay you on my return." Which of these three seems to you to be the neighbor of the one who fell among the ruffians?' 'The one who had mercy on him,' said the lawyer. And Jesus told him, 'Go and do the same.'"

Isabelle couldn't remember ever hearing the story before, though she, like most everyone else she knew, had more than once referred to some particularly kind person or another as a "good Samaritan." *So this is where the term comes from,* she mused. But as the pastor launched from the Gospel reading into his sermon, she realized that he, at least, thought of this Good Samaritan as more than a cliché. He spoke as if he expected everyone within range of his voice to indeed "go and do the same."

Isabelle had often wondered what ministers actually said to their parishioners on Sundays. She had met Marcel's pastor once. In fact, it had been Pastor Westphal who had driven her to the Boussant farm last fall. He had, of course, spoken to her of God, but not in any way that qualified as a sermon in her opinion. Now here she was listening to her first sermon and it was not at all what she had imagined. Somehow, she had expected a good sermon to be nearly as mysterious as she found God to be.

So she was puzzled by the straightforwardness of what the pastor seemed to be saying. Could it be so simple? If the words of Jesus were indeed true, then the two most important things God expected of her were to love Him and to love people. And the Good Samaritan story made clear the point that love isn't to be reserved only for those closest to us. Obviously, God expected action toward those in need. It made perfect sense, and confirmed her decision to get involved in the needs of the other refugees.

That was the easy part. The hard part was knowing how to love God. How could she truly love someone she couldn't see, someone she didn't really even understand, someone she hadn't even believed existed until a few months ago? What did loving God feel like? She couldn't imagine.

But what if she simply focused on helping people, doing acts of kindness? That, after all, was something she could understand, something she could actually do. And perhaps that was what God really wanted from her, anyway. And if that was what He wanted, then surely, in the course of sowing seeds of charity, she would reap the sense of closeness to God that she so longed for—the sense that He was smiling on her. He would almost have to smile if she did what He wanted, wouldn't He? And then, too, she felt sure He would answer her prayers.

For just a moment, Isabelle allowed herself to wonder what life would be like if her prayers were answered. And if she knew God would answer, would she dare to pray for someone to love her once again? Would she beg for the return of Marcel Boussant? Or would she ask for a new start for herself and Alexandre, far away in America?

⚜ ⚜ ⚜

Michael pulled back the drapes and blinked repeatedly as the morning sun poured through the window into his tiny room. It was Sunday, and he had allowed himself to sleep late—perhaps a little too late, judging by the dull ache in the back of his head. The lumpy, cylindrical pillow provided by the hotel left a great deal to be desired, in his opinion. After the first night in Geneva, he had asked to exchange it for a rectangular pillow such as he was used to at home, only to be told that there was a war on, as though that explained every possible inconvenience. And though he was trying his level best to get used to it, most mornings he still awoke with a slight kink in his neck.

Donning his robe, he rubbed the remaining sleep from his eyes, grabbed his shaving kit, and headed for the bath at the far end of the dimly lit hall, hoping he wouldn't have to wait too long while one of the other guests took a leisurely Sunday morning soak. On the way, he thought about his parents' house, and how wonderfully convenient and abundant everything was there. He made a mental note to send a postcard home.

Thirty minutes later, scrubbed and shaved, Michael returned to his room to find that an envelope had been slipped under the door in his absence. Tearing it open he found a brief note written on the hotel stationery:

My dear friend Michael,

M. de Rocher has agreed to meet with me at his home Tuesday evening. Would you be so kind as to join us? I will come to the hotel for you at 7:00. I am grateful for your help.

Your friend,

Heinrich Rosen

Michael, unable to suppress a grin, folded the note carefully and shoved it into the pocket of his robe. This was going to be a good week, he reasoned. Gerard had promised him the day off on Friday, and now he would get to accompany Mr. Rosen to yet another meeting in support of the Italian refugee evacuation plan. The real bonus was that further contact with the de Rochers might just lead to seeing their incredibly beautiful friend.

Isabelle was her name, Isabelle Karmazin. He let the sound roll off the end of his tongue. *It sounds good,* he thought. *It sounds Jewish. Mother would like that.* Michael loved it from the moment he first heard it. In fact, he liked everything about her—her gray-green eyes, her thick brown hair, the sound of her voice—everything. And he knew he would give just about anything to meet her again.

He wondered if Rosen were aware of just what this meeting with de Rocher could mean to him. Of course, it was tough to tell what Rosen was aware of sometimes. He seemed almost entirely fixated on the success of his evacuation mission. Not that that was a problem for Michael, not in the least. He believed in it wholeheartedly, and wanted to do whatever he could to make it a success. But that hadn't kept him from noticing Isabelle Karmazin.

The one thing that puzzled him about Rosen was the older gentleman's unwavering habit of introducing him to people as Michael Dreyfus of the Red Cross. Michael hadn't noticed it at first. Not really. But after a while, he almost wondered if his employer were more important to Mr. Rosen than he was, as though it gave a certain stature to his appeals to have someone on board from such an important organization. In the end, however, he guessed it was more likely that Mr. Rosen didn't know another way to introduce him comfortably. And it probably didn't matter, anyway. He was proud to be associated with such a worthy cause.

As for the meeting with de Rocher on Tuesday, Michael was counting the hours already. Hopefully, it would lead to something big for Rosen's committee. Somehow, he was sure it would also lead to seeing Isabelle again. He fingered the note in his pocket, unable to believe his good luck. It was practically too good to be true. The only thing better would be to find that Isabelle, too, was visiting the de Rochers on Tuesday!

⚜ ⚜ ⚜

"So," Justine asked, "what did you think of it?"

She and Isabelle had descended the steps of the cathedral into the sun-drenched courtyard, little Alexandre wide awake in his mother's arms. Robert lagged a few steps behind, deep in conversation with a friend.

Isabelle squinted against the sun's glare and placed a hand near Alexandre's face to shade his eyes. "It—it was very interesting," she replied hesitantly. She had a thousand questions for Justine, but she wasn't at all sure where to begin. "It wasn't like I thought it would be."

"I imagine it must have seemed quite different from a synagogue," Justine suggested helpfully.

Isabelle looked away for a moment. "I don't really remember, to tell you the truth," she said, as much to herself as to Justine. "My father didn't have much use for God or religion, so mostly we stayed away."

"But when you married—"

"No, there was no rabbi at our wedding." She laughed uneasily. "Adam—my husband—was a communist, and he wasn't any more interested in God than my father was. And at the time it didn't matter to me, either. Besides, in France only the civil ceremony is legally binding, anyway."

"How do you feel about that now?" Justine probed gently.

Isabelle hesitated a moment. "I think my father and Adam were both wrong," she replied at length. "And so was I."

"About the wedding?"

Isabelle almost missed seeing the twinkle in Justine's eye. "That too," she grinned quickly. Turning serious again, she added, "But what I really meant is that we were all wrong about God. I don't really know for sure why neither of them believed, but for me, it mostly had to do with all the bad things that kept happening to me."

"I can certainly understand that. What changed your mind?"

She smiled down at Alexandre. "Lots of things, really," she said, "and this little bundle was one of them." She poked playfully at the baby, who responded with giggles and squeals and a great deal of wriggling. "Actually, I think I always knew that God was there, somewhere, but I was so angry that it was easier to pretend He wasn't. But when Alexandre was born, I was so overwhelmed with gratitude for such a beautiful gift that I was finally able to see past my anger."

Justine suddenly grew very quiet, and Isabelle could see tears in her eyes.

"Oh, I'm so sorry, Justine. I didn't mean to—"

"It's all right," Justine whispered hoarsely, forcing a thin smile. "My time will come. I know it will." She dabbed at the corners of her eyes.

"It doesn't seem fair, Justine," Isabelle said softly. "You've believed in God all your life, haven't you, and He doesn't give you the thing you want most. And I was about as skeptical as a person could be, and I—"

"Don't, Isabelle," pleaded Justine. "You mustn't think like that. I'm sure there's a very good reason why I'm unable to have a child. I don't know what it is yet. But I won't stop trusting in Him just because I don't have everything I want."

Isabelle sighed and said nothing more. Just when she thought she was beginning to understand a little better, everything seemed confusing all over again. The trouble was, she knew she couldn't go back to the way things were before. Not after everything she had been through. Perhaps she simply needed to be a little more patient. Then maybe things would become more clear.

Chapter 14

Marcel lay fully clothed atop a well-worn cot and thumbed aimlessly through the pages of *L'Aigle de Mer.* He had read the seafaring novel at least twice before, but though it had long been one of his favorites, he just couldn't seem to concentrate on anything this morning. He had far too much on his mind, and he was anxious to be up and about. That, of course, wasn't possible for the time being, so mostly he just turned the pages, reading a few lines here and there by the light of the small kerosene lamp next to his bed.

The attic room he had occupied for the past few days was divided in half by a hastily constructed curtain made of blankets suspended from a long cord. On his side were the cot and a small table on which the lamp sat. On the other side, three children lay sleeping—two brothers and a sister—who had lost their parents in a Gestapo roundup. The room was normally illuminated by the tiny windows at each end of the attic, but heavy black paper was taped over them each night so that neighbors would not become suspicious if it became necessary to use the lamp. Marcel had decided to wait until the children awoke before removing the paper.

The attic and the rooms below comprised the Lyons presbytery where Pastor Roland de Pury lived with his family along the steep, winding Montée de la Boucle. This morning the house was empty, except for the attic's four occupants. Madame de Pury had just left with the children, judging by the silence below. But since it was Confirmation Sunday, Marcel guessed that the pastor would have been at the *temple protestant* on the Rue Lanterne for some time already, preparing the catechists for this most joyous of days. He wondered what de Pury would say to them as they readied themselves for the confirmation of their faith.

He couldn't help thinking back, if just for a moment, to his own confirmation. He had been so nervous that morning that he could barely eat. It had been a day like any other, in many respects. But like no ordinary day, it had marked his coming-of-age as a follower of Christ. It was an unforgettable day of celebrating his brief journey of faith and demonstrating to the assembled congregation that he understood, as far as he was then able, both the journey and its destination—that his faith was not completely blind. But just now, Confirmation Sunday seemed like a lifetime ago.

"Monsieur Marcel!" The words, though whispered, sounded unusually urgent. Marcel twisted around to see the cherubic face of a little girl peering around the far end of the wall of blankets.

"Good morning, Léa," he said softly, just above a whisper. "What's the matter?"

He couldn't help but notice the impatience registered in the six-year-old's great round eyes. It was such a change from the pain and sadness he usually detected there.

"Isn't anyone ever going to wake up?" Her exasperation was evident in spite of her whispering. "I don't want to stay in bed all day, you know."

Marcel stifled a grin. It wouldn't do to have her think he was mocking her. She seemed so completely serious.

"Are your brothers awake?" he asked.

"I am," answered a voice from the other side of the partition, "but Victor's still sleeping." Théo, at twelve years of age, was the oldest of the three children with whom Marcel shared his temporary attic home.

"Let him sleep, then," said Marcel, responding more to the look on Léa's face than to her brother's announcement. "He's probably tired."

"But he's always sleeping," Léa grimaced, "and I want to eat something. I'm hungry."

"Well, we can't go downstairs this morning, because no one is home. But I suppose I can sneak down and get some bread if you'd like."

"And can you open the windows? It's too dark in here."

Marcel put his book down and swung his long legs over the side of the squeaky cot. "All right then, I'll uncover the windows. But you mustn't make too much noise." Leaning over the lamp he blew out the flame, plunging the room into total darkness. Then he gingerly edged his way across the short and by now familiar distance to the tiny southern window and carefully removed the heavy paper. Sunlight flooded the makeshift hideout as he prepared to descend the stairs to the house below.

When Gilles Théron brought him here to the de Pury's under cover of darkness three days ago, Marcel had not expected to stay much longer than overnight—just enough time to get a decent meal and a few hours of sleep. By the time twenty-four hours elapsed after his escape, the Germans would have called off any all-out search—at least that was what he was counting on. Then he figured he would find a way out of Lyons on his own. It would be less dangerous that way.

The meal Madame de Pury offered him that first evening had exceeded his fondest dreams. After the thin soup, dried-out sausage, and stale bread of Montluc Prison, almost anything would have tasted good. But the thick slice of smoked ham that accompanied the usual potatoes, bread, and cheese rendered him almost speechless with gratitude. A gift from the farm of a parishioner, Madame had explained, one she could not serve to her other guests. Marcel needed no further explanation, and so he asked no questions. He had hardly given her comment any thought, even when he climbed exhausted into bed.

Much to his dismay, he did not awake until late the following afternoon, forcing a delay in his plans to leave. It was only then that he realized the extent of his fatigue and the effects that prison had had on him—both mentally and physically—in spite of the relatively brief time he had spent there. The de Purys tried to convince him to rest a few more days until Gilles could return for him and eventually, he had agreed.

The trouble was, the attic was beginning to feel like just another prison cell. Quiet, comfortable, and safe, to be sure, but confining nonetheless. And Marcel ached for a return to the outdoors where he had always felt most at home. It was in his blood, he reasoned. His love of the farm, the wind and sun weathering his face, his body steeled by hard work—these traits had been passed on to him by his father, and his father before him. When the war was finally over, he would return to carry on what Papa had started some twenty years earlier. No more dehumanizing prisons, no more suffocating attics, no more fear of arrest and brutality. Just a family to love, a farm to work, and sweet, uninterrupted peace.

And, except for when he slept, or when the three children wanted to talk, that is how he had passed the time. He reminisced about his father, missing since the outbreak of war with no news of any kind as to his fate. He wondered about Maman, Françoise, and Luc, whom he had not seen in over two months. They were trying to stay out of harm's way with his grandparents in Ardeche. He sometimes wondered if he wouldn't have been better off to have joined them.

He thought a lot about Isabelle Karmazin too. By now she would be settled into her new life in America, he guessed. He often tried to imagine what that would be like. He remembered the pictures he had seen, and the subtitled movies from Hollywood. He supposed it would be quite grand, especially for a woman as beautiful as Isabelle. And then, invariably, he tried to imagine what life without her was going to be like once the war was over. And that is when he wanted out of the attic most of all.

"Monsieur Marcel?" It was Léa again. She had already eaten her share of the bread he had found neatly sliced and waiting for them downstairs, and was now standing at the foot of his bed. "Your book is upside down. How can you read it like that?" she asked, as serious as if he might actually explain how it was done.

Marcel closed the book and laid it aside. "I guess it is kind of hard to read like that," he admitted. "Do you want to talk?"

All three of the children seemed to have accepted Marcel's presence from the very beginning. In fact, they seemed to appreciate having someone older to talk to. Perhaps they felt safer with him around, though they never said it in so many words. Théo, of course, probably felt he was quite able to take care of himself, though occasionally Marcel thought he noticed a fleeting look of fear in the boy's eyes. Victor and Léa were still young enough to appreciate a strong arm around them, and were less worried about maintaining a façade. Marcel imagined that would come soon enough.

Léa remained at the foot of the cot, not looking directly at him, yet neither was she looking at anything else, really. She just shifted her weight from one foot to the other, rocking back and forth slowly, rubbing the palms of her tiny hands together.

"What is it, Léa?" he asked gently.

"She's scared," said Victor, his head suddenly appearing between two of the suspended blankets. "She doesn't like it when the others go away."

"He wasn't talking to you, Victor," said Théo, still hidden behind the homemade partition.

"It's okay," said Marcel. "Sometimes I'm scared too."

"When you're all alone?" asked Léa.

"Yes," he replied, "especially then."

"What do you do when you're scared?" Victor was now standing beside his sister.

"Do you really want to know?"

"Yes," they answered in unison. And out of the corner of his eye Marcel caught a glimpse of Théo, standing just at the edge of the partition.

"Well," he said slowly, "whenever I get scared I say a prayer. That's what I do."

Léa, a look of pleasant surprise on her face, stopped rocking back and forth. "That's just what Maman always told us to do," she exclaimed.

"And do you remember to do that?"

"Sometimes I forget," she said, her brown eyes once again reflecting a haunting sadness.

Marcel averted his gaze. "Me too," he mumbled, trying to shake off the feeling of guilt that once again nipped at the heels of his heart. "Me too."

⚜ ⚜ ⚜

Half an hour later, all three Lévy children sat quietly on the edge of Marcel's cot, listening intently as he read aloud from the pages of *L'Aigle de Mer.* It was amazing to him how quickly his fellow fugitives had taken a liking to him, in spite of the circumstances—or perhaps because of them. In any case, he found all three to be pleasant company, though little Léa tended to ask too many questions at times. But that seemed to irritate Théo more than it did Marcel. Perhaps he was afraid she would annoy their newfound friend, the one person they saw more than any other.

Marcel had just reached the part where Captain Blaise Leduc was about to be pulled from the icy waters off the coast of South America by a harpooner, when the sound of a door shutting could be clearly heard below. Marcel stopped in mid-sentence, and no one made a sound, each straining for the sound of a familiar voice.

"*Allo!* Is anybody home?"

The voice didn't sound like it belonged to anyone Marcel knew. He cast a questioning glance at Théo, hoping for some sign of recognition on the boy's face. There was none.

"*Allo!* Are you here? I have to talk to you."

Marcel put his finger to his lips, then slowly rose from the cot and padded softly toward the attic door. Kneeling, he placed his ear against the door and listened. But all he could hear was the sound of his own heart beating a tattoo on his eardrum. As he glanced back at the children his heart nearly skipped a beat. They sat huddled together in the middle of the bed, silent and still as tombstones, their faces nearly as gray, their eyes wide yet unseeing.

"Please answer me!" pleaded the unknown voice below. "It's very important."

A tiny sliver of a thought began slowly wedging its way into Marcel's brain. Why, he wondered, would someone enter the house and call out to them if he didn't already know that they were here? And why would he announce his presence if he intended to do them harm? For all the intruder knew, they might be armed after all. And for a moment, Marcel wished it were so, even though he knew that the pastor and his wife would never have approved. Still, if he were at least able to protect the children . . .

Lifting the attic door as quietly as possible, he lowered himself onto the steps below. He attempted to signal to the children that everything would be all right, but couldn't tell whether they understood or not. They looked so scared.

⚜ ⚜ ⚜

Théo watched Marcel descend into the house below with a mixture of terror and disbelief. For a second, he wasn't sure whether he was more angry or scared. The truth was, after only three days or so, he really didn't know that much about the man. Sure, he was on the run from the police too. But would he turn them in in order to save his own skin? He guessed he would know the answer to that question in a matter of minutes.

Strangely, Marcel was pulling the door closed behind him, and Théo's world was once again reduced to the suffocating space beneath the rafters, isolated completely from whatever was going on downstairs. He felt trapped, with no place to go and no one to share the burden of care he bore for the two little ones. He was beginning to think that discovery was inevitable, eventually. There were, after all, only so many places they could hide. And without transportation, his options were further limited. He had considered taking a train to Nice where the Italian occupiers were reportedly much more humane than their German counterparts. But he realized that unaccompanied children would raise more than a few eyebrows. Besides, he had no money.

Léa's lithe body was pressed tightly against him, and he could feel her trembling. He wanted desperately to comfort her, but he didn't dare open his mouth, even to whisper. Victor, eyes darting wildly about, looked as though he might be sick at any moment, and Théo cringed at the thought of how much noise that was likely to make. He regretted the reflection instantly, however, knowing all too well just how scared Victor had to be. It was a wonder they hadn't all been reduced to hysteria after what they had been through these past weeks.

Muffled voices could now be heard from below, their indistinct sounds penetrating the attic door. He could not recognize one of them, though it seemed anxious, even urgent. But one certainly belonged to Marcel. Was he leading the stranger to their hiding place, or making up some kind of story to lead him away from them? It was impossible to tell since he could only make out an occasional word. Théo's stomach knotted tightly as he waited and listened. The house fell silent.

Then, with a suddenness that startled all three of them, the attic door was flung open, and Marcel's head appeared in the opening, his face completely drained of color. Léa's hand flew to cover her mouth, and Victor let out a low moan. Théo felt as though someone were squeezing all the air out of his lungs.

"Get your things," Marcel said slowly, "and come downstairs." There was a slight tremor in his usually strong voice.

"Wh-what's going on?" Théo stammered. Neither he nor the children moved so much as an inch.

Marcel looked tired, the bruises on his face and neck suddenly more visible, even though the light was poor. "We have to leave now." He said it gently, but his voice was insistent.

"B-but—"

"*Allez*, hurry, Théo," Marcel was more urgent now. "We don't have much time. The Gestapo just arrested Pastor de Pury, and they'll be here any minute."

Chapter 15

Marcel wondered if he would ever be able to get it out of his mind. The image of Léa and Victor huddling close to their brother, like chicks cowering under a hen's protective wings, had been burned into his mind. The expressions on their faces, a mixture of fear and utter disappointment, reminded him of how he had felt at the moment of his own arrest, some weeks earlier. But these children were far too young to have to experience such a cruel life, he told himself. Each new shock, each hardship, robbed them of a piece of their childhood, a piece impossible to recover once lost. He could only hope that they would become stronger in the process, that in growing older they would not also grow bitter.

For his part, Théo had first looked scared and then angry. And maybe he really was angry—or just maybe his anger was an attempt to put a manly face on a twelve-year-old's fear.

Marcel could relate to both the anger and the fear, for he was feeling both at the moment. He was angry at a system that would so devalue a race of people that even the children were herded into inhuman holding pens and then shipped by train to the east, like so much cattle to the slaughter.

Oh, the authorities all denied that anything so vicious was taking place. The children were simply being reunited with their families in a resettlement effort, they said. But Marcel knew differently. He had seen one of the trains, crammed with human cargo, and instantly knew in his heart that those on board were not intended to live—not in France, not anywhere. And he was afraid that the very same fate awaited his young charges if his efforts to get them out of Lyons were unsuccessful.

He hadn't planned what he was about to do, hadn't anticipated it in the slightest degree. Not once during his brief stay at the de Pury's had he considered involving the children in his own escape—or vice versa. But here he was, lying flat on his stomach in the tall grass near the rail yard, peering through the fence, waiting for night to fall, trying to form a plan of escape for the four of them. There simply hadn't been time to formulate a careful plan, nor had there been time to enlist additional help. The news of de Pury's arrest had come so suddenly, so unexpectedly, that everyone connected with the activist pastor had been caught off guard.

He had known immediately that he couldn't risk the busy Gare de Perrache, with its crowded quays and passenger trains. Police would be everywhere. So with the children in tow, he had made his way here, where freight cars were assembled into long trains for the trip north to Paris, south to Marseilles, or east to Grenoble.

The cool breeze whispered through the tall grass, bending it ever so slightly. The sun, which had beat down on them relentlessly all afternoon, was beginning its descent toward the western hills. The lengthening shadows made it harder to distinguish details in the rail yard from this distance, but Marcel was confident that by now he pretty much knew where everything was—everything, that is, that wasn't on wheels. Many of the rail cars had been moved from one place to another more than once. And once darkness fell, he knew that it would be almost like starting over again—except that he now knew where the soldiers patrolled and how often.

Théo, Victor, and Léa remained behind him, some fifty yards or so, where he had left them in a tiny abandoned shack. It would be the end of their hopes and plans, fragile as they were, if any of them were to be seen anywhere near the yards. He would return to get them once it was good and dark.

⚜ ⚜ ⚜

Jean-Claude Malfaire sat in his car a few houses down and across the street from number 30, Montée de la Boucle, and rubbed his aching shoulder. He watched with intense interest, as he had all afternoon, the stream of people who came and went from the presbytery, making notes occasionally in a small notebook that lay open on the seat beside him. He wasn't exactly sure what he was looking for, but something told him that with patience, he just might learn something of value.

The strange thing was that the people who came and went from number 30 didn't look like there was anything amiss. Everyone seemed calm, though perhaps somber, and no one seemed to be acting secretively or suspiciously. He would never have imagined that the pastor whose home it was had only this morning been arrested by the Gestapo if he had not witnessed it with his own eyes.

Malfaire had been outside the *temple protestant* on Rue Lanterne when the Gestapo agents arrived, and had watched with somewhat mixed emotions as they brought the bespectacled pastor out in handcuffs and drove away with him. It was a little cowardly to arrest a man of God, it seemed to him. On the other hand, knowing as he did that a fair number of Protestants, including pastors, were collaborating with the so-called Resistance, he guessed they had to be considered fair game. Still, he had hoped to question the pastor regarding the escape and disappearance of a certain young Protestant, Marcel Boussant. When the Gestapo interfered, he lost his chance.

He had been reviewing his file on Boussant when he remembered the Protestant connection. And while he had never been able to prove it, he suspected that the boy had been helped in the past by members of his church, and there was every reason to think that it might happen again. Besides being rather unorthodox in their beliefs, these Protestants were somewhat clannish, in Malfaire's view. Perhaps it came from being so few in number; he didn't really know. But he felt sure that they were not to be trusted.

That is why he had decided to question Pastor Roland de Pury this morning. Perhaps he could have shed some light on Boussant's whereabouts, though probably not without some incentive; everyone has his price. But now that the Gestapo no doubt had him locked up in Montluc Prison, there would be no way to discover what he did or did not know about anything.

Oddly, the Gestapo had not made an appearance at the presbytery. Odd, because Jean-Claude had found that it almost always paid to search the house of an arrestee. You never knew just what you might find, and more often than not, you found something incriminating. But here it was, hours after the arrest, and no Gestapo.

Even without the Gestapo present, however, Malfaire was reluctant to go into the house himself. The distraught wife would have undoubtedly made for a very fruitful interrogation, but he didn't want to chance it. One word to Klaus Barbie that he had been nosing around one of their cases, and the butcher would have his head on a platter. Even his old friend Philippe Darnand would be unable to protect him then.

So he waited and watched from a distance, hoping that something would turn up, but expecting it less and less as the day wore on. Finally, as twilight approached, he gave up, heading down the winding street toward home. Tomorrow, he decided as he massaged his shoulder, he would drive to Grenoble. If Marcel Boussant had somehow managed to slip out of Lyons, he felt certain that he would turn up in one of his old haunts. The sooner he discovered which one, the sooner he could settle an old score.

⚜ ⚜ ⚜

It was so dark inside the tumbled-down shack that Théo could hardly see Victor and Léa, sitting only a few feet from him. He couldn't decide whether it would be lighter, or darker still, once Marcel returned and they were able to join him under the stars. Hopefully, it would be just light enough for them to find their way, and dark enough to keep them from being seen by any of the soldiers, or police, or whoever might be patrolling the rail yard at this time of night. He just wished they could get going. Waiting here in this ramshackle place for much longer was likely to drive him mad, to say nothing of the effect it was probably having on the children.

"Théo!"

Théo started at the whispered sound of his name.

"Théo, it's me, Marcel. Are you all okay?"

"Yes. Is it time to go?" Théo could feel his pulse quicken the dull ache in his stomach was suddenly sharp.

Marcel's hand was on his shoulder then, and he could feel

Léa and Victor within arm's length as well.

"It's time," Marcel said in a low voice as they all huddled around. "I've found a place where we can wriggle under the fence, but we're going to have to be very careful. Does everyone understand?"

"Where are we going?" asked Victor.

"I don't know for sure. I can't tell which trains are going where. But don't worry, Victor, the most important thing is to get out of Lyons. And that's what we're going to do."

Théo wished he could feel as sure of that as Marcel sounded. He knew that they needed to get out of the city. But it was his city. He never felt really lost in Lyons, no matter where he was. Papa had made sure of that, often asking him to take the bus here and there on little errands. Théo loved it, even though he knew that some of the errands were of almost no importance. Papa had simply wanted to make certain that his eldest son knew the city. But surely Papa never envisioned why such knowledge would one day prove so invaluable. He couldn't have known. No one did.

In spite of his familiarity with Lyons, Théo was sure he would get lost on the very first day in any other city. And then what? What would become of Léa and Victor? Would they survive to see Maman and Papa again? Would they all be arrested and sent to one of the camps?

"You take Victor with you, Théo," Marcel was saying. "Make sure he stays right with you. And make sure to do exactly as I say. *D'accord?*"

"*D'accord,*" he responded numbly. He felt Victor's hand grasp his forearm, squeezing it tightly.

"I'll take Léa with me," Marcel continued. "If we get separated, don't panic. Stay where you are and I'll come find you. If the guards find any of us, take Victor and run for the fence. Once you get on the other side, just keep running as fast and as far away from here as you can."

Théo nodded, trying to keep from meeting Marcel's gaze straight on. He couldn't help feeling that if Marcel could see his face clearly, he would see the fear written in bold letters there. And he wondered if the young fugitive he was about to follow was half as frightened as he was.

⚜ ⚜ ⚜

Getting the children under the fence was easier than Marcel had expected. He had trenched out a shallow depression through which he could wriggle under the wire mesh. But it had only occurred to him as he was scooping out the last few handfuls of loose soil that even Théo was enough smaller than he was to make passing under the wire a snap. So, one by one the three Lévy children crawled through the opening and then crouched, waiting for Marcel to join them inside the enclosure.

"See that first line of wagons?" Marcel asked Théo when they were all together. The freight wagons were clearly silhouetted against the pale overhead lights in the center of the switching yard.

Théo nodded quickly.

"We've got to make it over to them and then sneak along until we find an empty one. But keep to the shadows as much as possible. If we get near the lights, we're in trouble." He looked from one wide-eyed young face to the next to be sure they understood before he continued. "Théo, I want you and Victor to stay here until I get up next to the wagons with Léa. Then come as quietly as you can."

He turned to Léa, then, and reached for her hand. It was damp and trembling, and in spite of the dark he could see that her eyes were as round and shiny as silver coins. She looked smaller than usual tonight, and frail.

Perhaps it was just the dark, but he couldn't help thinking how she reminded him of his sister when they were young. Françoise would get so frightened every time there was a thunderstorm. But Maman and Papa were always there to console her, to hug away the terror she felt. They would take her into their bed where she would snuggle between them until the storm had passed. It seemed so unfair that Léa had no parents to calm her fears, and doubly unjust that hers was no mere passing storm. *Why,* he wondered, *why does it have to be so hard on the children?* Yet even as he considered the question in his mind, he knew that there was no good answer. What he did know was that for the moment, he would be her comfort, her strength. And not just hers, but her brothers' as well.

"Climb on my back," he said, and without a word, she crawled up on him, encircling his neck with surprisingly strong arms. Crouching as low as possible, he set off quickly for the nearest rail car. He set Léa down again as soon as they reached the tracks, and helped her crawl under the car to lie in the space between the rails.

The smell of creosote filled his nostrils as he lay beside her, his lanky body stretched over the ties, the sharp gravel between threatening to pierce his knees and elbows. He shifted onto his side and peered cautiously toward the source of the light. His view, however, was partially blocked by another train parked on a siding parallel to the one on which he lay. The light was evidently coming from somewhere beyond it. He surveyed the narrow empty stretch between the trains, as much as the shadows would allow. Somewhere there would be guards, hopefully without dogs, and he wanted to get an idea of where they were, and where they went, before he ventured any further.

The boys arrived a moment later, sliding under the rail car just a few feet from where Marcel and Léa were.

"Sshhh!" he hissed, irritated. This was never going to work if they couldn't be quieter than that, he grumbled to himself. Their chances weren't very good even if they were all as silent as stones. But if they were going to be noisy—

"They didn't mean it," whispered Léa, breaking her silence. And the irritation building in Marcel crumbled as the glimmer of distant light revealed the glistening of tears in her eyes. They were just children, he reminded himself—scared and homeless. He reached out a hand and gently wiped away Léa's tears.

The crunch of boots on loose gravel sent a shock wave rippling through Marcel's body. He motioned to the children to lie flat against the rail ties and then did the same. The sound seemed to come nearer, then stopped. *Someone's searching under the wagons!* Marcel couldn't tell for sure whether the sound had come from the rail bed where they lay or from the set of tracks nearby. Either way, he hardly dared breathe, for fear of being overheard, and he hoped that the children too were holding their breath.

After a few seconds, the footsteps resumed, ever nearer, before stopping abruptly once more. Moments later a beam of light splashed haphazardly across the side of a nearby rail car, then spilled onto the ground only yards from where Marcel and the children lay. The guard had to be carrying a torch, Marcel decided. And he lay his head flat on a rail tie, to keep as low a profile as possible. Still he could see the light swinging closer and closer as the boot-clad guard approached.

"*Hallo*, Johann!" From out of the dark, a man's voice called out, almost pleasantly.

The footsteps ceased and the pool of light, only a few feet from exposing Marcel and his charges, suddenly swung away, leaving them gratefully in the dark again.

"*Was ist los?*" The man with the torch sounded mildly annoyed.

Marcel raised his head just enough to see the lower half of the man's body silhouetted against the light from his torch. But he couldn't see where the beam of light was aimed.

"*Ich habe etwas dass ich dir zeigen möchte.*"

Marcel tried to remember some German from his days in the lycée, but without much success. He wished he had paid more attention in class. He had picked up a word or two listening to the guards in Montluc Prison, but most complete sentences still escaped him. He was sure he could have done much better if it were Italian being spoken.

Muttering under his breath, the man with the torch shuffled back in the direction from which he had come, toward the sound of the second man's voice. The other man seemed to keep up a rather one-sided conversation. In an instant, Marcel knew that this was their chance to move to a safer location. If they could work their way along the side of the train away from the guard, traveling in the opposite direction, perhaps they could avoid being seen.

"Let's go," he whispered, "and try not to make any noise."

Taking Léa's hand again, Marcel crept along beside the train, stepping carefully from one rail tie to the next to avoid the noisy gravel between. Glancing over his shoulder, he could see that Théo and Victor were several yards back, but keeping pace as they too stepped from tie to tie. Marcel crouched low at regular intervals to peer under the wagons, making certain that no one was following along the opposite side. He couldn't see very well in the dark, but he figured that since one guard had a torch, any others would as well. And as long as they used them, he would be able to see them from a distance and would therefore have them at a disadvantage. It was likely the only disadvantage they had, however, and he took little comfort in it.

Trying the latch on the sliding door of each rail car they

passed, Marcel soon began to wonder if they were all locked. Not one of them had budged so much as a millimeter thus far, and he couldn't even guess how many more cars there were—or whether they were making their way to the front or rear of the train, for that matter. They would just keep trying until they had exhausted all the possibilities. Surely there had to be an empty car somewhere in this vast freight yard. Or if not empty, at least open.

Then another idea struck him as he passed a coupling. He wasn't at all sure it would work with the younger children, but it might be worth a try. At the end of each car was a ladder, leading to the roof. If they could find a train that was preparing to move out, they could mount to the top and lay flat, provided there was something to which they could hang on. That way they could avoid being spotted as the train left the yard, especially if its departure took place while the sky was still dark.

He pulled Léa into the space between the cars, next to the coupling, and waited for the boys to arrive. Then he motioned for all three of them to remain still while he climbed the rungs to the top of the freight car in front of them.

Once on top he snaked his way forward, groping all about him for a hand hold, anything that would keep the children from sliding off once the train was moving. But although he found that he might be able to hang on for some distance—and Théo too, though perhaps not for long—nothing he could feel with either hand convinced him that Victor and Léa stood a chance of surviving such a trip. Disappointed, he decided he would just have to keep looking for an unlocked door.

Slithering back toward the ladder, Marcel was startled by a sudden loud hissing sound. He looked up to see a silvery geyser of steam pouring into the night sky some fifty yards or so ahead, then heard a steam engine roar to life. He smiled at his own frightened reaction. At least now he knew where the front of the train was. Of course, this meant that extra caution was in order, since the train's crew would not be far off.

He dangled his feet over the edge of the roof, feeling for the ladder's top rung. Once he felt his weight firmly supported, he began to descend, slowly so as to remain as quiet as possible. He still wasn't sure what had happened to the guard, since he had not seen him—or the glow of his torch light—for quite some time now.

"Need some help, monsieur?" a man's voice asked calmly.

Marcel froze, just two rungs from the bottom of the ladder. His hands, suddenly damp with sweat, threatened to lose their grip. He wanted to descend, but his legs felt so weak he wasn't sure they would work properly. Gingerly, he managed to turn his head toward the sound of the voice. And there, arms folded across his chest, stood a man in a railroad uniform, sleeves rolled up above his elbows. Sweat glistened eerily on his powerful forearms and coal-smudged face as he stared evenly back at Marcel.

The children were nowhere in sight.

Chapter 16

"*Les enfants!*" Marcel's voice sounded hoarse. "What have you done with the children?" He had dropped to the ground the instant he realized that Léa and her brothers were gone. Now he faced the railroad man squarely, a mere half dozen feet separating them.

"Keep your voice down!" The man put a finger to his lips. "Do you want the *boches* to hear you?" Then he bent at the waist and pointed to the rails beneath the car Marcel had just dismounted. "They're safe," he said, a half-smile playing on his lips, "right behind you. They crawled under there when they saw me coming."

Marcel kept a wary eye on the railroad man as he too knelt to see that the three Lévy children were indeed hiding under the train, just as the man said. He reached a hand toward them, motioning for them to come out. Slowly, reluctantly, the three crawled out of their cachette, keeping Marcel between them and the stranger.

"Are you all right?" he asked them, alert to any sudden movement on the part of the man.

They nodded in unison.

Marcel turned to face the stranger again. "What are you going to do with us," he asked flatly. "Turn us over to the police?"

"Is that what you think?" The man's smile suddenly disappeared. "We're not all collaborators, you know."

"What, then? We don't have much money." He considered the few francs in his pocket. The money had been hastily stuffed into his hands by the man who had come to the de Pury's house to warn him. Little as it was, it was going to have to buy them food, somehow. Extortion hadn't entered his mind, until now.

But the railroad man shook his head, holding up his hands in protest. "I'm only trying to help you. I don't want your money."

"What are you suggesting?"

"This is my train." He said it with pride, as if he actually owned the locomotive and its caravan of freight wagons. "I can offer you safe passage to the Italian zone—as far as Grenoble, that is. But after that, I'm afraid you're on your own."

Marcel could hardly believe his ears. In fact, it sounded too good. How could he trust this man—engineer or not—without knowing anything about him? How could he entrust the children to him? "How did you find us?" he asked.

"I saw you come in under the fence," the engineer replied. "And there is only one reason I could think of that would bring you here at night—especially with small children. So I distracted the guard and came looking for you." He paused. "It wasn't all that hard, you know."

"Finding us?"

"Distracting the guard. You see, I keep a small bottle of

l'eau-de-vie for emergencies." He smiled broadly. "And tonight seemed like an emergency."

Marcel couldn't suppress a grin himself. *So that's why the guard hadn't reappeared yet.*

"What do we do now?" he asked, aware that sooner or later someone would resume patrolling the area.

"Follow me," said the engineer, "but be careful. If we get caught they won't hesitate to shoot us all."

⚜ ⚜ ⚜

Inch by excruciating inch the locomotive gathered speed—if it could actually be called speed at that point—straining against the cargo-laden wagons strung out behind it. Théo's fingernails dug into the palms of his hands as he willed the train to accelerate, to put as much distance as possible, as quickly as possible, between them and the freight yard. At the rate at which they were going, the last car probably hadn't yet cleared the barbed-wire perimeter. He couldn't tell for sure, because he couldn't see a thing. *Please, God! Let us get away!*

Théo was used to trains. He had ridden many of them with his family. Once he had even been allowed to ride by himself as far south as Nîmes where a summer camp monitor had met him at the station to drive him into the mountains. This, however, was shaping up to be the most exciting train ride of his life—and by far the most uncomfortable. Exciting, because in spite of leaving his beloved Lyons, they were also leaving behind the Gestapo. No more hiding in attics. And maybe he would be able to get some news about his parents.

But he, his brother and sister, and Marcel were not seated securely in the first class car, as he had so often been with Maman and Papa. In fact, a cattle car seemed preferable to where he found himself at the moment. Oh, the engineer had assured the four of them that this was perfectly safe, but within minutes of climbing aboard, Théo had begun to harbor doubts. And with each turn of the locomotive's wheels, his doubts increased.

Pressed tightly together in silence against the outside wall of the coal tender, the four sat in pitch darkness under a large musty-smelling tarpaulin. Dust from the loose chunks of coal the engineer had piled protectively over the tarp sifted down over them each time one of them moved, making what little air there was difficult to breathe. The chalky powder soon permeated everything, and Théo wondered if they would ever be clean again—or ever again take a deep breath.

Léa began to cough suddenly and couldn't seem to stop. The air really was becoming unbearably thick. It was a wonder they weren't all coughing. If only there were something he could do for poor Léa. At least they were away from the dangers of the freight yard by now. The steady hum of the wheels on the iron rails and the loud drone of the locomotive engine assured him that they were traveling too fast to still be in the city.

And then a wave of cool, clean air swept over him as the tarpaulin was drawn awkwardly back. There, silhouetted against the open firebox stood the engineer, his back to the fireman who shoveled fresh coal into the hungry flames.

"Thought you might like some fresh air," the engineer announced loudly, in order to be heard over the engine noise. "Is everyone all right?"

"Yes, I think so," Marcel yelled back.

"I'll leave you in the open until we near Grenoble. Just don't move around too much, and stay out of sight." And he turned to resume his customary place at the controls.

Léa's coughing was beginning to subside, but the initial surge of cool air had been replaced by blasts of heat from the firebox. Théo couldn't imagine why anyone would want a job standing so close to such an oven. Of course, it probably didn't feel so bad in the dead of winter, but this was nearly June. Perhaps they got used to it, after all, and didn't give it much thought. Watching the two men, however, he couldn't help but admire the way they worked together with hardly a word between them. It was obvious that they had teamed up before—many times, probably. He wondered how many times they had smuggled people out of Lyons together, or if this were the first. And he found himself hoping that they were as good at smuggling as they appeared to be at operating the giant, steam-belching locomotive.

The train had slowed to little more than a crawl when Marcel felt a corner of the tarpaulin being lifted once again. This time they had all known what to expect in its sweaty, dusty, smelly confines, and it hadn't seemed quite so bad as in the beginning. Still, the fresh air tasted wonderful.

"Do you know the area?" the engineer was kneeling beside him speaking into his ear so as not to have to raise his voice.

"I live a few miles from here," Marcel replied, though he hadn't actually been home to nearby Domène since the first of the year. He hadn't dared.

"Don't go home," the engineer cautioned, "and don't go anyplace where people are likely to know you."

Marcel didn't respond right away. How then, he wondered, was he going to find a hiding place for the children? It wasn't as if he could drop them off just anywhere, with just anyone. In his mind, though he had not mentioned a word of it to them, he had counted on leaving them in the capable hands of the Westphals. Surely the pastor and his wife would be able to ensure their safety. They had, after all, done as much many times before. If that didn't work he had figured on taking them to Professor Lambert.

"Where am I supposed to—"

"They'll be watching for you, my friend. They always do."

"But the Gestapo can't operate freely in the Italian zone," Marcel protested.

The engineer smiled grimly. "The Gestapo, no. The Milice, yes. Once they know you've escaped, they'll be waiting for you to make a mistake—like going to see friends."

Marcel was taken aback. "How did you know I escaped?" he asked.

"Gestapo handcuffs leave pretty nasty marks sometimes. I suggest you keep your sleeves down for a while."

Marcel looked down at his forearms, bare from just below his elbows where he had rolled his sleeves because of the heat. The man was right. Even in the dim light cast by the control lights on the engine, he could see where the flesh torn by the handcuffs had not yet healed. Self-consciously, he began to unroll his sleeves.

"Listen," the man said, "hide along the bank of the Isère, just below the Pont de Charènnes. I'll send someone for the children in the morning." He stood without waiting for a response and replaced the tarpaulin, plunging Marcel and the three silent Lévy children once more into total darkness.

Théo wasn't sure how much longer his legs would hold out. Victor, who had his left hand in a vise-grip, wouldn't be able to continue much longer either, at this pace. Fortunately, Léa was riding on Marcel's shoulders or she would have long since collapsed. It felt like they had been either running or walking for hours, though he knew it couldn't actually be that long. Still, all he really wanted was to lie down somewhere—anywhere—and close his eyes.

No one had slept on the train. It had simply been too uncomfortable under the tarpaulin. When the train had finally come to a full stop, and the coal-covered canvas had been removed, Théo had felt a kind of rebirth at being out from under its oppressive weight. But the exhilaration had soon been replaced by fatigue. After scrambling from the train, shrouded by an enormous cloud of steam that hissed and curled all about them, they hadn't stopped even once to rest. He would have asked Marcel to stop—or, at least to slow down—if only he hadn't been afraid that someone might overhear. The pace had slowed some, of course, once they had left Grenoble's train yard behind. But it still felt too fast to Théo. And he had no idea how far they had yet to go.

The sky overhead was clear, but the stars provided precious little light in the absence of the moon. Still, Marcel pressed doggedly on, and Théo was left to assume that he knew where he was going. Keeping up, however, seemed far more important at the moment than where they ended up. Getting separated in the dark, in a strange place—he didn't even want to consider the possibility.

A few paces ahead, Marcel stopped abruptly and swung Léa to the ground.

"The river is just ahead," he whispered to Théo when the two boys had joined him. "Can you hear it?"

Théo had been too preoccupied to even notice, but now that Marcel mentioned it, he could indeed hear something. Almost immediately he could envision himself lying on his back beneath a canopy of trees, lulled into endless sleep by the lazy lapping sounds of the river as it flowed to some faraway sea.

⚜ ⚜ ⚜

Unable to sleep, Marcel leaned his weary body against a tree stump, keeping a vigil over the shadowy forms of his three charges, waiting for the first glimmer of daylight. The gurgling of the river as it glided past them masked the sounds of measured breathing coming from the children. *Les pauvres,* Marcel mused. *They must be absolutely exhausted.* They had fallen asleep, all three of them, almost before they were stretched out on the ground. He hated the thought of awakening them, but dawn wasn't far off, now, and they would have to be ready for whoever came for them.

He didn't like the situation—not even a little. He would have preferred trusting someone he knew, like the Lamberts or the Westphals. But the engineer was probably right about the need for caution. The Milice could very well be watching to see where he might turn up. And the last thing he wanted was to endanger the children all over again, not to mention his friends. And if he never saw the inside of Montluc Prison again, it would not ruin his life!

The trouble was, he had no idea who was coming for the children. All the engineer had said was that he would send someone. And while the man had proved to be trustworthy, Marcel knew all too well that he couldn't automatically count on everyone else, no matter who they were connected with. He hadn't yet come to terms with the fact that he himself had failed. At best he had demonstrated a lack of judgment. At worst—well, at worst he had betrayed an innocent woman, and it continued to weigh heavily on him.

Even asking God's forgiveness hadn't eased his mind much. He certainly didn't feel forgiven. And from what Gilles had said, Hervé didn't sound as though he were in a particularly forgiving mood, either. Perhaps that was to be his punishment, to endure Hervé's displeasure—and God's too, perhaps—until he had atoned for his error. The problem was in knowing how to do that, especially if Hervé prevented his free access to the network again. And he suspected he would. Maybe Gilles could help. If all went well today, perhaps he could arrange to meet his old friend somehow.

The sky was beginning to glow in the east as Marcel rose and walked quietly down to where the gravel met the water. Looking toward the city, he could see the dark silhouette of the Pont de Charènnes spanning the river. On his left, the hillside rose steeply from the Isère to where the fortress of La Bastille stood watch over the ancient city. Beyond the bridge, rooftops and steeples stood stark and somber against the dawn sky. In the distance the Belledonne Range rose majestically above the Gresivaudan Valley, its flanks blue-gray in the dim light of early morning, its peaks the creamy color of as-yet-unmelted snow. It was hard to believe that this beautiful valley, like the rest of his beloved France, lay under a heavy blanket of oppression and tyranny. What was it going to take, he wondered, and how long, to throw off that blanket? Would he live to see it happen?

A rustling in the brush high on the riverbank above interrupted his thoughts, and he quickly dodged among the trees to keep out of sight. Keeping one wary eye on the sleeping children, he climbed the slope a few yards downstream of where the noise was coming from. Perhaps he could get a better view from higher up. He just didn't want to be caught too far from the children in case something went wrong.

The bushes at the top of the bank continued to rustle gently until all at once he thought he heard a woman's voice.

"*Oh, mais ce n'est pas possible!*"

He couldn't tell if she were talking to herself, or if there were two of them. And he had no idea what she thought was impossible. He couldn't see her at all.

"*Ça ne va pas, non?*" She sounded positively frustrated.

And then she was sailing past him—or at least someone was—arms and legs flying, as she hurtled down the slope toward the water's edge. Marcel reached out to break her fall, but too late. A moment later, she rolled past the sleeping children, coming to rest abruptly, and apparently painfully, against a tree. The waters of the Isère couldn't have been more than a half dozen feet beyond.

"Aiiiee!" she wailed. "I knew they should have sent someone else. This happens every time!"

"Are you all right?" Marcel asked, trying to hurry down the embankment without following in the woman's footsteps.

"Of course I'm all right!" she said rather brusquely as she rose and dusted the moss and twigs from her long black dress.

Marcel couldn't help but stare. Unless the dim light was playing tricks on him, he was looking at a nun! A young nun, by the looks of her, but a nun all the same. Why would a nun be wandering along the river at this hour of the morning?

"Who are you?" he asked, taking a step closer, "and what are you doing here?"

"I'm Sister Marie-Moïses from Notre Dame de Sion. And I've been sent to find three children. Have you—" She stopped in mid-sentence as she caught sight of the three, undisturbed in their slumber by all the commotion of the sister's arrival.

"These are the three?" she asked. Then without waiting for a reply she added, "They're filthy. What have you done to them? And just look at you! Monsieur, you look as if you've been sliding down chimneys!"

"Mademoiselle—"

"Sister Marie-Moïses, monsieur!"

"Of course, Sister Marie-Moïses," Marcel complied, suddenly a little flustered himself by the nun's interrogative style. She was not at all what he had expected when the engineer had promised to send someone. The convent of Our Lady of Zion did sound vaguely familiar, though it was not a part of his own network. And what sort of a name was Marie-Moïses, anyway? Did she get extra indulgences for including both sexes as well as using names from the Old and New Testaments? For a split-second, he considered asking her, but immediately thought better of it.

"We have not been sliding down chimneys, Sister," he said, perhaps more emphatically than necessary. "We came on the train."

"*Ah, oui*," she said, comprehension evident in her eyes, "with Monsieur Remy. Well, lucky for you, I brought a bar of soap and some clean clothes. I hope they fit." She looked around as though she had lost something. "Now where are they?"

"Perhaps you dropped them, Sister," offered Marcel, "when you fell down the bank." He paused, but she was still searching the ground around her feet, mumbling to herself. "I'll go have a look," he said.

Climbing back up the slope, Marcel found nothing until he reached the very top. There, stuck in the crotch of a low-spreading tree, was a cloth bundle tied with a bit of string. Reaching down to grasp it, however, his gaze fell on a piece of paper lying beside the base of the tree. He picked it up and turned it over in his hands. It was an identity card. Sister Marie-Moïses must have dropped it when she lost her balance.

Opening it up, Marcel couldn't quite comprehend what he saw. There had to be some mistake. The photo was of the nun he had just met, all right. But judging by the letter "J" stamped in black ink across the top of the card, Sister Marie-Moïses was a Jew!

Chapter 17

The longest walk Michael Dreyfus could ever remember taking was the fifty feet or so between the passenger side of Heinrich Rosen's Mercedes and the front door of Robert and Justine de Rocher's house on the Boulevard St. George in old Geneva. Rosen was rambling on about international bank deposit transfers or something of that nature, but all Michael could think about was how he could discretely inquire after a certain Mademoiselle Isabelle Karmazin.

Would the de Rochers think him rude, he wondered, or too forward, if he asked about Isabelle straight out? But, unless he did so, how could he expect that she would ever come up in conversation? Especially a conversation that was obviously going to center on the financial concerns of Rosen's evacuation project, judging by everything the older man had said since they left the hotel. No, it wasn't going to be easy to be discrete about this. Perhaps if he could find a way to bring up the meeting where he had first met Isabelle and Madame de

Rocher. Yes, that was it! It would seem perfectly natural then to inquire after the younger woman's well-being.

Rosen hesitated a moment before the de Rocher's front door, and Michael realized the old German was looking at him.

"Have you heard a thing I've said, Michael?" he asked pointedly.

"I, uh, I don't understand international banking all that well, Mr. Rosen," he stammered lamely.

Rosen blinked and said nothing for a long moment. "Well, let me and de Rocher do the talking, and perhaps you'll learn something," he said at last. And with that, he turned, grasped the door knocker, and gave a couple of sharp raps on the carved oak door.

The door opened a few moments later to reveal a smiling Justine de Rocher.

"Monsieur Rosen, how good to see you!" She motioned the men inside. "And Monsieur Dreyfus, welcome to our home. Please, make yourselves comfortable while I get my husband. He's upstairs with the baby while Isabelle helps me with dinner."

It took every ounce of control he could muster for Michael to suppress an ear-to-ear grin. Isabelle was here! She was really here! What amazing luck! Or could it be possible that Isabelle knew he was coming and arranged to be here as well? He hardly dared hope for something so incredible. All that mattered was that he was about to see her again.

Momentarily, a tall, fair-haired, well-built man, looking to be in his early thirties, descended the stairs. He was dressed impeccably in a tailored charcoal suit. Close behind him was Madame de Rocher, carrying a rather lively, dark-haired baby. Rosen stood to his feet as they neared the last steps, and Michael followed suit.

"Monsieur Rosen," beamed the man, extending his hand, "I'm Robert de Rocher. I guess you've already met my wife." He reached an arm around madame and drew her forward to stand beside him.

"I have had that pleasure, monsieur." Heinrich Rosen bowed slightly toward madame and then turned to indicate Michael. "And this, monsieur, is my friend, Michael Dreyfus of the Red Cross."

Michael felt himself flush just a little as he reached out to take de Rocher's hand.

"A pleasure, monsieur," purred de Rocher.

"Likewise," said Michael a bit more softly than he had intended. He turned and smiled at madame.

"What a handsome child," Rosen offered cautiously. "Will the young man be joining us for dinner?"

"Oh, no!" laughed Justine. "He'll be fed shortly and put to bed." She looked straight into the boy's eyes. "You've already had a long day, haven't you, Alexandre?" Then to the men, "Please excuse me while I take him to his mother." And having said that she crossed into the dining room and disappeared.

"The boy is not your child, monsieur?" Rosen looked at least as puzzled as Michael felt.

"We have no children," de Rocher replied, "but we've come to love him as if he were our own." Michael thought he caught a hint of regret in the man's expression. "Little Alexandre belongs to our friend Isabelle," de Rocher continued, lowering his voice. "She lost her husband to the Nazis before the child was born."

"I see." Rosen nodded sympathetically. "She must have suffered a great deal."

"More than she lets on, I can tell you that."

Michael suddenly felt as though a heavy object had been lowered none too gently onto his chest. He had felt something like this when he saw the Jewish family being turned away at the frontier, and again when he stood watching the refugees inside the wire walls of the camp at Le Bout du Monde. But it was more intense this time, and somehow more personal.

What unspeakable pain this beautiful woman must have endured. A widow, at her age. So young, and already a child to raise—alone. All alone. The boy must be a daily reminder of her loss, he told himself. And while he knew he couldn't begin to imagine the depth of her pain, he wanted desperately to comfort her, to somehow let her know that it mattered to him. It was strange to be so utterly affected by someone after one brief meeting, but he couldn't seem to help himself. He only hoped it would prove to be more than pity that he was feeling.

"Would you care to join me in the salon while we're waiting for dinner?" de Rocher offered politely. Michael followed numbly along behind the other two men, completely oblivious to their conversation. As the minutes passed, a feeling of intense sadness settled over him like a shroud.

⚜ ⚜ ⚜

Dinner conversation always seemed rather superficial to Isabelle, especially dinners like this, where the guests were hardly known enough to be considered acquaintances. Business, of course, would be discussed later, and it was pretty clear to her that Monsieur Rosen's reason for being here was business—or at least money. Fortunately, everyone seemed to be enjoying the roast duck that she and Justine had prepared. It had been the major topic of discussion up to this point.

"So, Monsieur Dreyfus," Robert de Rocher began, "what is it that you do for the Red Cross?"

"Please, monsieur, call me Michael—if you don't mind, that is."

"Not at all, Michael. So, what do you do?"

"I'm an aide to Gerard Richert. He is here representing the interests of the American Red Cross. We're trying to find ways to reduce the losses in our shipments of POW packages."

"I take it the losses are large, then?"

"Very large, and getting worse all the time."

"This Monsieur Richert, is he American?" asked Justine.

"No, madame, he's Swiss actually. But he's married to an American, and he has worked there for perhaps twenty years."

"And you?" she probed. "You don't have an American accent."

"No, I'm Swiss too," he confirmed, poking aimlessly with his fork at a morsel of duck. "But I live in New York. My family moved there from Lausanne when I was little. Even so, my parents have always insisted on speaking French at home. To tell the truth, I never expected it to be so useful."

Finally, thought Isabelle, this conversation might become interesting after all. Perhaps she would be able to find out about America from someone who actually lived there. The trouble was, Michael Dreyfus had hardly spoken to her all evening, had hardly spoken to anyone except when asked a question. Not that she was looking for attention, but she had hoped for a little more conversation. Perhaps he was only deferring to his older colleague. And Mr. Rosen didn't seem much for small talk.

"Well, I guess Robert and I are the only ones who haven't lived anywhere but Geneva." Justine looked at her husband and winked. "We're awfully boring, don't you agree, *mon chou*?"

Robert only smiled in return.

"Isabelle used to live in Paris, you know," continued Justine.

Isabelle darted a reproachful glance at her friend, but

Justine seemed not to notice. What Isabelle really wanted was to hear more about Michael's America.

"Ah, Paris is a lovely city, mademoiselle," said Monsieur Rosen, entering the conversation for the first time. "Did you live there long?"

"Since I was twelve," Isabelle replied a bit awkwardly. "My father took me there from Warsaw."

"Well, I am from Hamburg," announced Rosen. "But I used to have business interests in both Paris and Warsaw in addition to my office in Zurich. It is a shame what has become of Hamburg," he added somberly, "and to Warsaw and Paris, and even Berlin. Thank God one can still live decently in Switzerland. These Nazis are swine. They ruin everything they touch."

There was a faraway look in his eyes as he said that, and Isabelle wondered if he too had suffered personally at the hands of Hitler's henchmen.

"Is your family with you here in Geneva?" she ventured gingerly.

Heinrich Rosen shook his head slowly from side to side. "No one," he said softly. "They were all taken away before I could move them to Zurich. My wife, my children, even my grandchildren. That is why I work so hard to save as many of the others as possible. You understand."

"Yes," she replied softly, "I believe I do."

"Fortunately," he continued, "the Swiss allow me to pursue my initiatives because of my previous business dealings with the government. But frankly, business isn't very important to me these days."

The room grew quiet at that, with only the occasional clinking of a glass, or the scrape of a fork against bone china to break the seemingly eternal stillness. Isabelle wanted to say something cheerful in the worst way, but feared that to do so would be to disregard Mr. Rosen's pain. So she remained silent with everyone else. From across the table she thought she felt Michael Dreyfus' lingering gaze. Glancing his way, she caught a glimpse of his furrowed brow and wondered what he must be thinking.

⚜ ⚜ ⚜

Michael washed and dried his hands methodically, but without giving the process much thought. He was too frustrated over the fact that he had been stuck in the salon with Rosen and de Rocher ever since dinner, unable to fully grasp their discussion of the intricate financial details of Rosen's plans, and cut off from any possibility of talking to Isabelle. She and Justine had entered the room once, to serve the men coffee, but for all he knew she had since retired for the evening.

Leaving the hall bath, however, he had only taken a step or two in the direction of the salon when he heard the gentle timbre of women's voices. Unless he was mistaken, the sound was coming from the dining room. He took another step to rejoin the men, then turned and walked cautiously in the opposite direction. Michael figured that Rosen would be so wrapped up in his subject he would never miss him, at least not for a while. And if he didn't at least try to talk to Isabelle, he might not get another chance.

The two women looked up in apparent pleasant surprise as he hesitated in the doorway. They were seated opposite one another at the dining table. The table, now bare of dishes and polished to a fine dark sheen, held several bolts of fabric of various colors.

"Come in, Michael," Justine invited. "Is there something I can get for you? Another cup of coffee, perhaps?"

"Oh, no. I'm fine, really. I just—"

"Let me guess." She scowled teasingly. "Robert started talking about some complicated international banking theory and you were hoping for some real conversation."

"Something like that," he admitted, unable to prevent a grin. "What are you working on," he asked, indicating the yards of fabric on the table between them.

"Clothes for refugee children," Justine replied. "I don't know if you've ever seen any of them, but most arrive with very few personal belongings. When winter comes around again, many will have outgrown what few things they brought."

"I've seen a few," he admitted, "and I know what you mean. But doesn't the government give them what they need?"

Justine shook her head. "These children need far more than what the government can—or will—do for them. This is a small thing, but at least it's something. It would be shameful not to share some of what we have with them. Don't you agree?"

Michael nodded. Somehow, he hadn't imagined Justine and Isabelle involved in the refugee situation in this way. It seemed perfectly natural, now that he understood what they were doing, but he had only focused on Heinrich Rosen's way of approaching things. And that was to create a huge solution for an even larger problem. It had never occurred to him that individual people could make a difference, however small, and that it would matter.

"Well, since you're here," Justine said, "you might as well know that we've been talking about you." She looked at Isabelle, who seemed to color just a bit. "We're both curious to know what it's like to live in America."

"I'm afraid I don't know what to compare it to, since I don't remember living here at all," he began apologetically.

"Is it true that you can travel all the way from New York to

California without a passport?" asked Isabelle, who suddenly seemed far more animated than she had during the dinner conversation.

"I can travel anywhere I like, as often as I like, and no one has ever asked me for a passport." He smiled. It seemed so normal it had never occurred to him before.

"And anyone can start a business, even if they weren't born in America?"

"Yes, I suppose so. My father owns a business, and no one seems concerned that he's Swiss."

"And what about teachers and university professors? What if they're foreigners, or even Jews?"

Michael was beginning to understand what she was asking and why. "I know some teachers who are Jews," he said. "In fact, several of my professors at Columbia University were Jews."

"Is Columbia a good university?"

"It's one of the very best," he replied.

"I wish my father could have taught there," she said, wistfully. "Perhaps then things would have been different."

Michael didn't say anything right away, not wanting to pry or disturb her clearly private thoughts. Justine too seemed to sense Isabelle's need for a moment alone with her memories.

"Would you like to come to America someday?" he ventured some moments later.

Isabelle looked up, and in her eyes he swore he saw a glimmer of hope. "It's what I've dreamed of for months," she said.

Michael had to muster every ounce of his self-control to keep from laughing right out loud.

Long after Michael Dreyfus and Mr. Rosen had taken their

leave, Isabelle sat beside Alexandre's crib, gazing at the angelic features of her sleeping son. Sometimes she wanted him to stay just the way he was forever. She knew it could not be, knew it should not be, really. He too needed to grow, to change, to mature into manhood eventually. But sometimes she felt so inadequate for the task of being both mother and father. And then, too, she often felt afraid—afraid of the kind of world in which he would grow up. Would his world disappoint, betray, deny him the way hers had? Would he lose the ones he loved?

Perhaps if she could take him away from Europe and the powers bent on dominating the entire continent. Maybe then she could raise him with more confidence, more hope. She so wanted him to experience opportunities she never had, to know freedoms she only dreamed of. But was that possible here in Switzerland, ringed as it was with hostile nations?

If she were alone, she reasoned, she might be willing to settle for the relative security of this mountain confederation. She had wrestled with this very thing time and time again, and had resolved to put it aside. It wasn't as if this were a bad place to live, after all. And she was certainly being well cared for. But what of Alexandre? Shouldn't he have every advantage she could possibly give him? Wasn't that her responsibility as a mother? Especially in view of the fact that he had no father to provide for him.

Michael's descriptions of America fascinated her. He painted such a compelling picture, without really trying, as far as she could tell. The opportunity it afforded; the promise of freedom to come and go, to choose one's own course; its immensity and diversity. It sounded almost too good. What a country in which to raise a son!

And the rescue Mr. Rosen was preparing—it was such a noble idea. If it worked, thousands of frightened people would find themselves safe and secure on American-held soil in North

Africa, free of Nazism's terror. Perhaps from there they would be allowed to immigrate to the U.S. itself. She hoped Rosen and his friend Michael would be able to raise all the money necessary to pull it off successfully.

If only she could be a part of such an operation. Then maybe she could reclaim her dream of living in America. Of course, the Jews living in France and Italy were in far more danger than she was, and she understood why their plight had to be the priority. But she had prayed so hard. Surely God wouldn't deny her requests forever.

And even as these thoughts tossed and turned in her mind, she wondered if Michael Dreyfus just might be the answer to her prayers.

Chapter 18

Any illusions Marcel might have harbored of a return to a peaceful, if not entirely normal existence were dispelled within hours of leaving the Lévy children alone with the nuns of Notre Dame de Sion on Wednesday morning. Strange as it had seemed that nuns should be Jews—or Jews, nuns—he knew he had no choice but to trust the gregarious Sister Marie-Moïses. She had graciously allowed him to remain hidden at the convent the past couple of days, but he had agreed to be on his way to keep from adding to whatever danger the nuns were already in.

The children had been reluctant to see him go, of course. Léa, most of all. And seeing a tear course down her pale cheek as he said good-bye made him wonder, if only for a moment, if he were doing the right thing. She looked so forlorn, so utterly lost. But the truth was that he couldn't continue to run from place to place with three *gosses,* no matter how attached he'd become to them—or they to him. His mind accepted that fact in spite of the seeds of doubt sown by his heart. So, assured for the most part that his charges were in good hands, safe from prying eyes behind the convent's high stone walls, Marcel set out in search of Gilles Théron.

It took him a little while to decide where he would be most likely to find his friend. The railroad engineer's warning had made it clear to him that he needed to be extremely cautious. Professor Maurice Lambert and his wife, Claudette, were friends of the Thérons as well as the Boussants, and the professor would almost certainly know how to get in touch with Gilles. Lambert had been responsible for getting both Marcel and Gilles into the network in the first place. But trying to visit or phone him would put the professor and his family needlessly at risk.

Pastor Charles Westphal was another possibility, but with his prominence in the ongoing rescue of illegal refugees, that too would be an unwise choice. Few of the rest of Marcel's old contacts remained in Grenoble, most having taken to the mountain hideouts of the *maquis.* The rest had either been arrested or killed.

Of course, there was one means of contact he hadn't tried before, perhaps because it seemed too obvious. Now, however, he was running out of options and he really needed Gilles' help. The clothes provided by the nuns were clean and in good repair, but they were so ill-fitting he was immediately self-conscious. And the few francs in his pocket would not last long if he hoped to eat even one meal a day.

So, making sure he wasn't being followed, he made his way to the industrial area between the old St. Laurent cemetery and the sweeping arc of the Isère River northeast of downtown. There, in an unadorned squat gray building, the import-export business of Compagnie Théron was identified only by the small brass plate beside the front door. Marcel hadn't been here in years, and was grateful to find that it looked exactly as he remembered it. He rang the bell and waited.

When no one answered, he rang again, depressing the small round button a little longer this time. Still there was no response from within. It was early, he reminded himself, but not too early judging by the number of workers he had seen making their way along nearby streets. Thinking that perhaps the bell was broken, he tried again, listening carefully at the door. But no, from somewhere inside the building he could hear a faint buzzing sound that began whenever he pushed the button and ceased the instant he released it. Surely Monsieur Théron was in his office by now!

Looking all around to make sure he wasn't being watched, he peered in the small window beside the front door. Pressing his face as close as the wrought iron grillwork would allow, he was unable to make out anything clearly, other than the fact that an office light was on. Someone had to be inside. So, why weren't they answering the bell? He tried the door latch, surprised that it moved easily under his touch. Glancing once more over his shoulder, he slipped inside and closed the door softly behind him.

The outer office was unoccupied. Its three desks and assorted shelves and file cabinets seemed almost to mock him as he looked first one way then another. Two doors led from the room. As nearly as Marcel could recall, one would open into the warehouse, the other into the office occupied by Monsieur Théron. Marcel decided to try the latter first, and pushed the door silently inward.

A few cautious steps into the inner office and Marcel stopped short, his knees suddenly weak. A wave of nausea swept over him as he found himself gaping helplessly at a man's body sprawled on the floor behind the very large desk. Blood had seeped from a wound on the back of the man's head, matting his blond hair and beginning to cake on his neck just below his right ear. Marcel's shock passed in an instant and two long strides brought him to the man's side where he knelt to see if he had arrived too late. Rolling the body gently onto its side, the weakness and nausea returned with a vengeance. He was staring into the swollen face of Gilles Théron's father.

⚜ ⚜ ⚜

Jean-Claude Malfaire sat reading his newspaper and sipping a steaming cup of ersatz coffee. Every now and again, he pressed the back of his right hand to his lips, half-consciously gauging the tenderness in his knuckles. He chided himself for having left his leather gloves behind in Lyons.

From his table in front of the little café, he could see the pedestrian traffic in all directions. Grenoble's Place Grenette was a busy place this morning, he remarked to himself. Everyone hurrying, zombie-like to their jobs—those lucky enough to have jobs, that is. The rest, well, they were probably either looking for work or, as was the case with many of the women he saw, they were queuing up at the bakery or the grocer's in the hope of purchasing basic food items before they disappeared from shelves already far too bare. Luckily, Marie didn't have to go through such a tedious daily ordeal, he reminded himself. His wife deserved better and he saw to it that she got what she deserved, even though it wasn't always easy.

He took great pride in having built a career on making certain that everyone got what he or she deserved, especially those who preyed on honest citizens, or who threatened the public order with their petty criminal activities. What they deserved varied, of course, depending on the nature and severity of their offenses. But it all boiled down to separating the sheep from the goats, as he liked to think of it. Goats didn't belong with sheep. And while some could possibly be domesticated for a time, complete separation—forcible, if necessary—was ultimately the only solution. Good and bad simply could not coexist—not if society were to be safe and orderly. Not if the culture were to be maintained.

The war had complicated matters, even more the German occupation. Suddenly, people who previously wouldn't have defied the government, even in the smallest matter, were siding with communists and all sorts of other political perverts. Perhaps they found it easy to justify because few, even in the government, really liked the Germans. But why couldn't these otherwise good citizens see what they were doing to France? Malfaire wondered. Their subversive acts, however small, would lead to anarchy just as surely as responsible behavior would bring about stability and prosperity. It was only a matter of time.

There wasn't the slightest doubt in his mind that the people who stood to gain the most from anarchy, the same ones responsible for promoting the growing level of terrorism, were either communists, Jews, or both. It had to be. No right-thinking Frenchman would be so willing to sacrifice his country's stability in order to pursue some misguided effort to defeat these seemingly invincible Germans. Yet, amazingly, they managed to convince a few unstable citizens to do just that.

This young Marcel Boussant was a good example. Like most French youths, he had no doubt been pretty much law-abiding—that is until he had allowed himself to be influenced by Jews. And unfortunately, the influence was obvious. What was even more unfortunate, however, was that Boussant had somehow managed to convince a handful of other fools to go along with him. And now the mighty Gestapo had let him slip from its clutches. Malfaire snorted at the thought. Somehow, he would have to put a stop to this, himself. Someone had to.

Malfaire had been in Grenoble since Saturday, and had been joined by his young Sergeant Poulain on Monday morning. Together, they were keeping an eye on the people and places that might still have some connection with the young terrorist. This would be good experience for Poulain.

Jean-Claude had been here many times before, and while he still thought of Grenoble as a bit too provincial for his taste, he was also aware of how deceptively enchanting it could be. Its surrounding mountains, for instance, kept a spectacular watch over the sleepy Gresivaudan valley. But hidden in those same mountains, he knew, were dangerous gangs of thugs and terrorists. *Maquis*, they called themselves, after the troublesome thorn bushes of Corsica. One day, he mused, as he took another sip from his cup, one day they would all come to a bad end. A very bad end.

Sunday, he had thought he was finally making progress. The *temple protestant* had seemed a likely place to focus his efforts since he was well aware of how devout the Boussant family was. These Protestants were a rather close-knit lot. And even though the boy's family had vanished, chances seemed good that someone among the faithful would have received word of him, now that he was on the run from the Gestapo.

So Sunday morning he had waited outside the *temple*, far enough away to be inconspicuous, close enough to see who came and went. And he had waited a long time, for most arrived before ten and stayed until well after noon. He couldn't imagine why anyone would sit through anything so long. It had lasted even longer than old Father Benoit's pointed homilies. And if it had been half as provocative—well, it was little wonder that these Protestants were so peculiar.

When the crowd had finally spilled out onto the street, they had mingled like so many turkeys, milling about and chattering, children dashing up and down the front steps of the *temple*. Only one middle-aged couple seemed too preoccupied to stay and talk. With hardly a word to anyone they had hurried down the street to within a few yards of where Malfaire crouched in his car. Climbing into a sleek, late model Citroën sedan, they sped off toward the outskirts of the city. And Malfaire had followed them—and watched them until this morning.

Judging by the size and quality of their house—not to mention the man's business—these were not needy people. That could turn out to be a good thing, he had decided. Poor people had so little to lose.

Malfaire took another sip of the ersatz brew and smiled bitterly to himself. Surprisingly, the man had decided to play dumb when he and the always eager Sergeant Poulain had confronted him at his office early this morning. Claimed he hadn't seen Boussant in weeks, maybe longer. Well, no matter. Even if the man were telling the truth, which was doubtful, neither he nor his friends would be likely to take Milice Captain Jean-Claude Malfaire lightly from now on. And sooner or later the prospect of losing what they had would persuade someone to talk.

Malfaire grimaced slightly as he flexed the swollen fingers of his right hand. He had only just begun, but he would get what he wanted this time, no matter what it took. The Thérons had not heard the last of him.

Marcel was sweating profusely. Not willing to call the police and risk his own arrest, he had decided to take Gilles' barely breathing father someplace where he could get him some help. What to do, however, proved far more easy than how to do it.

While not a heavy man, Monsieur Théron was nonetheless bigger than Marcel and completely unable to offer any assistance in his present condition. Marcel had rolled him carefully onto his back after swabbing the worst of the blood and dirt from the wound on the older man's head. Then, reaching his hands under Théron's limp arms, he lifted the man's upper body off the floor and dragged him backward into the warehouse and toward the back door. It took longer than Marcel had anticipated, mainly because he was forced to stop and catch his breath more than once.

Once he reached the back door, he laid the unconscious man against the concrete floor, being careful not to injure him further, and peeked cautiously outside. A building, similar to the one he was in, stood across a broad alley, its back door directly opposite, not more than thirty feet away. No one seemed to be about, but the Théron's Citroën was parked a few feet away, as was another car, a Peugeot. Marcel wondered for an anxious moment whether it belonged to Théron's assailant, but quickly decided that only a complete fool would remain close by after such an attack—especially when his victim was still alive. But then, maybe his attacker didn't realize he was alive. All the more reason to move him elsewhere, and fast.

Scared that he would be discovered at any moment, Marcel half-pushed, half-pulled his friend's father into the back seat of the Citroën. The ignition key was in the older man's vest pocket, and as soon as the engine fired he slammed the car into gear and tore away from the industrial zone toward the Théron's home.

"Is he going to be all right?" Marcel did little to hide his anxiety. He was all too aware that another blow to the head, another hour waiting for the doctor, another—he didn't like to think about how close Gilles' father had come to not making it home alive. And it wasn't yet clear that he would pull through.

"It's too soon to tell," replied Dr. Billot, obviously making an effort to remain calm. "He's lost too much blood, if you ask me, and he's still pretty unresponsive. We'll just have to wait and pray. I'm afraid there's not much else we can do without taking him to a hospital."

Madame Théron remained silent, but her white-knuckled grip on the family Bible and the lines in her once-smooth face spoke loudly of her concern for her husband. She had called for the doctor, who was actively involved in the Resistance, just minutes after Marcel arrived with her badly beaten husband. Billot's presence had seemed to give her strength. But Marcel couldn't imagine how the situation could have been any more difficult for her. Used to depending on her husband for strength, she now had to be strong for him. Their son Gilles wasn't expected back until later in the day, and by then it could well be too late to decide whether to risk hospitalizing the elder Théron.

Marcel could once again hear the injured man's ranting coming from the bedroom and he cringed involuntarily. What he had at first considered a welcome sign of life, had quickly turned his blood cold. Babbling about someone "going undercover" and then something about "smuggling money"—at least that's what it had sounded like to Marcel—Monsieur Théron had resisted all efforts to quiet him. Even in his unconscious state his moaning seemed insistent, anxious.

Flushing red at the sound, Billot strode from the room to return to the bedside of his incoherent patient. Apparently he wasn't yet willing to force madame into a decision. Perhaps the crisis would pass and she would no longer be faced with the dilemma now staring at her. To leave him here could mean his death, while taking him to the hospital might mean saving his life. But it might also mean arrest—or worse—if anyone overheard his fevered rambling and took it seriously. And it might mean trouble for the entire resistance network.

I don't know what to do, Marcel confessed silently, his eyes fastened on the Bible in Madame Théron's hands, *but I know how hard it is to lose a father. Please, God, don't let Gilles lose his too.*

Nagging at Marcel's thoughts was the anger he was feeling over who had committed this brutal act—and why. He was certain it hadn't merely been a robbery; nothing in Théron's office appeared to have been touched. Neither were his watch and wallet missing. Someone had wanted to hurt the man, maybe even kill him. And that someone had known where to find him alone this morning. Or maybe he had been followed to his place of work.

It wasn't likely that the assailants were *caribinieri.* Whatever else they were, it simply wasn't the style of the Italian occupiers to be so brutal. They would have arrested him, certainly, had they suspected him of or caught him in some illegal activity, but they wouldn't have beaten him and left him for dead in his office. Marcel had nearly ruled out the Gestapo, as well. They seldom crossed into the Isère or the Savoie, apparently out of deference to their Italian allies. That didn't always stop them, however. There were some fascist locals eager to do the Gestapo's bidding—especially when the Gestapo could practically guarantee them immunity from prosecution.

But Marcel couldn't help wondering if somehow the attack were connected to his escape from Lyons. Had the local *miliciens* been warned that he was likely to return to familiar territory? It wouldn't have taken much detective work, after all, to establish a connection between him and the Théron family. Was it possible that the crime was carried out just to find out where he was? Gilles knew, of course, but had he told his parents?

Of course, whether or not they had previous knowledge of his escape, suddenly mattered little to Marcel. The fact was that he was here now, and it occurred to him that every minute he remained exposed them to even greater danger.

"I—I'd better be going," he said, suddenly feeling ill-at-ease.

Madame Théron appeared shaken. "But you—where will you go?"

"I don't know, but I can't stay. What if they find me here? They'll arrest all of you, and I can't let that happen. I've caused enough trouble already."

"Don't talk nonsense, Marcel." Dr. Billot stepped into the room, the strain of trying to keep his patient alive—and quiet—showing in the lines on his face. "If you hadn't happened along, he would probably be dead by now," he scolded, waving an arm vaguely in the direction of the room where Théron lay. "And the fact is, I may need your help to keep him alive."

"Yes, that's right," madame chimed in eagerly. "Besides, no one has come to the house. Perhaps they don't know anything. Perhaps they mistook my poor Henri—" She made a little choking sound. "I'm sure Henri didn't tell them a thing."

"Of course. Henri would never have told these *cochons* anything at all. Not a single word."

Rather than feeling reassured, Marcel worried that Billot's intense gaze would bore right through his soul. Did the doctor know about what had happened in the Ecole de Santé? Had Gilles or one of the others told him? What else would explain the way he was looking at him?

"Stay at least until Gilles returns," Billot continued. "Then we'll decide what to do next. You'll be safer here than out running for cover somewhere. Besides, you're going to need some new identification papers. In the meantime, keep a lookout at the front of the house while I try to keep Henri alive."

"But—"

"I'll call you if I need you."

Marcel turned and walked into the salon. From there he could look out over the street in front. He knew Billot was probably right. In fact, he had been secretly hoping the Thérons would provide him with a place to hide, at least for a while. He was sure he couldn't count on Hervé and Babette to take him in again. They wouldn't want him coming around—not after what he had done. And he couldn't return to Domène. It was so small that virtually everyone knew him by sight. He really had no choice but to wait for Gilles. He only hoped it wouldn't be long.

A car passed by on the street below the house just then, a late-thirties Renault sedan. He followed it absently with his gaze as it crept along and then turned a corner a hundred yards or so farther along. Moments later, however, the car reappeared, having reversed its direction. Again it crawled past the house slowly, almost as if the driver were looking for something—or someone. Marcel tried to see if the plates were issued in Grenoble or elsewhere, but couldn't tell through the lace curtains that covered the window.

"That's the car!" Madame Théron's voice behind him almost made Marcel jump.

"What do you mean?" he asked, as she drew alongside him. "Where have you seen that car before?"

"That's the same car we saw yesterday—and the day before," she replied, a look of terror in her eyes. "I told Henri to be careful this morning. He thought I was overreacting!"

Marcel reached an arm awkwardly around her shoulders and tried to comfort her as she put her face in her hands and sobbed.

Chapter 19

Marcel listened skeptically as Gilles Théron outlined his plan. He wasn't surprised that it promised to be difficult. He had participated in dozens of difficult schemes over the past months. And he had seen firsthand that with careful planning, what on the surface appeared impractical could often be broken down into manageable tasks, each rather straightforward and perfectly feasible. Hervé Chassin, for one, was a master at reducing very complicated operations to a series of childishly simple steps—simple, that is, in comparison to the whole. Perhaps Hervé's ability was due to his years of experience in masonry. In any case, all that was needed for success was to execute each simple step to perfection.

This plan, however, wasn't just difficult. It wasn't even particularly complicated. What Gilles was proposing seemed practically suicidal.

"You want me to walk out the front door and let whoever is in the Renault recognize me? Have you lost your mind?"

"Ssshhh!" Gilles hissed. "I don't want Maman to hear us."

"I can see why," Marcel replied wryly. "She'd undoubtedly agree that you're mad."

Gilles had waited until dark before sneaking into the house through a back door. Earlier, he had spotted the unfamiliar Renault parked just down the street and had decided to err on the side of caution, even if it turned out that one of the neighbors was only having out-of-town guests.

"Don't be ridiculous, Marcel. I'm not suggesting that you walk straight out into the street so this guy can recognize you. But unless he knows for sure where you are, he's going to keep watching the house."

"But what if it's not me he's after?"

Gilles shot him a reproving glance. "The police don't know about me or my father—not yet, anyway. Maman doesn't even know most of it. So who else would they come here looking for? You said as much yourself, not thirty minutes ago."

"All right," Marcel agreed, raising his arms in mock surrender. "It's probably me they're after. So why not just let me slip quietly out the back in the middle of the night. He'll never know a thing."

"He needs to know that you aren't here, that's why. My parents are in enough danger already, as you've seen. Papa can't be moved yet. And after what happened to him this morning, it's only a matter of time before this maniac searches the house. If he suspects you were here, we could all be dead tomorrow." Gilles paused for a moment. "What I'm proposing, Marcel, is a way to convince whoever he is that you never arrived."

"I don't want to put your parents at risk any more than you do, Gilles. It's just that I'm not sure this will work."

"Trust me, Marcel. It will work. It has to."

Marcel mulled it all over for a few moments. It was crazy, all right. But then maybe they didn't have that many alternatives, after all. They might be able to overpower the man in the Renault. But then what? Kill him? Marcel wasn't anxious to kill anyone—for any reason. Take him to Hervé and the *maquis?* Someone, somewhere undoubtedly knew what the man was up to and why. If he turned up dead or missing, Gilles' family would pay an awful price. And Marcel had to admit that by simply walking out he would solve little for himself, not to mention the risk to the Thérons. It seemed like a hopeless situation.

"Okay, suppose we manage to pull it off. What do I do then? I can't come back here, and I have no other place to go."

"Where did you plan to go when you left here, anyway?"

Marcel exhaled a long, slow breath and looked down at the backs of his hands. "I don't know. I've thought about it a lot, but I haven't really come up with anything that's likely to work."

"Well, I've been thinking about it too," Gilles said, a secretive smile curling up the corners of his mouth, "and I think I've got an idea."

Marcel looked up again, a spark of hope battling for a foothold among his doubts. "You're not thinking of some monastery or something, are you?"

The smile flickered and then vanished as Gilles leaned close to Marcel, lowering his voice as though fearful of being overheard. "One of my father's associates has taken ill, and I think you might be just the man to replace him."

"What? How am I—" Marcel stopped in mid-sentence. "Look, Gilles, this is getting a little too crazy. I don't know the first thing about your father's business. I know farming, remember? Let's just figure out how to get me out of here without making any more trouble for your parents. Then I'll go wherever you think is best—if I live that long, that is."

"We may not have much time," Gilles said soberly, "and

I've got to see to your travel documents before we leave."

"Travel documents for where?" asked Marcel.

Gilles raised his eyebrows. "Ever been to Geneva?"

⚜ ⚜ ⚜

By eleven-thirty, there was a bit of a chill in the night air. Jean-Claude Malfaire had donned his jacket around ten in anticipation of the drop in temperature, and so he was not at all uncomfortable, in spite of the fact that the driver's side window was rolled down in his Renault sedan. He liked to keep the window down so he could hear as well as see what was going on about him among the fashionable residences scattered along Rue Voltaire. But with their gates long since closed, and their windows shuttered, there was little to see or hear at this late hour. Only the occasional barking of a dog broke the stillness of the evening.

It was the three-story stucco house at seventeen Rue Voltaire that really held Malfaire's interest. Fifty yards ahead and to the left, its entrance was shielded from the street by a high gated wall, constructed of stucco-smeared stone matching the exterior walls of the house. A great granite block anchored each end of the front wall, and a slim, chiseled pair of stone columns offered support to the massive wrought iron gate. Only by looking in at the gate could passersby readily glimpse the well-manicured garden and lawns which surrounded the handsome home of Monsieur Henri Théron.

Tonight, as the moon rose slowly in the June sky, Jean-Claude Malfaire could make out little of the detail. Still, the house remained an imposing sight, and he couldn't help but admire Théron's good taste—and good fortune—in spite of everything he despised about the man.

He wondered, as he had the previous night, and the night

before that, what it would be like to move Marie and Dédé into such a house. He smiled as he imagined the stunned look on Marie's face as he carried her lightly over the threshold and into what was surely a magnificent entry hall. And Dédé would no doubt squirt past them both, racing pell-mell from room to room until he had thoroughly explored the entire house.

Malfaire looked at his watch once more and yawned. He would wait a few more minutes and then drive to his hotel. By then Poulain would have arrived at the other end of the street. The younger man would remain until noon, at which time they would begin the cycle all over again.

He had made little attempt to hide his presence. On the contrary, he wanted the Thérons—and whoever else might be inside—to know that he was watching. Especially after his rather unpleasant business with Monsieur Théron. Fear was Malfaire's ally, and the more reason they had to fear him, the better.

Of course, had this house been in the German zone, he would have resorted to more direct tactics in confronting the people inside. But the Italians were unfathomably squeamish when it came to roughing up the locals in their zone. Perhaps he had gone a bit too far with Théron already, but since he had heard no official complaints as of yet, he would just keep applying the pressure. Sooner or later, something would have to give. It nearly always did.

A motion in the street ahead caught his attention, and Malfaire pushed all other thoughts quickly from his mind. It had happened too quickly to tell exactly what it was, but his first impression was that it was something—or someone—creeping along beside the wall a hundred yards or more up the street. There was nothing out of the ordinary, nothing out of place that he could see now, however—no dog or cat—nothing at all. He rubbed his tired eyes, wondering if fatigue had caused him to imagine something. And then he saw it again.

This time there was no mistaking it. It was someone, all right. And whoever it was had crouched low, and was stealing furtively along the wall on the right side of the street. Malfaire leaned his head out the Renault's side window in order to see more clearly. He considered giving chase in the car, but quickly discarded the idea. The sneak obviously had no idea of his presence, or he would be running for cover. Better to follow on foot, Malfaire decided, and try to get as close as possible. That way he might actually stand a chance of catching him.

But as Malfaire slipped as noiselessly as possible from the front seat of his car, the figure stopped his flight. As Malfaire crept closer, he could barely make out what the man was doing. First standing, then stooping, then standing again, he appeared to reach for something, both high and low. Then, as if he had seen Malfaire approaching, he turned and fled down the street, making no effort at all to camouflage his retreat. Malfaire watched, annoyed, as the unknown man rounded a corner and disappeared from view.

A moment later, Malfaire's determined stride brought him to where the man had stood. There on the stucco wall, outlined in glowing white chalk, was a cleverly drawn pig whose face bore a remarkable resemblance to the mustachioed Führer.

Malfaire shook his head at the sheer idiocy of what he had just witnessed. To risk arrest for such a ridiculous—not to mention ineffective—act of defiance made no sense to him. And he realized anew that he would never understand these fools of the so-called Resistance. But as he turned and retraced his steps toward the car, he couldn't help but chuckle just a little. It was probably just some mischievous boy.

Jean-Claude Malfaire rose at six o'clock the next morning, as usual. Wasting little time, he shaved and dressed, then descended the two flights of stairs to the tiny lobby of the Hotel du Quai. On the way he decided to take a light breakfast at the adjacent cafe, rather than walking the half-dozen blocks to the Place Grenette where he had eaten the past three mornings. The time he saved would be spent later making a few telephone calls to Lyons. He checked at the desk for messages, then headed next door.

Last night he had reached the conclusion that Poulain could handle the surveillance of the Thérons if he had a little help. So, this morning he would arrange for the rest of his Milice unit to join them in Grenoble. That would free him up to generate other leads, and at the same time give him a little extra manpower with which to pursue them.

He also needed to check in with Marie. He had been gone since Saturday, and by now she would be getting worried. The fact that she worried actually pleased him a little. He had known colleagues who bragged that their wives never worried about them, as though he should be jealous of them. The trouble was, those same officers were usually the last to discover that they were the ones with reason to worry. He never really understood such people and consequently, had little sympathy for them.

Breakfast was bread and jam and ersatz coffee, along with a copy of the local newspaper, all served at a small round sidewalk table. Jean-Claude scanned the pages of the paper slowly as he sipped his coffee, looking for something—anything—of interest. The war news sounded mundane but positive, as it always did, thanks to the German and Italian censors. Perhaps it was better that way, he reasoned. There was no use in getting people all upset every time some little thing went momentarily awry on the Russian front.

The metallic squeal of worn brakes diverted Malfaire's attention from his paper and he looked up to see a taxi pulling up to the curb in front of the Hotel du Quai. A moment later, a young man in a charcoal suit exited the hotel lobby and sauntered across the sidewalk to the waiting car. Pivoting to his left, the man seemed to look directly at Jean-Claude Malfaire before climbing into the back seat. Then the driver gunned the engine and the taxi pulled quickly away.

Malfaire stood to his feet, barely noticing as his chair crashed over backward onto the sidewalk. Throwing a handful of coins onto the table, he bolted from the cafe, his heart and head both suddenly throbbing. He would have sworn under oath that the man he had just seen leaving his hotel was none other than Marcel Boussant! Perhaps he had been mistaken about the Thérons after all.

Racing into the hotel lobby he went straight to the clerk's desk, elbowing aside two men who were waiting there.

"The man who just called for the taxi," Malfaire demanded. "Where was he going?"

The elderly clerk stiffened. "Monsieur," he said indignantly, "you must wait your turn like everyone else. *S'il vous plait!*"

Malfaire jerked his identification badge from the inside breast pocket of his jacket and fairly shoved it in the man's face. "Milice!" he hissed, as he leaned over the desk. "Now where did the man go?"

His face suddenly ashen, the old clerk began to stammer. "I—I, uh, he said something about a train, monsieur."

"A train? Which train?"

"V-V-Valence, I believe."

Malfaire didn't wait any longer, but spun on his heel, colliding with the two men who had been standing at the desk when he entered.

"Get out of my way," he growled, and strode out the front door. At last, he told himself, I've got him at last. If he hurried, he would arrive at the Gare de Grenoble before the train for Valence departed. Once on the train, Marcel Boussant would be his. This time, heaven itself could not prevent it.

But when he reached his Renault a half-block away, Jean-Claude Malfaire felt a chill descend over his entire body. Unable to believe what he saw, he circled the sedan twice, more than enough to confirm that all four of the tires had been slashed to ribbons.

Marcel Boussant watched in nervous silence as the train pulled slowly out of the Gare de Grenoble, bound for Geneva. He pulled a kerchief from the pocket of the suit Gilles had lent him and mopped the moisture from his brow. It was time to relax, he tried to tell himself. In another couple of hours, if everything went according to plan, he would be over the border and out of reach of the Gestapo, the Milice, and whatever police agencies might still be after him. Until then, however, too much relaxation was highly unlikely—and not altogether wise.

He had to admit that, crazy as it had seemed, Gilles' plan had worked almost to perfection, though neither of them had managed a moment's sleep during the night. Just before twelve o'clock Marcel had crept up behind the watcher and marked his rear tires with chalk, while Gilles lured the man from his car with a daring display of graffiti art. The car, Marcel confirmed, was registered in Lyons.

The two were barely inside the garden wall again when another car arrived from the opposite direction and parked. Not having anticipated a second watcher, they determined to exercise extra caution. Apart from that, there was little they could do.

Gilles, whose artistic skill had first gained him entry into the resistance network as a forger rather than a graffiti propagandist, had spent the first few hours after midnight fabricating the documents Marcel would need to begin his new life in Switzerland. In the meanwhile, Madame Théron had altered one of Gilles' suits to fit Marcel's more lanky frame.

Marcel pored over a directory of Grenoble's hotels, marking all those that seemed likely for an out-of-town police agent. Then, using a city map, he plotted their locations and prayed that they would find the right one before breakfast. They would be breaking the curfew, of course, but as long as they could reach the hotels on foot, they felt they had a chance.

Fortunately, the fourth hotel they checked was the Hotel du Quai. A mere half-block from the front door, they spotted a black Renault sedan with chalk marks on its rear tires. Slipping into the hotel by a rear entrance, they convinced the night clerk to rent them a room (at a premium, of course) where they could complete their plans. But when a few extra francs revealed that the man they were looking for was Jean-Claude Malfaire, Marcel had almost decided to abandon the whole idea.

Staring into the *milicien's* eyes a couple of hours later had taken Marcel back to their first encounter, near the Swiss border, an encounter that had resulted in both being wounded by gunfire. And until recently, Marcel had believed it to be an encounter which had ended with Malfaire's death. So he had felt a strange premonition as he stepped into the taxi, fearing that the nightmare would be relived, that this time, too, Malfaire would find a way to follow.

Now, staring out the window at the granite peaks of the

Belledonne Range as the train steamed its way through the spring-green fields of the Gresivaudan Valley, Marcel felt the premonition fading. It was over, finally over, and he needed to forget that he had ever met this Malfaire. There was a lot more he wanted to forget as well, but he knew it would take time. Maybe in Switzerland he would have the time to make some kind of sense of all he had experienced in the past year, to put it all into some sort of perspective.

"Excuse me," an oddly familiar voice interrupted Marcel's musings. "Is this seat taken?"

Marcel's heart skipped a full beat when he looked up to see Didier, his cell mate from Montluc Prison, standing in the aisle looking down at him, his little round glasses sliding down his nose, his mouth curved into a broad grin.

Chapter 20

"I heard about your escape," Didier said with a conspiratorial wink. He flung his satchel into the overhead luggage rack and slid into the open seat before Marcel could respond. "*Chapeau!*" He clapped Marcel on the shoulder. "I don't know how you pulled it off, *mon ami*, but I've got to hand it to you. You really twisted those *boches* into little knots!"

"Ssshhh!" Marcel gave the owlish little man a warning glare. "Do you want everyone to hear? What are you doing here, anyway?"

"What's this?" Didier lowered his voice and pushed his spectacles back into place on the bridge of his nose. "You think you're the only one clever enough to outwit the *boches*?"

Marcel managed a sardonic smile. "I didn't outwit anyone, Didier. My friends may have, but I sure didn't."

"That's what I heard too. You must have some pretty powerful friends."

Marcel only shrugged, not wishing to discuss it further.

There was something about Didier that bothered Marcel, something more than the little man's loose tongue. He recalled the day he had been returned to his cell at Montluc after his interrogation at the hands of Klaus Barbie. Didier had been unusually agitated, almost accusing Marcel of having sacrificed him to the Nazis. Marcel could hear it now. *Look*, Didier had said to Mouyon, *the third man in the cell, I don't know you, and you don't know me. So we can't really hurt each other with the boches, right?* Then he had turned and pointed an accusing finger at Marcel. *But he's seen me before. More than once. He won't say so, but I know he has. And I don't want to find out that he's been talking about me.*

Marcel had seen Didier a time or two on the Lyons-Grenoble train, but he had no idea who he was or what he did. Still didn't, for that matter. But something about Didier's accusation rang rather hollow, though Marcel had never been able to put his finger on exactly what it was.

"So, how did you hear about my escape?" he asked.

"That's all everyone talked about for days," Didier laughed. "Even the guards. *Punaise*, what a bold stroke! Gunning down a dozen stinking *boches* in broad daylight. I'll admit it, I wish I had friends like yours, *mon ami*. Of course, they made the rest of us pay for it later, you understand." He gave Marcel a meaningful look.

Marcel felt his face flush. He had tried not to think about that, though he had known all along that it was a possibility. Of course, he couldn't be sure Didier was being truthful, given his obvious penchant for gross exaggeration. Still, it bothered him that others should suffer because of him.

Life was seeming more and more like a bizarre series of acts and repercussions. He could accept the fact that his actions held consequences for himself. He had been told from the moment he joined the network that offering assistance to Jews could mean his arrest—or worse. And he had paid a price. But each indignity, each scar, even his arrest, had only served to make him more determined than before.

What had become clear lately, however, was the fact that his actions also affected others: his own family, Dominique Raspaud's widow, Gilles Théron's family. And here was Didier telling him that prisoners—fellow resistants—had suffered simply because his friends had decided to break him out of Montluc Prison. Was it possible to do anything, even something good, that didn't jeopardize someone else's life or liberty? Marcel had serious doubts, but now was hardly the time to think about them.

"How did you get out?" he asked Didier, less interested in the answer than in redirecting the conversation.

"Pretty much the same way you did," Didier replied casually, "only I didn't have any well-armed friends to bail me out. I just jumped out of the truck on the way to the Ecole de Santé and ran for it."

"Just like that?" Marcel was incredulous.

"Listen, *mon ami*. They've known all along that I'm smarter than they are. Now they know I'm faster too."

Marcel could barely keep from laughing out loud. How, he wondered, had Didier managed to survive Montluc Prison? His tales were so outlandish, so preposterous, that few children would believe them, let alone the Gestapo. Was he really so naïve, or was it all an act? Whatever the case, he was obviously out of prison, free to come and go, and apparently no worse off for the experience.

It occurred to Marcel that there was another explanation for Didier's freedom, an explanation he didn't like at all. But, much as he disliked it, it was a lot more plausible than Didier's farfetched version of things. He determined to be careful about what he said, and he hoped Didier would get off the train soon. It wouldn't do to have the little man too close by when it came time to cross the border.

When the conductor announced that the next stop would be Aix-les-Bains, Didier stood and retrieved his satchel from the luggage rack above Marcel's head.

"Well, *mon ami,* this is my stop," he said, holding out his hand. "It's been a pleasure seeing you again." He cracked a smile. "Try to stay out of jail."

Marcel frowned, but took the hand he was offered. "Don't be a fool, Didier."

Didier turned and lurched down the aisle laughing, holding on to the seat backs for support as the train braked noisily to a stop. For the first time since the trip began, Marcel breathed a deep sigh of relief.

⚜ ⚜ ⚜

No sooner had Jean-Claude Malfaire replaced the receiver on its cradle after talking with Marie than the phone jangled.

"Yes?" he said into the ebony mouthpiece.

"You have a call from a Monsieur Didier Hebert, monsieur."

"Put it through."

He hadn't heard from Didier Hebert since the little man's release from Montluc Prison. He had assumed that the former stool pigeon simply wanted to lay low for a while. So why would he be calling now? And how did he know where to reach him?

"Capitaine?"

"I'm listening."

"Capitaine, you don't sound very happy to hear from me."

"How did you know where to find me?"

"I called your office in Lyons, and they told me. Listen,

Capitaine, I've got some information I think you'll want to hear."

"Why haven't you called me before now, Didier? You could have at least told me where you were." Malfaire wished the two were in the same room so he could shake the little worm.

"I've been busy with a few errands for our German friends. You understand. They were good enough to let me out, and now I'm returning the favor."

So that was it. Malfaire hated sharing information with the Gestapo, but it was better than having no information at all.

"What do you have?"

"What can you pay?"

"Why, you ungrateful little—"

"Things are different now, Capitaine. I have protection from people far more powerful than you. What I need, however, is money—about a thousand francs, to be exact."

Malfaire put his hand over the mouthpiece and swore. It had been so much easier before, when he had a string of petty crimes to hold over Didier's head. But Didier was not only ungrateful, he was completely without scruple. Perhaps he'd have to play along.

"I have to know something before I'll pay you a single centime," he said, trying to sound as menacing as possible.

"Do you know a young *paysan*, a *maquisard* named Marcel, who broke out of Montluc a couple of weeks ago?"

"What about him?" Malfaire tried to sound disinterested in spite of his rising pulse rate.

"Do I get the money?"

"Yes. Yes! Now what about this Marcel?"

"His train just left the station here in Aix-les-Bains. I'd be willing to bet that he's headed for Switzerland."

"Are you at the station?"

"Of course, Captain. Why do you ask?"

"Stay where you are. I'll bring your money to you in a couple of hours."

He slammed the receiver down, missing the cradle completely and gouging the top of the polished walnut desk. Then, reaching inside his jacket, he withdrew the 9mm Luger from its holster. Ejecting the magazine, he checked to make certain it was full before slamming it home again with the heel of his left hand.

⚜ ⚜ ⚜

The border crossing between Bellegarde and Geneva went much more smoothly than Marcel had anticipated. The Italian *caribinieri* gave the impression that his departure was a welcome event, as if in leaving French soil he somehow reduced the burden they were called upon to bear. The only hitch had been a couple of questions regarding the nature of his business, posed by the Swiss police who had come aboard at the frontier. Fortunately, Gilles had briefed him on the basics of the export/import business during the night, and the officer seemed satisfied with his answers. After meticulous scrutiny, his papers were returned to him, and within minutes, the train was waved through the checkpoint.

Marcel had nearly disembarked in Bellegarde, but decided against it at the last minute. It hadn't been part of his original plan, but ever since running into Didier, he had begun to reconsider his plans. In the end, however, he had chosen to stay on the train, and knowing that he was safe in Swiss territory at last made him glad he had.

With his one small valise in hand, he left the train at the Gare de Cornavin to find a bus that would take him near his hotel. But when he stepped outside, he forgot all about the bus. The mid-day sun seemed brighter, the sky above a more brilliant blue than he could remember, and suddenly he wanted nothing more than to stand right where he was and breathe in the precious air of freedom. Even though he knew that the soil on which he stood was nothing more than a tiny island in a sea of fascism, it was free soil. And at this moment, all his surroundings looked, sounded, and smelled of freedom.

It was delicious, this freedom, knowing that tonight he could sleep without fear of the Gestapo or the Milice. How long had it been? For a moment he wondered if this were how Isabelle Karmazin felt the night she crossed into Switzerland. Had she felt it afresh the day she stepped ashore in America? Had that moment evoked the same bittersweet memories for her that this day conjured up for him? Only the memories kept Marcel from a sense of complete euphoria as he paused to lift a silent prayer of thanksgiving to heaven.

By the time Marcel awoke on Sunday morning, the sun had long since crested the eastern horizon. A light breeze fluttered the curtains through the open hotel room window, making shadows dance playfully along the far wall. It took a moment, as it had the past two mornings, to remember just where he was.

The Hotel du Midi was magnificent in Marcel's estimation, by far the finest hotel he had ever stayed in. Not that he had actually stayed in many, of course. He was aware too that there were plenty of hotels in Geneva of far superior quality. But the Midi had a certain nostalgic charm to it, the air of a once-fashionable establishment now slightly past its prime. Its white stucco exterior, wrought iron balconies, and red tile mansard roof must have provided a welcome sight to the stylish visitors who came to enjoy a holiday near Lac Léman. The fact that the carpet was a bit worn in places, or that the wallpaper curled ever-so-slightly here and there, did little to detract from the Midi's essential beauty. Marcel was glad to be here.

Living here, he had discovered, would be the easy part. Business, however, was another matter altogether. The tiny office of Compagnie Théron, located in a bank building a couple of blocks from the hotel, was in chaos when he arrived on Friday morning, due, he guessed, to the illness of Théron's previous employee, Jacques Vallin. But unless he was very much mistaken, Vallin must have been ill a very long time. And last night Marcel had begun to wonder if order was even a possibility.

The important thing was that the flow of goods and money should begin again as quickly as possible. Henri Théron depended on it, and consequently, so did his employees. What Gilles revealed just prior to Marcel's departure, however, was that Hervé Chassin's *maquis* was also funded in large part with money that passed through this office. The revelation that he would continue to play an important resistance role pleased Marcel. But the burden of responsibility it brought threatened to overwhelm him at times. He wondered if Gilles had been crazy to hand him the job in the first place.

Today, however, he was going to try to put business out of his mind. It was Sunday, after all, and he hadn't been in church in weeks. And after church, he planned to walk to Reformation Wall before taking a leisurely lunch and an afternoon stroll around the lakefront. Here in Geneva, he was free to come and go as he pleased, and he intended to take advantage of it.

Finding St. Pierre's Cathedral was easy enough, since it dominated the city's Old Town from atop the hill. The peal of the bells sounding ten o'clock was just fading away when he reached the square in front of the church. Joining a handful of other late-arriving worshipers as they climbed the broad steps to the main entrance, he nearly felt, rather than heard, the strains of a hymn surging from the massive organ pipes. He slipped silently into a pew near the back of the vaulted sanctuary. Awestruck by the grandeur of St. Pierre's, Marcel spent the first several minutes drinking in the sight of the colorful stained-glass windows, and marveling at the size of the congregation. He closed his eyes and let the music wash over him.

People began filing past him the minute the service was over, but Marcel remained seated, savoring the organ's final fading notes. He thought back to all the Sundays he had shared a pew with his family in Grenoble's modest *temple protestant.* It hadn't always seemed as meaningful as today, especially when he was younger. He recalled how Papa would give him "the eye" whenever he squirmed too much—which was pretty often, or so it seemed. Just now, though, he wondered what had become of Papa, and if he were even still alive. It had been three years without a shred of news.

For her part, Maman was no doubt sitting with her parents at this very moment in the tiny church in Ardeche where she grew up. She too was undoubtedly thinking of Papa. Françoise would be right beside her, all attention focused on the sermon, all the young men watching her. Luc, of course, would be sitting nearby, though he probably needed someone to give him "the eye" from time to time. How Marcel wished this infernal war would end so they could all be together again.

The cathedral was nearly empty when Marcel finally stood to his feet and turned to leave. His stomach was growling and he had decided to delay his visit to the Reformation Wall until after lunch. But as he stepped into the aisle, his heart caught suddenly in his throat. For there, not twenty feet in front of him, looking as if she had seen a ghost, stood the woman who had haunted his dreams for five long months!

Chapter 21

Marcel, is it really you?" The words came out breathlessly, and Isabelle was suddenly more self-conscious than she could ever remember. Lips trembling, she tried her best to smile.

"Isabelle," was all he said, his usually strong voice little more than a whisper. But the look on his face mirrored the splendid bewilderment that enveloped her whole being. *Was this moment real? Dear God, could it be?*

For what seemed an eternity, neither spoke again. Isabelle had almost missed seeing him as she headed for the door. But something about the man in the charcoal gray suit seated all alone in the back of the church had caught her eye. Of course, she knew what it was, now. But she cringed inwardly at what she had very nearly missed.

Now her thoughts raced through a litany of questions she longed to ask: about his life these past months, about his mother, his sister and brother, about his feelings for her—

about what went wrong at the border. But staring across the distance into his warm chestnut eyes, her lips grew dry and refused to move. It was Marcel's voice that finally broke the silence.

"I-I don't, I mean, how did you—" His face flushed red. "What are you doing here, Isabelle?" he blurted at last, taking a step closer. "I thought you'd gone to America."

Isabelle, feeling her own face grow warm, shook her head. "It didn't work out," she said, lowering her gaze. She wanted to add "at least not yet," but thought better of it. It felt so good to be standing here, in spite of the awkwardness, that she didn't want to spoil it by telling him she still planned to go. The future could wait. There were more important things to say—and to hear—at this moment.

"I can't believe you're still here," he said softly, moving still closer. "I never thought I'd see you again."

"I know," she managed to whisper. "Me too." She had lived and relived this scene in her mind a thousand times over the course of the past five months without the slimmest thread of hope that it could ever come to pass. She wanted so badly to be strong, to say all that was in her heart. But now that the longed-for moment had arrived, she had to bite her lip to keep from crying.

She wanted to be happy. She was happy. But fear and confusion threatened to overwhelm that happiness at any moment. So many questions remained unanswered—so many yet unasked—so much she did not understand.

Then Marcel was standing next to her, reaching a gentle hand up to caress her cheek. She could hardly bear to look into his eyes, but couldn't look away. And finally, his unexpected nearness and the warmth of his touch conspired to weaken her resolve, and before she knew it, she had buried her face against his shoulder, hot tears flowing unrestrained.

⚜ ⚜ ⚜

For the longest time, Marcel just held Isabelle in his arms. Her nearness was like a balm, bringing healing and warmth to a heart he feared would only grow cold in her absence. He didn't even mind her tears, knowing the depth of feeling they represented, and a little envious of the release they provided.

He thought back to the very first time he ever held her. Arriving at his farm in the dark, she had been startled by the dog and had twisted her ankle in the loose gravel of the driveway. Just as she was falling, he had managed to catch her. And her touch had worked magic on him ever since.

The last time he held her they were standing together at the edge of a snow-covered field, awaiting the signal for her to attempt the dangerous crossing from France into Switzerland. She had cried then too and he had kissed away each tear, promising that he would join her as soon as he could. He had planned to follow in a matter of minutes. He had no way of knowing that it would take more than five months. But to be with her now made the delay seem inconsequential.

"I missed you, you know," Isabelle whispered, her tears all but spent, "and I was afraid you'd never come."

Marcel opened his mouth to reply when a woman's voice interrupted.

"Isabelle? Are you all right?"

Isabelle took a step back and wiped her tear-streaked face with careful hands. "I'm fine, Justine," she replied, sniffling just a little. "I'd like you to meet someone."

Marcel turned toward the voice to find a pretty woman, perhaps ten years his senior, smiling indulgently at the two of them.

"Justine de Rocher, this is Marcel Boussant. Marcel, Justine and her husband Robert are the ones who rescued Alexandre and me after we crossed the border. And they've been kind enough to let us stay with them."

"What a pleasure to finally meet you, Marcel," Justine said as she offered Marcel her manicured hand. "Isabelle has told us so much about you. And we're so grateful you sent her to us. She has become a dear, dear friend. And little Alexandre has absolutely stolen our hearts!" Her steel blue eyes fairly sparkled as she talked.

"*Enchanté*, madame," Marcel said, taking her hand a little awkwardly.

"Please, call me Justine." She turned to Isabelle. "I know you must have a lot to talk about, Isabelle, but did you invite Marcel for lunch? We'd love to have him join us. Of course, if he has other plans—"

Suddenly embarrassed, Isabelle looked expectantly at Marcel.

"No other plans," he admitted, nothing important, anyway. He could see the Reformation Wall another day—any other day, for that matter.

"It's settled then," said Justine. "I hope you don't mind walking, Marcel. We don't live far, and we seldom drive to church in fair weather."

"I don't mind at all," he said. "I enjoy walking." And he really meant it. Growing up he had walked nearly everywhere *except* to church. And after spending time in a prison cell, stretching his legs felt like a luxury. The fact that Isabelle would be beside him would make it an absolute pleasure.

"Come meet Robert," Isabelle invited, as they followed Justine to the door of the cathedral. To Marcel's surprise, she slipped her slender hand into his, squeezing it lightly. "And wait 'til you see Alexandre. You won't believe how much he's grown."

⚜ ⚜ ⚜

By mid-afternoon, the table conversation had begun to die down, and Isabelle excused herself in order to take Alexandre upstairs to his room for a nap. When she returned, Justine was alone in the dining room, clearing the table, humming softly to herself.

"Asleep already?" asked Justine, seeing Isabelle enter the room.

"I wish it were this easy every time," Isabelle sighed, stacking the empty plates. Some days it seemed that her little boy would never go to sleep. And invariably, those were the days she most needed rest herself. Thankfully, Justine was always ready and willing to lend a hand. She didn't know what she would do without her.

"One day he won't be taking any more naps, Isabelle. He'll be riding his *vélo* up and down the street with his friends on Sunday afternoons."

Isabelle laughed and followed Justine into the kitchen. "Someone else will have to teach him that. I've never been very good on two wheels."

"Perhaps when the time comes, Marcel will teach him." Justine gave her a meaningful look.

Isabelle felt her cheeks flush hot. "I don't even want to think about that, right now."

"Why not? What better time to think about your future than now?"

"I am thinking about my future—and Alexandre's. Especially his. I want him to grow up away from all this—this evil and violence, so he won't have to live in fear the way I have. Is that so wrong, Justine, to want a better life for my little boy?"

Justine was silent for a moment before answering. "No," she said at length, "it's not wrong, Isabelle. But *how* you raise your son is far more important than *where* you raise him."

Both women were silent then for several minutes as they finished clearing the table and began washing the dishes. Isabelle knew her friend meant well, but there were some things Justine would never be able to understand. Losing her mother, her father, her husband, for starters. Being pregnant and alone, tracked down by the police, forced to hide in an attic, subjected to scorn and discrimination at every turn. How could she possibly understand why leaving Europe—even idyllic Switzerland—was the only reasonable solution?

Isabelle hardly dared to think what that might mean between her and Marcel. Until today, she had harbored less and less hope that she would ever see him again. In a way, her dying hopes had given birth to new ones—hopes for a new start across the Atlantic. And while she had come to terms with her lot here in Switzerland for the short term, she had continued to feel that deep-seated unrest that kept her new hopes alive. Seeing Marcel again, however, rekindled all the fire she had previously felt for him—and added unbelievable complications to her life. *Why now?* she wondered. *Why not five months ago when I was counting on him?*

"Listen, Isabelle," Justine said, interrupting her thoughts, "I can finish these dishes by myself. Why don't you and Marcel go for a walk. You must have a million things to talk about."

Isabelle nodded. They did have a lot to talk about. She dried her hands and went to find Marcel.

The blue waters of Lac Léman, shimmering in the afternoon sun, had a mesmerizing effect on Marcel as he gazed out past the *jet d'eau* toward the mountains beyond. And sitting next to Isabelle on a park bench along the Promenade du Lac only added to the sensation that he was dreaming. He thought briefly about pinching himself, but realized that if this indeed were a dream, he never wanted to wake up.

He had said little on the walk to the lake, choosing instead to indulge himself in the luxury of her presence, a luxury that, in the space of just a few short moments, had made up for all the months of deprivation since last he saw her. She too had not seemed anxious to say much of substance, preferring to point out various sights that were by now familiar to her. He had never enjoyed small talk more.

Realizing that Isabelle was watching him, Marcel turned to face her and saw that her eyes were shining.

"What happened at the border, Marcel?" she asked. "Why didn't you come with us?" There was nothing in her tone that suggested an accusation, yet he sensed that she had been waiting all day to ask. He had known it would come up sooner or later. In fact, Robert had asked the same thing not more than an hour earlier.

"I wanted to come with you," he began slowly, trying to decide exactly what to say, "and I would have." He paused for a moment. "Do you remember the car that followed us?"

"How could I forget? I was scared they would catch us before we could reach the fence."

Marcel looked out over the lake again. "There was a policeman in the car. I was watching you crawl across the field when he caught up to me."

"Oh!" Isabelle covered her mouth with her hands. "We heard gunshots. Was that—"

He nodded. "Thank God, Hervé and a couple of his men came along."

"Hervé?"

"Babette's husband. The woman who took you across. If it weren't for him, I wouldn't be here."

"And Babette?"

"She got away too."

Isabelle looked away and let out a long slow breath. "I knew that something must have gone wrong. It's just that I was so scared and disappointed that you didn't join us." She turned to face him again. "It must have been awful for you."

He smiled weakly. "The worst part was losing you and not being able to explain what happened. I didn't want you to think—"

She laid a finger across his lips. "It wasn't your fault, Marcel. And now I know."

He kissed her finger, and then again, before she smiled shyly and pulled it away.

"I got your letter," he said.

"I didn't know. Robert said he knew some people who might be able to get it to you. But without an address—"

"Babette brought it to me." He smiled sheepishly. "I must have read it at least a hundred times."

"A hundred times?" Isabelle laughed. "You must have worn it out."

"Almost," he agreed.

He loved the sound of her laughter, and wished he could hear more of it. Perhaps one day they would sit in their very own salon and tell stories and laugh together until late into the night. Until then, however, he would just have to be satisfied with her presence. Once the pain of the past couple of years of her life began to recede, he knew she would find a great deal more to laugh about.

"I bet you didn't expect to find me in church, now did you?" There was a hint of a tease in her voice.

"I didn't expect to find you at all. But now that you mention it, I guess it's not all that surprising."

"Really? Why do you say that?"

"Because I say a prayer for you every day." He smiled self-consciously. "Sometimes more than once."

"Don't you think God will get tired of hearing about me?" It was hard to tell if she was serious or not.

"You're just as important to Him as anyone."

"I want to believe that," she said, "but it sure isn't easy. Some days I feel as though I'm beginning to understand, but other times I still have a million unanswered questions. Justine tries to help, but I guess I'm just a slow learner."

"I'm sure He's in no hurry, Isabelle, so keep asking. But if you're like most people, you'll always have more questions than answers. Faith is more about acting on what you know than what you don't know."

"Hmm. That sounds like something your mother would say."

"She's right, you know."

"So, how is she?" Isabelle asked, changing the subject. "I miss her. And Françoise and Luc too."

"They were fine the last time I saw them. They miss you too, you know. They think of you as part of the family. We all do."

She smiled, a kind of faraway look in her eyes. "You have such a wonderful family, Marcel. But then I guess you know that already. Do you see them often?"

"Not very. When you and I left for the border, Gilles took them to my grandparents' place in Ardeche. It's kind of remote, but they should be safe there until the war is over."

"Will it ever be over, Marcel?" she asked, and suddenly she sounded very tired. "Will it ever really be over?"

"It can't last forever. The Germans are losing ground in the east, and the Allies have crushed them in North Africa. It's only a matter of time before their whole rotten empire collapses, and then we can go back to France and start over again. You'll see." He wanted to believe it himself as much as he wanted to convince her. Maybe she had been right to want to go to America. France was certainly not the place to be raising a son alone these days. Without an all-out invasion by the Allies, the German occupation was likely to continue for quite some time. And as long as it continued, neither of them would be safe going back.

Isabelle leaned her head on his shoulder and stared out across the lake in silence. Something was obviously on her mind, and for a while Marcel was tempted to ask what it was. Rather than pry, however, he settled for the simple pleasure of having her near.

When Marcel walked Isabelle back to the de Rocher's house, a young man in his mid-twenties was sitting on the front steps. Seeing them approach, he stood to his feet and met them coming up the walk.

"Good afternoon, Isabelle," he said, with a schoolboy grin. "I hope you don't mind me coming unannounced, but I had some news I thought you might want to hear. Madame de Rocher said you were out for a walk, so I was just leaving."

"Hello, Michael." Isabelle looked a little flustered. "Um, I'd like you to meet my friend Marcel Boussant. He just arrived from France a few days ago." She turned to Marcel. "Marcel, this is Michael Dreyfus." She hesitated, then added, "from the Red Cross."

"Pleased to meet you." Michael, tall, dark, and well-groomed, seemed distracted as he shook the hand Marcel extended.

Marcel forced a smile in return.

"So," said Michael, turning once again to focus his attention on Isabelle, "do you want to hear the good news?"

"Perhaps we could talk later, Michael." Isabelle, looking increasingly uncomfortable, cast a sideways glance at Marcel.

"Monsieur Rosen has approved our plan, Isabelle. It's all set."

Marcel looked first at Isabelle, then at Dreyfus. Whatever was he talking about? What plan? And who was Monsieur Rosen?

"Well, I really should be going," suggested Michael. "We'll talk about the details later." He turned to Marcel, holding out his hand. "Nice to meet you, Marcel. *Au revoir.*" And he fairly bounded down the sidewalk.

Neither Marcel nor Isabelle spoke until Michael Dreyfus was out of sight. It was impossible to tell how Isabelle felt about the whole interchange. Her expression revealed little. And Marcel wasn't sure exactly what to make of it himself. But he wasn't going to ruin a near-perfect day by demanding some sort of explanation. He had no right. She would tell him when she was ready. He was sure of it.

"I guess I'd better be going too," he sighed, not knowing what else to say or do. "I've got a lot of work to catch up on tomorrow."

"Marcel—" Isabelle reached out to touch his arm, then paused. "Will you come to dinner on Tuesday? I'll explain everything then, I promise."

He tried to look into her eyes, to read something—anything—in them that would help him understand, but she looked away. So, bending slightly at the waist, he leaned toward her and kissed her softly on the cheek. "Until Tuesday, then." And he turned and walked away.

A block down the boulevard, he turned to see that she was still standing where he had left her, watching him go. Tuesday seemed like a lifetime away.

Chapter 22

Happy birthday, Léa!"

"*Bon anniversaire!*"

Théo Lévy watched with satisfaction as Victor and a half-dozen black-and-white clad women gathered round his wide-eyed little sister, congratulating her on having reached the age of seven. If she preferred a house full of playmates closer to her own age, she didn't show it. Even as the shock of surprise faded from her face, a look of pure pleasure took its place. This was turning out even better than he had hoped.

Across the room, hovering like the queen bee over all the other nuns, Sister Marie-Moïses winked at Théo and gave him a "thumbs up." He smiled and returned the sign. It hadn't been easy, he told himself. But then, keeping anything from the curious Léa never was. And it would have been impossible without help from Sister Marie-Moïses. She had made all the preparations, organized the other nuns, and somehow managed to keep Victor from giving it away. He had the hardest time keeping secrets!

"Oh, she's so pretty! Look, Théo. Isn't she the prettiest ever?" Léa had torn the wrapping paper from a beautiful porcelain doll in a fancy ball gown and was holding it up for Théo to see.

"She's *très belle*," he agreed, a bit overwhelmed. He had asked Marie-Moïses to try to find a little doll for Léa with the few francs Marcel had given him. But never had he imagined that anything so fine could be had so cheaply. Obviously, the nuns had taken up a collection of their own, though he couldn't imagine that they had much to give, either. He was a little puzzled as to just how nuns got money in the first place. However they did it, he was forced to admit that he hadn't seen Léa this happy in a very long time.

"I think she looks just like you, Sister," Léa said, holding the doll up to compare with Marie-Moïses. The others all laughed good-naturedly.

"I think she has too much hair to look like a nun," Victor announced quite seriously, "and too much of that red stuff on her lips." A few of the nuns snickered. "She looks more like a singer, to me."

"Well, I don't care about that, Victor," Léa retorted. "Besides, if the sisters can make her a black dress and one of those long hats, she'll look exactly like Sister Marie-Moïses, no matter what you say."

Marie-Moïses leaned down close to Léa. "Don't you think she's pretty the way she is?" she asked. "I do."

"Yes, but she doesn't look like anyone I know," replied Léa, matter-of-factly. "If she looks like you, then I will always remember you. And I will always remember this very special birthday." She looked into the nun's suddenly tear-filled eyes. "Can you make her a nun dress, Sister?"

Marie-Moïses looked across at Théo, as if for permission.

He didn't like the idea very much, but the last thing he wanted to do was to spoil his sister's birthday. Reluctantly, he agreed.

"All right, then." The nun turned back to Léa. "You'll have your 'nun dress.' But around here we call it a 'habit,' and Sister Miryam is the one who does all the sewing."

"Oh, thank you, Sister." Léa was positively gleeful, hugging the nun and the doll at the same time. "Can you make her one of those gold things with the little man on it to hang around her neck too?"

"We'll see, *mon chou.* We'll see." Marie-Moïses looked warily across at Théo again. This time he didn't say a word. He was certain she knew what he was thinking.

"There's a telephone call for you, Jean-Claude."

"Who is it, Marie? Unless it's Marshall Pétain himself, I really don't want to talk to anyone." Malfaire was stretched out on the settee in his robe, a broadcast of the national orchestra on the radio, a half-empty glass of *pastis* close at hand.

"It's Colonel du Puy, Jean-Claude. He says he needs to talk to you right away."

Du Puy was a *casse-pieds,* as far as Malfaire was concerned, an incompetent pain-in-the-neck aristocrat, whose wife's money had garnered him various political appointments over the years, most recently that of colonel in the Milice. The old man didn't know the first thing about police work, and his brief commission in the army during the Great War had been a fiasco, according to those unlucky enough to have served under his command.

Malfaire sighed audibly, rising from the comfort of the settee. He stumbled a little, but waved Marie off when she tried to steady him. He was fine, really, he told himself. He just hated having a quiet evening disturbed by his commanding officer, that's all.

"Malfaire here," he intoned into the receiver.

"This is Colonel du Puy, Captain." The voice at the other end of the line sounded strained. "I trust you won't find my intrusion too inconvenient."

"Not at all, Colonel," Malfaire lied. Everything about the pompous old fool was inconvenient. His existence was inconvenient.

"Captain, I've been called away to Paris on urgent business and I won't be back for a few days. But something has come to my attention that I thought we should discuss before my departure."

"Yes, Colonel?" What could be so important that it couldn't wait a few days? Du Puy never knew what was going on, anyway.

"I understand that you have deployed several of our men in the Grenoble area. Is that true, Captain? And if so, may I ask for what purpose?"

Malfaire pulled a chair up quickly and sat down. So, someone had complained to the colonel about his little surveillance operation.

"It's really only a handful of men, Colonel, and we should have our mission completed in a few more days. Certainly no more than two weeks, at the most."

"Do you mean to tell me that there isn't enough to keep you busy right here in Lyons?" The tension in the colonel's voice was increasing. "Who was it exactly who gave you this 'mission,' as you call it? I don't recall hearing a thing about it!"

This is just like him, fumed Malfaire. He hates to be bothered with details, but when something doesn't suit him, he wants to know why he wasn't given the details. "I'm terribly sorry, Colonel," he said aloud, "but there simply wasn't time to fill you in. I've been pursuing a key member of a major terrorist network. He escaped from the Gestapo right here in Lyons recently, but I think I know a way to reel him in." He paused for a moment, gritting his teeth before adding, "With your permission, of course."

"Just who is this man you say you're after?"

"His name is Boussant, Colonel. Marcel Boussant. He's been interfering with our efforts to process and deport Jews for some time now."

"How many men does he command?"

"I-uh, I can't say, exactly. But I can assure you that he is a very dangerous man. The sooner he is eliminated—"

Du Puy cut him off. "Call the men back to Lyons, Captain."

"Colonel?"

"Call them back immediately. And from now on, restrict your activities to Lyons and the Rhône department—unless, of course, you obtain my permission in advance."

"But, Colonel—"

"I can't have every officer in the Lyons Milice chasing petty criminals all over France. Especially when the Gestapo just arrested this fellow they call Max, who may be the head of the whole terrorist movement, and we knew nothing of his whereabouts. We risk being viewed as incompetent and wholly unnecessary. And I, for one, will not stand idly by and watch that happen. Have I made myself clear, Captain?"

"Colonel, if you would allow me—"

"That was an order, Captain!"

"Of course, Colonel. Will there be anything else?"

"That's all, Captain Malfaire. *Bon soir.*" And the line went dead.

Malfaire, still holding the receiver to his ear, looked casually up at Marie, who had remained in the room for the entire conversation. The last thing he wanted was for her to think that he was having any sort of problem in the Milice, especially after having lost his post with the police not six months ago.

"I'll do everything in my power to bring him to justice, Colonel," he said. "You can count on me. *Bon soir.*" Only then did he replace the receiver on its hook.

"*Chérie,* would you be so kind as to get me another drink?" he asked Marie.

"Is everything all right, Jean-Claude? What did the Colonel want?"

"Nothing you need to worry about, *chérie.* Now be a dear and get me that drink."

That old fool is going to ruin everything! Malfaire had already begun to feel a slow burn in the pit of his stomach as Marie stepped into the dining room to pull a bottle from the liquor cabinet. He's worried about saving face with the Germans, while criminals and Jews are roaming the streets! No wonder things are going from bad to worse. Well, the good colonel hasn't had the last word on this yet.

Malfaire picked up the receiver and dialed the operator. When his call finally went through, he tried to keep his voice down. The less Marie heard, the better.

"Didier, it's Malfaire. Look, something has come up and I need your help."

"You need my help? What, no threats, no ultimatums?"

It galled Malfaire to no end that Didier had him at a disadvantage. The fact was, however, that the ungrateful little worm had protection from the *boches.* That alone had kept him from blowing Didier's head off the last time they had met. But given the chance, Malfaire wouldn't hesitate again.

"Forget about what I said before. I'm telling you now, some things have changed."

"Well, you know me, forgive and forget, I always say. And

you know I'm happy to help my friends in the Milice. What can I do for you this time, Captain?"

"Keep an eye out for Marcel Boussant, and let me know the moment you spot him."

"Really, Captain, I thought I told you he went to Switzerland. I doubt he'll be back."

"He was probably taking more Jews across the border. He's done it before, you know."

Didier laughed. "He wasn't smuggling any Jews this time. He was alone, like I told you, and I don't think he's coming back."

"Don't be so sure about that, Didier. He's a lot smarter than you think. And he's got some pretty resourceful friends."

"You're right about his friends, Captain."

"Listen," said Malfaire, "I think he'll return to get more Jews. I don't know when, but I'm sure he'll come back. And when he does, I want to know about it. Understood?"

"And you understand that the price is now double?"

Malfaire grinned wickedly to himself. "Oh, you'll be paid in full, *mon ami*. Don't you worry about that."

⚜ ⚜ ⚜

"Sister, we need to talk." Théo stepped out into the corridor and closed the door softly behind him just as Sister Marie-Moïses strode past. She almost always seemed to be hurrying somewhere.

"What is it, Théo? Can it wait until later? I mustn't be late."

The birthday celebration was over and the nuns were on their way to the chapel for evening prayers. Victor was trying mightily to read the fables of La Fontaine to Léa in the upstairs room that had become the children's temporary home. But

Théo had other things on his mind.

"It's about Léa."

"Is she ill? She didn't have too much cake, did she? Oh, I knew we shouldn't have made it so sweet. It's just that we thought a little sugar would be a treat, what with the rationing and all."

"She's fine, Sister. And she really enjoyed the party. Thank you for being so nice to her—to all of us."

Marie-Moïses smiled and put a hand on his shoulder. "You're very welcome. We don't get to have parties here very much. It was nice to have an excuse, really. Besides, we all love your little Léa so much."

"That's what I wanted to talk about. Léa admires all the sisters—you especially. Now she wants her doll dressed like one of you. I'm afraid she'll want to stay and become a nun herself."

The nun tried to suppress a giggle. "Oh, I don't think you need to worry about that. She's only seven, after all. We don't accept novices until they are much older."

"Well, I wish you wouldn't make it seem so, well, so nice to be a nun."

"Would it be better if I acted like some sort of black-and-white ogre, who's eager to eat young children?"

Théo looked away, embarrassed. This was harder than he thought it would be. "Of course not," he said. "But you said you wouldn't try to make us into Christians. You promised."

"And you're afraid Léa might want to become one?" Marie-Moïses leaned against the corridor wall and folded her arms across her chest. "I made a promise to God to give shelter to any Jewish children He brings our way. And I promised the rabbis that if they trusted me with their children, I would trust their souls to God. I have never tried to make anyone into a Christian, as you call it." She stopped for a moment and looked directly at Théo. "Besides," she continued, "you can't force anyone to become a Christian. It's strictly voluntary."

"Well, Léa's a Jew just like Victor and me," Théo said, as emphatically as he could manage, "and we don't want to be anything else."

"I respect that," she said, as she turned to go. "In fact, I used to think the very same way myself."

Now what did she mean by that? Théo wondered.

Chapter 23

Standing in front of the mirror that hung over his hotel room bureau, Michael Dreyfus fumbled with his tie as though his fingers were frozen. For some reason, the double Windsor knot he normally tied without thinking refused to cooperate even after three attempts to bring it under control. So, untangling the tapered length of dotted red silk, he began again, whistling tunelessly in spite of his mounting frustration. There were still twenty minutes before it would be time to leave.

It was going to be an important evening; he could feel it already. And for the first time it had nothing to do with Red Cross business, or Heinrich Rosen's plan to evacuate refugees—not directly, anyway. Perhaps that was why he was so nervous, even a bit clumsy. Tonight he was going to pay a social visit to the home of Robert and Justine de Rocher—at the request of Isabelle Karmazin, he was sure. He had only known her a short time, but his efforts on her behalf were beginning to pay off already, in more ways than one.

Returning from work on Monday evening, he was on his way to his room in the Hotel des Cignes when the desk clerk handed him the message:

Dear Michael,
Please do us the honor of joining us for
dinner at eight o'clock tomorrow evening
at our home, boulevard St. Georges.
Kindest regards,
M. & Mme. Robert de Rocher

Michael could hardly believe his luck! Naturally, Isabelle was behind this. She had to be. She was simply too shy, or too proper, to make the invitation herself. That suited Michael just fine. He had always preferred girls with a strong sense of decorum, girls who were, in fact, just a bit old-fashioned. He was beginning to feel that his trip to Switzerland, in spite of the hazards, was becoming a journey of destiny.

The one thing that troubled him, however, was his brief encounter with Isabelle and this Marcel Boussant fellow on Sunday evening. At the time he had been so excited about his news—not to mention feeling a little awkward about showing up uninvited and unannounced—that he hadn't paid much attention. But the more he thought about it, the more it bothered him. Who was this Marcel, anyway? A friend from France, Isabelle had said. But what kind of friend? And why did it seem as though he couldn't take his eyes off of her?

Michael finished straightening his tie. After all the grief it had given him, it finally looked nearly perfect. He slipped on his jacket and looked at his watch. There was just enough time to walk downstairs before the taxi was due to arrive. Perhaps he worried too much, he told himself, as he locked the door behind him. There was no reason to spoil a perfect evening before it had even begun.

⚜ ⚜ ⚜

Marcel took his jacket off and slung it over his shoulder as he strode purposefully along Rue de Candolle. The still air this June evening was warmer than he had expected, and he didn't want to risk perspiring heavily before arriving at the de Rocher's house. He was nervous enough as it was, without worrying about that too. Fortunately, he didn't have much farther to walk.

He welcomed any opportunity to spend time with Isabelle, of course, but he couldn't shake the notion that this evening would probably be far less pleasant than Sunday afternoon had been. Not that Isabelle was likely to be any less captivating. Certainly not! Seeing her again after more than five months of separation had made it hard to concentrate on his work the past two days. He imagined that he would be no less enthralled with her this evening, no matter what.

But Isabelle's promise to explain her puzzling Sunday night conversation with this fellow, Michael Dreyfus, was eating away at Marcel. To begin with, he hadn't quite comprehended why she didn't just tell him what it was all about right then and have it over and done. Surely that would have been far simpler than dragging it out for two agonizing days. What could be so hard about that? But he had to admit that she had a perfect right to keep her own counsel, and that regardless of any understanding they might have had, she really didn't owe him any explanation at all regarding her future plans. After five months of separation, she would have been foolish not to make *some* plans, wouldn't she?

It would have been a whole lot easier to swallow, however, if it weren't for the involvement of this Michael Dreyfus character. Marcel had seen the way the tall stranger looked at

Isabelle, and he didn't particularly like it. Who was he, anyway? Red Cross, according to what Isabelle had said, but that could mean almost anything. And what about that little hint of something in his accent? Maybe he was imagining things, but it didn't sound local to Marcel's ear.

A taxi whizzed past just as Marcel was making the turn onto the Boulevard St. Georges. A couple more minutes and Isabelle would be able to divulge her secrets. He wasn't sure if he was prepared for what she would say or not.

Isabelle smoothed her khaki skirt over her slender hips and took one last look at her reflection in the hall mirror, turning this way and that before descending the stairs. Her cheeks looked a little flushed, she thought. Perhaps it only appeared that way because of the pale rose blouse she wore. Better her guests' attention should be drawn to her cheeks, however, than that they should notice the red lines in her eyes. She hadn't slept much in the last two days, thinking about what she would say tonight. Unfortunately, she still wasn't sure.

Michael Dreyfus' arrival in her life had come at a moment when she had given up all hope of leaving Switzerland for the safety of some faraway place. And just when she had resigned herself to an indefinite stay under the seemingly tenuous protection of the Swiss flag, Michael had offered to get her out of Europe—and quite possibly to America. She only wished he had come along sooner.

What worried her, however, was the suspicion that Michael might be a little too fond of her—that this was not a purely humanitarian gesture he was making. Oh, she was flattered by his attention. Who wouldn't be, as tall and handsome and charming as he was? But she felt little more for him than profound gratitude for his offer of escape from this brutal continent.

Michael had certainly known how to get her attention. As a fellow Jew, he sensed the anger she felt at the way she had been forced to live the past three years. Too, he had seemed to understand the fear she lived with as a result of her string of personal losses: loss of family, of freedom, even of dignity. She just wanted to get as far from it all as possible and somehow, Michael saw that right away. What was better, he had the means at his disposal to do something about it.

At this very moment, four ships purchased with money from Monsieur Rosen and his associates were tied up in the port of Genoa. As soon as American or British authorities gave them permission to land in Allied territory in North Africa, 30,000 Jewish refugees would board the ships with the blessing of the Italian government. Michael, with his Red Cross connections, would provide Isabelle and Alexandre safe passage from Geneva to Genoa where she too would board one of the ships. After that, she would be on Allied soil in a matter of hours—a day at the most. Once there, she would be in a more favorable position to make application for entry to the United States.

She knew it wasn't without risk, but she couldn't simply turn her back on what he offered, if for no other reason than that she owed it to Alexandre to get a fresh start, to go where she could raise him free from fear and turmoil. He deserved a chance at real freedom, and she intended to give it to him. Michael stood ready to make that happen.

On the other hand, her most passionate, persistent prayers had been answered when Marcel Boussant walked back into her life on Sunday morning. It was almost more than she had dared hope for, after months believing he was either dead, in prison, or some other equally horrible fate. She could hardly believe it even now, and caught herself smiling just thinking about it. If she had harbored any lingering doubts that God was indeed good (and she certainly had), they were pretty much put to rest on Sunday.

A single look from Marcel's deep chestnut eyes had reignited in her the flame she had feared was extinguished for good. Something about him made her feel as if she were the most important person on the planet. And, indeed, her safety had very nearly cost him his life, as she discovered just two days ago.

He would never make such a claim, she was certain, but in her heart she knew that she owed him her life. And Alexandre's too. Yet somehow, she knew she couldn't turn away from the future—hers and Alexandre's—for the love of a man. Not even Marcel's love. The funny thing was, she knew he would never ask her to. That, among a host of qualities, was what she loved about him.

It would be much harder for her to go, now that he was here. There was no denying that. But she had a feeling that his stay in Switzerland was only temporary, anyway. Sooner or later, when things calmed down a little in France, when the police or the Gestapo grew tired of looking for him, he would return to do what brought them together in the first place. And that was to save as many of her people as possible from certain death at the hands of the Nazis.

She hoped both Marcel and Michael would understand. And she prayed that neither she nor Alexandre would ever be faced with such a difficult choice again.

"Anyway," Isabelle concluded, after what she feared had been a rather disjointed explanation of her intentions, "that's what I think I should do—for Alexandre's sake, you understand."

No one said a word. Robert, at the head of the table, continued to eat the remaining few morsels of his *lapin roti* in silence. Marcel, seated to Isabelle's left, was staring at his plate, pushing his food aimlessly back and forth with his fork. Michael, seated across the lace-draped table next to Justine, refilled his water glass for at least the third time without looking up. Justine, whose gaze Isabelle had felt the entire time she was talking, finally cleared her throat.

"Well, it looks to me as though everyone is nearly finished with the *lapin*," she said. "I'll just slip into the kitchen and bring out the cheese. Is there enough bread left for everyone?"

A chorus of vague murmurs communicated what she needed to know, and she rose to begin clearing the plates from the table. Uncomfortable with the stony silence, Isabelle too got up from her chair and began to help. For a moment she thought Robert was about to speak, but instead, he just gave her a little smile, filled with reassurance. She flashed a quick, uncertain smile in return, then followed Justine into the kitchen.

"I've probably ruined everything," she blurted, as soon as they were alone. She fought to keep back the tears.

"I doubt that very much, Isabelle." Justine put down the plates she was carrying and put her arm around Isabelle's shoulders. "Anyway, it's better to have everything out in the open, don't you think? Besides, you can't let the rest of us determine what you should do. You're the one who has to live with your decisions."

"I know, but I don't want to hurt anyone, either. Especially not Marcel. I owe my life to him, and I'm afraid he's going to feel betrayed by all this."

"I'm sure Marcel did what he did out of love for you, not

because he expected anything in return. Of course he'll be disappointed, but if he truly loves you, he'll want what's best for you, no matter what."

"Do you really think so? Love like that seems too good to be true. Won't he expect me to stay here with him?"

"Sacrifice is what real love is all about, Isabelle—being willing to pay any price for the good of another. It's the kind of love God demonstrated to us, and it's how He wants us to act toward each other. Romance quickly fades unless it's based on a giving kind of love."

Isabelle wondered if she had ever felt that kind of love toward anyone else. It seemed so wonderful, so noble, yet so rare. Sure, she had given up a lot in her marriage to Adam, but she often felt that she had no choice, that somehow it was her duty. Alexandre, on the other hand, could count on her to give up anything and everything for his benefit. She didn't even have to think about it. Maybe the love of a mother for her child was as close to the real thing as she would ever get. And Marcel? She was sure she loved him, but what was she supposed to do to prove it? What about how she felt? Didn't that count for something?

"What about Michael?" she said suddenly. "I can tell that he thinks of me as more than just another Jewish refugee. Don't get me wrong, I appreciate what he's doing for me. But I don't love him. What if he expects more from me than I can give him?"

"It's like I just told you," said Justine, squeezing her shoulders warmly. "If he really loves you, he will want what's best for you, no matter what."

"So what do I tell him?"

"Just be honest with him. He seems like a good man. I'm sure he can take the truth. If not, it won't take you long to find out."

Isabelle felt the tension inside her beginning to melt for the first time all evening. Maybe, just maybe, Justine was right about this. Maybe everything wasn't ruined after all. Of course, she still had to face reality, knowing all too well that things hoped for don't always turn out in the end.

"Now there's a dinner that won't be soon forgotten!"

Marcel looked across the back seat of the taxi at Michael Dreyfus and smiled in spite of himself. Sharing the taxi ride back to their respective hotels had not been his idea, but when Michael offered, he could see no good reason to refuse. They would only be together for a few minutes, in any case.

"What did we eat, anyway?" he asked jokingly. "I can't seem to remember." There was no point in letting the conversation turn serious.

"Me neither," Michael chuckled. "I didn't eat enough of it to find out, whatever it was."

"It must have been good, though," quipped Marcel. "Robert ate enough for both of us."

They both laughed. Then neither said anything more for several blocks. Only the rise and fall of the engine's hum disturbed the quiet as the driver guided his car through the sparse night traffic of Geneva's Old Town.

"I didn't know anything about you when I first met her," Michael said, suddenly serious. "I wouldn't want you to think—"

"It's okay," Marcel interrupted. "You had no way of knowing."

There was another long pause.

"She'll probably feel better once she can take Alexandre away from here," Marcel ventured, not sure that his heart could ever accept what his mind found possible. "She's really been through a lot."

"I hope you're right," Michael replied thoughtfully. "I'd hate to see her disappointed all over again. It just wouldn't seem right."

Something in the way Michael said it gave Marcel pause. Had he been too quick to judge? he wondered. Those certainly didn't sound like the words of some cavalier Don Juan, bent on yet another amorous conquest. He had to admit that Michael actually seemed like a decent guy. Perhaps reason had been clouded more by petty jealousy than by love, after all. Not that it made the situation all that much easier to live with. It certainly didn't curb his profound sense of disappointment. But it did give him some food for thought.

"Hotel des Cignes," announced the driver, as the taxi glided to a stop at the curb.

"Perhaps we could have lunch sometime." Michael actually sounded hopeful as he opened the car door.

"Perhaps." Marcel nodded. He would need some time to think about that.

Strange how things turn out sometimes, he mused, as he stepped out of the taxi a minute later. *It's only been two days and I'm losing her all over again.*

Chapter 24

Alexandre Karmazin squealed gleefully as the wheels of his navy blue *poussette* bumped noisily across the cobblestones in front of St. Pierre's cathedral. Church was over and Robert and Justine de Rocher had walked on ahead toward home, leaving Isabelle and Marcel to follow at a more leisurely pace with the baby.

"Have you heard anything from Gilles?" Isabelle asked, once the *poussette's* wheels were rolling quietly over the smooth surface of the sidewalk. "How is his father?"

"He's going to be all right," said Marcel. "He's going to have to take it slow for a while, though. At least that's what the doctor says. I'm just not sure he knows how to do that. He's a very hard-driving man."

"How are things going with his business here in Geneva? Are you feeling settled yet?"

"Things are going all right, I guess," Marcel replied, "as nearly as I can tell. There is so much to learn. Two weeks ago, I hardly even knew the machine tool business existed. Now I'm having to deal in it every day, and it's even harder than I thought it would be. The hardest part is that there's no one around to show me what to do. I have to figure everything out as I go. I just hope I'm doing it right. I don't want to let Gilles down—or his father either, for that matter."

"I'm sure you won't. It'll just take time to get used to it, that's all."

He shrugged. "I suppose you're right, but I'd really rather be farming. At least I feel as though I understand plants and animals."

Isabelle laughed. "Maybe Gilles' father could get into the dairy business, instead of importing machine parts, or whatever you call them."

"At least I know which end of a cow is which!" Marcel grinned at her. "With some of these parts, I can't tell if they're right side up or upside down. It's very confusing. Fortunately, I only see samples. If I had to work in a warehouse full of these things, I'd go absolutely crazy."

"Come with me to one of the refugee camps sometime, if you want to see something that drives me crazy," Isabelle said. "It's kind of like a warehouse for people."

"How often do you go?" asked Marcel, his face suddenly stone serious.

"About once a week. Often enough to be grateful I don't live in one. Some of them are not much better than the detention camp I was in back in France."

"Do you enjoy your work for the refugees?"

"I love to sew," she replied, "and it means a lot to me to provide for people who have nothing—or next to nothing. But I don't enjoy going to the camps."

"Why do you go, then? You could have Justine take the clothes to the camps without you, couldn't you?"

"Yes, I guess so. But in a way, going there helps me to remember how fragile my freedom is. It keeps me from taking what I have for granted, becoming complacent. And it reminds me that as long as I stay, they can take everything away from me in the blink of an eye." She really hadn't intended to say all that. It had just come out. She was never actually sure why she went back to the camps. Not until she said it, that is.

"And that's why you want to leave?" Marcel slowed the *poussette* to a mere crawl, his gaze fixed on Isabelle's face.

"I'm tired of losing, Marcel." She tried not to return his gaze, afraid she might cry if she looked into his eyes. "I want to go someplace where I don't have to worry about being left with nothing—with no one."

"There isn't any place like that, Isabelle. Not on this earth, anyway."

"What do you mean?"

"Going to America isn't going to protect you from loss or hardship or even from death. Only heaven can promise that, and you have to die to get there."

"Am I supposed to just wait around while God decides whether or not I've suffered enough? I have to do something, and I don't know what He wants from me."

Marcel stopped in his tracks. "Just trust Him, Isabelle. That's what He wants."

"And then everything will work out fine?" Even to her own ears, Isabelle's tone sounded more sarcastic than she had intended. "I'm sorry, Marcel, but I've tried. It's just not that easy for me."

Marcel didn't reply right away, and they continued on for several blocks in silence.

The warmth of the sun and the motion of the *poussette* had conspired to put Alexandre to sleep. *He looks so completely peaceful,* Isabelle mused. *He has no idea what I'm going through.*

And he would never have to know, if she had anything to say about it.

Marcel, on the other hand, had a look of sadness about him that Isabelle had never seen before. She hadn't intended to hurt him, but what did he expect from her? She couldn't very well just sit on her hands when she had the chance of a lifetime, could she?

"Are you angry with me?" she asked as they reached the Boulevard St. Georges.

"Angry?" Marcel's expression registered surprise. "Why would I be angry with you?"

"For wanting to leave."

"I guess I am pretty disappointed," he said, "but I don't feel angry with you. It's just that I was getting used to the idea of having you near again. It's hard to see you go."

"Oh, Marcel, it's hard for me too, don't you see? I don't want to leave you. I am just trying to do the best thing for my future—for my son's future. And I don't see any future for us here in Switzerland."

"Why not wait until the war is over?" he pleaded. "Just tell me you'll think about it, Isabelle. Please, at least think about it."

"Please don't make it any harder than it already is!" Isabelle could feel a familiar knot beginning to twist at her stomach. "You said I should trust in God. Well, maybe God has been watching out for me lately, after all. Maybe He sent this opportunity along at just the right time. And what if this is my only chance for real freedom? I have to try, at least for Alexandre's sake. I don't want him to have to suffer the way I have."

Marcel stopped and looked up, as though scanning the sky overhead. Isabelle couldn't tell if he was looking at something or simply avoiding her gaze. Slowly, he turned his face toward her and she could see that his eyes were shining. Tilting her chin slightly upward with his hand, he looked straight into her eyes. "I don't want either of you to suffer, Isabelle. I love you too much for that. If you're sure about leaving, I won't stand in the way."

Isabelle's heart skipped a beat. "Wh-what did you say?"

"I won't stand in the way of your leaving—if that's what you really want." He took his fingers from her chin, but she didn't move.

"I heard that," she said, the beginning of a smile tugging at the corners of her mouth. "But what did you say before that?"

For a moment, he looked puzzled. Then, as the light of comprehension began to dawn, his face flushed red. "I-I guess I said that I love you, Isabelle. I thought you knew that already."

Without thinking, Isabelle raised up on tiptoe and kissed him squarely on the lips. Warmth flooded her entire body as she lingered there for just a moment. And as she withdrew, she realized that she had wanted to do that for a very long time.

"I don't understand you, Isabelle Karmazin." Marcel looked at her over a lopsided, bewildered grin. "I really don't understand you at all."

Isabelle wondered if she understood herself. Leaving this man behind was shaping up to be the hardest thing she had ever done, no matter how good her reasons.

⚜ ⚜ ⚜

"When will you know for sure?" Isabelle couldn't believe what she was hearing. The telephone receiver felt like lead in her hand as she tried to make sense of the news Michael Dreyfus had just given her.

"It shouldn't be long," he was saying. "Monsieur Rosen says that a delegation has gone to visit the American authorities in Tunis. They should have an answer in a matter of days."

"What if they refuse to let the ships land?" she asked.

"Then the delegation will try to persuade the British to cooperate. They occupy a good bit of North Africa, as well as Palestine."

"Michael, I'm really not interested in going to Palestine."

"Neither am I," he said quickly. "A lot of Jews are, though. Some of them have even tried already, but the British have set up a naval blockade just to keep people out of Palestine. They're afraid that an influx of Jews will stir up trouble with the people already living there. But you don't have to worry about that. Monsieur Rosen says he probably won't need to approach the British at all. He thinks we have a better chance with the Americans."

"Well, I wish it would hurry up and happen." Isabelle was feeling the knot in her stomach again. "The longer it takes, the more nervous I get."

"Nervous? About what?"

"About everything!" Isabelle was incredulous. "I have a baby to think about, Michael. I would never forgive myself if anything happened to him. And frankly, I dread saying good-bye to the de Rochers. They've been absolutely wonderful to me, and it won't be easy leaving them."

"Are you nervous about saying good-bye to Marcel?"

Stunned into silence, Isabelle clapped her hand over the telephone's mouthpiece. Why would he ask such a question? And how was she supposed to answer? *Just be honest with him,* Justine had advised. *I'm sure he can take the truth. If not, it won't take you long to find out.*

"Yes," she said at length, "I'm very nervous about that."

"I can understand that." His voice sounded sincere.

"You can?"

"Of course. He's a nice fellow and, according to Monsieur

de Rocher, he saved your life. I wouldn't expect you to look forward to saying good-bye to him."

"There's more to it than that, Michael."

"I see." He was silent for a moment. "Well, in any case, it shouldn't be long, now. I expect to hear from Monsieur Rosen almost any time."

"Let me know the minute you hear anything."

When Isabelle hung up the phone she walked up the stairs to her room and began to pack a few of her things into a suitcase. It wouldn't hurt to be ready when the call came.

⚜ ⚜ ⚜

The crèperie Michel had but one outside table available when Michael arrived a few minutes before noon. He agreed to take it in spite of the fact that it was somewhat less protected from the sun than most of the others. It was too nice a day to eat indoors. Besides, he liked to sit where he could watch people as they came and went, and this table was perfectly situated for that. He glanced around at the other patrons, some sitting quietly alone, others chatting with friends, colleagues, or lovers. It was the kind of scene of which he never grew tired.

When Marcel Boussant arrived a few minutes later, Michael stood and waved him over to the table.

"I'm glad you could come," he said, motioning Marcel to an empty chair.

"Thanks for the invitation," Marcel responded, once he was seated.

The waiter broke the awkward moment of silence that followed by offering each a menu and suggesting a couple of the house specialties.

"I'll have two of your *crèpes aux champignons*," said Michael, without looking at the menu.

"Excellent choice, monsieur," the waiter congratulated him before turning to Marcel. "And you, monsieur? What would you like?"

"I'll have the same."

"*Merci,* messieurs. I'll be back shortly with your lunch." He collected the menus and disappeared.

"So," Marcel began casually, "how are things at the Red Cross?"

"Busy," Michael replied, happy to have something mundane to talk about. "And getting busier all the time. The Allies are flying more and more bombing missions over Germany, which means more men shot down. Which, of course, leads to more prisoners in German camps, and that keeps us busy getting packages to them."

"And what is your role there?"

"I'm an aide to Gerard Richert, who's here from the U.S. investigating the huge amount of pilferage we suffer in shipments coming from the States."

Marcel's eyebrows raised perceptibly. "You're an American?"

"No," said Michael. "Actually, I'm Swiss, but my father moved his business to New York when I was just a *gamin,* so I grew up over there. And you?"

"French, as I'm sure you know," replied Marcel. "My family has a small farm near Grenoble."

"That's not too far from here, right? I came through there on the train. Say, come to think of it, there was some problem with the tracks and we were delayed near Grenoble. Sabotage, they said." He chuckled. "Friends of yours?"

"Could have been." Marcel grinned. "Those things happen from time to time."

"Did you ever do that sort of thing?" Michael was suddenly curious.

"Not blowing up things, if that's what you mean."

"Robert de Rocher says you saved Isabelle's life, that you helped a lot of Jews. Wasn't that dangerous?"

"I suppose it was, at times," said Marcel, without pretense. "We just tried to be careful and help as many as we could."

"Well, I appreciate what you've done for my people. I only wish there were more like you."

Marcel's face colored a little, and he looked down at the tablecloth.

"What brings you to Switzerland, then?" asked Michael. "Surely not farming!"

Marcel laughed. "No. Actually, I represent a friend's business here in Geneva."

"So, you're a farmer and a businessman?"

"Not much of a businessman, I'm afraid. But my friend needed someone, so I came."

"Let me guess," said Michael. "Your friend needed some help, and you needed to lie low for a while, right?"

"Something like that."

"Would you ever do it again—help Jews escape, I mean?"

Marcel nodded. "If I could, I would."

The waiter arrived just then and placed a plate in front of each of them. On each plate were two identical crèpes, lying in a spoonful of rich burgundy sauce, and topped by a dozen tiny, but perfectly formed whole mushrooms.

"Bon apetit!" The waiter backed quickly away before turning to serve a couple at a nearby table. The woman reminded Michael of a slightly older version of Isabelle.

"Have you heard that the evacuation from Genoa is supposed to happen fairly soon?" Michael asked between bites. "We don't know exactly when yet, but it looks as if it won't be long."

Marcel nodded, continuing to eat his crèpes. It was impossible to read his expression, but Michael had a pretty good idea that this was not Marcel's preferred topic of conversation. Still, for his own peace of mind, he needed to get it out in the open.

"I know it's none of my business, Marcel, but do you love her?" No sooner were the words out than he wished he had taken a different tack. He really didn't want to put Marcel on the defensive.

Marcel paused a moment before answering. "Yes, I do," he said softly. "I love her very much. But if you're really asking if I'll stand in the way of her leaving, the answer is no. I want her to be happy, and since she's become convinced that her happiness depends on leaving here, I have to let her go."

"And you think I've convinced her of that?"

Marcel shook his head. "No, I think she's convinced herself. She's scared, Michael, and she doesn't see any other way to conquer her fears."

"I take it you don't agree that this is the best thing for her."

"It doesn't really matter what I think, but no, I think she's making a big mistake. She's been running for a long time, and she's had good reason to. But she has to stop running sometime, and now seems like the right time, to me. Of course, it's not my decision to make."

"Do you plan to keep seeing her?" Michael wanted to know.

"Until the day she leaves."

There was a firmness in Marcel's last declaration, a sort of defiance that Michael admired, in spite of the complication it posed for him. He knew he couldn't expect the young Frenchman to simply fade out of the picture, especially given Isabelle's fondness for him. But if he were patient, he could prove himself just as worthy of Isabelle's affection as Marcel—maybe even more so, if shared heritage meant anything to her. And once Europe was behind her, Marcel would begin to fade into memory.

In a way, Michael felt badly for Marcel. He was a good man, brave, devout, and loyal. He actually liked Marcel, liked being around him. It seemed an unfortunate twist of fate that they had both fallen in love with the same woman.

Chapter 25

September 1943

The summer months passed all too quickly for Marcel. His days were mostly filled trying to keep abreast of the flow of paperwork required by Swiss and French authorities for the shipment of machine tools to the Compagnie Théron warehouse in Grenoble. He was finally getting the hang of the business, thanks in part to occasional bits of advice from Michael Dreyfus, whose father happened to be in the same business in New York. That, and the time-honored method of trial and error, enabled him to become fairly efficient. Some days, he actually didn't mind this line of work.

Once each week, usually on Thursday, he withdrew a certain amount of currency from a special account in the bank in his building. The amount was different each week, signaled to him by a special coded notation in the cables he received from Gilles. Late the same night, a nameless visitor would come to his room to deliver instructions, claim the money, and then transport it across the border, presumably to Hervé Chassin.

Marcel was never told exactly, but he suspected that at least part of the money came from British or American sources. He couldn't imagine where else the *maquis* could get such sums.

Whatever time was left after taking care of his obligations, Marcel spent with Isabelle and the now-crawling Alexandre. There was still no word on their departure for Genoa, but Marcel tried to treat each week as if it would be their last together—no easy thing after so much waiting and wondering. Secretly, he had begun to doubt that it would ever happen, but Isabelle remained hopeful, though increasingly frustrated at the delay.

Just after 6 P.M. on Thursday, Marcel locked the door to his office and with his valise securely in hand, headed down the street toward his hotel. The strain of the past weeks, both personal and professional, was beginning to take its toll, and tonight all he wanted to do was wash up, eat dinner, and go to bed. Unfortunately, his shadowy visitor would be arriving around ten o'clock, so there would be no rest until after the man was gone.

Five minutes later, Marcel was turning the key in the lock of his hotel room door. Shouldering the door open while he dropped the key back into his pocket with his free hand, he found himself staring at a stranger, seated on the end of the bed.

"What are you doing here?" The question was more a reflex than anything else.

"Come in, Monsieur Boussant. I've been waiting for you." The man with the silky voice smiled benignly, revealing a gleaming row of perfect white teeth. His right hand, however, was wrapped around the butt of a semiautomatic pistol which was casually aimed in Marcel's direction.

Marcel could feel his pulse rate begin to climb, but he remained where he was. "Who are you?" he demanded. "How did you get in here?"

"I didn't mean to frighten you, Monsieur Boussant," the silky voice intoned, as the man set the gun down beside him on the bed, "but I was told to meet you in your hotel room. The door was unlocked when I arrived, so I made myself at home." He flashed another toothy smile.

"What is it you want?" Marcel asked, still wary. He was sure he had locked the door this morning. He wondered if perhaps the maid had left it unlocked, but he dismissed the thought as unlikely.

"I've come for the valise," said the man, rising from the bed.

"Where are my instructions?" He could feel the hair on the back of his neck begin to rise. The instructions always came first. Always. And he never gave the courier his valise, only the money inside.

The stranger's smile faded. "Come inside and shut the door, Monsieur Boussant. Your friend won't be coming to see you again—ever. I'll be coming from now on, and you will give me the money you've been giving him. And if you do or say anything foolish, I will personally see to it that you die a very slow and painful death." The smile returned, though it was anything but benign this time.

"You can have the money this time," Marcel said, reaching slowly into the valise, "but once my people realize it's missing, they'll find someone else to do the job. You'll never get another franc!"

"Just hand me the money, Boussant!" The silk was gone from the stranger's voice as he took another step forward. "I'm sure you'll think of some way to keep it flowing."

As Marcel pulled a small handful of franc notes out of his valise, he heard voices in the corridor behind him. With a flick of his wrist, he launched the paper money into the air in the direction of the stranger, then took two quick steps backward. Turning to his left, he raced down the corridor toward the sound of the voices.

"Help!" he shouted as he ran past a middle-aged couple fumbling with their door lock. "I've been robbed!" Fright was the only way to describe the look on their faces.

Down two flights of stairs and through the lobby, Marcel sprinted as fast as he knew how, afraid to turn and see how close behind the stranger was. Pushing his way brusquely through a small knot of people milling around the main entrance, he burst out onto the sidewalk. Now where? His mind was racing, nearly out of control. Think! He had to think. And he had to find someplace to hide—at least until he could decide what to do next. He dashed off down the street, dodging cars and pedestrians alike. And every few yards he cast an anxious glance over his shoulder to be sure he was no longer being followed.

After a few blocks, Marcel slowed his pace. There was no sign that he was being followed, and he needed to catch his breath. Besides, he had no idea where he was going. He thought briefly about reporting the incident, but decided that calling the police wasn't the best option. He was carrying an awful lot of cash for a twenty-year-old foreigner. How would he explain that?

He couldn't simply return to his hotel. What if the gunman came back? He didn't dare go back to his office either. If the man knew his hotel and room number, it wouldn't take much more to discover his business address. Hopefully, the night watchman would keep him out of the building, but Marcel wasn't willing to stake his life on that.

Looking up, Marcel found himself across the street from the Hotel des Cignes. For some reason, the name caught his eye. Hotel des Cignes. He didn't recall ever being there. And then suddenly, it occurred to him. It was Michael Dreyfus' hotel. This is where Michael had come the night they shared the taxi. What if . . . He shook his head and kept walking. There was no point in dragging Michael into this. Somehow, he would just have to figure this one out by himself.

⚜ ⚜ ⚜

Michael Dreyfus took off his jacket and placed it carefully on a hanger in the armoire. Then he sat down in the wingback chair by the window and stared pensively out toward Lac Léman, quickly mesmerized by the eerie red and gold glow of the water in the fading light.

Today had been a long day, filled with reports and hearings, as usual. But it had been made especially long by Michael's conversation with Gerard Richert just after lunch. Richert was unhappy with him for what he described as "Jewish distractions." When Michael had tried to defend himself by suggesting that what he did on his own time was his own business, Richert had become furious, accusing him of using his position with the Red Cross to gain influence with Rosen and other Jews. Michael had denied it, of course. The truth was, he suspected that it was his connection to the Red Cross that interested Rosen, but he had never made an issue of it. Richert apparently wasn't in a mood to see it that way, however. They would be wrapping up their inquiry into the shipping losses in another week or so, the older man had announced then, and he should prepare to return home to New York and forget all this evacuation nonsense. The threat of losing his job was veiled, but it was definitely there!

All afternoon, all Michael could think of was the fact that he only had a week in which to insure that Isabelle got out of the country. And Heinrich Rosen wasn't due back until late

Saturday, so he had no way of knowing how the evacuation plans were going.

The summer had passed quickly it seemed to Michael, in spite of the seemingly interminable delay in Rosen's plans. He had been given very little time off, and in retrospect, staying busy at work had probably kept him from going crazy with impatience. Still, there had been many evenings when he would have enjoyed some company—Isabelle's company, in particular—but had to content himself with dreams of the future. The last thing he wanted was to incur any sort of resentment for coming between her and Marcel. That chapter would end soon enough by itself.

Besides, he really liked Marcel. He couldn't help it. And he suspected that if things had been different, the two would have actually been friends. He had even offered Marcel some business advice from time to time. Not that he was any kind of expert, but he had spent several summers working in his father's company while attending Columbia University.

Now, however, everything he had known over the past few months would be coming to a rapid close. It would be good to get home and see his parents after so much time away. He knew his mother was worried about him. She would keep worrying, too, until he was back where he belonged, as she liked to think of it. He figured his mother wouldn't relax until he finally got married. And he was sure she would be absolutely thrilled with Isabelle Karmazin.

Lost in thought, Michael was startled momentarily by the ringing of the phone. Walking to the nightstand, he picked up the receiver.

"*Allo, oui?*"

"There's a Monsieur Boussant here to see you, monsieur. Shall I send him up, or will you come down to the lobby?"

Marcel, here? Now? "Uh, send him up, I suppose." He

hung up the phone. *What is this all about?* Marcel had never once visited him here at the hotel. And why tonight?

A few minutes later, Michael opened the door and showed Marcel into the room.

"I'm sorry to bother you like this," Marcel began, "but I'm in a little bit of trouble." He looked tired.

"What kind of trouble?"

"I-uh, I was robbed. Er, that is, someone tried to rob me. I need a place to hide while I figure out what to do next."

"Sit down, you look tired." Michael moved the wingback chair away from the window and motioned for Marcel to sit in it. "Have you gone to see the police?"

"I can't." Marcel looked out the window. "I know it sounds crazy, but I can't."

"I don't understand," said Michael. "How are you going to make sure the thief is caught if you don't tell the police?"

Marcel sighed. "Look, it's pretty complicated, Michael, but I have a lot of money in my valise, money that belongs to someone else. If I go to the police, I'm the one they're likely to arrest. They probably wouldn't even believe the robbery part."

Michael was confused and said so. And then he listened slack-jawed as Marcel told him the whole story. He had never been so close to anything so dangerous—and exciting—in his entire life. And he couldn't get over the way Marcel was so matter-of-fact about it all. Sure, Marcel was scared. Who wouldn't be? But he didn't seem to find his circumstances at all unusual. Upsetting, yes, but not unusual. Michael was spellbound.

"What are you going to do?" he asked when Marcel had finished.

"I'm not sure, yet," said Marcel. "One thing is sure, though. I have to find a way to get a message through to the *maquis.* Their courier is dead, and if they don't find out the truth soon, they'll send someone looking for me."

"And if they find you?"

"That depends," said Marcel somberly. "If they think I've stolen from them . . ." His voice trailed off.

"Don't they trust you?" Michael asked. This *maquis* sounded like a heartless bunch.

"What do you expect them to think if the courier has been killed, and the contact man and the money are both missing? They'd have to be crazy not to suspect something."

"What if you just take them the money yourself?"

Marcel looked doubtful. "What do you mean?"

"Just go back to Grenoble, or wherever, and hand the money over. Tell them what happened. Then they'll know you didn't try to do anything crooked." He paused. "You know where to find them, right?"

"Of course I can find them," said Marcel, "but I can't leave Switzerland yet. What if your refugee evacuation happens while I'm gone? I want to be there when Isabelle leaves."

Michael was incredulous. "What are you thinking? You're hiding because some fool threatened to rob and kill you! If you don't get word to the *maquis*, they may come after you too! How safe is Isabelle going to be with you around, Marcel?"

Marcel put his head in his hands, but he didn't respond.

"Look, nothing is going to happen before Monsieur Rosen returns from his trip to Zurich. And he isn't due back until Saturday night. If you take the train in the morning, you can be back by tomorrow night. Tomorrow is only Friday. You won't miss a thing, I promise."

"I—I don't know, Michael. The man I need to give the money to may not be all that happy to see me. I let him down once before. I'm afraid I let a lot of people down."

"Don't you think he would respect you for taking charge and going straight to him? At the very least he'd see that you aren't a quitter or a coward. Besides, I can't think of a better way to get the money to him. Can you?"

Marcel looked thoughtful for a long moment. "I'll think about it," he said at last. "Just give me some time."

"Take all the time you want," said Michael, hardly able to suppress a smile. "I'll call down to the lobby to see if the concierge knows the train schedule." He could feel a tingle of excitement running all the way up and down his spine.

At six o'clock the next morning, Marcel stood in line at Geneva's Gare de Cornavin to buy a ticket for the 6:30 train to Grenoble.

"Grenoble, *aller-retour*," he told the man behind the glass when it was his turn. He paid for the round trip ticket, then walked slowly toward the police checkpoint. The Swiss police would check his papers here, and make sure he wasn't carrying any contraband before allowing him to cross into the area reserved for trains arriving from and departing for France.

Out of the corner of his eye, he could see Michael still waiting in the ticket line, and something inside him wanted to rush over to him and call the whole thing off. They had stayed up until 2 A.M. figuring out how to get the money across the border, but in the cold light of day, it seemed like a stupid idea. He could have kicked himself for letting Michael talk him into it. The trouble was, if he didn't get going, the plan would fail for sure. He kept walking.

A few cursory questions, a quick check of his papers and his valise, and Marcel was through the Swiss checkpoint. Now he simply needed to board the train and wait. Michael would join him in a moment, transfer the half of the money that he was carrying, then return to the station just before the train departed. That way, the more thorough Swiss would be circumvented, leaving Marcel with only the Italian checkpoint to worry about on his own. It wouldn't be easy, but he would worry about it later.

Marcel found an empty seat and waited, hoping he didn't appear as nervous as he felt. The other passengers seemed not to notice, but he had trouble sitting in one position for long. Like Michael, he had filled his wallet with money, thinking that to the border police, a certain amount of traveling cash would appear perfectly normal. The rest of the money, however, they had hidden in their shoes, and in their underwear, reasoning that only the most suspicious of police would venture to search so thoroughly. But now that the cash had been in place for nearly an hour, it was beginning to be more than a little uncomfortable.

Marcel looked at his watch. Only five minutes until departure! He knew that Michael still had to find an unoccupied W.C., unburden himself of the money he carried, and deliver it to Marcel, all before the train pulled out of the station. Under the best of conditions, it would take several minutes, and he was not yet in sight.

Seconds, and then minutes, ticked steadily away, until Marcel felt as if his pulse were racing well ahead of his watch. He heard the conductor's boarding call—and still no Michael. Marcel pressed his face against the cool window glass, straining to see along the platform. What could be keeping him? Had he been detained by the border police? Or had he simply given up and gone back to his hotel?

The couplings creaked and groaned as the train began to inch forward. And there at last, sprinting as if his life depended on it, was Michael Dreyfus, chasing alongside the string of rail wagons, grabbing a handrail and leaping aboard as the train began to pick up speed.

When he appeared in the doorway of the passenger car a moment later, Michael looked frightened and out of breath. But his eyes lit up when he spotted Marcel, and he broke into a broad grin.

At least he made it, thought Marcel, *but now what? This isn't how it was supposed to happen at all.*

Chapter 26

The surge of adrenaline Michael experienced didn't really begin to subside until he could see the Italian checkpoint receding into the distance. Never had he imagined himself involved in anything so dangerous and frightening—and so exciting—as smuggling money across a hostile frontier. If only his fraternity brothers could see him now! He smiled to himself. They'd never believe it—not for a New York minute. But then, if he hadn't pinched himself a time or two in the past half-hour to make certain he wasn't dreaming, he wouldn't believe it either.

Marcel, who was just now returning from a trip to the W.C., seemed to be taking everything in stride. Of course, the Frenchman was a more practiced hand at this sort of thing, Michael reminded himself. Still, it must have given him a bit of a scare when Michael nearly missed the train. But there was no way either of them could have known that a fresh-faced policeman would suddenly feel the need to scrutinize all

Michael's papers, down to the finest detail. Only the Red Cross identification card convinced the youthful Swiss to ease up.

"Whew, that feels much better!" Marcel sighed as he sat down facing Michael.

Michael chuckled softly. He couldn't wait to remove the money from his own clothing, but Marcel had suggested he stay put a little while before walking to the W.C. There was no point in attracting attention.

"How much farther?" he asked.

"An hour and a quarter," Marcel replied, glancing at his watch. "Maybe an hour and a half. It's hard to say, exactly. I didn't notice how long we were stopped at the border."

"Me, neither," said Michael. The fact was, he had been too excited to notice. But the *caribinieri* who came aboard seemed to have little enthusiasm for the required check of documents. Searching for contraband hardly seemed to be on their agenda, either. They had asked almost no questions at all.

The train swayed and rumbled along the floor of the narrow valley that sliced through the mountains of Savoie. Here and there along the hillsides, tiny patches of color appeared where trees were just now beginning to don the red and amber jewels of autumn. Vineyards, espalier orchards, and fields of corn formed a patchwork quilt that blanketed the valley and lower hills. And every few miles a tiny village appeared, its hardy dwellings invariably huddled around a church.

Michael had passed this way back in May, but he had been so anxious to arrive in Geneva that he wondered at how much of its beauty he had missed. Too, he realized that the change of seasons can enhance or diminish certain qualities of a place, but he almost felt as if he were seeing France for the first time.

"It's beautiful," he said aloud, his gaze transfixed by the passing scene.

"Yes, it is." Marcel sounded almost wistful.

"Do you miss it?"

"Always," Marcel replied, a little hoarsely. "Every single day."

"Will you ever come back here to live?"

"Just as soon as I can." He lowered his voice. "Just as soon as we've crushed the Nazis."

Michael marveled at Marcel's resolve. The tide was turning in this hellish war. There were signs of it in Africa, in the east, and more recently, in the Allied offensive in Southern Italy. But in spite of all that, France lay firmly in the Nazis' grip and was likely to remain so for a very long time to come. But there was something in this youthful Frenchman that seemed to view his country's freedom as inevitable. It wasn't bravado, but a kind of confidence that Michael admired in him.

"Next stop, Aix-les-bains," sang the conductor as he passed among the passengers. "We'll be stopping for two minutes only."

Michael watched as several passengers gathered their belongings and trudged through the aisle toward the doors. He wondered how many of them shared Marcel's vision of freedom, and how many had simply given up all hope. The looks on their faces suggested that, at least for many of them, freedom was nothing more than a fading memory.

⚜ ⚜ ⚜

Jean-Claude Malfaire was perspiring as he strode across the street to the Gare de Grenoble. He looked at his watch one last time, reassuring himself that he hadn't come too late, only to be startled by the whistle of an inbound train. Was this the one? He had driven at breakneck speed all the way from Lyons to meet the train from Geneva, and for once it looked as if his luck were going to hold. He broke into a slow trot, not wanting to miss even one of the disembarking passengers.

Didier Hebert, unscrupulous though he was, had come through for him one last time. If the little worm's information was correct, it would be well worth the 2,000 francs he had demanded. If not—well, Didier would not be able to run far enough or fast enough. If it weren't for the fact that he could be of some use, Malfaire would have taken him down long ago. And no one would have missed him. In Malfaire's opinion, Didier was such an arrogant, annoying little sewer rat, his own mother had probably disowned him.

The call from Aix-les-bains couldn't have come at a better time, except for the fact that it afforded little time to actually get to Grenoble. Colonel du Puy was once again in Paris, at least through the weekend, and he would never know that his orders were being carefully ignored. Malfaire smiled to himself. Du Puy was one cat who hardly knew what the mice were doing even when he wasn't away! Keeping this little excursion a secret from the old colonel wouldn't be all that difficult.

Jean-Claude arrived on the platform just as the train was braking to a full stop, bells clanging, engine rumbling, brakes hissing, wheels squealing against the iron rails. He found a post he could stand behind, one which he could peer around, but which was large enough so that no passenger descending to the platform would have an unobstructed view of him. He had gone to a lot of trouble to get here, and he certainly didn't want to spook his quarry now.

One by one, the passengers got off the train, some laden with bags, others with little or nothing in their hands. It was hard to watch all the passenger exit doors at once, but eventually everyone had to file into the terminal at a single point not thirty feet from where Malfaire stood. He watched them all carefully, men and women, afraid that some attempt at a disguise might not be readily apparent. He saw no one he recognized. No one at all.

Three minutes passed, then five, before all the passengers had deserted the platform, and still there was no sign of Marcel Boussant. Malfaire was beginning to feel his anger well up inside, like a volcano waiting to spew molten lava. He had waited all summer long for some word of Boussant's reappearance from exile in Switzerland. At least that is where Didier claimed he had gone. But there had been nothing until today. And apparently there was still nothing.

He remained in place a few more minutes, watching desperately, before finally giving up. Didier would pay for this, he fumed as he walked the few yards back into the terminal. He would arrange a meeting place to pay him off, some quiet little out-of-the-way spot, and then he would simply put a bullet between the weasel's eyes.

A porter, pushing a large empty wheeled cart, brushed past Malfaire on his way out of the terminal, nearly causing him to lose his balance.

"Hey! Watch where you're going!" He was in no mood to be pushed around by the likes of a common laborer. But the man ignored him and continued pushing his cart toward the standing train.

Malfaire was about to accost the man when it dawned on him that the train from Geneva probably terminated in Grenoble. That would explain why no one had seemed in a particular hurry to disembark, and why not a single new passenger had boarded. And that was why the porter was only now unloading bags from the baggage car. Of course, that was it! And all this time he had assumed it was just a ten-minute stop before continuing on to Lyons.

Forgetting all about the porter, he dashed to the car at the end of the line and climbed aboard. Drawing his 9mm Luger from its holster inside his jacket, he began walking the aisle, looking carefully in and under each seat. There was no one there. The car was empty.

He opened the doors at the end of the aisle and entered the second car. There, ahead and to the right, someone was slumped over in one of the seats, all but hidden from view. Very clever, my young friend, Malfaire thought to himself. You almost had me fooled. Aiming the Luger at the point where the boy's head would appear when he sat up, Malfaire took a couple of cautious steps forward.

"Hands in the air, Boussant," he barked. "This time it's over."

Hands reached into the air above the seat back, then a conductor's hat came into view, followed by the ashen face of the conductor.

"Please, don't shoot," he pleaded the moment he saw the gun. "I was just picking up some money one of the passengers must have dropped. Here, you can have it!" He began to extend his left hand, which was clutching something that looked like a fifty franc note.

"You fool! You could have been killed," roared Malfaire as he lowered his gun.

The conductor looked as if he had received a last-minute reprieve from a date with the guillotine. "Please, take the money, monsieur," he gushed, his hands trembling. "Really, it's not mine. I don't even want it."

Malfaire was no longer paying any attention. Out the window, he could see Marcel Boussant hurriedly entering the terminal alongside another, taller man. Thrusting the Luger back into its holster, he spun away from the cowering conductor and bolted for the door. There was no time to lose. Boussant and his friend would be out on the street in a matter of seconds.

⚜ ⚜ ⚜

"Just try to act natural," Marcel cautioned as he and Michael exited the main terminal. He led the way down the sidewalk to where three buses sat waiting, their diesel engines idling noisily.

"Which one do we take?" asked Michael.

"The first two."

"What do you mean, the first two?"

"Keep your voice down, Michael, and listen carefully." Marcel tried to sound as calm as possible. It wouldn't do to panic at this point. "We've got to split up. You get on the first bus in line. It's number 12 and it will take you as far as Place Verdun. If you get there before I do, find a *cabinet téléphonique* and call 76-22-43-28. Tell whoever answers to have Gilles meet us there in an hour."

"But how will he know it's not a trap?" said Michael. "And where will you be?"

"Tell him you're a friend of Isabelle Karmazin. He'll understand. I'll meet you there soon, but I'm going to take a different bus to try to throw Malfaire off, if he follows. If I get there first, I'll call Gilles, myself, but don't assume that I'll get there first. Have you got the number?"

Michael repeated the digits perfectly.

"*Allez!*" Marcel clapped him on the shoulder. "Be careful!"

Marcel waited just outside the door of the second bus, designated No. 17, until Michael was safely aboard No. 12. Only then did he turn his attention back in the direction of the station. He expected Malfaire to emerge at any moment.

"I'm leaving, monsieur," called the bus driver. "Are you getting on?"

"Don't you have to wait for the No. 12, first?" asked

Marcel. The first bus showed no signs of going anywhere, as of yet.

"I'm not responsible for No. 12, monsieur, only No. 17. Are you coming or not?"

Marcel climbed aboard and paid the fare, then found an empty seat near the rear of the bus. Why wasn't No. 12 moving yet? Was something wrong with it mechanically? Had he simply used poor judgment in separating from Michael? He grabbed hold of the back of the seat in front of him as No. 17 pulled away from the curb and eased past the still idle No. 12 before accelerating into the morning traffic.

Peering out the rear window, Marcel shivered involuntarily. Jean-Claude Malfaire had emerged from the train station and was scanning the street. *He's walking toward the bus!* Marcel groaned almost audibly. And still, the No. 12 bus did not move.

No. 17 swayed around a corner in the direction of Grenoble's centre ville, nearly unseating a distracted Marcel. By the time he was able to steady himself, the No. 12 was no longer visible. And suddenly, he felt as if the wind had been knocked out of him. Michael Dreyfus was trapped.

⚜ ⚜ ⚜

Michael watched in horror as the man Marcel had identified as Jean-Claude Malfaire, climbed aboard the No. 12 bus and started down the aisle.

"Your ticket, monsieur," the driver called after him. "I need to see your ticket."

Malfaire turned half-way around. "Milice," he growled, pulling some sort of identification badge from his jacket which he thrust in front of the driver's face. "Satisfied?"

"Of course, Capitaine." The driver looked shaken. "Are

you just looking, or would you like to ride, Capitaine?" he added.

"What difference does it make to you?" Malfaire took a couple more steps up the aisle, scrutinizing the faces of the passengers.

"No difference," said the driver hurriedly. "It's just that I must begin my route now."

"Not until I tell you." Malfaire sounded almost bored as he said it, as though his power were so absolute that there could be no questioning it. He continued pacing slowly toward the rear of the bus, coming ever closer to where Michael sat. *Did he see me with Marcel, somehow?* Michael wondered.

Michael swallowed hard as the dark, piercing gaze of the solidly built Malfaire settled ominously on him, looking him up and down. It was as if the little black marble-like eyes were looking right through him. He felt tiny beads of sweat forming on his upper lip, and he wished for all the world that the moment would end. There was something evil about this man, and the total silence on the bus attested to the fact that others sensed it too.

Malfaire turned suddenly and called out to the driver.

"You can go now," he said.

"Where would you like me to go, Capitaine?" The driver's voice was subdued, a little frightened.

"Where you always go," Malfaire chided him. "Have you forgotten where that is?"

"No, of course not."

Malfaire sat down then, directly across the aisle from Michael, as the driver slipped the bus into gear and pulled away from the curb. Michael tried his best not to look in the captain's direction, but something told him the black marble eyes were still prying, still peering at him. What did the man hope to gain by this? he fumed. If there were something to accuse him of, why not just say it?

Michael wiped the back of his hand across his mouth. Funny, he thought, how the inside of his mouth could feel dry and parched as old newsprint, while his face and neck were damp with perspiration.

At each stop, a few passengers got off the bus, and a few more climbed aboard. The names of the stops all seemed unfamiliar to Michael. He was listening for Place Verdun and little else. The trouble was, unless Malfaire decided to call a halt to the little game he was playing, there would be no opportunity to follow Marcel's instructions once he arrived. He recited the phone number to himself. Did he have it right? He wasn't sure.

He tried to think through what he would do if Malfaire actually attempted to arrest him. But arrest him for what? He hadn't done anything. Nothing that is but to associate with a wanted *maquisard.* He was struggling to think of ways to get rid of the valise when the driver called out the next stop.

"Place Verdun is the end of the line," he announced. "Everyone please exit the bus."

Chapter 27

Place Verdun was in chaos when Marcel arrived. Scores of people, perhaps more, stood or walked along the walkways which cut diagonally across the park at the center of the Place. An even larger crowd lined the sidewalks that formed the park's perimeter, and dozens more were arriving from the side streets by the minute. Shouts went up from various points in the crowd, some angry, some provoking roars of laughter and approval from the crowd, but from where Marcel stood, it was impossible to tell what was being said. All eyes, however, seemed riveted to the Prefecture, the seat of government for the Isère region.

Marcel pressed into the crowd, trying to see what was going on, worried that it was just another obstacle to the rather sketchy plan he had proposed to Michael Dreyfus. There was no way Gilles could meet them here now. The way the crowd was growing, he would never get within blocks of the park.

And how would Michael find a phone in this mess, anyway? Of course, there was a chance he might not show up at all, especially if Malfaire recognized him somehow.

Thinking it would help to at least know what all the fuss was about, Marcel caught an older man by the elbow.

"Excuse me, monsieur," he said as the bearded man spun around to face him. "What's going on? Why is everyone gathering here?"

The old man looked at Marcel as if he had taken leave of his senses. "Where have you been all morning, young man? Haven't you heard?"

"Heard what?"

"The Italians surrendered to the Allies, that's what. They're moving out, going home to Maman." He chuckled. "And good riddance, I say! They can't leave fast enough to suit me."

Marcel was momentarily speechless. The occupation forces leaving? Finally, after ten long months of Italian domination, some good news!

"What's going to happen now?" he asked the bearded man.

"Today, I'm going to go home and uncork a bottle of champagne," said the man, a smile of anticipation on his lips. "Tomorrow," he added, his smile fading to a look of sober reflection, "who knows what tomorrow brings?" And he wandered off among the growing crowds, muttering to himself.

Trying to see what was attracting so much attention in front of the Prefecture, Marcel edged his way forward through the increasingly noisy throng. By now it was easy enough to tell what was being said—insults mostly, directed toward the as-yet-unseen Italians. And much as he was happy to see the occupiers depart, he cringed at the obscenities being hurled in their direction.

A group of four or five youths stood atop a nearby park bench, looking out over the crowd, and cheering wildly as if at a soccer match. Students, no doubt, Marcel figured. The university buildings lined the square opposite the Prefecture and it wouldn't have taken much of a commotion to draw the students away from their classes on a sunny fall morning. He pushed his way to the bench and clambered up beside the others. They hardly seemed to notice, so engrossed were they in the spectacle.

From his new vantage point, Marcel immediately understood what had attracted the crowd. Dozens of Italian soldiers were frantically hauling boxes of files and armloads of supplies out of the Prefecture, depositing them haphazardly into the backs of waiting trucks, then dashing back inside, only to reappear with more. Even from where he stood, more than fifty yards away, most of the soldiers looked hardly more than frightened boys. Ranged along the street in front of the Prefecture, a score of *caribinieri* struggled to keep the taunting crowd at bay, brandishing their machine guns menacingly while their countrymen finished loading the trucks.

From somewhere deep in the crowd, someone hurled a bottle. Arcing its way over the mass of onlookers, it smashed against the hood of a transport truck, spraying two nearby soldiers in a shower of glass shards. As the pair instinctively dove for cover, a split-second of shocked silence descended over the square. It was as if no one had really expected the taunting to turn to violence—any kind of violence. As if some invisible moral line had been crossed, some understanding violated.

Without warning, the silence erupted in a burst of gunfire. Not waiting to see who was firing—or at whom—Marcel plunged from the bench into the swirling, screaming crowd. Fighting to keep his feet amid the pushing and shoving of the terrified onlookers, he began pressing toward the perimeter of the park. Progress was brutally slow, and he found himself struggling against a rising tide of panic. *Focus*, he reminded himself. *Think about what you have to do—nothing else.* And suddenly it dawned on him that what he had to do above all else was to find Michael Dreyfus.

Straining to catch a glimpse of bus No. 12, Marcel wondered if Michael had made it this far. He didn't want to think about what could happen if Malfaire caught him. Michael had to get there! That's all there was to it.

⚜ ⚜ ⚜

As bus No. 12 had approached Place Verdun, a disturbance of some sort had caught Jean-Claude Malfaire's policeman's eye. Keeping one eye on the nervous young man across from him, he noted that the tree-lined park directly ahead was brimming with people. Even the street around the park seemed more like a pedestrian zone than lanes suitable for automobile traffic. Puzzled, he tried to imagine what would bring out such a crowd on a day like this, seeing that it wasn't a holiday. But then, this didn't look much like a holiday crowd.

If this were Lyons, he mused with satisfaction, no such crowd would dare to gather—not with the threat of German troops in the city. But here in Grenoble, the Italians undoubtedly took their usually sloppy approach to things. He guessed that their Latin temperament worked against them when it came to orderliness and organization. It was a wonder they could manage an occupation at all.

Entering the crowded square, the bus driver swung the bus hard to the right, slowly and skillfully weaving his way through the milling throng to the designated bus stop. The passengers, who Malfaire's mere presence had cowed into silence, were suddenly abuzz as the cause of all the commotion became apparent. From the elevated vantage point of the bus windows, it appeared that Italian soldiers were streaming in and out of the Prefecture, loading various items into trucks and other military vehicles. There was an air of urgency in the soldiers' movements, accentuated by the machine-gun-toting *caribinieri* who formed a barrier between them and the crowd.

Momentarily forgetting about the young man across the aisle, Malfaire rose and strode to the front of the bus.

"What is this?" he demanded. "What's going on here?"

But before the driver could answer, the dull murmur of the crowd outside exploded with the sound of gunfire. Outside the bus, chaos reigned as the panicked crowd suddenly scattered in a thousand directions. Inside too, passengers screamed and began bolting for the exits, jostling one another in their rush to get away, very nearly bowling Malfaire off his feet.

Somehow, in all the confusion, Jean-Claude Malfaire lost sight of the tall young man he had been watching so carefully. Leaping from the bus, he looked in every direction, but it was almost impossible to focus on anyone. Everyone was running, seemingly oblivious to where they were going. Some, in fact, seemed to be running in the direction the gunfire had come from. But they all ran.

Patiently scanning the crowds, Malfaire soon had his reward. Few Frenchmen were as tall as the young man who had gotten off the train with Marcel Boussant. And half a block away, his height betrayed him.

With a wink at fate, Jean-Claude Malfaire started after him at a slow trot. When the young man hooked up with Marcel Boussant again, he would be right behind.

The moment the bus doors had come open, Michael had made a break for the street. Like everyone else, he had been frightened by the sound of gunfire, but even a riot, or whatever was going on in the square, seemed worth risking if it meant he would be out from under the watchful eye of Jean-Claude Malfaire. He would have said that the man gave him the creeps, but it was worse than that. There was something sinister about him.

Running away from the bus, trying to keep from being swept away with the crowd, Michael hadn't traveled more than a few dozen yards when he heard his name faintly over the cacophony of crowd noises.

"Michael, wait! Michael!"

Turning toward the sound he saw Marcel Boussant waving frantically, pushing his way through a knot of frightened people.

"Am I glad to see you!" Marcel exclaimed, as he got closer. "Are you all right?"

Michael nodded. He found himself fighting back the urge to grab Marcel and hug him, he was so happy to see a familiar face, one he knew he could trust.

"Come on," Marcel shouted. "Follow me." And he began forging a path through the crowd, running whenever possible, walking when necessary.

It was all Michael could do to keep pace, in spite of his longer legs. Perhaps it was the fact that Marcel knew where he was going. Perhaps Marcel was just more used to walking, growing up on a farm, and all. But before long, they turned onto a side street, rue de la Liberté the sign said, and progress was much faster than before.

"Did he follow you?" Marcel asked, slowing to a brisk walk.

Michael shook his head up and down. "Scared me to death," he admitted.

Marcel looked sympathetic. "I'm sorry about that,

Michael. I expected your bus to take off first. Then it would have been me trying to lead him on a merry chase. I just never thought—"

"It's over, Marcel," Michael said. Cracking a smile he held up his hands. "See? I survived. Stop worrying."

Marcel looked relieved. "Where did you lose him, anyway?"

"I got off the bus when the gunfire started," Michael said. "I didn't see him after that."

"Just now?" Marcel's face went white, and immediately, he twisted around to look behind them. Michael turned as well, only to find that Malfaire was keeping pace with them, a half-block back.

"H-how did he find us here?" he blurted.

"I don't know, but he always seems to know just where I'll be!" Marcel sounded exasperated. "And he never gives up!"

They increased their pace, turning left onto another street, more of an alley, really, and still the *milicien* followed. They turned left again, and yet again, and then right onto rue de la Liberté, retracing their steps back toward the chaos of the Place Verdun. Malfaire remained a half-block behind.

"I guess you never had a chance to call Gilles?" It was more a statement than a question.

Michael shook his head. Under the pressure of Malfaire's scrutiny, he had forgotten everything else.

"Me neither," said Marcel, "but I think it's time we did. How fast can you run?"

"Fast enough, I guess. Where are we going?"

"Someplace safe, I hope," said Marcel, setting a brisk pace. "Just stay with me."

⚜ ⚜ ⚜

Marcel was still breathing heavily as he rang the bell at the gate. Even at this late hour of the morning, the convent of Notre Dame de Sion seemed completely deserted. Of course, some might have preferred to describe it as completely serene, but when no one answered the bell right away, Marcel feared that the nuns were simply gone. But so little of the convent could actually be seen from outside the walls that it was hard to tell what might be going on inside.

"Are you sure this is the place?" Michael asked. He too was out of breath after their race through the streets.

Marcel gave him a sideways glance. Of course this was the right place!

Running had certainly been the right thing to do, Marcel decided, even though he hadn't felt this exhausted in quite a while. Young as they were, he and Michael had easily outdistanced Jean-Claude Malfaire, and within a matter of blocks he had disappeared from view completely. Of course, they had taken a circuitous route just to be on the safe side, but it probably hadn't really been necessary. Marcel wondered if Malfaire were even now sitting on the curb somewhere, wheezing from the exertion.

After several minutes of waiting—and several more rings of the bell—a nun whom Marcel didn't recognize slid open a small panel in the solid wooden gate and peered out at the two of them. She didn't say anything, she just looked from one to the other, as if waiting for someone to explain their business.

"I-uh, I'm looking for Sister Marie-Moïses," Marcel stammered at last.

The panel slid shut without a word from the nun and Marcel could hear her soft footsteps leading away from the gate.

"That was rude! Now what?" Michael seemed perplexed.

"She'll go get Marie-Moïses, I guess," Marcel replied. "But

she's probably taken an oath of silence, so she can't talk to us."

"And this Marie-Moïses, can she talk?"

Marcel laughed. "Oh, yes. She hardly ever stops talking."

Just then the gate creaked open enough so that they could see the silent nun standing half-hidden behind it. She motioned for them to follow her inside. Once they were beyond the gate, the nun closed it and then led the way into what appeared to be a receiving room where she indicated that they should sit. Legs and lungs aching, they were only too happy to comply.

Sparsely furnished with three rude wooden benches and a small table, the room was paneled in wood stained slightly darker than the floor, giving it a somber, austere atmosphere. Light from the only window fell across a Bible which lay open atop the table. Next to the Bible, someone had placed a vase containing a single pink rose, the room's only bit of color.

"Shalom, Marcel. It would appear that the Lord has brought you back to us, after all!" Sister Marie-Moïses burst into the room smiling. "He has obviously answered our prayers for your safety. Are you well?"

"I'm fine." Marcel couldn't help smiling as he rose to greet her. "And you?"

"I couldn't be better." She looked quizzically at Michael.

"Oh, excuse me, Sister. This is my friend Michael." Marcel hadn't really intended to use the word "friend," but now that he had, it really didn't seem like the wrong word.

"I'm very pleased to meet you, er, uh, Mademoiselle." Michael looked a little flustered.

"Sister Marie-Moïses, Michael," she said, holding out her hand, "and it's my pleasure. Welcome to Our Lady of Zion."

Michael shook her hand.

"How are the Lévy children?" Marcel asked. "They're still here, I presume."

"Still here, and doing wonderfully," Marie-Moïses responded enthusiastically. "They are such well-behaved children that we've hardly had any difficulties at all. And Léa, well, she's the favorite of all the sisters, as you might imagine."

"I can definitely imagine it." He hesitated a moment. "May I see them? I mean, if it's not too much trouble."

"Of course! It's no trouble at all. I'll go get them right away. They talk about you all the time, you know." She turned toward the door.

"Before you go, Sister," Marcel said tentatively, "we're in a bit of trouble and we need a favor."

Marie-Moïses turned back around. "Yes?"

"We need to call a friend to come get us. Do you have a telephone?"

"Come with me," she said. "While you're phoning your friend, I'll bring the children down."

"What are children doing in a convent?" asked Michael when Marie-Moïses had gone. The only telephone the nuns owned, it seemed, was here in the small office where she left them.

"I brought them here from Lyons over three months ago," Marcel said. "They're hiding until someone finds them a better place, someplace where they can move around more freely. They're just kids after all."

"Jews?"

"Of course."

"And it doesn't bother them to live in a convent full of Catholic nuns?"

"I don't know if it bothers them or not. Maybe you should ask them. But, frankly, it's better by far than going from place to place, scavenging for food, which is what they had been doing. The oldest one used to steal food from restaurant kitchens to feed his little brother and sister."

"I noticed that the sister said 'shalom' to you when she came in," said Michael. "That's Jewish, not Catholic. Do you suppose she picked that up from the children?"

Marcel picked up the phone. "She's probably been saying it all her life," he said, as he dialed Gilles' number. "She grew up Jewish like all the other nuns here. Their common background is what brought them all together—that and their faith in Jesus, of course."

By the look on Michael's face, it was hard to tell whether he was shocked or merely surprised.

Jean-Claude Malfaire indulged himself in a smile of satisfaction. The fact that Boussant and his friend had taken refuge in a convent was only a temporary setback, and perhaps not much of one at that. In spite of their attempts to throw him off their trail, he was right on top of them. And in spite of the fact that forcing his way onto church property, particularly a convent, would be dimly viewed by all but the most ardent Nazi, the boys were stuck—fenced in. He had made a tour of the walled perimeter of the convent and there was no way out except through the two front gates—one for pedestrians, the other for vehicles. All he had to do was wait for the pair to reemerge. Or, if push came to shove, he could wait until after dark and go in after them.

Tailing the two fugitives had been simple enough. When they began to run, he had merely hailed a passing taxi. So while they were wearing themselves out running across the city, he was comfortably seated in the back seat of a Peugeot, sometimes behind them, sometimes in front, but always with both of them in plain view.

Fifty francs had been enough to convince the taxi driver,

along with one of his friends, to deliver Malfaire's Renault from the train station while he watched the convent. So now he was all set. If the boys stayed, he would go in after them. If they left, he would be right behind them. One way or the other, he promised himself, it would all be over before the clock struck midnight.

Chapter 28

When Gilles Théron arrived at Notre Dame de Sion around two in the afternoon, he was not smiling. Nonetheless, Marcel introduced him briefly to Michael Dreyfus, Sister Marie-Moïses, and the three Lévy children, Théo, Victor, and Léa. Gilles was polite, as always, but obviously had something on his mind.

"Can we talk privately, Marcel?" he asked as soon as the formalities were over.

"Use the office, if you like," Marie-Moïses suggested. "You know the way."

So Marcel picked up his valise and led Gilles into the tiny office. Closing the door behind them, he placed the valise on top of the desk, and then sat down on the edge of it.

"What is it, Gilles?" he asked, as his friend paced back and forth in front of the door. "If it's about the money, I can explain."

"I certainly hope so," Gilles blurted. "When Hervé's courier didn't show up this morning at the usual time, he got worried and called me to see if I knew anything. What's going on? And what are you doing back here?"

Marcel cleared his throat. "Last night when I got back to my hotel, some man I've never seen before was waiting in my room—with a gun. He told me to give him the money. He hinted that he'd already killed the courier, and said that I would have to give him the money from now on. I didn't know what else to do so I ran." Marcel felt a tingle along the back of his neck just thinking about it.

"Did you give him the money?"

"Just enough to distract him, a thousand francs or so, I guess. Anyway, I lost him and eventually ended up spending the night at Michael's hotel. I didn't have anywhere else to go. Everything had always gone so smoothly I had never really thought about any contingency plans."

"Hervé has made this arrangement work for at least six months," said Gilles, shaking his head, "and nothing has ever gone wrong. I wonder what happened. He's going to be pretty disheartened over losing the courier. But I still don't understand what you're doing here."

"You didn't expect me to wait around for the gunman to come find me, did you? I couldn't very well go to the police, and I couldn't just sit there, so I decided to bring the money myself. Besides, I was worried about what Hervé would do when he found out that the courier and the money were missing, and that I was nowhere to be found, either. Don't you think he'd be a little suspicious?"

Consternation clouded Gilles' face. "Why do you think Hervé would suspect you of anything?" he asked.

Marcel looked away. "That's obvious, isn't it, after the way I failed him in prison? He probably wishes he'd never let you talk him into giving me another chance."

"I didn't talk him into anything, Marcel. It was as much Hervé's idea as it was mine."

Marcel hadn't expected that. He looked directly at Gilles again, who was nodding his head as if to confirm what Marcel was thinking. The assignment in Geneva, Hervé's idea? It was hard to believe. Hervé had been angry and disappointed, hadn't he? And with good reason. Marcel certainly didn't blame him for distancing himself. So why would he want Marcel in such a sensitive role? Did it mean that all had been forgiven? It seemed like too much to hope for.

"I'm sorry," he said at last, "I didn't know."

"Look, Marcel, you're too hard on yourself." Gilles put a hand on Marcel's shoulder. "Everyone makes mistakes and Hervé knows that. He's more worried that something has happened to you than about the money." He grinned. "But he would like to get the money. Do you have it with you?"

Marcel relaxed enough to permit a weak smile of his own. "Right here in this valise. Just don't ask how we got it across the border." He handed the leather cases to Gilles.

"We? You mean Michael knows about this too?"

"I needed his help to get this past the border police. He hadn't really intended to travel with me, but one thing led to another and he ended up coming along."

"How are you going to get back to Geneva?"

"The train, I imagine. It's how we got here."

"I'd reconsider that idea, if I were you," said Gilles. "The Italians have left, as you probably noticed. But the Germans are already moving troops into the city to replace them. I imagine they'll have the borders sealed off in a couple of hours. Maybe less."

Marcel's chest suddenly felt tight, as if he were being squeezed by some unseen force. "I guess I wasn't thinking about the Germans." For a moment he pondered the possibilities of such a development, none of which looked positive. Grenoble, it seemed, would soon know the severity of life under the heel of the Nazi boot.

"Has anyone warned the Jews?" he wondered aloud. "With the Italians gone, there may be no place left to hide."

"Not even a convent," Gilles added ominously.

Not even a convent. The thought echoed and reechoed in Marcel's mind. Gilles was right, of course, but what could he do? It would be hard enough to keep clear of the Germans on his own. What was he going to do about Michael Dreyfus and three Jewish children?

⚜ ⚜ ⚜

"Madame Karmazin?" said the voice on the other end of the telephone line, "this is Heinrich Rosen. Forgive me for disturbing you, madame, but I must know if you have seen Michael Dreyfus today."

"Michael? No, I haven't seen him all week." Isabelle was surprised to hear directly from Monsieur Rosen on any matter. But why would he be asking her about Michael? "Is something wrong?"

"Well, madame, I am not quite sure. You see, I returned a day early from my trip to Zurich, and when I called his office they said he had not come to work today. So, I called his hotel and I must confess, I became a little worried. It seems he asked about the train schedule to France last night, then left with another young man early this morning. According to the desk clerk he asked for a taxi to take him and his friend to the Gare de Cornavin. I thought perhaps—"

"I have no idea where he might be, monsieur," Isabelle cut in quickly, her mind racing. "What did his friend look like? Did the hotel clerk say anything about that?" she asked.

"Just that he was young, and that they seemed to know each other, that's all," said Rosen. "Listen, madame, since Michael is not around, I would like to come and speak with you personally. Something has come up—a slight change in our plans—that you should know about, so we can all make some decisions by tomorrow. Will I be disturbing you if I come by around 5 o'clock this afternoon?"

"I suppose that would be all right. You say there's been a change in plans?" Isabelle was curious and suddenly fearful at the same time. Would this, too, end in disappointment after all?

"I'll explain everything when I arrive. *A bientôt,* madame."

"*A bientôt.*" Isabelle was suddenly so preoccupied that she nearly missed the telephone cradle as she hung up the receiver.

"Who was that?" Justine's voice startled her.

"I didn't hear you come in," Isabelle said, recovering her composure. "It was Monsieur Rosen. He can't find Michael anywhere—not at his hotel or at work. For some reason, he thought I'd know where he was."

"Perhaps he just took the day off to go sightseeing. It wouldn't be the first time, you know."

"Someone at the hotel seemed to think he might have gone to the train station with another young man, said he'd asked for a schedule of trains—to France."

"France?" Justine looked more than a little skeptical. "Why would Michael go to France?"

"I can't imagine," Isabelle replied thoughtfully. "And no one seems to know who he went with, either."

"I'm sure it's nothing to worry about," said Justine. "Unfortunately, Monsieur Rosen seems like the kind to fret."

"Oh, that reminds me," Isabelle remembered aloud, and suddenly she felt a chill. "He's coming by about 5 o'clock. He said there had been a slight change of plans, and he wanted to talk to me about it."

"Monsieur Rosen? What do you think it is?"

"I don't know, but he said some kind of decisions need to be made by tomorrow."

"Are you nervous?"

"A little. Why do you ask?"

"Because you're trembling, that's why." Justine's gaze was sympathetic. "Do you want to talk about it?"

"I don't know what good it will do, Justine. We've been over it all before."

"It can't hurt, can it?" There was something reassuring in Justine's smile, something that told Isabelle she could say whatever she needed or wanted to say. And Isabelle wondered if she would ever again have such a good friend.

"What if it doesn't work out?" she began slowly. "The evacuation, I mean. What if Monsieur Rosen says that I can't go, after all?"

"Isabelle, I don't think—"

"But what if he does? I've been thinking a lot about this the past few days, Justine, and I'm beginning to wonder about some things. Like what happens if I can't go to America, after all? And what happens if Marcel goes back to the *maquis* in France? He might, you know, and I can't very well stop him. I can't even ask him not to go. Not after all he risked for me, and certainly not after the way he's been so understanding about this evacuation plan."

"You're asking good questions, Isabelle." Justine's brow furrowed just a little. "Have you reached any conclusions?"

"That's just it, Justine. I really don't know what to do. What I do know is that I don't want to keep living in fear. But I feel as if I've been running forever, and I don't know how to stop."

"Are you running to something or away from something?"

"Sometimes I think I'm just running away from disappointment," Isabelle admitted. "The other night, I was thinking about all the reasons I want to go to America. Most of them have to do with all the hardships I've known. I don't like pain and loss and disappointment I guess, and I want a future where I can avoid them as much as possible."

"We all do, Isabelle, every one of us, even though most of us haven't suffered nearly as much as you have. But we don't control the future."

"That's just it. What if I go to America, and I end up being just as disappointed there as I have been here? Where will I go then? There will be no place left to run." An emptiness settled over Isabelle at the mere idea that she might never really be happy. And talking about it didn't seem to be helping much.

Justine too seemed to sense the void. "Isabelle," she said tenderly, "you've got to stop running before you get to America. I hear it's a wonderful place, but it is just a place, after all. It doesn't have the power to solve your problems. Only God can do that. And He can only do that if you let Him."

"I want to, Justine, I really do, but I can't seem to understand how. It's so hard. Please, help me understand."

Justine was quiet for a moment. "This may not be easy for you, Isabelle," she said at length. "It may not even be what you want to hear."

"Why, because I'm a Jew and you're a Christian?" Isabelle asked without rancor. "Perhaps you should let me decide for myself."

"All right. The first few days after you came to Switzerland, you used to gaze at the Swiss flag whenever you were near one, almost as if you revered it. There was a time or two I thought you might actually kiss it."

"I remember," said Isabelle, sheepishly. "It seems almost

ridiculous, now. I guess I was rather enamored with it."

"Can you describe it, and what it represented?"

"Of course," said Isabelle. "It's a white cross on a field of red. And for me, it symbolized peace, a refuge, freedom from fear."

"And has it lived up to what you expected? Are you experiencing the kind of peace and security you'd hoped for?"

Isabelle didn't answer. The answer had been obvious for months to anyone who knew her.

"Isabelle," Justine continued, her eyes shining, "a nation, no matter what its flag, can offer you nothing more than temporary peace and external freedoms, and even then its power is limited."

"What are you saying?"

"That I think you want the kind of peace that lasts. You want a freedom that inhabits your very being, that doesn't depend on circumstances. And it's no wonder you've been disappointed. The Swiss cross is all well and good. But it's a very pale image of the cross that stood on a hill outside Jerusalem nearly 2,000 years ago. Perhaps you've been looking to the wrong one for help."

Isabelle sat in silence, letting the words sink in. Justine had been right; this wasn't going to be easy, no matter what choices she made.

⚜ ⚜ ⚜

When the convent gates began to swing inward for the second time that afternoon, Jean-Claude Malfaire could feel all his senses begin to function on high alert. Waiting was always the hardest part. He hadn't actually been sleeping, but he had trained himself over the years to conserve energy during the lulls, so that he could be fully energized when needed.

The shiny black Citroën that had entered the gates three hours ago was slowly gliding back out onto the street. This time, however, the driver had been joined by two other men, the very pair he had followed from the Place Verdun. Marcel Boussant was seated in the front passenger seat, while the tall one was alone in the back.

Malfaire waited until the Citroën had traveled to the end of the block before turning on the ignition in his own Renault. Then he pulled carefully away from the curb and followed at a discreet distance. If he played his cards right, this whole affair could be ended soon, and he could get back to placating the incompetent Colonel du Puy and his Gestapo handlers. More importantly, however, he could settle his months-old score, once and for all, with the impudent and far too lucky Marcel Boussant.

The Citroën driver didn't seem to be in a big hurry, maintaining his speed at or below the limit as he wound his way through the back streets of Grenoble. Traffic was light and the city unusually calm this afternoon, especially compared to the morning's turmoil over the chaotic retreat of the Italians, and within minutes the sleek black sedan had escaped the city limits. Malfaire held back even farther, since the open road made him far more vulnerable to detection. There were so few cars on the road here, however, that keeping the Citroën in sight was not at all difficult.

Winding through the hamlets of Gières and Murianette, it began to dawn on Malfaire that Marcel Boussant was headed for the village of Domène and home. He thought about all the criminals he had arrested over the course of his career. In the final analysis, they had all made his job easier by making stupid, predictable mistakes—mistakes just like young Boussant was about to make.

Malfaire smiled. His moment of revenge was at hand.

⚜ ⚜ ⚜

"Turn right at the top of the rise," Marcel instructed, as Gilles guided his father's Citroën sedan along Domène's serpentine main street.

"I hope you know what you're doing," said Michael Dreyfus from his seat in the back. "I want to get back in one piece."

"This is where I grew up, Michael. Believe me, I know my way around. If the Renault is following us, we'll lose it before long."

Gilles steered the car to the right where the road crested a rise in the center of town, and headed up the hill past the public fountain and the paper mill. There the road angled sharply to the left as it ascended steeply along the side of the foothills overlooking Domène. The view was spectacular, although broken from time to time by the trees that lined the two-lane blacktop.

Looking down on the village from above, Michael's heart sank as he watched the Renault approaching the fountain they had just passed. "He's following us, all right," he said. "How did he know where to find us?"

"It doesn't really matter now." Gilles' voice was amazingly calm even as he urged the car to more speed up the hill. "What matters now is that we don't let him catch us."

"Check on the *gosses,* Michael," said Marcel. "I want to make sure they're all right before we go any farther."

Michael pulled the modified center section of the upholstered seat back forward, revealing an opening leading to the Citroën's trunk. Inside, amid a mound of blankets and pillows, lay the three Lévy children.

"Are you all right back there?" Michael called to make himself heard over the road noises.

"I think so," twelve-year-old Théo shouted back. "How much longer do we have to stay here?"

"It shouldn't be long now, and then you can come up here with me." Michael hoped he was more convincing than he felt. With a car on their trail, who knew just how long it would be before it would be safe to have the children out in the open. Of course, they couldn't leave them back there for too long. "Tell you what," he called to Théo, "I'll leave this open for a while. How will that be?"

They had decided to put the children out of view simply to avoid the suspicion that might be aroused by the sight of three men traveling with three children. Out in the country, where there was less chance of being stopped, however, they wouldn't have to be so careful. Théo had seemed to understand, and Victor and Léa had gone along with the idea. Whether they approved or not was hard to tell.

After a series of sharp turns, the road to Revel had straightened out somewhat, though it continued to rise rapidly. Looking out the rear window, Michael caught sight of the Renault again. This time, however, it was much closer than before.

Leaning forward so as not to be overheard by the children, he murmured, "Do you see that?"

Marcel nodded as Gilles glanced in the rearview mirror.

"Take a left at the fork up ahead," said Marcel, then to Michael he added, "we're coming to Revel. It's only a tiny village, but it's the biggest one we'll see for a while. By the way," he added with a thin smile, "I forgot to point it out, but my farm was just a half-mile back. I'm sorry I couldn't invite you in."

Michael placed a hand on his shoulder. "Next time I'm through here, I'll stop in for a very long visit. I promise." He realized as he said it that he wasn't kidding. He really would enjoy a lingering, unpressured conversation with Marcel. After all, they would have so much to talk about. At the moment, however, the prospect of returning didn't seem likely. And the closer the Renault got, the less likely it seemed.

Chapter 29

The road was called the Balcone des Belledonnes, and as its name implied, it wound its way along the edge of the uneven foothills, offering an unparalleled view the length of the Gresivaudan Valley. Across the valley the near-vertical cliffs of the Chartreuse Mountains stretched from St. Eynard to the towering Dent de Crolles, giving the impression of an impregnable fortress, a bulwark against the encroaching hills.

Marcel never failed to marvel at this sight, much as he was accustomed to it, and today was no exception. Today, in fact, he desperately needed the momentary distraction of this panorama of grace and power in the face of growing helplessness.

Gilles was obviously pushing the powerful Citroën as fast as possible under the circumstances, as the squeal of tires attested. But the added weight of five passengers was proving a disadvantage in the race with the Renault. Fortunately, the twisting two-lane road had few straightaways, and thus far Gilles had managed to outmaneuver his pursuer. How much longer he could continue to do so was anybody's guess.

Marcel alternated between scanning the road in front and keeping a watchful eye on the driver of the Renault. Something urgent in his gut told Marcel that what he feared most was indeed coming to pass, yet he dared not alarm the others even further by voicing that fear. *If only the children were safe*, he thought, his mind reeling at the very idea that they—or even Gilles or Michael—should share his fate. And unarmed, he was powerless to protect any of them.

By himself, Marcel knew he might stand no better chance of survival. But then the risk of attempting the impossible would be his alone.

"Is he still gaining?" asked Gilles, unable to take his eyes off the narrow road ahead. Beads of sweat had appeared on his forehead.

"I'm afraid so," Marcel replied, trying to keep his voice low so as not to alarm the children. "Are you all right?"

"I'd be a lot better if I could get a little more distance on him. It's still a long way to Pontcharra, isn't it?" Gilles had phoned Hervé Chassin from the convent and the *maquis* leader was sending someone to meet them in the crossroads town of Pontcharra who would then take the five passengers on to the border.

"Maybe not all that far," suggested Marcel, hopefully. "If we can just stay ahead—"

His voice was lost in the report of a gun and simultaneous shattering of glass, as the rearview mirror on his side of the car disappeared.

"Get the kids up here on the floor!" he yelled to Michael, who had instinctively ducked his head below the level of the rear window. Michael stared uncomprehendingly back at him.

"Another bullet might pierce the trunk. If they're on the floorboards between the seats they're less likely to get hurt."

Understanding at last, Michael reached back behind the seat cushions and began pulling the frightened children forward. Clambering wide-eyed over the seat and onto the floor, they huddled out of sight under their blankets as Michael closed the unconventional seat back.

Marcel, his racing heart beating a tattoo on his ribcage, raised his head slightly to peer over the back of his seat at the approaching Renault. This time the car was so close there was no mistaking the crazed visage of Jean-Claude Malfaire, his right hand plying the steering wheel, a semiautomatic pistol clutched in his left. *Dear God, protect us!* Marcel breathed, knowing full well that it was the only hope they had left.

For a long moment, nothing happened. The only sounds were the high-pitched whining of the Citroën's engine, and the shriek of the tires as Gilles pushed them to the limits of their durability on each succeeding curve in the road.

The swaying motion never seemed to cease, leaving Marcel with the impression of being perpetually off-balance. He looked across to see Gilles, crouched as low as he dared, furiously cranking the steering wheel first one way and then the other. Making a poor target for the obsessed Malfaire was one thing, but a little too much sway, Marcel knew, would send the car careening out of control, over the edge and into the valley below. Malfaire would get what he wanted without firing another shot. Marcel hoped Gilles knew what he was doing.

The impact was so sudden that no one had time to prepare for it, least of all Marcel. Crouched down as he was, he was thrown forward, his right shoulder slamming into the dashboard as the Renault butted them from behind. Tires and children screamed in unison and out of the corner of his eye he could see Gilles fighting for control as the Citroën threatened to skid off the road.

Clutching his throbbing shoulder, Marcel dared a quick look out the rear window. Malfaire was closing on them again, and his face was plainly visible this time, his lips curling into a wolfish grin.

"Here he comes again!" Marcel yelled. "Brace yourselves!" He barely had time to heed his own advice before the next grinding blow rocked the Citroën.

"We can't take many more like that," Gilles muttered between clenched teeth.

"At least he's not shooting at us." Marcel almost regretted saying so, wondering how long it would be before Malfaire would try again. It had to be clear to him by now that they were not able to outrun him. Perhaps he was just toying with them. And if what he wanted was to terrorize them, he was certainly succeeding.

"Isn't there anything we can do?" asked Michael from the back. "We can't just let him keep smashing us!"

"I'm doing everything I can!" Gilles was irritated. "If we had something to shoot with we could at least force him to keep his distance."

"Maybe we could throw something at him, distract him a little," offered Marcel, an idea suddenly forming in his head. "Isn't there a tire iron in the trunk?"

"I'll get it," said Théo, speaking up for the first time. "I know right where it is."

"It's too dangerous. What if we get rammed again while you're back there?" Marcel didn't like the idea at all.

"Think about it, Marcel," said Gilles. "You and Michael can't very well squeeze back there, and it would at least give us something to try."

Marcel didn't move, but he could hear the seat back being lowered and Théo scrambling into the trunk.

"I've got it!" Marcel heard a moment later, just a split-second before the interior of the car exploded in flying glass. Instinctively, he closed his eyes and buried his head in his arms. He never heard the sound of a gun, but the tinkling of falling glass shards seemed to go on and on, as though they were falling from somewhere high in the sky.

When at last he mustered the courage to peek over the seat back, he saw the pursuing Renault through a gaping hole in the rear window. What little glass was left looked as though it were only hanging in place by the slenderest of threads. The rest was scattered everywhere. Michael looked stunned, his face and hands marked with tiny cuts that were beginning to seep red. Théo, apparently unharmed, looked out from the protection of the trunk, while Léa and Victor remained wrapped in blankets on the floor.

Marcel swept the glass from the back of the seat and lunged back to grasp the tire iron that Théo held out for the taking. Twisting back into his seat, he rolled the side window down. Without a word, he took careful aim and hurled the iron toward the Renault, now just a half dozen yards behind.

Malfaire swerved at the last minute and the spinning iron missed its mark, bouncing crazily but harmlessly on the pavement. But in the maneuver, the Renault began skidding violently sideways. Marcel watched in horrified fascination as the car rocked wildly, pitched up on two wheels, then tumbled over onto its roof. Instead of settling there, however, it continued to roll over another full turn, slowly grinding and twisting as if in a dream, before finally reaching the edge of the road and tumbling from view.

Gilles brought the battered Citroën to a stop, and he and Marcel jumped out, racing to the edge of the precipice. On the rocks 200 feet below them, Malfaire's car, by now a barely recognizable tangle of metal, had finally come to rest. Almost as if in a parting gesture, a single puff of black smoke rose from the wreckage, ascending reluctantly until it dissipated in the late afternoon sun.

The descent into Pontcharra had been uneventful, by anyone's standards. Shaken by the events of the past hour, no one in the Citroën had found much to talk about, least of all the children. Théo could hardly believe they had all survived.

The car wasn't in very good shape. Everyone had climbed out for a look at the destroyed Renault and then the men had quickly cleaned up all the loose glass they could. Gilles had even removed all the sharp pieces that remained in the rear window, just so they wouldn't look so conspicuous, he said.

Théo sure felt conspicuous, sitting next to Michael, whose face and hands were covered in scratches and cuts from the flying glass, and riding in a car with no back window, a rear bumper that was mashed against the car body, and a missing outside mirror. It was a good thing that they were going to change cars in Pontcharra. Hopefully, the rest of the trip would be a little less exciting.

He gazed at Victor and Léa, still clutching her doll, and wondered if they would ever sleep without nightmares again.

The doors to the barn opened as Marcel and his companions arrived on the small farm near Pontcharra, and a man he did not know motioned them inside. Gilles guided the damaged Citroën alongside two other cars that occupied the barn's dusky interior. Then the unknown man closed the doors behind them, leaving them momentarily in a sort of twilight.

Someone snapped on an overhead lamp a few seconds later, and harsh light flooded the center of the barn as the frazzled travelers exited the car.

To Marcel's astonishment, Hervé Chassin and his wife, Babette, emerged from the shadows to greet them. But while a part of him was pleased that they were there in person, this was a meeting he had been dreading. How could he ever make things right with Hervé?

"It's good to see you, *mon brave*," said the stocky Hervé, gripping Marcel's hand. "You had us worried there for a while. We thought something had happened to you."

Marcel lowered his eyes. "Look, Hervé, I'm sorry for what happened in the prison. I didn't know—"

"Hey, forget it, let it go. You had no way of knowing."

Marcel looked into the older man's face where a reassuring smile confirmed the longed-for words. Such a rush of relief swept over him that he could feel his eyes tear up. He didn't dare say anything for fear that he would be overcome with emotion. Somewhere deep inside, he could feel a dam burst, as if all his pent-up fear and anxiety had been released by Hervé's forgiveness. In human terms, he knew such an equation made little sense. But then, it had long been clear to him that humans don't always have the best perspective on things.

"You'd better rest here a bit before going over the fence," Babette whispered to Marcel. "Give me a few minutes to scout around."

He nodded agreement and let Léa slide down off his back. A few feet away, Michael followed suit, setting Victor on a tree stump before slumping against it himself. Théo was already seated on the ground nearby, obviously exhausted from the torturous trek they had just completed. Only the sound of their breathing and the faint rustling of leaves could be heard as Babette disappeared into the trees.

It was nearly midnight, a full two hours since they had left Babette's car. Clouds had rolled in during the early evening hours, obscuring the moon—and much of the landscape—and the threat of rain hung palpably in the cool night air. Switzerland, invisible on the other side of the clearing, seemed a very long way off.

The trip from Pontcharra to this secluded area northeast of Annemasse had taken far longer than Marcel had hoped, simply because they hadn't wanted to risk encountering any German checkpoints. Forced to avoid all the main roads and towns, they traveled miles out of their way in the process. Fortunately, Babette had prepared for this, and seemed to know exactly which routes to take and which to avoid.

Worse than all the detours, however, was having to leave the car so far from the frontier. German border patrols, just getting used to the territory, were likely to be extra cautious, Babette had warned, so she had insisted that the car be abandoned far enough away that it would attract no undue attention.

Théo, of course, managed to make the entire trek on his own, though not without stopping to rest from time to time. But Marcel and Michael had been obliged to carry the two younger children on their backs a good deal of the way. Now the five sat huddled at the edge of the clearing that marked the Franco-Swiss frontier.

It was impossible to tell what was going through the others' minds, but Marcel couldn't help but think about the last time he had waited in such a place. It hadn't been far from here, as nearly as he could tell, yet it had seemed much different. Snow had blanketed the clearing that first time, as Isabelle prepared to cross. Taking her in his arms, he had kissed her and then released her to begin the last dangerous leg of her journey to freedom. He could still see her crawling across the snow, Alexandre strapped to her back.

Suddenly, Marcel caught himself looking anxiously around, as if expecting Jean-Claude Malfaire to interfere as he had that first time. He shuddered then at the recollection of today's earlier disaster that insured the inspector-turned-*milicien* would never terrorize him or anyone else, ever again. Still, he knew it would be a long time before he would be able to stop thinking about him.

But even with Malfaire dead, there were a million ways for tonight's scheme to turn to disaster. There was no telling how frightened the children were, for one thing, or how they would react under pressure. And the Germans would certainly make the crossing more difficult than had the Italian *caribinieri*. Marcel was anxious for the night to be over, to wake up and find that he was safe in Geneva.

The crunch of dried leaves announced Babette's return, and Marcel rose to meet her.

"I can't tell where all the guards are," Babette confided, "but if you don't get started soon, it may be too late. They've already begun to string new wire on this side of the stream." She tugged at his sleeve, pulling him a few steps away from the others. "I don't want to frighten the children any more than necessary," she whispered, "but I'm pretty sure I heard dogs."

All of a sudden, Marcel had to fight the urge to call the whole thing off.

Michael Dreyfus couldn't decide which was more frightening: the wild car ride he had endured earlier in the day, or the moment he was living right now. Scared as he had been, crouched in the back seat of the careening Citroën, he was pretty sure that stealing across an open field patrolled by armed Nazi guards and their dogs was at least as bad. And his pounding pulse seemed to indicate the same.

Babette led the way across the open field. She would stay with them as far as the stream, before turning back to make good her own escape. Crouching low as she had instructed, Michael stayed as close to her as he could, while holding on to Victor's hand. Théo followed not far behind, while Marcel and Léa brought up the rear.

A single raindrop splatted against Michael's face, and then another. *Blast!* he fumed silently. It was hard enough to see more than a few feet ahead as it was. Rain would only make it worse. But in spite of his silent protests, more drops continued to find their way to the ground, quickly becoming a steady, drumming shower. Michael tugged Victor close beside him, in a vain effort to keep the boy from getting completely soaked.

Babette stopped just a few feet ahead of him, and as he closed the gap between them, his heart sank. She was examining what looked like an impossible tangle of barbed wire, trying to find a way through. The rain coursed down his face and neck, and he could feel his clothes beginning to stick to his back. This is crazy! he murmured to himself. We'll never get through this hopeless mess.

"Doesn't look good, does it?" Marcel whispered behind him.

Michael turned to see that all the others looked as drenched as he felt. "What are we going to do?" he asked. "We'll never get through this."

"There's no other way." Marcel shrugged. "We'll have to figure out something."

Babette rejoined them, her short hair plastered to her head, droplets of water clinging to each strand. "I think I see a way you can get through, but it won't be easy," she said in a low voice. "Michael, why don't you go first, then the children can follow you. Marcel, you make sure everyone gets through safely, then run for it. Once you make it across the stream you should be all right."

Michael froze. This was it. In a moment they would be on their own in a wet, dark, jagged jumble of steel wire, and it was up to him to lead them through. He wanted to go back. He didn't need to do this, after all. He had a Swiss passport. He worked for the International Committee of the Red Cross. He could simply hike to the nearest town and walk across into Switzerland. Oh, he would have some explaining to do, all right, maybe a lot of explaining. But he could do it.

"Michael. Michael!" Marcel's hand was on his shoulder. "Are you all right?"

Michael didn't answer. All he could see were the rain-soaked faces of the three Lévy children staring up at him. Of course he didn't have to go this way, he told himself. But they did. He looked at each desperate face. They had no other way out. And he couldn't very well leave Marcel to take care of them all alone.

"Where do I start?" he asked Babette. He knew he had to do it.

She smiled wanly through the falling rain and gripped his arm. "This way," she replied. "And please, be careful."

What Babette had discovered, as it turned out, was the place where two separate coils of wire had been hastily twisted together. Wriggling his way on his back along the muddy ground, Michael was able to avoid most of the razor-sharp barbs, and sooner than he had thought possible he was crawling out on the other side. Holding the last few strands of wire out of the way, he waited and watched as first Victor and then

Théo slithered under the tangled barrier and into the open field beyond.

He watched as Marcel appeared to coax Léa a bit before she seemed willing to follow. Then reluctantly, she lay down on her back and began to slowly worm her way through, just as she had seen her brothers do.

"*Allez*, Léa! You can make it!" whispered Théo from the other side.

It was taking her twice as long as the others.

"Michael!" Marcel rasped. "On your left!"

Michael whirled to look in the direction indicated, only to see two lights in the murky distance—two lights that seemed to draw nearer even as he watched. Guards? It had to be, the way the lights moved. He felt a violent chill wrack his body.

"Aiieee!" Léa wailed suddenly.

Michael turned back to see that one of the wires he had been holding had slipped from his grasp and tangled itself in Léa's rain-soaked hair. She was stuck, and no amount of her own efforts seemed to do anything but make the situation worse.

With Théo holding the wires, Michael found he could reach Léa, but nothing he tried would undo her hair from the barbed metal that bound it. He kept glancing in the direction of the lights, fighting down the panic that rose each time he noticed they were nearer than before.

"I'm coming to help you, Léa. Just lie still." Marcel's hoarse voice sounded reassuring as he began to squirm under the wires.

Michael backed away, knowing that too many bodies in the same location would probably result in someone else getting stuck. The rain was coming down harder than before, forming little pools in every slight depression, making the ground slick and soggy. It was also making it harder to see.

Marcel was beside Léa now, comforting her, trying to calm her. His fingers plied the offending wire. He twisted the locks of her hair. But he seemed to fare no better than Michael had. Reaching into his pocket, he withdrew a small penknife, and as Léa's eyes widened in fear, he simply cut off the hair that held her to the wire.

"Pull her out and go!" It was a command, not the request of a friend.

Still, Michael hesitated. He couldn't just leave him here.

"Go!" Marcel insisted. "I'll be right behind you," and as he said it he pushed the still-frightened Léa ahead of him and under the last of the wires.

Grabbing her hand, Michael pulled her all the way out, picked her up, and with the boys in tow, started out across the field. Glancing back he saw Marcel struggling to clear the last of the wires.

Heading in the general direction Babette had indicated before her departure, Michael ran blindly, slogging across the field as fast as he could. He stumbled on some loose rocks, but managed to keep his balance and slow down, just before his feet plunged into cold water over his ankles. The stream. It had to be the stream!

Shifting Léa up onto his back, he took hold of Victor's hand and waded out into the swift-moving stream. Keeping just downstream from Théo, in case the boy should fall, he moved steadily but slowly into the deeper water. The current tugged at him, and when Victor lost his footing, it was all he could do to hang on without going down himself.

Still he pushed on, until the water was lapping around his waist. A dog barked somewhere behind them, and then another, followed by shouting voices. Michael tried to increase his pace, but Victor simply couldn't go any faster in the current. Théo, abandoning all caution, plunged into the water headfirst and began to swim. Léa tightened her death grip around Michael's neck and started to sob.

In the midst of all the frenzy, Michael found himself in shallow water again. A few tottering steps and he and the Lévy children were clambering out of the creek bed onto soggy grass. Yet another dozen yards and they had reached a simple barbed wire fence. Here, at last, as the children climbed easily through to the Swiss side, he stopped to listen for signs that Marcel wasn't far behind.

What he heard were two brief machine-gun bursts, followed by a triumphant shout—in German.

Chapter 30

The sky was only hinting at dawn when Marcel, trembling violently from the wet and cold, dragged himself the last few yards to the door of an old, rundown farmhouse. He had no idea where he was, nor how long he had been walking. Torn and mud-soaked, his clothes hung on him like rags. Clutching his left side with both hands, blood oozing from between his fingers, he was too weak to pay much heed to the wary mongrel that circled him, growling.

The door to the house opened a crack, spilling a sliver of light into the yard, and someone yelled at the dog, to no avail. A second later, the door opened wider, and Marcel found himself standing in a pool of light, momentarily blinded.

"What in— Who are you? What do you want?" The voice was gruff, maybe a little frightened, but it didn't seem to belong to anyone.

Marcel tried to reply, to take a step forward. Something

didn't seem quite right. Vaguely aware of losing his balance, he marveled at how quickly the ground rose to meet him. The pain only lasted a split-second before everything turned silent and dark.

⚜ ⚜ ⚜

Théo Lévy fumbled nervously with the buttons on the sleeves of his shirt, and tried not to think about how poorly his clothes fit as Michael Dreyfus knocked on the door of the house on Boulevard St. Georges. The border police had scrounged dry clothes for him and Léa and Victor before releasing them to Michael's care. It had been wonderful to get out of the wet, muddy things they had worn across the border, but he was afraid they all looked ridiculous. He wished he had his old clothes back. Especially since the house looked like it belonged to people as rich as Papa and Maman.

"Hello, Isabelle," said Michael to the woman who answered the door. "I'm sorry for the disruption, but these poor *gosses* need something to eat, and I was wondering—"

"Michael, what happened to your face? Are you all right?"

"It's nothing. Just some scratches from a car accident. I'll tell you all about it later. May we come in?"

"Oh, I'm sorry! Please, come on in," the woman exclaimed, as she ushered them into the entry. The inside of the house looked even nicer than the outside. And big too.

"Who are they? Where did you find them?" Théo heard her whisper, as they were ushered inside.

"Let me introduce you to Théo, Victor, and Léa Lévy. They've just come over from France. Children, this is Madame Isabelle Karmazin."

Madame? She looked too young to be married, even though she was pretty enough.

"Did I hear that right?" interrupted another woman, a little older than Isabelle and almost as pretty. "You came over the border just last night?" she asked, looking the children over from head to toe. "Why, you must be starved. Come in the dining room while I fix you something to eat."

That sounded good to Théo, and a quick look at his siblings confirmed that it was unanimous. The border police had given them a little bread and coffee, but that had been hours ago.

"How did they get past the patrols?" Isabelle asked Michael as they all trooped into the dining room.

"Well, they *didn't* exactly," Michael began sheepishly. "Not on this side, anyway. But I told the police I had found the children wandering in the woods. I showed them my Red Cross papers, and said I was authorized to take charge of them. They apparently didn't want to be bothered, and they let me take them."

"You mean you *didn't* find them on this side of the border?"

"It's a long story, Justine," said Michael. "Perhaps we can talk about it another time."

Théo bit his lip. Michael had made him promise not to tell anyone that he had accompanied them from the French side.

"Well, thank God they didn't have to go to one of those awful camps." Justine shook her head in disgust. "Have you seen what they're like?"

"Unfortunately, yes," Michael replied. "That's why I lied to the police."

"What are you going to do now?" asked Isabelle. "Surely you aren't thinking of taking care of them yourself. You live in a hotel room. And besides, you won't even be here much longer."

Michael glanced at the children, then back at Isabelle, and

finally at Justine. "I-I was hoping maybe—could we talk in the other room?"

Théo usually found it annoying when adults had to talk in another room. Today, however, he was so busy eating the bread and chocolate that Justine had served, that he really didn't mind that much. But he couldn't help but notice the way Justine kept smiling at the three of them.

⚜ ⚜ ⚜

"We need to talk, Isabelle." Michael seemed awfully somber for someone who had just rescued three children from the Nazis and then arranged for a well-to-do Swiss couple to care for them.

"I know," Isabelle said quietly. "I've already talked to Monsieur Rosen. It's all right, Michael. In fact, I made up my mind not to go before he came over."

Michael looked puzzled. "Talked to Rosen? About what?"

"You don't know yet? The port of Genoa has been occupied by the Germans. They've seized the boats. The evacuation is off."

Michael looked stunned, staring past Isabelle as if she weren't even there. For a full minute, he said nothing. Then, suddenly animated, he slammed his fist down on the arm of his chair.

"I can't believe it! Thirty thousand people could have been—no, should have been saved! And all this time the American and British bureaucrats were just dragging their feet." He fell into a brooding silence, then suddenly looked at Isabelle again. "Did I hear you say you had already decided not to go? Why?"

"Because I realized I would be going for all the wrong reasons, Michael. I finally realized that I can't keep running away.

And that's what I would have been doing by going to America."

Michael lowered his head, but Isabelle thought she detected a tear in his eye.

"Please, Michael, it's nothing against you, it's just that—"

He held up a hand to silence her. "I know that you could never be happy going away with me. I don't understand why, exactly, but I've known it for some time, now," he said slowly, deliberately. "I-I know you love Marcel—and that's why I wanted to talk to you." He paused, grimacing.

"What do you mean? What are you talking about?" She really didn't understand what he was trying to say.

"Marcel was with me in France, Isabelle. It's a long story, but the children were friends of his. We were bringing them across the border together. We ran into some trouble, there were gunshots, and he—he didn't make it. I'm so sorry." Michael dropped his head into his hands and began to weep.

Isabelle felt as though her heart had been torn into tiny pieces and then crushed underfoot. *It can't be! It can't be!* her mind screamed, but her heart was too broken to hear. And little by little, a leaden numbness settled over her whole being like a heavy winter fog.

Somewhere in the background the phone was ringing, but Isabelle was too despondent to care.

⚜ ⚜ ⚜

Marcel Boussant could feel himself flying, soaring up and up toward the blinding brightness that seemed to hover just out of his reach. His body glowed with an eerie warmth, unlike anything he had experienced before. His limbs were bound tightly to his body in a kind of cocoon, almost a shroud, so that he could not move them even if he had wanted to. He had no desire to do so. Every vague sensation felt warm and soft and pleasant.

"Marcel."

Voices were calling him, beckoning him higher and higher toward the brightness.

"Marcel, open your eyes."

Angel voices, bidding him to look into the brightness.

"Marcel, it's me. Isabelle."

Isabelle? He tried to smile. Somehow, he had known she would be here too. He just hadn't expected her to meet him on arrival.

He blinked his eyes open for a split second, but the brightness forced them closed again.

"You opened your eyes. Oh, thank God you opened your eyes!"

He tried again to open his eyes, and this time the brightness wasn't quite so painful. He blinked, then blinked again. And there, looking down on him was the face of an angel, if ever he saw one.

"Marcel, can you hear me? Squeeze my hand if you can hear me."

He squeezed one hand and then the other. He squeezed both hands—just to make sure. And for the first time, he felt pain, searing pain that began on his left side and radiated throughout his body. Wincing, he nearly closed his eyes again, but he forced them to remain open, afraid he would lose contact with the angelic creature that held him by the hand.

"You're going to be all right, Marcel, but you need to lie still. The doctor said they found you just in time."

They found me? he wondered. *Who found me?* He vaguely remembered hearing gunfire and dogs barking. And then the stream. Had he fallen into the water, or had he jumped in? After that, he only remembered floating toward the light.

"Wh-where—" He struggled to form the words. His mouth felt and tasted like the inside of an old shoe.

"You're in the hospital. Robert brought you here after the people who found you called him. Apparently you gave them his name before you lost consciousness. Do you remember?"

He shook his head slowly. The fog was beginning to clear, and he had a vague recollection of someone carrying him into a house. Obviously, he must have said something to someone or he wouldn't be looking into Isabelle's face just now, but he couldnt' remember telling anyone anything, much less Robert's name.

"Michael?" Images continued to come back to him—the barbed wire, the dogs, the guards, then the water, and hours of darkness. "The children?"

"They're all safe. Justine and Robert are going to keep the children for the time being. They have plenty of room, and Justine is so excited about it." She paused and took a deep breath. "Michael is coming by later to say good-bye. He was thrilled to hear you were alive, Marcel. He thought you'd been killed." Then she added, "He's going back home at the end of the week."

"Home? What do you mean?"

"America. He's going back to New York."

"But what about your evacuation?" Marcel tried to sit up and was immediately rewarded with a spasm of pain in his side. Isabelle leaned over him and placed her hands firmly on his shoulders.

"You've got to lie still, or you'll be here a lot longer than either of us wants," she scolded gently. Her expression grew serious. "There's not going to be any evacuation. It's all been called off. And even if it were still on, I made up my mind not to go."

"You made up your—" Marcel began, when a glimmer of

something metallic caught his eye. At first he thought his eyes were deceiving him. But on closer inspection, he could see that Isabelle was wearing a chain around her neck—a woven strand of gold he had never noticed before. And when he saw the tiny cross suspended from that chain, he thought his heart would stop.

Isabelle, noticing that he was staring at it, took the cross in her fingers and carefully touched it to her lips. "A gift from Justine," she murmured, "to commemorate something else I decided." And then she smiled. "It's why I'm not running away anymore."

Unable to speak, Marcel just smiled back at her. And for a moment, he could feel no pain at all.

Still smiling, Isabelle leaned closer. "I love you, Marcel Boussant," she breathed, her gray-green eyes clear and intense, "and I want you to know I'm staying right here."

And then she kissed him—a tender, lingering kiss, her warm lips full of promise as they pressed against his own. If only for a moment, all the pain and exhaustion, all the uncertainties, melted away. And in their place, a deep gratitude washed over him for a thousand answered prayers, a dream come true, a whole new life.

The moment had to end, of course, and all too soon, as far as Marcel was concerned. He knew this time, however, that it marked the beginning of something that would bloom and grow for years to come. And he was equally certain that, in spite of all they had been through, and all they would yet face, life with Isabelle Karmazin would be the next best thing to heaven.

Historical Note

For nearly 30,000 European Jews, escaping into neutral Switzerland meant that they would survive the war years. But fearing an unmanageable flood of refugees, the Swiss instituted tight controls, including military-style housing compounds, some little better than concentration camps. Thousands of Jews were actually denied entry into Switzerland, and some border guards went so far as to hand them over to Nazi authorities in Germany and Occupied France. It is not surprising to discover that few of them survived.

Fortunately, many in Switzerland did not endorse the official policies. Members of the Evangelical Protestant Church, for example, did much to alleviate the suffering of the refugees. They housed Jews in their homes, raised money to clothe and feel them, petitioned the government on their behalf, and tried to arouse the social conscience of the Swiss people. Among others, theologian Karl Barth roundly denounced anti-Semitism as unchristian, rallying the people to the plight of the Jews under Nazism.

Switzerland, however, was not the only country with a less-than-stellar record of treatment of Jewish refugees. The boatlift described in the story was an actual event—or would have been, if only the U.S. or the British had given permission for the landing of refugees on Allied-held territories in North Africa. But because neither country would give such permission, 30,000 Jews fell into the hands of the Nazi occupiers in France and Italy—30,000 who might have easily been saved.

Pastor Roland de Pury, the Protestant pastor in Lyon, was a real person, as was Pastor Charles Westphal of Grenoble. De Pury was actually arrested near the end of May 1943, just as is portrayed in the story. The Gestapo held him in Montluc Prison for about five months before deporting him to his native Switzerland. He returned to the pastorate in France after the war.

All other characters in the story (with the exception of political figures and the notorious Nazi, Klaus Barbie) are of the author's own creation. Any similarity, real or imagined, to persons living or dead, is purely coincidental.